ERAFI

Book 1

The Jestivan

David F. Farris

www.erafeen.com

Written by: David F. Farris
Cover illustrated by: Alessandro Brunelli

This book is a work of fiction.
All material was derived from the author's imagination. Any resemblances to persons, alive or deceased, are simply coincidental.

Thank you.

Sphaira Publishing, 2015

IBN-13 978-0692606407
IBN-10 0692606408

THANK YOU

Mom, Dad, and AJ
for believing in me.

CJ and Pops
for all your help—motivational and financial.

Geoff
for editing my early drafts into a blood-bathed slasher film.

Joel
*for being the first to lay eyes on this story, and for all your support and
advice.*

Justin
*for introducing me to a world that became the catalyst to this idea.
Without you, this would not exist.*

·

INTEL KINGDOM
(LIGHT KNOWLEDGE KINGDOM)

PHESAW
(CENTRAL SCHOOL OF THE LIGHT REALM)

DEV KINGDOM
(DARK KNOWLEDGE KINGDOM)

Tames

TAMES FOREST

COSMOS RUINS

Cosmos

Teleplatforms

TAMES MTNS.

Shreel

REGION OF
DEMONS

Rence

NECROSIS
VALLEY

RENCE
FOREST

Cogdan

Prayoga

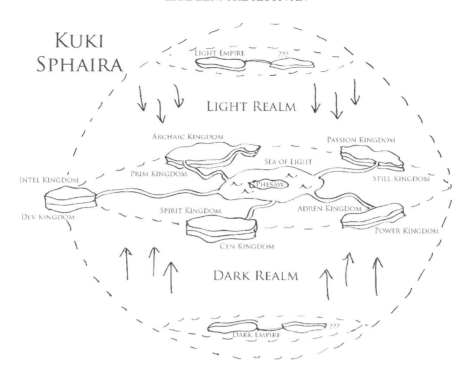

*This is a 3D module of Kuki Sphaira. There are no landscapes or structures because its purpose is to better position the reader in the world in respect to other kingdoms and realms. Arrows represent flow of gravity. "???" means it's unknown to the commoners. Dev, Cyn, Power, Still, and Prim Kingdoms (Dark Realm) hang on the underbellies of floating islands. Intel, Archaic, Spirit, Adren, and Passion Kingdoms (Light Realm) sit atop.

<u>Light Realm</u>

Intel Kingdom (mind, electricity):
Bryson, Simon, Lilu, Director Debo, Princess Shelly, King Vitio

Passion Kingdom (heart, fire):
Olivia, Himitsu, Director Venustas, King Damian

Archaic Kingdom (mind, ancients):
Agnos, Rhyparia, Director Senex, King Itta, Toono

Spirit Kingdom (soul, wind):
Jilly, Tashami, Director Neaneuma, Queen Apsa

Adren Kingdom (body, speed):
Toshik, Yama, Director Buredo, King Supido

<u>Dark Realm</u>

Dev Kingdom (mind, psychic):
The brothers, Prince Storshae, General Ossen

Cyn Kingdom:

Prim Kingdom:

Power Kingdom:

Still Kingdom:

1

A Vacant Tree

After a night of hiding beyond the horizon, the early morning sun climbed above the trees only to be greeted by a familiar, stubborn wall of dreary clouds. Another typical day in the Intel Kingdom.

Inside a quaint suburban home, a blond-haired sixteen-year-old boy sat in silence on the floorboards of the hallway that was dimly lit—for the most part. There was a small area that bathed in a radiant light, and he was sitting directly across from it.

It wasn't an ordinary light. There was no source. No candles. It simply existed on its own. The light didn't wane the farther out it stretched either. It stopped abruptly, as if there was an invisible wall holding it in.

Still, no matter how fiercely he stared down the oddity, the boy wouldn't dare to enter it. He studied it, but that was all. What was there to learn? He had already learned enough once before. A painful lesson he never wanted to experience again.

He took his eyes away from the light and gazed down at the vicious scars wrapping around the index finger on his right hand. Even with the passing of five years, it was a wound that had never fully healed …

A young boy stood next to the light he was told to never touch. Unfortunately, his curiosities were getting the best of him, leading him to a decision he would soon regret. He reached toward the light and when he was within millimeters of touching it, he yanked his hand back in fear.

Slapping himself several times to muster up some courage—something only an eleven-year-old boy would think of doing—he readied himself again. He decided that he would go straight in without hesitation, so after taking a deep breath, he thrust his finger into the unknown.

His skin popped and hissed. He let out a spine-chilling scream as he crumpled to the floor and desperately clutched his hand. Tears spilled down his cheeks and saliva stretched thin between the lips of his blubbering mouth.

Even after pulling his finger out, the burning sensation wouldn't cease. He felt it in his bones. It was pain that made him think of dying—a pain no eleven-year-old should ever experience.

A thunderous knock on the front door pulled him from his memories. As he stood up, he took one final glance at the shield of light. He knew who was at the door. Although that knock sounded frightening and loud, it came from a very small person.

He unlocked and opened the door. A young girl stood on the front step. Her eyes were blue and her hair was violet. It flowed down in waves from underneath one of her unique possessions—her kitten hat.

"Good morning, Olivia," he said.

She wasn't the one to respond. "What's up, idiot?" a deep voice asked.

He altered his gaze from Olivia's eyes upward to the sandy-brown kitten. "You know, Meow Meow? Considering the kingdom I live in, calling me an idiot seems kind of ironic."

Meow Meow was quick to retort. "I'm aware, Bryson. But the fact that you live in this kingdom is what's ironic."

Bryson chuckled. "Witty as usual."

The kitten's face became perplexed as he asked, "Why do you always greet her, but not me?"

"Why do you always insult me, but not her?" Bryson fired back.

Meow Meow's eyes narrowed. "Touché."

10

After Bryson winked at the hat, he looked back at Olivia. She still had yet to say a word, and her facial expression was as blank as always. Perhaps even calling it an "expression" wasn't fitting at all. She had never expressed any sort of emotion in her life, yet she resided in the Passion Kingdom. The people of this kingdom were known for their abnormally strong hearts and the ample amount of Passion Energy flowing through them.

So Olivia's placement in the Passion Kingdom was odd. She wasn't like any of her fellow Passion residents. Her face was the equivalent of stone. In fact, her personality bore more resemblance to her kingdom's natural rival—the Still Kingdom.

Bryson snapped out of his trance. He smiled at her and said, "Let's get going or we'll miss the biggest day the school has seen in the past three decades."

On the entirety of their lengthy walk to the Teleplatform, Olivia was fixated on the ground.

"What's wrong?" Bryson asked.

A long pause followed. As he realized that she wasn't going to avert her attention from the freshly cut grass, he sighed and said, "You're not one to show anything of what you're feeling, but since we left my house, you haven't said one word—or even made a noise for that matter."

"I am fine," she replied.

Bryson threw up his arms in shock and bellowed, "She's alive! Thank the Goddess, she's alive!"

"She's not fine," Meow Meow said. "She's upset because it's both of your birthdays today, and once again, you're ignoring it like every year prior to this—"

FWAP! The kitten hat's sentence was cut short by Olivia's soft fist. She looked away from the ground and stared blankly at Bryson. "Nothing is wrong," she repeated.

From the frown on Meow Meow's face, this was an obvious lie. Meow Meow knew everything that went on inside of Olivia's head. Essentially, his mind lived inside of her mind. No one knew how he came into her possession. When Bryson met her, she had the hat on. And while her possession of it was a mystery in itself, the strangest part was its existence at all. It went against all logic.

11

Ignoring the birthday comment, Bryson stared up at the sky as they continued walking. A game of peek-a-boo was being played by the sun, using the clouds as its hands, while the land of the Intel Kingdom glowed in childlike joy each time its mother's life-giving rays reached ground.

He suddenly became queasy. "A mother …" he muttered to himself as he switched his gaze toward the grass, sticking out his bottom lip.

They reached the teleplatform that would take them to the Light Realm's school, Phesaw. Based on the acronym FESAW, it represented the five powers of the five light kingdoms—Fire (Passion), Electricity (Intel), Speed (Adren), Ancients (Archaic), and Wind (Spirit).

Bryson and Olivia were starting a new journey at Phesaw this year. The two of them had coasted through years of typical courses that every student takes, but now it was time for them to meet the special eight other people who were chosen to be a part of a very prestigious group—a group that hadn't existed for thirty years.

Bryson climbed onto the elevated, golden platform enclosed by lightning-filled diamond rods. The cage began to gleam as Bryson reached down to assist Olivia up. He stumbled backward as he hoisted her.

"Are you getting weaker or is Olivia becoming a fat ass?" heckled a voice from the back of the cage. "She looks like she could pass for fourteen, so I'm guessing it's you."

A normal sixteen-year-old girl would have been offended by the accusations, but not Olivia. Unfazed, she looked at the boy and said, "Hello, Geno."

Bryson, on the other hand, straightened up, strutted toward Geno, and shoved him in the chest.

"Hey, jerk. I have been wiping the floor clean with you for the past five years. She would do the same if she wasn't so kind-hearted."

"Dude, I'm almost seven feet tall," Geno replied, which was scarcely an exaggeration. "You really think you could take me?"

"You're all attitude, no action. I hope you have fun drifting through another boring school year," Bryson smugly retorted as he reached up and jabbed Geno with his finger. "Olivia and I have new wonders to explore at Phesaw this year."

Geno just smirked at Bryson, who started to feel more and more ridiculous as he stood there with his scarred finger pressed against Geno's chest. Someone behind him snickered.

"You look like an idiot," Meow Meow said.

"Shut *up*, furball!"

For a brief second, Geno looked confused. Then he smirked again. Looking down at Bryson, he asked, "What do you mean by new 'wonders'?"

"I mean I'm in a different league this year, boy," Bryson said, his bravado a bit muffled by Geno's chest. "You'll find out what I mean in about an hour."

Geno rolled his eyes. "*Tch*, now look who's all attitude." He turned around and gave Olivia a look of disgust as he walked away from the confrontation.

Bryson, not ready to end the confrontation, darted after Geno. But he was quickly stopped short by the firm yet soft grip of Olivia's hand on his wrist. He looked back at her with angry eyes, but once they caught hers, they immediately softened. Nobody could look into the calm sea of Olivia's blue eyes and not feel tranquility.

"I'm going to make him pay, Olivia. He made us look like fools."

"Why must you care?" Olivia asked while staring at Bryson as if she was looking at nothing more than a brick wall. "You are stronger. You know this. Must you prove it? No."

She glanced at Geno, who was now standing with a group of friends. "You would look like a fool if you were to chase after him after the confrontation obviously concluded," she continued, still holding his wrist. "You will not move from this spot. Is that clear?"

Although her word-choice resembled a mother's, her delivery wasn't motherly at all. It was without affect as always.

"Okay," he said. It was as simple as that. He knew Olivia was right. That was her thing—being correct. She always had an amazing knack for common sense.

The Teleplatform, which resembled a massive bird cage, began spinning. Everyone grabbed hold of one of the many support poles scattered throughout. Most people took their positions casually, ready for what was about to happen. But it was obvious who were the weak ones or the newcomers. They were holding on for dear life with fear in their eyes.

Now brimming with excitement for what was to come, Bryson decided to let go of his pole and trust his balance. He couldn't help but think that this would thoroughly impress the first years and the pretty girls. Olivia shot a glance at him. When the platform hit maximum rotational speed, and the open field of grass engulfing them began to blur, regret flashed upon Bryson's face immediately. For a brief moment, sight became nonexistent, signifying the moment of teleportation.

As the platform began to slow, Olivia peered around the cage in effort to find Bryson, but her mistake was looking at eye level. A low murmur of giggles crept throughout the cage. Crumpled at the edge of the platform with his face pressed into the gleaming golden bars, butt in the air, and arms sprawled backward toward his toes, rested Bryson.

"His lack of sense is bewildering," Meow Meow said with a look of disbelief on his face.

"He tries too hard," responded Olivia coolly. She strode toward Bryson as he slowly pulled himself up to an attempted prideful stand. As she pushed through the crowd of onlookers, certain comments could be heard:

"That's Bryson, right?" asked a very young blond girl who looked to be around the age of eight. "The LeAnce kid? His dad created these Teleplatforms and he doesn't know how to ride in one?"

"Doesn't look like he's capable of being anything like his old man," an older man—probably the girl's father—responded. "His dad would be ashamed if he saw something like this."

Ignoring the jibes, Olivia grabbed Bryson's upper arm and pulled him toward the door. His yellow bangs had fallen in front of his eyes and he was holding his forehead. His eyes were unseen, but the thrum of his anger was palpable. From an onlooker's perspective, the reason for his rage would seem to be obvious—he had just made a complete fool of himself in front of a large crowd. But this was not the problem at all.

Gingerly, Olivia guided her friend down the steps, which stretched nearly five stories into the sky. They had arrived at Telejunction, a major landmark in the Light Realm that sat atop a hill and loomed over the school of Phesaw. The entirety of its vast campus could be seen from this vantage point. Two lines of multiple Teleplatforms ascended into the air as they converged toward the highest platform at the central corner. A staircase descended from each one toward the granite floor.

On the way down, Olivia spotted a few of her friends leaving their respective Teleplatforms, but there was no time for distraction. Bryson was not fit for any social encounter at the moment. While he was a dreary person at heart, when he was around other people, normally he knew how to put on a mask. And without his jubilance, nobody would want to be forced into the awkwardness of holding a conversation with Olivia alone.

Meow Meow squinted toward the direction of the vast granite landing. Scanning the area, his eyes finally rested on an empty spot where the floor met dirt, and patches of grass struggled to peek through the shade underneath a lone dead tree.

He didn't have to point it out to Olivia. The moment Meow Meow spotted the empty location, she saw it too. Not directly through her eyes, but indirectly through his.

Olivia nodded and sped up her pace down the steps. Weaving through the traffic of people and dragging Bryson behind her, her purple hair bounced with each step. Once at the bottom, she pivoted to the right and walked briskly toward her destination. A sudden blurt came from the crowd she had now distanced herself from.

"Olivia! Bryson! Come on, we'll head to Phesaw together!" shouted a tall, tan boy with black hair.

She ignored him and continued walking. The boy frowned and turned away. With their destination reached, Olivia sat Bryson against the tree. She took a seat on the lip of the granite floor and stared at her friend. Bryson's body was limp, and sniffling could be heard. As brittle and forlorn as he looked, it was like he was leaning against his own mirror image.

Bryson appeared defeated, but not because of embarrassment. His head hung low, but not because of shame. He was a boy struggling to grasp who he was. Fighting through his thoughts, he looked toward the sky, making his face visible for the first time since before their departure from the Intel Kingdom. It was the complete opposite of the smug look he had worn before. His head leaned back on the tree as he breathed sporadically. Each intake of breath caused his nostrils to flare. Olivia continued to look at him as if she was staring straight through him. Her mouth made a thin unreadable line.

Meow Meow gazed at the sky as Bryson did, where the crusted underbelly of a floating island hovered above them. With a face of understanding, the kitten hat broke the silence: "Do you think the answers are up there?"

Bryson didn't answer. "Often times, that's where people look to for answers," Meow Meow continued, still following the clouds. "You want to know who your father was. You hear from others that he was one of the greatest men to ever live—the Fifth of Five. So this makes you think that he's up there … Powerful and pure, strolling through the Light Empire as a Bozani. Who knows if that is actually the case? After all, becoming a Bozani after death is the ultimate reward, but also astronomically rare.

"Understand this, Bryson. Regardless of who your father was, his genes are inside you. You have every chance of becoming something even greater. I know that for everyone else, reading Olivia is like trying to translate a different language, but I know what she feels and thinks, and she has every ounce of faith in you."

Olivia stirred in her sitting position. Meow Meow looked down at Bryson with a rare comforting look.

"Everyone else knows more about my dad than I do, and I'm his son," Bryson said. "I can't even remember what he looks like. These people who claim to know who my dad was and who I am, trying to compare the two of us, are imbeciles. The ignorance they spit out of their pathetic mouths is complete madness, yet it still scars my heart."

Bryson looked down from the sky at Meow Meow. His eyes were glazed and red. "But they *do* know more about my father. Why? Because my father—supposedly fighting to protect the Intel Kingdom's precious princess—died in combat … I was four. I should have some inkling of memories that hold his image, but no.

"Am I supposed to live up to my father—a man I don't even know? There's so much pressure because he's a *legend* to the Light Realm. But people fail to realize—*I'M NOT MY FATHER!*"

It was a shout of frustration. There was a pleading look in his eyes. It was hopelessness. Bryson would never escape the shadow of Mendac LeAnce.

DAVID F. FARRIS

2

A Cracked Mask

Bryson and Olivia were the lone stragglers behind the scattered packs of students walking toward the front doors of Phesaw. Bryson had regained his composure and his conversation with Meow Meow had taken a turn in the opposite direction.

"Obviously, they think we're something special," Bryson said with a proud smile.

Meow Meow rolled his eyes. "They see *potential*. That's it. Whether you live up to that potential is a different story." Olivia's hand reached up to scratch Meow Meow's nose. "As of right now, you are weak—very weak. Believe me."

"What do you know?" Bryson snapped.

Meow Meow smirked and shook his head. "So young and so sure of yourself, yet so naïve."

Bryson's eyes narrowed.

"I suppose your residence and energy doesn't help," the kitten continued, ignoring Bryson's annoyance. "Born in the Intel Kingdom, you think you know everything. After all, intelligence is your strong point ... supposedly."

Bryson bent over to grab a pebble from the stone path. He stretched his right arm across his body to loosen up his shoulder. Tossing the pebble in his hand, he said calmly, "Keep mocking my intelligence and you'll realize that my arm can be more of a threat than my brain."

"Drop it," Olivia said in her monotone. "Simon is coming."

An eleven-year-old boy was running toward them through the crowd. His shoulder-length fiery red hair whipped behind him as he sprinted. His shirt was ragged and torn at the cuffs, and his green shorts reached mid-thigh.

Bryson braced himself, readying for impact. The freckle-faced boy leaped into his arms with a genuine smile, exposing his two front teeth, which were considerably bigger than the rest.

As Bryson gave the boy a friendly hug, he asked, "How are you, Simon?" He squatted low to allow Simon to climb onto his shoulders.

"I've been doing great! Long summer of working the fields with my dad, but I can't complain. We had a decent season for once!"

The four of them resumed walking again, and Simon reached across to rustle Meow Meow's fur, which the kitten allowed. Not many people could get away with treating him like an actual house pet, but Simon was a sweet kid.

"You ready for another grueling year?" Bryson asked.

"I'm just happy to have an excuse to not be plowing fields in the hot sun all day," Simon said. "My dad may make me work, but when Phesaw is in session, he understands what my education can bring me."

"Smart man," Meow Meow said.

"I've never doubted my dad," Simon said with the same wide smile. He leaned over, his hair dangling in Bryson's face, and asked with wide eyes, "What about you? What's the great LeAnce looking forward to this year?"

Bryson smirked and started digging in his pocket for his cherished letter—and got a prompt smack on the forearm from Olivia. She slowly turned her head and blankly stared at him. "No."

"Aww, Olivia, don't be a downer!" Simon said with an air of disappointment. The little boy bent sideways and reached for Bryson's pocket, causing him to nearly fall off head-first. He was saved when Bryson quickly readjusted his balance.

"Jeez, calm down. I'm not climbing those steps with a monkey attached to me," Bryson said while letting him down.

They started their climb to the front door. "Besides, Olivia is right," Bryson said as he stretched his shoulders. "You'll get the answer to your question at the ceremony. I promise you big things from me this year."

With this news, Simon's face lit up. After all, the ceremony was only twenty minutes away.

The four of them finished their climb in silence and walked through the thirty-foot-tall wooden doors where two men frowned at their tardiness.

They were standing in a gigantic lobby that curved off to the right and left, wrapping itself around the central auditorium with many polished, wooden doors scattered across its inner wall. The ceiling was high, and tall clear windows lined the upper half of the outer wall, allowing the space to bathe in rich sunlight.

The lush, soft carpet was a wealthy red. The walls were a creamy yellow. Covering the entire ceiling was a beautiful canvas—a singular work of art. Where they stood, above them were rolling flames of orange, red, and yellow with a few blues and blacks scattered among them. However, a student following the circular path of the lobby would realize that the painting would change from flames to golden lightning to wind to Ancient Pieces to vicious slash marks that represented the sword. Then that student would find his or herself under the flames again. It was a never-ending masterpiece.

It took four guards to shut the school's main doors. Simon gave Bryson and Olivia a quick hug and ran toward the auditorium. There were still patches of students lingering in the lobby, waiting for the last second before they took a seat inside. Olivia and Bryson sat on the floor under a portrait of an old balding man.

"If I were them, I'd be fighting my way to a front row seat right now," Bryson said smugly.

Meow Meow laughed and shook his head. "You ever stop to think that any of these people could have also received a letter?"

Bryson's mouth dropped with sudden disbelief. "I never thought of it that way!" He quickly sorted through the many faces peppered throughout the hall. Young, old, male, female, short, tall, skinny, fat. After realizing he didn't see anyone worthy of receiving a letter, he confidently said, "Nah, I don't know any of these people."

"So knowing them is a prerequisite?" Meow Meow asked.

Bryson looked at the kitten as if he were stupid. "Of course. I know all of the strongest people in this school."

As Olivia began playing with her toes, Meow Meow explained, "There are a couple flaws with your logic. One, there are way too many students in this school for you to know everyone. Two, why do you keep using the term *strongest?* This is the Light Realm, not the Dark. Our realm does not hold the Power Kingdom. If anyone is known for their brute strength, it's the people living in that kingdom. Plus, there are other factors to consider such as smartest, fastest, and most spirited ... to name a few."

"Most *spirited?*" Bryson pressed his forehead against his knees and laughed as he slapped his hand. "You really just said most *spirited?!*"

A disgusted look crept onto Meow Meow's face, but Olivia was the one to respond. "Spirit motivates. Spirit holds a group together. Spirit is something everyone should have a little bit of. Don't disregard it. The loveliest people have the liveliest spirit."

She continued playing with her toes with an empty look. A considerable amount of silence passed until she finally said, "Spirit is a tool that can rival your intelligence."

"Or *your* emotion." It was an impulsive response, and Bryson regretted it immediately.

Olivia's toes stopped wiggling, and she sat still for a moment. It wasn't a natural silence, but a forced silence. Bryson suddenly became aware that he and Olivia were the only two left in the lobby. He shot a nervous glance at his best friend.

She turned and passively looked at him dead in his eyes and said, "Spirit kept your father alive longer than he should have been." Then she pushed herself off the floor. The unreadable look in her eyes had not changed at all, but that didn't matter, for when Olivia walked toward the polished door, a single tear trailed from Meow Meow's eye. Despite her empty expression, somewhere deep inside her heart, Olivia was crying so hard that not even Meow Meow could completely mask the pain.

Olivia opened the door and entered the auditorium, her violet hair flowing behind her. The silence was drowned out by voices of the thousands of students occupying the seats inside. Then the door swung shut as the silence swallowed Bryson once again.

3

The Directors

A circular stage sat at the center of the massive auditorium. Row after row of mahogany benches stretched upward from the center. The only natural light came from the lone circle of glass in the ceiling directly above the center stage. Scattered throughout the audience were Intelights, which were handy sources of light that ran on Intel Energy. They only existed where there were people of the Intel Kingdom nearby to power them, which there were plenty of in a school full of students and teachers from all five of the light kingdoms. They were dim, but that was the purpose. The stage basking in sunlight was supposed to be the center of attention.

Leaning against the auditorium wall with one foot resting on the back of the last bench was Bryson. He had given up on the impossible task of pinpointing Olivia in the crowd. As he looked down the rows in front of him and across the room where faces on the other side were visible, there was nothing but an endless sea of people. Listening for a familiar voice proved useless. All that could be heard was the white noise of different conversations.

He shivered as he blew a strand of hair from his eyes. "Colder than usual," he muttered to himself.

The anticipation of the ceremony had dissipated for him, and all he felt was frustration. To bring up the topic of emotion to Olivia was inconsiderate. She never expressed herself emotionally. And while Meow Meow never had problems expressing his own, he made a rule of never allowing what Olivia was feeling to be seen through him. He did this out of respect for her. They shared the same mind, so he knew why she concealed her sentiment and he must have appreciated those reasons.

For Meow Meow to shed a tear on Olivia's behalf meant that Bryson had struck deep. He had only seen the kitten lose hold of Olivia's feelings one other time, and that was the first time Bryson spoke of Olivia's emotions. After that, he had made sure to never let the topic surface again … until today, at least.

Bryson's worry was interrupted by the extinguishment of the Intelights. The audience disappeared in the blackness, and all that could be seen was the pillar of light shining vertically through the arena and the stage glimmering underneath it.

A podium in the shape of a halo sat at the stage's center. It was designed for someone to stand inside of it and be able to turn and look at all sections of the circular crowd. Only one person was allowed to stand there, and he held the highest authority in Phesaw—the Grand Director. Surrounding the central podium were five, more traditional, podiums. These were intended to overlook their specific sections of the assembly, and they belonged to each of the five Energy Directors.

The stage was still vacant, but the students knew that would change very soon. The sudden lull of the crowd was a sharp contrast to the low roar from just seconds before.

Bryson looked toward the clock on the opposite wall: 8:59. A little less than one minute left. His anticipation returned. For the past eight years he had coasted through the basic routine of a student's life at Phesaw, but he was now headed toward a different path, and a very rare one at that. Only nine others would join him on this new journey, and soon he would meet them.

The clock struck nine. Five holes in the mahogany floor emerged behind the outer podiums. The crowd murmured as five heads began to peek through the stage.

As the Energy Directors' faces became visible, the auditorium roared. It wasn't loud—it was deafening, and the Directors didn't hide their appreciation. Although their postures didn't alter, a smile was still noticeable from each of them. As their platforms came to a halt and connected with the rest of the stage, the five directors simply stood tall, hands connected behind their backs, necks long, and heads up. And they pulled this off while still appearing relaxed.

Elation filled Bryson as Debo, a very special person in his life, occupied the podium facing Bryson's section of the crowd. Debo's dirty brown hair was messy and rustled as always. His short, untidy bangs framed his chiseled face in an irregular way. Two golden piercings studded his left ear, one at the top and the other through the earlobe. They matched his immense director's robes, which were also a golden yellow with a thick white trim, symbolizing the colors of electricity and his role as the Intel Director. He was the head of the Knowledge Wing of the school. Regardless of how many times he had seen Debo wear these robes, Bryson still found it odd to see him in such attire.

At the next podium in the circle stood a slightly hunched elderly woman with pure white hair woven tightly into a bun. A strand of hair fell on both sides of her face as her eyes squinted at her area of the audience. Her sky-blue robes draped over her shoulders and cascaded toward the ground. Although her physical attributes made her seem old and weak, the Spirit Director in charge of the Spirit Wing was the youngest at heart. She was the perfect example of what Olivia and Meow Meow were trying to lecture Bryson about earlier, and as he realized this, a sigh of disappointment escaped him.

Next was a tall dark-skinned man in silver robes that seemed to fit him more snugly than the others. They gripped to his body until the robe reached its hem, where it then frayed loosely a bit. Short charcoal-black hair lined at the edges framed his forehead in the shape of a square. He was the most physically fit of the directors because, quite simply, his position demanded it. He was the Adren Director of the Courage Wing. People of the Adren Kingdom were unrivaled in speed and swordsmanship, which explained the sleekness of his robes. They were meant to be aerodynamic.

A vast contrast could be seen in the next Director. He was not tiny, yet there was no denying he was short. Short enough to require his platform to be raised above the stage a sizeable amount. Lines of age crowded his face. Stringy, gray hair extruding in every direction possible enclosed a balding area in the shape of a crescent moon at the top of his head. His beard was just as unkempt, and his glasses sat crooked on his nose. His robes were a sandy-brown, almost the same color as Meow Meow's fur. It was hard to believe that this man was a Director, yet he was. The Archaic Director who led the Morality Wing had held his position longer than anyone besides the Grand Director.

Then came the most beloved of the five. Tan-skinned and dirty-blond, her bashful blush somehow fought through her already rosy cheeks. Her long, straight hair was tucked into the back of the blazing red robes that hugged her upper torso and fit snugly onto her curves. She was the Passion Director, leader of the Emotion Wing.

As the five Energy Directors held up their hands, palms facing the students, the clamor died out. A clearing of the throat echoed around the walls and ceiling.

Debo, the Intel Director, spoke first: "Ladies and gentlemen …"

The Passion Director spoke next in her high voice: "… boys and girls …"

"… please stand tall …" the Adrenaline Director continued in his deep tone.

"… but remain quiet …" the Archaic Director whispered loudly.

The Spirit Director enthusiastically finished the presentation: "… as we welcome back Grand Director Poicus!"

The five Energy Directors turned around to face the center spot, hands still behind their backs. A balding head peeked above the podium. As the platform rose, his pure white robes with silver trim began to show. He had a long white beard, but no mustache at all. The biggest oddity was his eyebrows, which were abnormally hairy, and the hair at the end of them hung down his face a little bit. He didn't stand proud and tall, but annoyed and slouched.

As his rise came to a halt, he reached his hand up to his face, rubbed his eyes, and sighed.

"Why must we make this ridiculous presentation?" he asked in a tired, soothing voice.

The Intel Director responded, "It is—"

"—*tradition*," Grand Director Poicus scornfully finished Debo's sentence.

Poicus tilted his head toward the audience and surveyed the mass of standing students. He then groaned, placed both elbows on the podium, and put his face in his hands.

"Sit down. I'm not one for theatrics and flashy presentation. I hate this tradition."

The students sat. Bryson remained leaning against the back wall. A smirk spread across his face. Poicus was as blunt as ever. Bryson was sure that if it wasn't for tradition, the Grand Director wouldn't even be wearing his Director's robes.

Poicus began the annual opening ceremony as usual. Nothing out of the ordinary occurred. He welcomed the first years, went over school rules, discussed upcoming events for the first semester, and even told a few jokes that were questionable for some of the younger students' ears. However, things soon became exciting.

"As we approach the conclusion of this exaggerated spectacle, residents of each kingdom will head to their respective wing of the school. Intel residents to the Knowledge Wing, Passion residents to the Emotion Wing, Spirit residents to the Spirit Wing, Adren residents to the Courage Wing, and Archaic residents to the Morality Wing. But—"

Poicus paused for a moment and smiled as he gazed throughout the assembly. "… We aren't finished yet."

Bryson's ears perked up. His head had been tilting to one side as he had kept dropping in and out of a bored sleep. The only moment he'd been waiting for had arrived.

"Over the course of the summer, the Energy Directors have been straining relentlessly over a couple decisions that could, potentially, sculpt the future. I have been a small part in these decisions, providing insight when needed."

Director Poicus reached under the podium and pulled out a glass of water. He took a sip then cleared his throat before continuing. "Ranks among the students are, typically, not something this school believes in. The only ranks that exist are those of a Director, Professor, and Student. However, there was a time once in the past when a higher rank among the students was granted.

"Thirty years ago, a group of five young men and women formed; one student per kingdom. Just like now, I was the one who triggered the founding of that group. It was a troubled time, as most of you know from countless lessons in history class and stories growing up. And though what you have learned only scratches the surface of that turmoil, we will not get into specifics here."

The director's face was grave as he delivered the climax of his speech: "Simply put, at the end of last year, the directors thought it wise to, once again, give birth to the Jestivan."

The once motionless students began to stir and murmur. Everyone knew the childhood stories. They were a group of students who became something far greater. They were heroes, and one was a legend.

The Energy Directors motioned for silence. Poicus thanked them and resumed speaking: "Thus, we prepared. We sorted through countless candidates, weeding out students based off intangibles, physical abilities, leadership, strength of spirit, emotional stability, and many other factors. Of course it is impossible to find someone who holds all these traits, but we felt as if our decisions were right. In the end, we decided on ten students— two students per kingdom. Yes, ten. With what is looming on the horizon, we felt that five wouldn't suffice. Ultimately, the decision for each kingdom's pair was made by their Energy Director."

Poicus spread his arms to his sides as he smiled down at the Directors. "With that said, I will allow them to introduce the second coming of the Jestivan."

The butterflies swelling inside of Bryson's stomach were overwhelming. He would soon hold the surname of 'Zana'.

Debo was first to speak. "Members of the Intel Kingdom hold a brain unrivaled, Intel Energy unique to that kingdom only, and electrical abilities capable of, literally, shocking the world. With much deliberation, my first choice as a member of the Jestivan is the second daughter of the king of the Intel Kingdom and the younger sister of Princess Shelly—Lilu ... Excuse me, I guess that would be *Lita* Lilu now."

Bryson's mouth dropped. They were going into this with a bang. Lilu was one of the more popular students in Phesaw, which was evident by the roaring of the crowd.

The sunlight that cut through the hole in the ceiling shifted toward the audience—now standing, as befits the presence of a Royal—opposite Bryson. He had a perfect frontal view of Lilu walking down the stairs. Her green hair split at her shoulders and cascaded down her back in waves, while a few strands fell loosely down her front side. A bright begonia was attached to the front of her hairline on the upper-left of her forehead. She wore a blindingly white dress with other, smaller begonias lining the straps that hugged her shoulders. It was a summer dress, reaching no further than the top of her knees. She looked every bit like the princess her older sister was.

When she reached the bottom of the stairs, she walked around the stage to the side closest to Bryson, where Debo stood waiting. She took hold of the Intel Director's hand and he gently pulled her up. Blushing slightly and wearing a cute smirk, she handed him her letter. Bryson caught himself starting to blush too, and then quickly readjusted his stare downward in attempt to calm the rush of heat to his face. She was not looking at Bryson, and he had never met Lilu before, but the beauty of that innocent face was infectious.

The clamor began to die down as Debo stood behind his podium once again. As he ran his hands through his messy brown hair, he let out a sigh and said, "This next student was a very difficult decision for me. I knew he would be a good candidate, but I wasn't sure what others would think. I didn't want to be accused of playing favorites, which isn't the case at all. Fortunately, Grand Director Poicus agreed that this boy was, in fact, the best candidate."

Bryson couldn't contain what he was feeling. It was time for him to follow in his father's footsteps—one of the original five Jestivan.

"This boy is a rowdy one. A boy who can be encouraged very easily, but on the flipside, can be discouraged to a point that makes you wonder if he has any spirit in him at all."

Bryson frowned.

"However, his drive to become one of the most talented beings outside of the Light Empire and the massive amount of Intel Energy inside of him allow us to look beyond that glaring fault ... which will still need to be addressed."

Debo paused and, for the first time, looked directly at Bryson at the top of the crowd. The director's eyes were gleaming of pride as he finished the introduction. "Please, welcome Bryson LeAnce into the Jestivan."

Bryson shielded his face with his arm as the spotlight redirected toward him. The students turned around in their seats to get a better look. Hesitantly, he began to walk down the staircase that seemed to stretch on forever. He didn't notice the reaction of the crowd, whether there were cheers or silence, for the anxiety swelling inside of him trumped any other sensation.

Lilu, daughter of a king and the younger sister of a princess, had handled this situation with complete composure, but Bryson wasn't used to this sort of thing. Beads of sweat dripped down his forehead and his legs quivered. It was just another example of Bryson's scared interior conquering the hard outer shell he always tried to maintain.

But then it got worse. He closed his eyes and took one nervous gulp, and when he reopened them, he found himself in a place he had seen in many of his dreams. It wasn't just *one of* his dreams—it was one of only two he had ever experienced.

It was peaceful. The air was crisp and the sky a deep blue—not a single cloud. He gazed straight above, knowing exactly what to expect. Pink petals danced in the wind above as he stared into the canopy of a cherry blossom.

Basking in the shade, he leaned his head back until it rested on the tree's base. His eyes closed for a brief second before opening again as he adjusted his stare downward. He was atop a hill that overlooked the entirety of Phesaw's campus. Luscious green grass blanketed the ground surrounding him. He put his right hand in the grass and gripped a chunk of it ... Soft, healthy.

Crowds of students, staff, and professors mingled on the grounds below. Based on their numbers, it had to be after-school hours. Alas, he already knew this. He had dreamt this same scenario thousands of times before.

Then he felt his head begin to turn to the left, and his heart began to beat faster. It felt like his neck moved at an abnormally slow pace. But then it happened.

Everything vanished into black, and the dream left him feeling the same way it always did ... wanting more.

4

The Jestivan

As Bryson slowly regained consciousness, the blurred image of giant, empty blue eyes began to come into focus. It was Olivia, and she was grasping his arm as she slowly pulled him to his feet. A grunt escaped his mouth.

"The dream again," Olivia said softly, holding Bryson's shoulders to support him. Meow Meow's gaze was stern.

"Migraine," Bryson answered. "Go back to your seat." He brushed free and continued down the stairs.

It was dead silent in the auditorium, and Bryson knew all eyes were on him as they questioned what they just witnessed. Did he go into shock from the overwhelming attention? If so, that didn't look good for the Intel Director. Debo had just finished explaining why Bryson was a tough decision, and now this.

These thoughts made it difficult for Bryson to look in Debo's direction as he approached the landing. However, as he stood at the stage's lip, he looked up through his thick bangs to see Debo smiling back.

As Debo's six-foot five-inch frame leaned over Bryson, the sunlight from the window above caused the director's ear piercings to shimmer.

"Always making things a spectacle," Debo whispered with a wink. "Hand over the letter, Bry, and go stand next to Lilu."

Bryson walked briskly to his spot in front of the podium. He couldn't tell if Lilu was worried or horrified. The only thing he knew is that he would jump off one of the kingdom's cliffs for her heart. Below would be a vast meadow of all the different flowery scents, exactly like the perfumes that were hitting his nose as he stood a hair's-breadth away from Lilu.

"… and now Lita Lilu and Zana Bryson will be taken below this stage where they will wait for the rest of the Jestivan to accompany them." Debo's voice beckoned Bryson's attention away from his daydream, saving him from more embarrassment as he realized he was leaning so close to Lilu that he was practically sniffing her hair.

Without turning his head, Bryson glanced to his right. To his dismay, Lilu was glaring at him in horror. She grabbed the hair falling down her left side and swung it to the other side, so that it fell down the front of the shoulder opposite of Bryson. But this only made it worse. Now her bare shoulder, collarbone, and long, elegant neck were exposed.

He felt the floor beneath him start to sink. The crowd applauded their induction as they disappeared beneath the stage, but the ruckus was swallowed by silence as the floor closed above them.

Another minute or two of silence passed by until Lilu finally broke it. "You are friends with Director Debo?" Her voice was angelic.

Bryson cleared his throat. "I guess friends would be a part of it. We're a lot of things. It's a bit complicated."

"Is that why you're here?" she asked.

The question—which was more of an accusation—wasn't unexpected. Being close with an Energy Director wasn't something that many students could claim, and Bryson wasn't mad at her for asking such a question. "I'd like to think that's not the case," he said. "You heard Debo say he had to consult with Grand Director Poicus, who agreed to make me a Zana of the Jestivan."

"*Director* Debo," Lilu corrected him, taken aback.

Bryson laughed. "I'm sorry. Habit."

They were talking into complete darkness—cramped together, almost touching shoulders. After a couple minutes, the platform started to pass window panes that, surprisingly, revealed water and fish.

"Are we descending through the sea?" Bryson asked incredulously.

"It looks like it," Lilu said. "We've been sinking for a while now. I wouldn't be surprised if a couple of the other pairs have already gone through their introductions and begun their descents."

"If we keep going, we'll end up on the underbelly of the island in the Dark Realm."

Lilu laughed, then snorted a little bit. It was cute.

Several long minutes passed before Bryson and Lilu passed through the ceiling of a large room. A massive carpet lay at the center, but besides that, the space was empty. Once the podium touched down on the balcony overlooking the room, Bryson hopped off and stretched his back while letting out a groan.

Lilu stepped off the podium like the Royal she was, delicately placing her feet on the balcony's floor, careful to not stumble in her pink high heels. They matched the pink begonia in her hair perfectly.

She and Bryson walked forward to the balcony's railing that overlooked the empty room. Lilu placed her elbow on the railing and her chin in her hand. Bryson could feel her looking at him suspiciously from the corner of her eyes. He knew what she was thinking.

"I'm not mental, you know," Bryson said. "I get really bad migraines. That's all."

Lilu's eyes narrowed. "Migraine, eh? That was more than a mere migraine. It was like you became possessed."

Possessed? Could that be it? Of course not.

Bryson laughed, leaning back with his hands still gripping the rail. "It sounds like you're suggesting someone has the Voodoo Relic, and I know you would never do that. It's impossible for anyone to have such a rare Ancient Piece, and even if they did, even the Archaic Director wouldn't have the Archaic Energy capable of using it."

"Do you think I'm *that* stupid? Of course that's not what I was suggesting."

"No, no, you're not stupid at all." He winked at her. "You're in the top of the ranks for the Knowledge Wing, after all."

She didn't smile in response, but her expression calmed a bit.

"What did you see that made you think I was possessed?" he asked.

"The change in your demeanor. Let me show you."

She walked to the top of the stairs and began to awkwardly climb down. She was nervous, hesitant, and uncoordinated. There were no signs of the grace she always walked with.

Bryson fought back a laugh. "You look like an idiot."

That brought a real laugh from her. "Oh, really? Do you even realize who I am right now?"

Bryson thought about it, then blushed. "You're mocking me!" he shouted.

"Therefore you just called yourself an idiot. However, you changed halfway down."

Her jittery walk transformed into a purposeful stride. All hesitation was eliminated. She continued this until she came close to the landing. But at the fourth step above it, she put the back of her hand on her forehead, took a sharp intake of air, and fell into a crumpled heap.

"You're quite the actress, Lilu."

Standing back up and adjusting the bottom of her shirt, she replied, "Yes, well, I may have overdone it there."

"May have?" Bryson asked with a smile.

They jumped as a spot in the ceiling rattled open. It was the second podium completing its journey from the auditorium high above. Bryson leaned with his back and elbows against the railing, eyeing the third and fourth Jestivan members as they sunk lower to the balcony. Lilu sat on the lower steps with her legs crossed, elbow on her knee and chin in her hand, lazily craning her neck to see who the pair was.

Bryson didn't recognize the boy, but when the girl stepped off the platform, his mouth dropped in disbelief. She was one of the more familiar characters in school, probably because she wore the same outfit every day.

A burgundy bandana covered the top of her brown hair and her sweeping bangs covered her forehead and completely blanketed one of her eyes. She wore an oversized beige shirt that split in the front at her waist. It was so long that it resembled more of a dress. However, the shirt was so dirty and worn, comparing it to a rag would be more like it. And then there was her umbrella, which she always carried at her side. Her name was Rhyparia, and she was also shoeless, as always.

She returned his expression with a pout. "Shocked to see me here?" she asked rhetorically. As her face turned to disdain, she said, "Don't worry. The rest of the school looked just like that when my name was announced. As if I could ever be deemed a lita. That arena was so quiet, I could hear my ears ringing."

Rhyparia trailed off as she noticed that Bryson's open mouth had yet to shut. She then glanced down the stairs to see Lilu staring at her—not quite as blatantly at least. She rolled her eyes and mumbled "Whatever" under her breath.

Bryson closed his eyes and turned to look at the boy. His hair was a deep black and a bit shaggy. While his hair was not long when it came to how far it fell down his back, there was a lot of it matted on the top and sides of his head. He wore a white robe with a rope tied around his waist, and though he was not shoeless like his Archaic Kingdom counterpart, he was the next closest thing: footed in sandals.

"Greetings, I am Agnos, resident of the Archaic Kingdom and seeker of the reason for our existence," he announced as he extended his right arm toward Bryson.

Bryson returned the polite gesture by firmly grasping his hand. As the two shook hands, Bryson said proudly, "I'm Bryson LeAnce, resident of the Intel Kingdom and err …" He thought for a second to think of something else. "And seeker of the secrets to not making myself look like an idiot."

Agnos smiled. "I assume you're referring to the show you put on up there." He looked at Bryson thoughtfully. "It seems you have a sense of humility. I admire that."

Bryson's posture rose. "Thank you. I try to find a laugh in everything."

"Now—" Agnos tilted his head toward Rhyparia, who was sitting on the steps with her chin on her knees in a deflated manner—"show me that you have a sense of character by undoing your first impressions with the lovely girl over there."

Bryson's shoulders fell as Agnos took the wind out of his sails just as quickly as he'd inflated them. It was a clever tactic. He built him up just to tear him down. Bryson realized he would have to be careful with this one. But he had to agree that he'd acted abominably.

Bryson took a seat next to Rhyparia and stared blankly across the room. Rhyparia, a bit shocked, turned to stare at him, almost as if she was trying to read his thoughts.

"Why the sudden change of heart?" she asked.

Bryson leaned back on the stairs. "I wouldn't classify it as a change of heart. That reaction wasn't a result of my feelings toward you." He paused, choosing his next words carefully. "I was, simply put, surprised."

Rhyparia's mouth curled with disgust. "'Surprised'? That sounds awfully shallow. You're judging me because I'm poor. I get it. My family is scum. I understand. I suck. Nothing new."

Bryson sat back up and looked at her seriously. "First of all, you wouldn't be here if you sucked. Who your family is doesn't matter. You are your own person. But I struggle with that myself. Secondly, yes, I was surprised, and maybe I shouldn't have reacted like that. However, I wasn't surprised in the way you're thinking. I just couldn't believe the school would choose two *supposed* good-for-nothings to be put into the Jestivan. I'm in the same boat you are. But this is my chance to prove them wrong, and you should look at it the same way."

Rhyparia's face softened a bit. "Thank you."

A third section in the ceiling opened. They all looked up as the next duo of lita and zana finished its descent. But before the platform reached ground, a flailing body—accompanied by a panicked yell—plummeted off its edge. It was followed by a resounding crash as the person hit the balcony's floor.

Lilu took off her heels and darted up the stairs. She knelt next to the boy and asked him if he was okay.

The boy, whose brown hair was perfectly parted on one side and combed across, opened his eyes. When he saw Lilu, he gave a suave smile and said, "Now I am." He grabbed her hand and kissed the back of it. "My name is Toshik, resident of the Adren Kingdom, known for my speed and abilities with a sword." He winked after the last part.

Lilu blushed a bit and stood up quickly. Looking down at him, she said shyly, "I'm Lilu, resident of the Intel Kingdom."

Toshik sat up. "Thank you for rescuing me from the wicked witch."

"I'm about to bury you in a wicked ditch," interrupted a new voice.

The podium finally reached the floor to reveal a girl who was obviously annoyed. She had purple hair, like Olivia, and her bangs flowed into a strand of hair that spiraled down the right side of her face. She wore a yellow headband and a yellow and black singlet. From the way it squeezed every curve of her body, it resembled a wetsuit. The only place uncovered was her head. And of course, as expected from anyone from the Adren Kingdom, she had a sheathed sword on her hip. She strode over to the staircase and strutted down past Agnos.

"What happened?" Agnos asked.

"He doesn't keep his hands to himself, so I pushed him off. And don't talk to me like we're friends, Agnos."

She walked to the bottom of the stairs and then toward the opposite wall of the room—far away from everyone. The way her hips swung in her elastic singlet caused Bryson to compare it to a pendulum.

He turned to look back at Lilu and Toshik. Childish jealousy was eating at his soul. He had never been comfortable talking to girls. The only one he had in his life was Olivia, but her lack of emotions made it easier for him to talk with her. Plus, he'd known Olivia for eight years. The only person he was more comfortable with was Debo.

Toshik finally stood up, and Bryson was caught off guard by his height. He towered over Lilu, forcing her green hair to fall back as she looked up with shocked eyes. He was tall enough to be eye-level with Debo, and his lean build intensified it. He wore a black and grey striped cardigan with a white V-neck underneath. His khakis were loosely fitted and straight-legged. And despite his fall, his hair was combed to perfection, making it look like it was molded with wax. This spelled trouble for Bryson.

"Anyways, I'm sorry for the scare," Toshik said, brushing nonexistent dust from his sleeves. "I'm perfectly okay. No need to worry." Toshik gave her a charming smile as Bryson scowled from his seat.

Rhyparia looked at him with a sly smile. "Since you got a stab at me with that rude expression you made when you saw me, I'll take a stab at you."

Bryson exaggeratingly poked out his lower lip and blew air into his bangs.

"Don't give me that," Rhyparia said. "It's only fair."

Bryson looked at her. "Fine," he mumbled.

"I would never have a chance with a boy like him." Rhyparia tilted her head in Toshik's direction. "You said you're looked down upon by everyone like I am, so why are you getting upset about a girl like Lilu, who you'd never have a chance with?"

Bryson glared at Rhyparia. "Thanks," he said coldly.

"Now we're even," Rhyparia said as she leaned back against the steps and gave a satisfied giggle.

There was a lot of socializing going on when the next space in the ceiling opened up. Lilu had brought Toshik down to Agnos, and as it turned out, the two boys already knew each other from a while back. While those three exchanged pleasantries, Rhyparia and Bryson continued their small talk, and the swordswoman from the Adren Kingdom was still seated by herself across the room.

There was a blond girl laying on the podium in fetal position and a boy with pure white hair leaning over her. The boy was slapping her cheek and saying, "Come on, silly Jilly. You're overreacting."

Toshik sprinted up the steps toward the podium with a look of fierce resolution. He took a knee in front of the girl. "Jilly, what hap—"

"*TOSHIK!*" she screamed as she jumped up and hugged him around the neck.

Toshik didn't respond very well to the enthusiastic greeting. He immediately stood up with an annoyed expression on his face as Jilly remained dangling from his neck.

"Get off me," he demanded.

"Guess what, Toshy!" She stared up at him with bright green eyes. Her face radiated sunshine, rainbows, and butterflies. "Guess what, guess what, guess *WHAT?!*"

Toshik looked down at her in defeat and reluctantly asked, "What?"

"On the way down, the boy with the snow hair and I saw something awesome!" she said as she hopped down. "I think we sunk through a ginormous FISH TANK!" Jilly spread her arms wide like a child to signify just how big *ginormous* was.

"It was the Sea of Light."

Jilly stared at him for a second or two before a look of understanding finally graced her face. "Oh ... I knew it!" she exclaimed as she pounded her fist into the open palm of her other hand. "That explains the shark!"

Rhyparia giggled, and Bryson shook his head in awe.

Jilly stuck out her bottom lip, placed her hands on her hips, and said, "There is no way that shark would fit in my fish tank. It needs a diet before it can be my pet fishy."

The things she was saying led Bryson to question her age, but she looked to be no younger than him. In fact, she was probably older.

"You can't have a pet shark," Toshik said simply.

Jilly gave Toshik a friendly look of disappointment. "Now, Toshy, if I really wanted a pet shark, I could get one." She flexed her nonexistent muscles and exclaimed, "I'll just have to get stronger!"

Toshik spun around purposefully and headed back toward Lilu and Agnos. Jilly stared at him blankly for a bit and then skipped behind him like she was frolicking through a garden.

As she started to follow him down the stairs, she completely froze in the position she was skipping in. Left foot on the ground and her right knee sitting in the air, arms frozen at her sides, she turned to look around the room. She resembled a statue until an unrivaled smile graced her face.

"Hi, everyone!" she shouted to the rest of the Jestivan members.

Everyone responded with a scattered and mumbled, "Hey."

Everything she did and said reminded Bryson of a child. Her playfulness, spirit, and zealous emotions were overwhelming. It was no surprise that she was from the Spirit Kingdom.

Jilly frowned. "Are we at a funeral or a celebration?" she asked. When nobody responded, she nonchalantly said, "Oh well."

She looked across the room toward the purple-haired swordswoman who was still sitting in solitude. Her eyes widened as she shrieked across the empty room, "I know you! Yama!"

Jilly darted down the stairs and tripped over Bryson's leg in the process. She stumbled a little bit, but recovered immediately, giggling at herself. "Whoops!"

Rhyparia was still laughing into her hand. "She'll be a fun one," Bryson said as he watched Jilly stretch out her hand to greet a baffled Yama.

Then came the jarring noise as the last section in the ceiling opened up, followed by a startled scream from Jilly as she jumped backward and fell into the arms of Yama, who, in turn, quickly pushed her back upright.

Bryson darted up the stairs, ready to greet his friend. This was the last platform carrying the ninth and tenth members, so he knew they were from the Passion Kingdom. This meant Olivia would be occupying this platform, and he desperately wanted to apologize.

As the final members reached the balcony, and Olivia's empty, blue eyes became visible, Bryson hurled himself at her with a warming embrace. She took it like she always did—unfazed and expressionless. She did not hug back, but she never hugged back. This didn't bother Bryson though. Meow Meow's reaction, however, was a little bit different.

"Get your big, empty head away from my face," the kitten hat whined as he struggled to push Bryson's face away with his dangling paws.

"But I love you too, Meow Meow!" Bryson said as he gave a quick peck to his furry cheek.

Meow Meow immediately stopped struggling. He became completely still, stared Bryson down with an evil look and said, "You must have a death wish. Don't you ever kiss me again."

As Bryson released his hug, he caught a glimpse of the other member from the corner of his eye. It was the tall tan boy who tried getting Bryson and Olivia's attention at Telejunction that morning.

"Well hello, Himitsu," Bryson said warmly. "I'm sorry about earlier. I wasn't in the right state of mind to interact with anybody at the time."

Himitsu slid his hand over his sleek black hair. "No big deal, man. I figured something was up." He put his hands on Bryson and Olivia's shoulders and said gravely, "I'm just happy to see two familiar faces. At least with you two, I can be myself ..." He paused for a couple seconds and then added with a sinister wink, "... for the most part."

Meow Meow stared at Himitsu with a twisted face. "Do you have a creep switch on you that I can possibly turn off?"

"Still the same smart ass," Himitsu replied. Meow Meow stuck out his tongue.

Himitsu returned his attention to Bryson and Olivia. "Anyways, happy birthday to both of you," he said with a happier tone.

"Thank you," Olivia responded. Bryson's face soured a bit as he mumbled his thanks under his breath.

Himitsu looked around the room. "Well, time to go make my fake greetings with everyone."

As Himitsu walked toward the trio of Agnos, Toshik, and Lilu sitting on the stairs, Bryson turned to face Olivia. "I'm so sorry, Olivia," he said sincerely.

She blankly stared at him for an uncomfortable amount of time. During the lengthy silence, Bryson noticed Meow Meow had fallen into one of his many, random catnaps, but that was typical of the kitten hat.

After several seconds passed, Olivia finally said, "Okay."

Bryson smiled. That was the best response he would get from her and he knew that.

Things were beginning to liven up a bit as the ten new Jestivan got to know each other better. Yama seemed to have control of her temper regained by the hands of Jilly. They were still alone across the room.

The biggest group occupied the left staircase. Lilu was seated next to Agnos, who was in the middle of morally questioning everyone in the group. Toshik and Himitsu were both standing a couple steps below, looking at Agnos in a confused way. They towered over the rest of the Jestivan—Toshik was somehow even taller, if by only the smallest of margins. And then there was the snowy-haired boy who was on the platform with Jilly. With all the insanity behind Jilly's entrance, he had been sort of overlooked, and now he was standing awkwardly with the group.

The opposite staircase was occupied by the last three members— Bryson, Olivia, and Rhyparia. They were talking about Rhyparia's Ancient Piece—her umbrella.

"What is its ability?" asked Bryson.

Rhyparia opened it and twirled it in her hand. "I'm not sure. I don't have the ability to control my Archaic Energy yet." She closed the umbrella again and said with a sigh, "So it's basically just a prop for now."

"Same story here," Bryson said. "This is about all I'm capable of doing with my Intel Energy." He opened both hands palm up and a few lifeless sparks emitted from his fingertips.

Rhyparia shrugged. "At least that's something."

They were interrupted by a sudden exaggerated yawn. "You'd think his brain would make up for his lack of talent." Unfortunately for Bryson, Meow Meow was awake. "Sadly, that's not the case."

Bryson's face twisted with irritation as he replied, "I like you better when you're sleeping. I think I'll put you in a coma."

"Simon would be more threatening," Meow Meow said with a sly smile.

Bryson went to jump at the kitten hat, but Olivia stopped him with a hand to his chest. The impact caused him to gasp for breath.

Cringing in pain, Bryson turned to look at Meow Meow. "What's it like having a little girl be your bodyguard?"

"What's it like being subdued by a little girl?" the kitten retorted.

"You suck."

As Meow Meow smirked at his victory, Olivia continued to look blankly at Jilly across the room, who was enthusiastically trying to reach for Yama's sword with no success. Rhyparia had been staring suspiciously at Meow Meow ever since he woke up.

A little while later, a pair of doors opened up under the balcony. A voice carried through from the other room: "Litas and zanas of the Jestivan ..." There was a short pause. "... Come in."

5

A Predecessor's Grave

For the first time in what seemed like an hour, the newly titled Jestivan left the lobby they had been socializing in. Bryson entered the new room side by side with Olivia. Looking around, he saw high, elegant walls paneled with beautiful mahogany. A window looking into the depths of the Sea of Light wrapped around the room at the top of the wall.

"Please, may you all have a seat?" said a soft, gentle voice at the forefront of the room—Grand Director Poicus, who was flanked by the five Energy Directors. They stood next to a black drape that was obviously hiding something. Director Poicus gestured toward the square pillows scattered across the wooden floor. Each member chose a spot and knelt with both knees on the pillow, butts on their heels, and palms resting on their lower thighs. Yama and Toshik rested their swords in front of them while Rhyparia did the same with her umbrella.

Once everyone was situated, all six Directors knelt on their pillows, facing the students. The Adrenaline Director placed his sword in front of himself.

Grand Director Poicus was first to speak. "How does it feel?" he asked with a smirk.

No one spoke, but their smiles spoke for themselves. Olivia remained expressionless, of course, and so did Yama.

Poicus appeared pleased. "That's interesting. The smiles gracing everyone's face are very complex ones. It isn't a simple *happy* smile."

"I'm super happy!" Jilly blurted out, then quickly snatched both of her hands over her mouth as she realized her disrespect.

The Grand Director didn't seem to mind, and his smile spread wider. "Allow me to explain what I mean. Or, better yet, allow me to throw it to Passion Director Venustas. She'll be able to explain better, for she knows how to read a smile." He nodded to the head of the Emotion Wing.

"Your smiles show a lot about what each of you are feeling at this moment," Venustas said, "but if I were to sum it up in one word, it would be *anticipation*. You're unsure of what is to come and you are eager to find out, and that sense of wonder and exploration feeds you."

She glanced at the black curtain that was hanging to the side. When she continued speaking, her voice was somber. "However, that's because you look at this opportunity too narrowly. All you think of is the potential of success and fame, when, in reality, the potential of failure is far more likely." Bryson's stomach knotted up as the realization of what—or better yet, *who*—was behind the curtain hit him like a ton of bricks. "This is a unit, but there are possibilities of individuals inside of the unit not making it. After all, we don't know what the future holds."

Poicus took over where she left off. "In other words, if you're in this purely for the glory, you will fail. Glory isn't proper initiative. Can someone tell me what is?"

It went silent for a short moment before someone risked answering. "A greater good," Agnos said.

"Yes. And what is a greater good?" Poicus asked.

"Anything that will better those around you," Agnos replied again.

"Very good. The Jestivan is selfless. Glory—if it comes—is nothing but an insignificant byproduct. Names like Ataway Kawi and Mendac LeAnce are legends to us, but their glory comes from what they achieved. And what they achieved served a greater good."

Ataway Kawi and Mendac LeAnce. Two legends to their respective eras.

"However, one of these men—Mendac, an original Jestivan—wouldn't have lived long enough to achieve what he did if it wasn't for a girl." He said the last part weakly as he looked toward the black curtain. Then he turned back toward the students. "I'm sure you're all familiar with the stories of the original Jestivan." Everyone nodded. "Good. Director Debo, lift the curtain."

As Debo grasped the curtain, Bryson braced himself. If it weren't for what was behind that curtain, Bryson's dad would have died a lot sooner, and things like the Teleplatforms and Telejunction would not exist.

Debo pulled off the veil to reveal a diamond-trimmed sky-blue coffin. Shock plastered nearly every young face. Even Yama, who had been holding a stern expression since she sat down, faltered a bit.

The reaction that stood out the most, however, was Jilly's. Her jaw practically hit the floor as she let out a gasp. She straightened up and craned her neck to get a better look.

The Spirit Director was smiling at Jilly's reaction, causing the wrinkles around her mouth to sharply curve. "This must be quite a treat for you, Lita Jilly," she said.

"The stories say she was buried at the school, but nobody has ever actually seen her coffin or memorial," Jilly replied without taking her eyes off the coffin. "I can't believe my eyes. This is the grave of my *idol*, Director Neaneuma."

"That's no surprise," the old woman said. "She is the pride of the Spirit Kingdom and an idol to most of our people."

"I'd say almost every girl—no matter the kingdom—looks up to her, Director Neaneuma," said a voice from the back. It was Lilu. "She is the perfect example of what pure love is."

Bryson's mind was reeling. The woman resting in that coffin was the reason why his dad escaped death at an earlier age, but at the same time, his dad was the reason why she was inside there.

As Debo returned to his seat, Poicus cleared his throat. "Thusia. Resident of the Spirit Kingdom and one of the five original Jestivan. She held an immense amount of Spirit Energy inside her little body, giving her the ability to create tornado-like winds. She was also the driving force behind the Jestivan thirty years ago. She was absolutely necessary for the group's survival."

Olivia glanced at Bryson. Despite her blank expression, he knew that she was concerned for him.

"As you all know, a significant battle happened 27 years ago," Poicus continued. "It was a battle between Dev King Rehn—leader of one of the Dark Realm's five kingdoms—and two Jestivan—Thusia and Mendac. Thusia lies in this coffin while Mendac is buried in the Intel Kingdom's Palace. They are the only two original members of the Jestivan whose whereabouts are known.

"Puddles littered the mud and grass as the sky was shrouded in gray. Roars of thunder shook the ground while bolts of lightning sporadically lit the somber sky. Thusia and Mendac were winning the fight against Dev King Rehn, and despite the bleak weather, everything seemed to be in favor of the Light Realm. The Dev King was wounded and struggling for breath. But Mendac was also suffering from severe injuries.

"While he was recovering, Thusia was in the process of finishing off the Dev King, whipping him with vicious gusts of wind. He keeled over on one knee on the verge of death, but before Thusia could land the finishing blow, the ground violently cracked between them.

"She stumbled backward with her hands over her ears, for the sound of the crust fracturing beneath them was intense … but even that proved to be nothing compared to what she heard next.

"A roar. A deafening roar that caused the tiny hairs on her skin to stand tall. A roar that overpowered the torrential thunderstorm they were amidst. And as she crawled backward, for the first time in her life, she witnessed something that made her face twist in horror—a mighty and powerful demon had risen from the crust. Masses of rubble rolled off its broad shoulders and rained to the ground below, causing Thusia to scramble in every direction to avoid being crushed. The demon roared again as it began smashing the ground with heavy fists, grabbing chunks of land and tossing it away.

"It then set its eyes on the injured Mendac LeAnce, who was slumped

47

against a boulder. Thusia jumped in front of her partner and knocked the demon's swiping hand away with a blast of wind. She then immediately followed up with another, stronger burst of wind directed toward its face, knocking it onto its back. Thusia stayed in her fighting stance while Mendac attempted to stand with no success.

"The demon sprang high into the air, aiming to crush Mendac with its feet. Thusia decided to act on an impulsive plan. She sprinted toward Mendac and leapt above him like a salmon. As her back arched, she acted as a shield. She had accepted her fate, but she had to stall for a little more time, so at the crest of her jump, she released the largest gust of wind she had ever summoned toward the bottoms of the demon's feet.

"The demon's descent was slowed, but its massive weight continued to bear down on them. Mendac begged her to move, but she ignored him and explained what she was about to do—release all of the Spirit Energy in her body into Mendac's, and while it would not give him the ability of wind, he would temporarily have the spirit and drive to fight at his fullest potential without the pain of his injuries holding him back. She then instructed him to dive out of the way from where the demon was about to land.

"Mendac pleaded against her plan. He knew that special ability of a Spirit resident had a terrible downside—complete paralysis. But she had already made her decision. After all, Mendac was the man she loved.

"So she closed her eyes and shifted all of her focus on releasing her Spirit. As she did so, her wind began to weaken, and the demon began to fall faster. Mendac's spirit began to ignite and he felt a sudden drive to persevere. As he dove away, he released some of his electricity into one of the metal rods from his waistband, and tossed it into the puddle next to him. As he did, Thusia's wind disappeared, her eyes became faint, and the demon's feet crushed her stomach, chest, and head on impact."

At this point, Meow Meow was failing miserably at holding back tears.

"As the demon landed," Poicus continued, "it howled as it was electrocuted. Ignoring the pain from the demon's burning skin, Mendac climbed onto its chest. He spit in its face, grabbed his second metal rod, reached high in the air with two hands, and rammed it through the demon's heart as he unleashed a final surge of electricity into it.

"At this point, he still had hope that Thusia was alive. He had thrown the metal rod into the puddle for two purposes. If Thusia had somehow survived the impact, the electricity could act as a reboot to her body's nervous system. Granted, this would have caused unparalleled pain for Thusia since all feeling would be returned to her body, but life would have been worth it.

"Mendac slid down the demon's belly, his feet making a splash in the soft mud. He saw Thusia's forearm and hand extending from underneath the demon's leg. He slipped and fell in the slop as he ran to her. Tears streamed down his face over the probability that the woman he loved was dead.

"But as he slid through the mud toward her hand, there was cause for some hope. Her fingers were weakly grasping at the air. She wasn't paralyzed. Mendac thrust his shoulder into the demon's massive thigh, but he couldn't brace himself against the sludge. He tried every stance, but nothing worked.

"Finally, he fell to his knees and put his hand in hers, and as he did, she grasped it firmly. He wanted to see her face. To feel her touch, but not have it accompanied by the sight of her loving smile, felt like death in its own right. He began crying harder as he felt her grip start to weaken.

"Mendac kissed her fingers, begging her not to leave … but her hand went limp in his. He cried and cried and cried. It was a display of such raw emotion that Mendac had never shown before. He had a reputation for being a little cold-hearted, but Thusia could always mend that fault. He slouched over the ground and Thusia's lifeless hand, not even realizing the king of the Dev Kingdom had used that opportunity to flee."

Grand Director Poicus looked at the coffin after he finished the story. Lilu, Rhyparia, and Jilly were wiping tears from their eyes. Olivia was wiping tears from Meow Meow's eyes. But Toshik was scowling and shaking his head.

"You don't seem pleased, Toshik," Spirit Director Neaneuma said.

"As a member of the Adren Kingdom, I see no nobility in letting a lady die for you, Director Neaneuma."

She frowned. "So you don't respect what she did?"

"I have respect for what she did, but she shouldn't have had to do it. I have zero respect for Mendac. The man should protect the lady."

"Why must you always think that way?" Jilly retorted. "A lady can protect a man!"

"Quiet, Jilly," Toshik snapped. "I've been protecting you since the day you became my Charge and it will always stay that way."

Jilly scrunched up her face. "You never let me protect myself."

Director Neaneuma smiled. "So that explains your logic, Toshik." She glanced at the Adren Director to her right. "You Adren people are so dutiful."

"I'd hardly describe him that way," Yama sneered. "He only cares about Jilly when she's in danger. Otherwise, all of his attention is on any girl with a heartbeat. He can't even fight properly unless there's a pretty girl watching."

Toshik snorted and teased, "Your attitude may be beastly, but, physically, you would still fall in the pretty girl category."

A sharp gust of wind smacked Bryson in the face, which was odd since he hadn't seen Jilly or the snowy-haired boy make any gestures to conjure their wind abilities.

"Yama, go back to your seat and put it down," came a deep, demanding voice. It was the tall, dark Adren Director.

She was squatting behind Toshik's back with her sword drawn across the front of his neck. Bryson realized that the wind was actually from how quickly Yama moved. All he had seen was a blur of colors. To the other, more untrained eyes, she had probably seemed to have disappeared. It was an intimidating show of her explosive power.

Even still, Toshik didn't falter. His face was relaxed as he sat with a leisurely posture. "You're feisty," he said with a sly smirk.

"You're disgusting," Yama fired back. She sheathed her sword and returned to her cushion.

Poicus cleared his throat. "We're off to a great start." He clapped his hands together. "Back on topic. You've all heard this story countless times throughout your childhood, so why would I tell it again?" He paused, but no one answered his question. "Because there is a valuable lesson—a lesson that will hold the ten of you together. You must know that each of you is important to the unit in your own unique way. When Thusia died, the Jestivan died. It could not persevere without her spirit. She was its engine.

"It's not all about raw ability." He looked at Himitsu. "Or speed." He looked at Yama. "Or who your parents were." He looked at Bryson. "Or your sense of duty." He looked at Toshik. "Or intelligence." He looked at Lilu.

"The Jestivan's survival must also rely on essential factors such as composure." He looked at Olivia. "And modesty." He looked at Rhyparia. "And wisdom." He looked at Agnos. "And prudence." He looked at the unnamed boy with white hair. "And, of course, spirit." He looked at Jilly.

"What I'm saying is, don't take any of your fellow litas or zanas for granted. Treat each other as equals. Do you understand?"

"Yes, Grand Director," they responded in unison.

Poicus's face brightened. "Superb! Now we can get to the fun stuff. Tomorrow will be an interesting day to say the least. The Directors decided to split the group into two teams. For now, we'll name them Team A and Team B since the Energy Directors didn't like what I came up with." He frowned. "You will be able to decide on your actual names when the teams come into fruition. So if there are ten of you, and we will be splitting you into two groups, how many people will be in each group?"

The room went silent, for nobody wanted to give the obvious answer to the silly question—except perhaps for Jilly, whose face was contorted with concentration as she counted her fingers. Math was obviously not her strong point. Honestly, when it came to her mind, there probably weren't many strong points, but Bryson gave her the benefit of the doubt.

It took a while, but eventually realization dawned on her face. She raised her hand violently and started making huffing noises in order to be recognized.

Grand Director Poicus and the Adren Director smiled while the rest of the Energy Directors couldn't hold back their chuckles.

"Yes, go ahead, Jilly," Poicus said.

"*Five!* Five to each group, Grand Director Poicus."

"That is correct."

The directors clapped softly, which would make anyone else think they were being mocked, but Jilly seemed elated as she brushed a strand of hair behind her ear, exposing her blushing cheeks. The room's atmosphere had shifted to positivity now that Mendac and Thusia's story was done. It was a welcome change for Bryson.

Poicus stood up. "It's good to know we can all do math." The Jestivan giggled. "Tomorrow, teams will be chosen. Two people will be assigned the role of captain for each team. As for how the captains will be determined … I'm not telling you—*yet*.

"It could be the two tallest. Or, perhaps, the two cutest." Poicus stroked his chin. "And if that were the parameters, and if I was a betting man, which I happen to be, my money would be on Olivia and Jilly."

"*Director!*" Director Venustas said as she smacked him on the back of the head. A chorus of laughter followed while Poicus rubbed his skull.

The Archaic Director, head of the Morality Wing, rose from his seated position. He probably could have stayed seated, for standing barely increased his height. "I think I will finish this off in fright of our lovely Grand Director having another shameful slip of the tongue.

"Captains and teams will be chosen tomorrow, and that is the extent of what you need to know. You all are dismissed. Have an ethical day."

6

A Scorching Light

Bryson gazed into the dreary, gray sky as he walked toward the front door of his house. He loved his kingdom for this reason. For 46 years, the sun had never shined in the Intel Kingdom. It was always clouds—dark, depressing clouds. They put him at peace. While his jubilance shined bright in a social setting, on the inside he was always a loner. Honestly, all he needed were a total of three people … Well, two people and a cat.

Upon entering the house, Bryson removed his shoes and rested them next to the baseboard. He felt an urge to release some creativity, so he headed toward the family room. He wiggled his toes in the lush white carpet. He loved the soft feeling after a long and exhausting day.

As he sat down in front of the piano, he relaxed his shoulders and breathed deeply, allowing his creative juices to start flowing. Considering the fact that the Intel Kingdom was more known for factual and logical expression, it was odd that Bryson had a creative outlet such as music. It was just another thing Meow Meow would tease him for. He smiled at the thought.

He placed his fingers on the keys and started playing his favorite song. It represented a three-step, psychological evolution and it began with a subtle tapping of one key for fifteen seconds—*seclusion*—before entering a more complicated tune, but still at a turtle's pace—*sorrow*. Slow and somber. Melodic and captivating. It was as if the piano was crying.

During the slow part of the song, Bryson stared down the hallway at a wooden door that led to an unknown closet. It was a door he had never stepped through during his eleven years of living in this house—not because of a lack of interest, but because it was impossible. A light shielded the door day and night.

And that wasn't the end to its oddities. The light had no visible source. There was no wick, and no Intel Energy was being pumped into it. But perhaps the most interesting aspect of the light was the danger it presented. And at that thought, Bryson looked down at his right index finger as it continued to dance across the piano keys. *What was in there, that he would risk my life to protect?*

Bryson's mind went blank as he approached the fastest section and final psychological step of the song—*spite*. His golden bangs fell in front of his face as his body started shifting aggressively with the dynamic harmonizing of the piano.

"'Phases of S,' eh?" The unexpected intrusion jolted Bryson back into reality. The question came from a man leaning against the doorway. He had slipped into the house while Bryson was attentively vulnerable.

"Always the same song—so predictable," the man added with a smile.

Bryson returned the warm smile while a bead of sweat ran down his forehead. "I'm definitely not spontaneous."

"No wonder you have no luck with the ladies."

It was a more recognizable Debo. Instead of his golden robe, he had on a bluish sweater that hugged his long torso, and loose-fitting dress pants to accompany it.

"Interesting day," Bryson said.

"You're right about that. But we'll talk about it during supper." Debo rolled up the sleeves of his sweater. "So what do you want me to make?" he eagerly asked.

Bryson stood up and stretched. "Something that you're not going to royally screw up."

Debo winked. "Then I guess I'll try surf and turf!" he exclaimed before bolting toward the kitchen.

Bryson laughed and shook his head. But when he turned to look down the hallway toward the closet door again, his expression became stern. He walked away while gripping himself from the sudden chill.

Later that night, Bryson and Debo were sitting at the dining table with a generous portion of steak and lobster on their plates. The tableware was nothing fancy. Actually, it was very plain for a household that belonged to someone of Debo's stature. Despite it being past sunset, the window that nearly covered the entire side wall was open, allowing the approaching autumn air to cool down the dining room. And to make the moment even better, Bryson could taste the juices in the meat. He wasn't biting into charcoal, unusual for one of Debo's steaks.

"Cheers. Your cooking is actually decent this time," Bryson said as he shoved another bite into his mouth.

Debo raised an eyebrow. "I guess that's a compliment. Thank you."

"Not quite."

Debo stared intently at Bryson as he ate for several more seconds before he said, "So, about today."

"You mean when I collapsed?" Bryson asked through a mouthful of lobster.

"Yes, when you collapsed. Same dream as usual?"

"Since when has it been anything else? I haven't had the nightmare since I was young." Bryson pushed his plate away from him, leaned back in the chair, and belched. "That was satisfying," he said with a grin.

"This was the first time it happened while you were awake?"

"Well, you're a straight shooter tonight. You don't want to talk around in circles for a bit first?"

"No."

"Shame." Bryson sighed. "Yes, it was the first time."

Debo was playing with one of his ear piercings. "Interesting. I wonder what drew it out during such a time."

"No clue."

Debo tapped his fingers on the table. "Well, your dream occurs in the outskirts of Phesaw's campus, looking down at it. When you collapsed today, you were in Phesaw. The school could be a connection."

"Any guesses beyond that?" Bryson asked.

"I think this is where I fail you," Debo said as he got up to start clearing the table. "I guess I'm a poor excuse for an Intel Director."

As the night came to a close, Bryson lay in bed and stared at the ceiling. He was thankful that his birthday was over and especially grateful that Debo didn't try any surprises this year. No cake, no parties, limited birthday wishes.

He altered his gaze from the ceiling to the light-shielded closet directly outside of his room. Reaching over and grabbing a quill from the nightstand, he twirled it between his fingers before throwing it toward the light. It soared through the air—the quill unaware of its pending doom. Once it made contact, it caught fire and burned to a crisp. As its ashes fell to the ground, Bryson thought back to when he first learned about the glowing door ...

"Listen here, Bry," Debo said. "I've always told you to never touch this light. That it can hurt you badly. I've always warned you about my Intel Energy and the dangerous electricity it can create."

"And that's why you've never shown me them," said an enthusiastic seven-year-old Bryson. "You're super strong!"

Debo smiled. "Correct. This will be the only time I ever show you what my Intel Energy is capable of. You're getting to the age where you're going to start acting on your curiosities and not listen to what I say. Pretty soon, locks on the door won't keep you from opening them, so I have to be extra careful."

Bryson stood on his tip-toes in anticipation as Debo continued speaking. "You know what Intelights are." He nodded in the direction of a newly formed shield of light. "This is an Intelight—an everlasting and very powerful Intelight. I told you to find a twig this morning. Do you have it with you?"

The young boy shoved his hand deep in his pocket and pulled out a small twig. Debo took it from him. "This will do nicely," he said. "Now, watch closely."

Debo held the end of the twig and slowly pushed it toward the glowing orb. Bryson expected the Intelight to act, literally, as a shield. However, this was not the case. As the twig touched the light, it disintegrated into ash. The boy's mouth dropped in disbelief. It was a level of power he had never witnessed before. He was taught that the people of the Passion Kingdom were the only ones capable of burning because of Passion Energy, but Debo was proving this wrong. This Intelight, created by a member of the Intel Kingdom and his Intel Energy, was burning this twig to ash.

"You see? Do not touch this light. It must be strange that I will be keeping something so dangerous in the house, but my intentions are not to hurt you." Debo gripped Bryson's shoulder as he stared him in the eyes. "I love you. I always have and I will always take care of you. What's the number one rule in this house?"

Bryson looked back at him with large, curious eyes. "Do not touch the light."

Debo rustled Bryson's long blond hair. "Good," he said with a satisfied smile …

Bryson rolled over in his bed and closed his eyes in effort to finally fall asleep, but thinking about the light prevented any of that. He decided to think of something worth dreaming about. His mind drifted to a beautiful Royal girl with green hair and a pink begonia, and with these thoughts, Bryson dozed off with images of Lilu in his mind.

7

The Captains

The following day, Bryson and the rest of the Jestivan found themselves inside the same room they were in the day before during the story of *Thusia's Sacrifice*. Today, however, Thusia's coffin and the pillows were gone, leaving the room bare.

The ten Jestivan stood in a line against the wall while the Directors stood in the middle of the room. Grand Director Poicus was standing in the center spot as usual.

"What makes a good leader?" he asked.

"Power," Bryson answered quickly.

Poicus tugged at his beard. "Well, a leader has power, but what *gives* him that power?"

"I think he meant power as in physical ability, Grand Director Poicus," Yama corrected. "And if that's what he meant, I would agree."

"Ah, I see," Poicus said. He smiled and rubbed his open palms together.

"Then this test seems only fitting for that of a captain! If a leader requires strength to smash his foes, then we planned accordingly, Directors. Today's test will be a measure of your power—or ability and talent I should say. Your energies will be put on display."

Bryson's stomach dropped. He had never managed to emit more than mere sparks from his fingertips. Debo always told him to master technique and speed before moving onto his energy. He was going to utterly fail this test.

"Rhyparia, you may have a seat near the wall over there since you already had your turn earlier this morning."

Confusion crept its way onto most faces as they watched Rhyparia separate from the pack. *Why did she get a private test?*

Poicus ignored the perplexed looks. "We randomly chose the order this morning and Zana Himitsu, you are first. Please, come stand in the center of the room, state your name and kingdom, and give us a splendid show!"

The Directors backed up against the far wall while Himitsu strolled out to where they had been standing. Tall and tan-skinned with sleek black hair, he had an alarmingly commanding presence thanks to his height and perfectly erect posture.

"I am Himitsu, member of the Passion Kingdom, possessor of Passion Energy and wielder of fire," he said in a creepily calm voice.

"Very well then. Let's see it," the beautiful Director Venustas instructed.

Himitsu rolled up one of his long robe sleeves. He pointed at the ground, and as he did so, a flame about half his height sprouted—a black flame. This caused eyes to widen around the room—including the Directors'. Venustas, however, smiled as Himitsu proceeded to circle his pointed finger around himself until he was enclosed in a short wall of black fire. It emitted no smoke and no light.

Venustas looked at Poicus with a satisfied smile. "And you didn't believe me."

"I must apologize. When someone approaches me with the claim that he or she knows an assassin-blooded teenager with control over his or her ability, I tend to think they're a bit crazy."

Poicus told Himitsu to have a seat next to Rhyparia. Spirit Director Neaneuma then called on the next student. "Lita Jilly, it's your turn, dear."

Jilly raced to the center of the room—or hobbled the best she could in her heels.

"Jilly . . . Why heels?" Neaneuma asked.

"Yesterday, Grand Director Poicus said the competition could be a battle between who is the cutest, so I tried to look extra cute today! These heels are cute, right?" she asked while looking down at them.

Neaneuma glared at Poicus, who ducked his blushing face in embarrassment. The Spirit Director turned back toward the girl and said sweetly, "Take them off, hon. They aren't necessary."

Jilly gave a sigh of relief and threw her heels to the side. "Thank bhavatama."

Neaneuma nodded for her to begin.

"I am Jilly, resident of the Spirit Kingdom, possessor of Spirit Energy, and wielder of wind."

The moment her sentence ended, a blast of wind shot upward, enclosing her body. Its power forced her to hold down her dress as her face rippled. Her long, blond hair looked like it was being pulled by a vacuum from above. This went on for close to a minute, and Bryson began to wonder if she even knew how to stop. Toshik's face was in his hand. He obviously wasn't amused.

Finally, the wind halted abruptly, and Jilly's hair fell into a frizzy mess. She was smiling from ear to ear. Once again, just like every other time when Jilly was the focal point, the directors appeared amused.

"Very good. You may have a seat," instructed Neaneuma.

Passion Director Venustas spoke next. "Ms. Olivia Lavender."

Olivia walked deliberately to the center of the room. With an expression of stone, she said, "I am Olivia, resident of the Passion Kingdom, possessor of Passion Energy, and wielder of fire."

She stood still for a few moments. The only movement came from Meow Meow wiggling his nose. For any other student, failing in front of the directors would have been extremely embarrassing. But this was Olivia. If she couldn't do something, she wasn't going to shy away from that fact.

"What's wrong?" Venustas asked.

"I have no knowledge of how to use my fire abilities. I have never shown any signs of any kind of ability," Olivia blandly explained.

Venustas gave her a warm smile. "And that's perfectly okay. You may take a seat."

The next four Jestivan did fairly well in their tests. Toshik and Yama both showed off their impressive speed and swordsmanship. However, Yama was definitely the faster of the two. The boy with pure white hair, who was introduced as Tashami, exhibited his wind abilities. He didn't show as much power as Jilly did, but he definitely displayed more control. Then there was the beautiful Lilu. She had rubbed her hands together viciously until an electrical current engulfed them, and when she pulled her hands apart, the electricity stretched and entwined around itself. The control was masterful.

Now there were only two left to test, and Bryson was the next up. "Come on, Bryson," Debo said. "Let's see what you can do."

Bryson walked toward the testing area in a surprisingly calm state, for he had already accepted the fact that this was going to be a letdown. He cleared his throat. "I'm Bryson, resident of the Intel Kingdom, possessor of Intel Energy, and wielder of electricity. I shall dazzle you all with my talents."

Upon saying this, he pathetically raised his hands in front of him as to receive a bowl of soup. As he did so, a few, weak sparks discharged from his fingertips and quickly died out.

He scanned the director's faces. They were unreadable. He supposed that was better than scorn. Debo's face broke into a smile. "Thanks for wowing us, Bry."

"That'll be twenty pintos," Bryson said in a deadpan. "And tips are always welcome."

Debo chuckled. "Go have a seat."

It was down to one person left. Agnos strolled to the spot in the same white robes and rope tied around his waist that he wore yesterday. With each step, his sandals made a hollow noise that echoed against the walls.

"I am Agnos, resident of the Archaic Kingdom, possessor of Archaic Energy, and wielder of ancients." He reached in his pocket and pulled out a pair of black glasses with perfectly circular frames. While putting them on, he explained, "These glasses are my Ancient, and they are in the highest tier of rare pieces—a Relic. This isn't an Ancient you simply stumble upon in a shop. I could sell these glasses for an amount that would allow me to never have to work a day for the rest of my life."

Bryson didn't believe it. He sat there, laughing to himself.

"However, that would be against my morals," Agnos continued. "I strive for a deeper meaning to this world, and these glasses provide access to that meaning." He paused again as he pulled out a book from his robes. "Here I have a book from the Cyn Kingdom—perhaps the most notorious of the Dark Realm's kingdoms in regards to inflicting fear. Most of you know it better as the Void. This is incredibly difficult to get a hold of, but it's important for my demonstration. In the Cyn Kingdom, they speak Cynnus. It's a very unique language that sounds similar to a mixture of a snake's hiss and a ghost's howl. Only a handful of people in the Light Realm know it.

"I myself, have never practiced other languages. I know one language, and that's Sphairian. But this doesn't matter. Why? Because this Ancient allows me to interpret any language, no matter if I'm reading or hearing it."

Agnos walked toward the directors and showed Grand Director Poicus the book. It only took a mere glance for Poicus to realize he didn't know what he was looking at. "Yes, that's definitely not Sphairian," the old man said as he handed it back.

"Listen," Agnos commanded. He licked his index finger and flipped through a few pages until he found the one he wanted. "'I came here to save them. I came here to spread the warmth that ignited my soul. I was a fool. I was once known around the Light Realm as the Unbreakable, but now I'm completely shattered. There is no hope in this world … Everyone should die. That's the only way to escape. No existence … Nothing. That is the only perfect world. To live is to suffer. With death comes comfort. I failed myself … Or perhaps, the world failed me.'"

Reverberating silence followed his reading.

"You're all probably wondering how I have a book written by someone who has not been seen or heard from in almost 28 years. Well, I had a long talk with one of our fellow Jestivan last night. When this person learned about my ability, they asked me to read a book they had possessed for nearly six years.

"As interesting as this is, however, I have even greater aspirations of learning about bigger, more complex stories. Stories that were documented hundreds—maybe even thousands—of years ago. Stories written in ancient text. Ancient text that can only be read by someone with these glasses I'm currently wearing. The lone problem is finding these ancient documents."

Bryson was impressed. Agnos may not be a fighter, but there was no denying this boy's intelligence.

"Extraordinary," Grand Director Poicus said. "I think I can speak on behalf of all the directors when I say one of the most rewarding perks of being a teacher are those rare moments when a student teaches us something. We seldom get to experience the wonder of gaining new knowledge such as that. Simply splendid. Thank you, Agnos. You may have a seat."

While Agnos took a seat with everyone else, the directors began whispering among themselves. Bryson decided he was okay with not being a captain. Besides, he didn't want the pressure and would probably make for a horrible leader.

As the ten students began adjusting where they were seated to better accommodate who they wanted to talk to, Bryson sat in front of Olivia and Rhyparia. "I guess us three are definitely not captain material," Bryson said.

Rhyparia smiled. "That's perfectly fine with me. It's not like any of these people would actually respect me as a captain anyways."

"You're a downer," Meow Meow snorted.

Bryson gave Rhyparia an exasperated look. "Stop being like that. You're obviously special." He then sat up intently and asked, "Why else would you have gotten to take the test by yourself and not embarrass yourself like Olivia and I did?"

"I didn't embarrass myself," Olivia said.

"Well?" Bryson pressed.

Rhyparia adjusted her bandana and looked to be thinking for a second. She then said, "I'm not sure. Like I said yesterday, I have no clue how to link my Archaic Energy with my artifact."

Bryson decided to drop it. She was being suspicious, but he didn't care enough to press the subject any further. Besides, Jilly's obnoxious shouting was distracting him. Yama, who was at the other end of Jilly's conversation, was somehow taking it in stride.

Bryson let out an enormous yawn. "Rhyparia, do you want to hang with me and Olivia after school today?" he asked.

She smiled awkwardly. It was obvious she wasn't used to that sort of offer. "Of course."

"I'm not sure what we would do, but we'll figure out something," he said with a shrug.

Rhyparia started to say something, but was cut short by Grand Director Poicus. "Attention, young ones," he commanded firmly. "We have made our decisions." He paused and asked with a smile, "Can I get a drum roll?"

Immediately, Jilly began excitedly slamming her hands on the hardwood floor—she was the only one.

"I appreciate that, Lita Jilly," Poicus said. "The captains of the two teams will be …" He made an unnecessary pause for dramatic effect while Jilly's ear-rattling pounding of the floor continued.

"Bryson and Olivia!" Poicus shouted.

Crickets—or at least that's what would have been heard if there were any. Olivia appeared unfazed, but Bryson and the rest of the Jestivan were dumbfounded. The two names Poicus just announced seemed to still echo off the walls of the empty room. Or perhaps they were echoing between each person's ears as their brains tried to make sense of this.

It was still silent. A minute had passed and the directors all seemed amused. It had to be a joke. That was the only explanation.

"Aha, you got us, Grand Director Poicus," Toshik chuckled.

Poicus fixed his eyes on the tall swordsman. "I'm serious."

Toshik's face twisted a bit. He seemed to be offended, but before he could speak up again, Agnos interrupted: "It makes sense. Grand Director Poicus, you made it very clear yesterday that our success won't rely solely on strength or speed or smarts. There are other factors to consider." He looked at Olivia and a shocked Bryson before adding, "They displayed the least talent, but that doesn't mean they are any less important to the group. I am going to make the assumption that this is going to be a test of our loyalty and camaraderie. You want to see if we can still push forward without discrimination. Am I correct in saying this?"

Poicus smiled. "A student who makes more sense the more he opens his mouth. I wasn't aware such a specimen existed."

"I appreciate that, sir."

"Everything Agnos said is correct. This is why Bryson and Olivia will be the captains. Every single one of you will have no objections to this." He paused and scanned their faces. "Is that clear?"

Not everyone answered and Toshik was still visibly upset, but Poicus ignored this. "Good, as for the teams, they were chosen at random earlier today. Also, we decided to keep the team names simple. Team Bryson and Team Olivia." Toshik rolled his eyes.

Poicus instructed the newly appointed captains to stand at two separate spots on the floor. Bryson felt ridiculous, yet a part of him was excited to prove something.

Pulling out some parchment, Poicus cleared his throat before announcing the rosters. "Joining Olivia will be Yama, Tashami, Agnos, and Lilu."

Bryson's heart sunk when he heard Lilu's name. As he visually followed her dazzling smile toward Olivia, he noticed the flower in her hair today was a lily, and of course the rest of her elegant outfit matched its brilliant white color.

Fortunately, there was a silver lining with Toshik's name not being mentioned. At least the two of them would be separated.

"As for Toshik, Jilly, Rhyparia, and Himitsu, you four will be joining Bryson," Poicus said.

Bryson made an effort to read their body language as they walked toward him. To his pleasure, Himitsu, Rhyparia, and Jilly appeared elated to be joining him. Rhyparia wore a wide smile, Jilly skipped pleasantly in his direction, and Himitsu gave him a creepy wink. Toshik, on the other hand, was noticeably reluctant, as it took him a few seconds before he decided to lazily push himself off the wall and disgruntledly walk toward the group. It was a rather snobbish and unattractive look, but Jilly put an end to it when she hopped up and flicked him in the ear.

"Dammit, Jilly!"

"Be nice!" she snapped back.

"Wise words from your Charge, Toshik," said a deep voice. It was the Adren Director, who was normally a very quiet man. "You're coming off as prissy, which is the complete opposite of what our kingdom is about."

Toshik's face deepened to a cherry red.

"Take a look at the four people standing with you," Poicus said. "During the beginning of your tenure as a Jestivan, your team will be your family. Now, this doesn't mean you can't mingle between groups. In fact, we encourage you to do so. The groups are simply there for mission purposes. These will be the people you carry out tasks with."

As he took a look at his group, Bryson felt confident. He liked his lineup. Toshik was going to be stubborn, but he was still very skilled with a sword. Himitsu had assassin blood inside of him. Black flames had always symbolized an elite killer. While Jilly didn't have full control over her wind, she still demonstrated good power with it. And her personality was the icing on the cake. Then there was Rhyparia. She claimed to not know anything about her Ancient, but there was reason for doubt. But with that said, she was the only person—outside of Olivia and Himitsu, whom he had known previously—he had gotten to talk to, so he felt comfortable with her.

Olivia's group was probably even more formidable. She had Yama—perhaps the scariest Jestivan in regards to technique, speed, and fighting ability. Bryson could recall not blinking once during her test. Then there were Agnos and Lilu—the two most intelligent of the Jestivan. Agnos had a different sort of intelligence. He was wise. Lilu was factual. However, Agnos's downside was his uselessness in battle. Her final member raised the biggest question mark. Bryson struggled to remember his name … Tashami—that was it. He demonstrated decent control of his Spirit Energy, but everything about him screamed "decent."

"That's it for today," Poicus said. "I insist that all of you get to know each other over the next four days. Training will start next week. We will not meet down here, but back above ground." There were a few sighs of relief in response to the last statement. It did feel sort of claustrophobic down below the sea.

"And you will be meeting with your specific Energy Directors," Poicus continued. "We won't meet as a group. Any questions?"

"Why are we getting four days off?" Lilu asked.

"Two reasons. One, we want you to get to know each other without distraction. Two, training will not be an easy task—physically or mentally. All of you, as well as the directors, need time to prepare for what is to come."

And with that, he gave an evil grin before dismissing them.

8

Lilac Suites

The plan for Bryson's team to stick together and hang out for the night didn't last long. Before fifteen minutes had passed, Toshik peeled off to meet up with one of his many lady friends. To be honest, Bryson didn't mind. The only thing that bothered him was that he could sense Jilly's mood dampen a bit when he left. She did well in masking it, but it still showed.

Bryson, Rhyparia, Jilly, and Himitsu were walking around the lively perimeter of the school. Phesaw's campus was continuously bustling with activity, for there was no curfew inside of the grounds. While a fair amount of the students, such as Bryson, commuted to and from school, most were housed in dorms. Because of this, there were many fun attractions and areas of interest circling the school, including the different dorm buildings.

The group had just entered Phesaw Park, a serene field of rich green grass blanketed in patches of pink petals that had fallen from the cherry blossom trees scattered throughout. These canopies stretched for miles, drowning the park in a cooling shade.

Jilly's red kimono flowed with each bounce as she hopped from one clear spot of grass to the other, careful to not step on any of the petals on the ground. She claimed they were lava and shrieked in fake horror each time someone stepped in it. Himitsu made a point to purposely and teasingly step on every pink spot they passed, and he would make sure to accompany it with a sinister smile. She retorted that he was a, in her own words … a "big butt face".

Bryson soaked in the environment's beauty. Typically, he didn't like this sort of scenery, but with friends, it felt different. He glanced to his right and, for some reason, finally realized just how gorgeous Rhyparia was. Her umbrella was open and resting on her shoulder. He couldn't find the logic behind it being open while walking through the shade, but he didn't care. It was an elegant look for someone wearing clothes comparable to rags.

They approached a stretch of the park that was clear of cherry blossoms and took a seat in soft grass that felt more like clouds. This was a popular area, as students would come here to participate in playful duels after school. Their timing was perfect, for two students were mid-brawl with a couple friends from each side cheering them on.

One was using electricity—an Intel student. The other was using wind—a Spirit student. Bryson was impressed by their fighting ability. They demonstrated more skill with their energies than Bryson ever could—and he was supposed to be a Jestivan.

However, they weren't capable of emitting their energies through space. In order for their abilities to strike home, they had to use hand-to-hand combat. Although it was still a notable skill, it was common and expected from an advanced student at Phesaw. Expelling their abilities through space was something that only a handful of students could accomplish.

They also lacked quickness, making their movements slow and predictable. Bryson couldn't use his electricity in combat yet, but he had elite speed. He had Debo to thank for this. Debo always taught him speed and technique first; the energy would come later. In fact, the Intel Director pointed out that not even *he* used his electricity in fights. He had to be pushed to his limit before turning to his Intel Energy. It was a last resort.

As Bryson observed the fight, he thought of something funny. "I would pay to watch Yama fight one of them."

"I think you meant eat one of them for breakfast," Himitsu said.

Jilly frowned. "Don't say that. Yama would never eat anyone."

Bryson slapped his face. "Jilly … sarcasm."

Jilly ignored him, stood up, and yelled, "Let's go, boys! I believe in you!"

The two duelists' eyes lit up as they saw who it was. When they started fighting again, they turned the intensity up while their friends whispered and glanced in the Jestivan's direction.

The students knew who Bryson, Jilly, Rhyparia, and Himitsu were. Of course. After the spectacle yesterday morning, who wouldn't?

Fists were thrown harder and kicks were narrowly dodged. The Spirit student swung a kick that had a hefty gust of wind following it. His opponent ducked under the kick, but he straightened up too quickly and the whiplash of wind struck his face. It was a common mistake with amateur fighters—loss of awareness.

The Intel student hit the ground with a thud, and his friends quickly hurried in his direction. "That's enough!" Rhyparia shouted. "There's no need to try to knock each other out for our entertainment. You're not here to hurt one another. You're here to have fun and practice."

Himitsu pouted. "Spoil sport."

Rhyparia gave him a stern look. "You're twisted if you found that fun."

"Why thank you," Himitsu said. "But since when is suffering a minor wind burn equivalent to getting hurt?"

"Look at him. He's lying on the ground in pain. He's obviously hurt," she said.

Himitsu nonchalantly leaned back on his elbows. "He's weak. Him being hurt is a byproduct of him being weak."

Bryson smirked at the intriguing logic.

"You're as big a poop as Toshik," Jilly said.

Bryson found himself amused more by his fellow teammate's bickering than the duel he'd just witnessed. In an odd way, the bickering was a good sign. You don't bicker unless you feel comfortable with the people around you. Constantly being nice is fake—something only needed when dealing with simple acquaintances.

As late afternoon progressed into evening and the sun began to sink below the horizon, the group decided to visit the dormitories of the Jestivan who'd chosen to live on campus this year.

It turned out being a Jestivan came with many perks. Their rooms were in the most lavish of dorm buildings, the Lilac Suites. Violet-shuttered windows lined each level of the four-story brick building, and the glass doors on the fourth floor led to private balconies.

The Lilac Suites sat in the most beautiful—and expensive—section of Phesaw's campus; northeast of the school. Four perfectly laid cobblestone paths converged in front of the building, one of them exiting from Phesaw Park. It was a place where nothing came cheap, and it only took a few minutes of exploring to learn this. Even Tabby's, a quaint gift shop, stocked nothing under twenty pintos—not even their chocolates. This was probably because their chocolates came from the plantations of the Passion Kingdom's western volcanoes. The bar wasn't really a bar. It was more of an elegant lounge with a band of string instruments as entertainment.

This part of campus was referred to as Wealth's Crossroads, and it had a reputation for representing the snobs of the school. Bryson wanted to dismiss this as just a stereotype, but to be fair, he'd been told that this was where Toshik lived for the past several school years.

When they walked into the Lilac Suites, they were greeted with a relatively empty lobby. It wasn't late enough for most people to have come home yet. Students were either training, attending afterschool activities, or hanging out with friends.

The lobby was expansive. A piano sat to the far left, and next to it was a small indoor pond with a miniature waterfall crashing into it. A bar sat at the center of the back wall with several tables and chairs scattered in front of it. The receptionist desk was to the right along with some very luxurious violet-colored furniture.

The interesting thing about this building was that even though it was four floors high, the lobby's ceiling extended to the roof. As Bryson gazed upward, he could clearly see every level. Each floor circled the perimeter of the building's walls. Ivory white railings ran along the edges, so a person could lean over and look down into the lobby from above. However, the most stunning aspect of the Lilac Suites was the massive, sparkling white chandelier that dangled from the ceiling, passing all three floors until it stopped directly above the lobby.

Rhyparia looked around, then bounced her fists against her hips. "I think it's a smidge too much." She glanced down at her clothes and smirked ruefully. "Then again, I also wear this rubbish."

"I tried swinging on it yesterday, but the receptionist yelled at me," Jilly said, waving her arm in the direction of a young lady at the counter to the right.

Bryson gave Jilly a dumbfounded look but decided to not question her common sense—or lack thereof. He scanned through the few people scattered throughout the lobby and spotted two Jestivan sitting at the bar—Agnos and Yama. Neither of whom looked to be enjoying themselves. Bryson couldn't hear what they were saying, but their aggressive postures made it obvious that it was not a pleasant conversation.

Jilly followed Bryson's eyes and opened her mouth to shout a greeting, but he alertly covered her mouth. He wanted to know why they weren't with the rest of their group. He pointed to the farthest table from Yama and Agnos. "Sit down. Don't draw attention to yourselves."

To Bryson's surprise, they obeyed. Jilly whispered a hearty "Yes, sir!" which he found amusing.

This was when Bryson's problem with always being cold came in handy. He wore a hooded jacket wherever he went, which he put up now to conceal himself. He silently made his way toward the bar and took a seat on a stool a few spots down from the arguing duo. When the balding barkeep approached him, Bryson waved the man off. Bryson cinched the drawstring of his hood as an extra precaution. He had no need to look in their direction. He only needed to hear them, so he leaned to his left a tiny bit.

The first voice he heard belonged to Yama. "I told you. It *can't* be him. It's *not* him."

Agnos responded in an irritated tone that Bryson hadn't heard from him before. "He works there, Yama. Get that through your thick skull."

"So what if he works there? There are plenty of people who work there."

"You don't know him like I do. I was his best friend for years. He was only your Charge … which was unfortunate for him. Toshik protects his Charge better than you could."

Then glass shattered, for Yama had squeezed her glass to its breaking point. She had lost all awareness of where she was or she simply did not care. "Stop blaming me for what happened, prick," Yama hissed. "I had no control over that. He chose his own way."

"Incorrect. He chose that *woman's* way, and you allowed it. Once she came into the picture, he completely changed. I know he robbed the Archaic Museum yesterday. And I know it was because of *that woman.*"

"Anyone in Kuki Sphaira could have robbed the museum."

"False," Agnos said. "The only way that place could be robbed during the night hours is by someone inside. There are far too many important Ancient Pieces in there."

The constant denial of Yama's rebuttals pissed her off more. "He has no need for such a dark relic."

"That was once true—back when he was someone I looked up to. Then you came in and failed at your job. And you're the reason why he's gone. He is no longer the Toono we knew."

Bryson braced himself for the retaliation, but he didn't hear one, so he decided to take a subtle peek. Yama simply sat there, looking blankly at the bar in front of her. The bad-ass woman was now struggling to hold back tears.

Agnos seemed unconcerned. He put money on the table for the barkeeper and walked away.

Bryson slipped out of his seat and retreated to his group's table, welcomed by the inquisitive glares of his teammates. He could tell that Jilly was really battling hard to not run to Yama's rescue.

"Go ahead, Jilly. She could probably use a friend," Bryson said in a deflated tone.

"Thank you." She said it without a smile. It was his first sighting of a serious Jilly.

Jilly took a seat next to Yama and put her arm around Yama's waist, pulling her inward slightly. Yama's head rested on Jilly's shoulder, her purple hair falling next to Jilly's golden tresses.

"What's this I'm hearing about the Archaic Museum being robbed yesterday?" Bryson asked.

Rhyparia looked at him, stunned. "Is *that* what they were arguing about?"

Bryson nodded.

"Agnos shouldn't be discussing that with her. That news isn't to leave the Archaic Kingdom," Rhyparia said with disgust. "Reckless."

"And why is that?" Himitsu asked.

Rhyparia fidgeted for a moment before leaning in and whispering conspiratorially, "An ancient piece was stolen from the Archaic Museum last night, which is news in itself." She leaned in closer. "However, such a big uproar was made about it that people are beginning to speculate that it was a relic—a very dangerous relic. But that's all there is as of right now … speculation. Only the museum's higher staff knows exactly—along with Archaic King Itta."

Himitsu stared at her. "Hold on," he said. "Didn't Agnos say his glasses are a relic? They don't seem so dangerous."

"Not all ancient pieces have to be dangerous or combat-oriented. Some can be tactical. Some can even be fun and harmless. There are three tiers to ancients. You have the fossils, which are very basic and common pieces. They usually impart weaker abilities. Then there are the artifacts, which are the mid-tier. My umbrella would fall into that category. The relics are rare and powerful."

She leaned back in her seat. "A few would tell you there are four tiers, but most would call B.S. on that."

Himitsu thought for a bit, then asked, "Wouldn't something like that be insanely protected?"

Rhyparia raised a finger. "And *that's* the mystery. It's heavily guarded—understatement—at all hours. That goes triple during the night, making last night's robbery even more baffling."

"Agnos said it was from a person who worked within the walls," Bryson said. "One of the security guards."

Rhyparia tapped her fingers on the table. "That would make sense. Heh, that Agnos … he's a really smart guy."

9

The Theft

The Archaic Museum was closing to the public and the graveyard shift was about to begin. A young man who looked to be in his early twenties walked through the front doors and into the entrance hall as the final visitors straggled out. His most distinguishing feature was the bandage circling the upper portion of his head.

He walked through a tall, arching hallway before reaching his designated station. Known as Relic Alley, it was the most important area of the museum and probably the most revered landmark of the Archaic Kingdom. It was his responsibility to stand guard in this cavernous corridor displaying some of the rarest ancient pieces known to exist.

The clock struck 10 P.M., signaling the end of the third shift. As the young man approached Relic Alley, he nodded to the guard he was relieving.

"Try not to fall asleep," the departing guard said.

"Tell that to the head officer," the young man said lightly.

He received a smile from his coworker. "Indeed. Don't work too hard. Have an ethical night, Toono."

Ethical—if only he knew. Shrouded in darkness, Toono prepared as he always did. He grabbed his own ancient piece from within his cloak. It was a bubble wand like the ones children played with during the summer months. However, this was a grander version, rivaling the length of a sword. It was wooden and had four holes—three at the top that were each a different size and one at the bottom of the handle.

A bubble wand. Admittedly, it sounded silly, but it was exactly why he was the museum's premier guard outside of the head officer. He inhaled deeply then blew into the wand's second hole from the top, causing a modest-sized bubble to escape, roughly the size of a wardrobe. He then waved the bubble toward one of the displays, which it swallowed completely. He repeated this process until every relic occupied its own protective home.

The night went as routinely as any other would. He appeared to be fulfilling his duties, but in reality, he was simply stalling for the right time.

A couple more hours passed, and the head officer was supposed to start his scheduled rounds. His job was to make sure everyone was still alert and not slacking off. Unfortunately for the museum, they hired an incompetent and hypocritical man who frequently slept through the night. Toono was hoping this would be the case tonight.

He left his post and swiftly headed down the moonlit hall, his cloak softly billowing behind him. Snoring became gradually louder the closer he got to the front lobby. And sure enough, when he looked into the man's office, he was knocked out in his chair.

The young man immediately returned to Relic Alley. He craned up his neck toward his exit route. The ceiling was high, and at the top of the walls were open windows that allowed the moonlight to shine through, but they were barred and too high to reach. He blew into his wand again, this time into the smallest hole. A pebble-sized bubble escaped and floated upward until it passed through the window and out of sight.

Now he was forced to wait patiently. He continued to stare at the window until his neck grew tired. Glancing toward one of the museum displays, his eagerness began to swell at the sight of five white gems.

A noise akin to eggs being cooked in a pan startled him from his trance. He looked back up to the same window—this time with good news. She had responded to his signal. A corrosive substance was eating at the bars.

He had to move quickly. The nitric acid didn't care about stealth, so it continued to crack and sizzle. Toono approached the display he'd had his eyes on for the past year as he created another bubble from the middle hole. This time he enclosed his own body in it, and in the process, scooped up the five gems and hurriedly stuffed them inside of his cloak.

Alas, it was too late. The head officer was staring Toono down from the corridor's entry way. His daunting height and lean build dwarfed Toono's more modest frame.

"Please ... Just let me leave." It was a placid request from Toono.

The officer glared at the thief. "I can't believe you, Toono. I cannot allow that."

Toono glanced toward the now open window. The acid had finished its work. "I don't like killing. Even when I started with rodents, it tore me apart. But if you oppose me, I'll have no choice but to mark you as the first tally on my already long list of murders. Don't make me do this. Unlike the others, your death would be unnecessary. It would serve no purpose than allowing me to escape."

Despite the warning, the officer ran toward the thief with his sword drawn. A man of the Adren Kingdom in charge of protecting a building inside of the Archaic Kingdom ... *typical.*

Even when opposed by a man who possessed such staggering speed, there was no fear reflecting in the blue eyes of Toono. It was as calm as the tranquil breeze of an autumn night. The officer lunged at Toono with an aggressive swing of his sword, but the thief did not move, for when the sword made contact with the bubble, it ricocheted backward so viciously that the blade's spine hit the officer between the eyes.

While the officer staggered backward, the bubble-shielded Toono sprinted in the direction of the far wall. The man recovered himself and gave chase. Without breaking stride, Toono leapt toward the wall feet first, making his body parallel to the floor. As his soles connected with the stone, his knees bent while the bubble surrounding him flattened a bit. Both instances were to act as springs. Toono launched viciously in the opposite direction at a speed that rivaled the officer's. With no time to react, the officer was blasted by the impact. His flailing body flew violently across the room with such velocity that there was no arc to his trajectory. He hit the far wall with a sickening thud, and like a bug splattered against a fly-swatter, held there for a moment before sliding to the ground.

The young thief stared gravely at the bloody, crumpled mess. This sight was the first alarming signal of him transitioning into a person he never thought he'd be. Regardless, he had done what was needed of him.

Bouncing a few times to gradually gain height, he continued to observe the lifeless body. However, his anguish was only a fleeting sense before he soared through the open window, excited about the progress that was just made and, more important, the opportunity to finally share good news with the woman waiting for him outside.

10

Speed Percentage

The next four days made Bryson realize just how much fun having friends could be. He decided to sleep over in Himitsu's dorm room instead of going home. This allowed him to see Lilu on a regular basis, though he could never quite work up the courage to talk to her. The only face that was missing frequently was Olivia's, as she always had to go straight home before dark.

Bryson had learned very little about Himitsu during his stay. He tended to keep his personal matters to himself. However, he was able to learn a bit about Jilly and Rhyparia.

Jilly's mom was dead. She died giving birth to her. Her father was a major in the Spirit Army, which was why Toshik was appointed as her protector at a young age. Her father was constantly away from home, so Toshik was supposed to fill the role of an older brother—which he fulfilled in a certain sense.

Rhyparia was different from the rest. Both of her parents and all of her siblings were alive. She had five siblings, and Rhyparia was the second oldest. They all still lived under the same roof—if you wanted to call it a roof. Supposedly it was a collection of large blankets sewn together. Their house was a shack with three rooms: a kitchen, a bathroom, and an open space where they all slept together. Bryson felt terrible imagining seven people trying to live in a three-room shack—and it turned out that Rhyparia wished that there were less of them to crowd the space.

As they sat in the lobby of the Lilac Suites during lunch on their last day of break, Jilly made an envious remark about Rhyparia's mother through a mouthful of Tabby's chocolates. But Rhyparia stopped her cold, saying, "I'd rather my parents were dead."

The tension that followed was as stiff as the wooden chairs they sat upon. Jilly was flabbergasted and Bryson didn't know what to think. Himitsu smirked and said, "Ooh, you are an interesting one."

Bryson thought about it for a second and asked, "Doesn't that completely go against what your kingdom is about?"

She rested her head on the table and looked out the window. "Ha, *morality*. In this case, I don't care. They deserve it. Hopefully, fate will get them."

Although curious, Bryson decided not to further press the subject. "Okay then … no more of that," Jilly said.

Himitsu casually leaned back in his chair. "I can't wait to train tomorrow. And by the Passion Director herself." He smiled. "I should learn a lot."

Professors typically handled students. The directors were more like the school's board of executives. They were highly skilled and revered, but to be taught and trained by one was a privilege that not many students got to experience. Bryson, however, had been trained by Debo his entire life, so it wasn't anything new to him.

"Debo is going to work me and Lilu like dogs," Bryson moaned.

"It's so weird when you don't address him as 'Director,'" Jilly said.

Bryson shrugged and looked back at Rhyparia, who was still staring out the window. Mentally, she was off in a dark place.

*　　　*　　　*

The next morning, Bryson found himself waiting in the common area of Phesaw's Knowledge Wing, where the Intel students gathered for breakfast, lunch, and dinner. But this morning it served a different purpose, as the room was cleared for the two Intel Jestivans' training session.

Bryson was stretching when Lilu strolled out of the lady's restroom. She had gotten changed out of her gleaming golden dress and into an outfit that surprised him—a pair of white training boots, loose athletic shorts, and a white t-shirt. Her flowing green hair was now in a messy bun—and flowerless.

"Nice look," he snickered as Lilu began stretching.

She looked up as she reached down to her right foot. "I may seem like a high-maintenance girl, but I'm not an imbecile. As much as I prefer heels and a dress, I can't train or fight properly like that."

"Always taking everything as an insult to your intelligence. The hostility."

"I'm proud of the kingdom I live in and I want to represent what it's about to my fullest extent. That's all."

Bryson watched her stretch for a second, thinking about what she said. "I don't know if I feel the same way. Our kingdom has done some shady stuff in the past."

"Are you impugning the king—my father?" Lilu snapped.

"Correct," he said—a little too casually.

Lilu opened her mouth to quickly retort, but Bryson corrected himself: "*Partially* correct, I mean. I'm impugning *our* fathers … both of them."

She frowned. "They did what was best for the Intel Kingdom."

"They also hurt people in the process."

"People from the *Dark* Realm," Lilu said, shocked.

"They're still people."

The door to the commons swung open, halting the conversation. Intel Director Debo entered, but he was followed by a trio of unexpected faces: Adren Director Buredo, Toshik, and Yama.

Bryson rolled his eyes, for he knew exactly what this meant. He wouldn't be learning how to hone in his Intel Energy and electrical abilities, and he was an idiot for thinking otherwise. Lilu, apparently not yet realizing what a farce this was going to be, looked totally confused as she watched the three guests place their swords against the wall.

"I talked to Grand Director Poicus this morning," Debo said. "We'll be conducting joint training sessions with the Adren Director. Director Buredo was kind enough to agree to this."

Bryson could not help but notice how tall Director Debo, Director Buredo, and Toshik were. Each of them were pushing six-foot-six.

"I don't understand, Director. Do we not have our own energies and abilities to polish?" Lilu asked. "Toshik and Yama must focus on their Adrenergy in order to perfect their speed. Bryson and I must do the same for our Intel Energy to perfect our electrical abilities."

"Bryson must have not told you how I train my pupils, Lita Lilu," Debo said. She shook her head.

"Your Intel Energy isn't that important. In fact, none of the energies are important at the beginning." Lilu's eyebrow rose a bit. "Your abilities bloom naturally. While training to control your energy may help somewhat, it is really more of a natural thing than anything else. When the time comes, you will be able to wield your electricity effectively. So let's forget about our energies and focus on something you can improve—your speed and technique."

Bryson sighed a bit louder than he meant to.

"What is it, Bryson?" the Intel Director asked.

"This is so bland! This is all you've ever taught me since I was five. This same old spiel."

"And obviously you still haven't heard it enough." Debo turned to Director Buredo. "When do children in the Adren Kingdom start learning how to fight, Director Buredo?"

"At the age of two," he replied in a deep tone.

"And what are they taught?"

"How to be fast and agile, yet make every move a calculated one."

"Precisely!" Debo said. "I couldn't have said it better myself. *That* is what makes the swordsmen and swordswomen of the Adren Kingdom so fearsome." He looked at Bryson and Lilu. "Did you know most of their speed doesn't actually come from their Adrenergy?"

"Really?" Lilu asked. She was heavily invested in Debo's lecture. Bryson, however, had zoned out.

"Yes, Lilu," Buredo said. "Only a small percentage of our speed comes from our Adrenergy. The rest of it is from the years of work we put into perfecting our bodies and natural fighting abilities."

Lilu's face lit up. "I'm aware of the concept of speed percentage. I was never really taught about it though, as it's more relevant to the Adren students."

Director Buredo nodded, but Lilu continued her little lecture. "The scale is obviously 0 to 100%. The 100% is equivalent to max speed, which is based off the fabled two-second mile, but nobody actually knows who ran that. It's more of a measuring stick. How much of that 100% can be achieved without Adrenergy?"

"It is believed to be 70%," Buredo replied.

"Wow," Lilu paused in shock. "So people of any kingdom can become fast? And the other 30% is limited to the people of the Adren Kingdom?"

The Adren Director smiled. "Technically, yes. But most of our warriors can barely tap into their Adrenergy, just like most of your people can barely tap into their Intel Energy. A typical student can only reach an average of 32% of max speed—29% of that due to the years of physical training and 3% being our Adrenergy."

"So I could potentially reach the speed of most Adren Kingdom warriors?"

"Perhaps," he said, "if you had been training from the age of two. What is your speed now?"

Lilu blushed. "I've never had it measured."

"It's time to change that," Debo cut in. "Today, we will be recording each of your speed percentages. Then at the end of the school year, we'll measure it again.

"We'll pair the girls together and the boys together. You'll time your partner to see how fast it takes him or her to run across the length of this room."

Bryson gazed up at Toshik as the warrior handed him the clock. "Hey, man. We really didn't get to talk much during the break. Glad we're going to get to work together."

Toshik sneered. "Just focus on timing me." As he turned away to walk to the opposite wall, he added, "Don't blink."

Slightly offended, Bryson frowned. He couldn't harness his electricity, but when it came to speed, he was well trained. He smiled inwardly. *Finally, a chance to gain this snob's respect.*

While Toshik and Yama crouched into ready position, Bryson prepared himself to time correctly. He knew how quickly he would have to click the stop button after pressing go. You needed insane reflexes to time a talented Adren resident, for they'd be at the finish line in an instant. To the untrained eye, they would disappear.

"Bryson and Lilu, you ready?" Director Debo asked.

They nodded with intense concentration.

He smiled. "I hope so." Then he raised his hand and shouted, "Go!"

As expected, Toshik was fast, but not to the point where Bryson couldn't see him. He timed it perfectly, pressing the stop button exactly when Toshik reached the finish line. He knew by looking at the time that Toshik had done well, but he wouldn't know the exact percentage until he calculated the conversions.

Toshik started to say something to Bryson, but Debo's laughter cut through the room. He was laughing at a distraught Lilu, whose green hair was blown out of its bun and laying in a frizzy mess down her back.

Bryson and Toshik couldn't hide their amusement either. Lilu wasn't ready for Yama's speed since her eyes and reflexes weren't accustomed to this sort of thing.

Debo finally regained his composure and said, "I'm guessing you didn't get the time."

Lilu shook her head, her eyes still wide with awe.

"I'll do it," Director Buredo said. As he took the timer from Lilu, Yama resituated herself at the starting spot.

"Go!" Debo shouted.

It was over in an instant. Now Bryson realized why Lilu was traumatized. It was like Yama teleported as if she was from the Dark Realm's Dev Kingdom. He caught a glimpse of a blurred trail of color—or maybe he just imagined it. She was significantly faster than Toshik.

"You really know how to get me going," Toshik said with a smile.

"Shut up," Yama snapped.

As the two began their typical bickering, Bryson and Lilu readied themselves for their sprint. Bryson had both hands resting on the floor and focused intensely on his first step. The push-off was critical. He thought about what Debo always told him:

Acceleration should be instantaneous, not steady. Eventually you should reach a point when the ready stance or even a slight bend in the knee isn't necessary. You should be able to push-off from any position and hit your speed percentage immediately. That is what will make you dangerous.

After replaying this lecture in his mind, Bryson decided to relax from the stance he was in. He stood up, his arms dangling casually. Toshik laughed, but Debo smiled—a sincere and proud smile. This would make up for his awful display during the captain's test.

For the third time, Debo shouted, "Go!"

When Bryson took the first step, he knew he was golden. While reaching the opposite wall, Toshik's face was still shifting from amusement to bewilderment. Knocking the smug look off his face pleased Bryson more than it probably should have.

Yama, too, looked a bit surprised. She must have noticed from the corner of her eye. Since Lilu was much slower, Yama had time to avert her attention.

The best reaction, however, was Director Buredo's. He was an unflappable man, so his arched eyebrows said a lot.

Bryson's ego swelled, so when he walked past Toshik, he swept his golden bangs from his face and asked, "Did you blink?"

Toshik stammered slightly before realizing there was nothing he could say.

After everyone calculated the times of their partner, it was time for their speed percentages to be announced. Director Debo opened up the first folded parchment. "With her first ever speed percentage test, Lilu ran at 20%, which is average for someone not from the Adren Kingdom. We'll definitely improve on that throughout the year."

Lilu's lips pursed in disappointment. "I'm sorry, Director. As royalty, I should be exceeding expectations in all categories."

"Don't be so hard on yourself," he replied. "Like I said, you were trained differently before now. We're not expecting you to be perfect, and you will improve. Director Buredo and I will make sure of this."

He opened up the next parchment. "Ah, Toshik. No surprise here. You clocked in at 42%. Very nicely done. You represent the Adren Kingdom splendidly, and, like Lilu, you will improve on that percentage."

Toshik gave a slight nod.

Debo moved on. When he opened the third parchment, he grinned wide. "Bryson, you clocked in at 41%."

Bryson couldn't hide his satisfaction. Meanwhile, Toshik seemed sick to his stomach.

Yama couldn't resist the chance to take a stab at her rival. "Take into consideration that three to four percent of Toshik's speed is coming from Adrenergy, it seems that Bryson's natural speed is faster than Toshik's." She winked at Toshik. "That's either very impressive on Bryson's part or very pathetic on Toshik's."

Deep resentment flooded Toshik's face. "Stop it, now," Director Buredo commanded to his two Jestivan.

Debo wiggled his fingers together in anticipation for the final parchment. "I already know this next number will be high." As he unfolded it, he shook his head and laughed. "53%. My goodness, Lita Yama."

Bryson's stomach dropped. That number was ludicrous for someone of her age—someone of *any* age, really.

"You're nearly three times as fast as I am," Lilu said, smiling with admiration.

"That's not how I look at it," Yama said.

"And how do you look at it?" Debo asked.

"I look at it as exactly what it is. I'm 53% of max speed, 47% short of my goal. I'm just scraping past the halfway mark."

The room fell silent for a moment. "You want to reach max speed?" Debo asked.

"Of course."

"Not even Director Buredo is close to that speed. No one is. Nobody even knows where the two-second mile came from."

"It exists for a reason," Yama said, frowning. "Someone achieved it in the past. Regardless of how far in the past it was, it still happened—and it will happen again. I must reach max speed."

Yama took several steps toward Debo and looked him dead in the eye. Although she was significantly shorter, he blanched as she asked, "Are you doubting me, Director?"

One side of his mouth curved upward. "Not at all, Yama. Your resolve sends chills down my spine." He put a hand on her shoulder. "I will cherish the time spent training you into what you want to become. You have a fighter's spirit."

"Thank you, sir."

The rest of the day was fairly boring. Because of Lilu, the training was basic. Bryson assumed the Directors didn't want to break her confidence by separating her from the others.

One of these drills was suicides—sprinting from the starting line to another spot and back, and then out again, each time to a further line. It was simplistic, but for Lilu, it was a type of conditioning she wasn't used to. Bryson spent a lot of the morning and afternoon patting her on the back as she puked into a trash can. He could only think about the surprise she was in for when they finally got to the real speed training.

When it came time to end the day, the Directors left and Jilly came to pick Yama up and take a walk around the school grounds. But Bryson, Toshik, and Lilu lingered in the commons. Lilu was sprawled on the floor. She had given up on attempting to stand, for each time she tried, her legs would not cooperate. She was moaning about how disgusting she felt, but Bryson found her as attractive as ever. He imagined wiping the sweat from her forehead, looking into her ivy green eyes. An exhausted lady of royalty looking up at him with a desperate longing for something that would distract her from a long day's struggles. He thought about what that something was, then boldly leaned in for the kiss.

Then a low moan dragged him from his daydreaming. It was Lilu. She was moaning with pleasure as Toshik massaged her shoulders.

Bryson felt like an idiot. As always, while he was imagining things, someone else *did* things.

"So Bryson, how'd you get so fast?" Toshik asked.

He couldn't believe Toshik had the nerve to casually strike up a conversation while touching Lilu, but he reluctantly answered anyways.

"Debo taught me everything I know."

"Impressive. At first, I was a bit pissed that you showed me up, but I respect that sort of skill. You had me nervous last week with that pitiful display during the captain's test." He gave Bryson a wide grin.

Bryson was unsure how to respond. Was that an insult, or a compliment? "Err, thanks?"

Toshik chuckled. "It was a compliment. I apologize if it sounded bad. I'm not good at praising guys."

"I understand." Bryson got up and put on his hoodie. Raindrops pattered against the building. "I'm going to head home. You two enjoy your night," he said dully.

Bryson walked out of Phesaw with a bittersweet feeling. On one hand, he hated Toshik for being bold enough to make moves on Lilu, but on the other, he was happy to have gained some of his respect. The most important part was making sure his teammates were on the same page as he was.

As Bryson lackadaisically strolled through the rain toward Telejunction, he heard someone shout for him from behind. "Bryson! Hold on!"

He turned around to see Lilu running toward him. Her green hair was sopping wet from the rain, and she was still in her shorts and t-shirt.

"Why are you out here like that?" he said. "You're going to get sick."

Her eyes narrowed. "You're not my mom. Anyways, I had a question."

Bryson's heart fluttered. "And what's that?" he asked as casually as he could as he took off his jacket and set it on her shoulders.

"Well—" she paused. Her eyes became fixated on his bare chest. On his right pectoral muscle was a giant scar in the shape of a *T*, and on the left was a similar scar in the shape of a *2*.

Lilu pressed a finger against his chest and ran it across the wound, and Bryson's heart fluttered again.

"What happened?" she asked, sounding sincerely concerned for him.

"I don't know. I don't remember a time when I didn't have this scar."

She looked at him with unease. "That wasn't on accident."

Bryson let out a laugh. "Obviously not." He reached behind Lilu and pulled up the jacket's hood for her. "Now, what did you want to ask?"

She paused. Bryson knew she wanted to discuss his scar some more, but he wasn't interested. Her shoulders slumped and she asked, "Can Director Debo help me with speed percentage training outside of class? I know he teaches you at home, so I'm wondering if I can come over some nights to learn with you."

This was his chance. "Of course," he said, trying to sound nonchalant.

"Awesome!" she shouted. "I won't come tonight because my body is dead, but I'll try one of these nights this week. See ya!" She turned around and sprinted back toward the school, splashing through puddles as she flew down the expansive hill. "I'll give your jacket back tomorrow!" she yelled.

While Bryson stood shirtless in the downpour and watched her disappear, all he could think about was how much he didn't want the jacket back. He liked the thought of her having a piece of him wrapped around her body. If only he was aware of the stupid smile on his face.

*   *   *

The sun sat high in the sky as the sizzling heat of midday beat down upon the grounds. Outside Phesaw's Morality Wing, a lone young man lay exhausted in the grass. His matted black hair was lathered in sweat and his breathing was heavy. Not experienced with physical strain, his body and lungs felt as if they would shut down at any second.

He wasn't a fighter, so being forced to train like one was frustrating. Having to wear athletic clothes only made it worse, and the humidity made it feel like he was layered in heavy wool.

He was staring at a gymnasium off in the distance. The door creaked open and an old man poked his head around the corner. It was Archaic Director Senex. He shook his head. "That will not do, Agnos. You must work. Although we're not counting on you to fight, you still must know the basics of it. And before we can get to the basics, you must train your body."

Agnos lay still for a second before he pushed himself up to his knees. "You always separate me and Rhyparia, Director Senex."

"And that's because my most important job is to keep my students safe." Director Senex looked at him gravely. "Do you want to get hurt?"

"No, sir," Agnos replied.

Senex smiled. "Good. Then I will continue to keep you separate from

Rhyparia while she learns. Back to your pushups, Zana Agnos," he said, then disappeared back into the gym.

It only took a couple pushups—if they could even be called that—before he put down his knees and cheated. Pathetic, yes, but he didn't care. He had no intentions to fight, nor did he believe in combat—unless it was that of the mind.

The ground shook violently beneath him, halting any of his thoughts. It would have scared him if he wasn't used to it. Then it shook again. Then it rattled for close to ten seconds. A few leaves rocked slowly to the ground below.

Agnos gazed toward the gym again. *What in the world was Rhyparia's ability?* Not only did Director Senex refuse to allow Agnos inside the shed while she was training, he wouldn't let him in at all. This sorely ticked him off. If there was one thing he hated more than anything, it was secrecy. He always wanted answers, and it explained why he cherished his ancient.

Agnos decided that the sporadic vibrating of the ground was an excuse to give up on exercising. He walked over to his bag and pulled out his glasses and the book by the Unbreakable. Nothing could distract him from reading.

*   *   *

On the opposite end of Phesaw, outside of the Spirit Wing, two more Jestivan were in the midst of their training session. Agnos would have been jealous, for this session seemed more like leisure than work. Spirit Director Neaneuma was strolling through the gardens while Jilly and Tashami followed closely behind her.

Neaneuma's wrinkled lips pursed together as she glanced at the destruction around her. "Jilly, look at what you've done to my flowers over the past two weeks," she said wearily.

Jilly bowed her head with a guilty look, further covering her eyes with her golden sunhat. "I'm sorry, Director Neaneuma. I'll get better with my control. It's just very diffi—" She was cut short as Director Neaneuma raised her hand.

"Go ahead, Jilly. Let's try this again."

The blond girl took a nervous gulp. She spread both arms and swung them forward, causing a heavy blast of wind to plow through the garden. Several plants were ripped up by their roots and tossed through the air. The most humiliating thing was the ripe tomato that slapped Director Neaneuma in the face.

The elderly woman wiped the juice from her eyes while Jilly resumed apologizing. "I'm always messing up! I'm so sorry!"

"It's not only you, Jilly. Both of you are frustrating. I have two students who are polar opposites. I have you, a girl who can't hold back." She then turned her gaze to the ivory-haired Tashami. "And I have you, a boy who *only* holds back. I have two extremes. There is no middle ground."

Tashami simply returned her stare as a gentle breeze blew past. "I know that's your breeze, Tashami," Neaneuma said.

"I like soothing winds," he said. "They're pleasing enough to be noticed and appreciated, but not violent enough to stand out."

"As much as I also love calm winds, I still must prepare you for combat, and calm winds will serve you no purpose then. You hold back so much."

The breeze rustled through Tashami's hair as he explained himself. "I hold back because there is nothing to be gained from bringing my power to the public's attention. I'm not headed down the same road as my father. This is especially dangerous for us people of the Spirit Kingdom. It's good to believe in perseverance, but too much faith can blind us from the reality of our limitations. That's how you bite off more than you can chew."

Tashami picked a rose from the garden. "This is my logic," he said. "The less power I exert, the stronger my belief of having less power becomes. I don't want to think I can succeed at everything. My dad thought that, and that was his downfall."

"Who was your father?" Jilly asked.

"'Was'? Physically, my dad is still out there … somewhere. Mentally?" Tashami tossed the rose away. "That's a different story."

*　　*　　*

Inside a large, dimly lit corridor, the silhouettes of three people could be seen dashing around. The curvaceous Passion Director Venustas stood at the center of the room. Flashing a white smile brightly contrasting with the darkness of the room, she casually dodged attacks from her two Jestivan.

Himitsu and Olivia were composing a sequence of synchronized techniques in order to land a blow on the elusive director. Himitsu fought from the far corners of the corridor, his black flames blending with the shadows.

Since Olivia wasn't capable of using her Passion Energy, her approach was the opposite of Himitsu. Venustas was slightly more careful in avoiding her forceful blows. If Olivia made contact, she knew she'd feel it for a long time.

While concealing his presence behind the flames, Himitsu waved his hand forward, launching a line of black fire at Venustas. The Passion Director wiggled her nose before casually stepping to the left, the jet of fire blazing just past her. The sound of heavy footsteps alerted her to snap her head to the right, and as she did so, she felt a stinging wind sweep past her cheek from Olivia's tiny fist.

But Olivia wasn't done yet. Venustas heard the girl plant her foot in the ground instantaneously after missing her punch. It was a loud pivot—even for Olivia—signaling the likelihood of a vicious kick. If it was any other student's, Venustas would simply catch it, but this was Olivia … she would break her hand. So she wisely ducked low to the ground. Her long hair untucked itself from inside her cloak as Olivia's foot shot over her head. Suddenly Venustas realized that she was actually being forced to try. As she pondered this, Himitsu hit her in the back and tackled her to the ground.

The Passion Director lay motionless on the stone floor. She was breathing much heavier than normal. Himitsu could feel the fullness of her chest rising underneath his head, and he quickly jumped to his feet. He extended a helping hand, which she graciously accepted. He was happy it was too dark for her to notice his face flushing red.

"Good job with that combo," Venustas said, waving her hand at the candles around the room as fires erupted on their wicks. "I lost focus on the smell of your flames because of Olivia's continuous attacks. She gave you the opening, and you took it."

"Thank you," they replied.

"Himitsu, what are you going to do when you're put in a face-to-face, one-on-one encounter? Do you honestly think you can stab every enemy in the back?"

He smirked. "If I do my job right, then yes. If I end up in a situation you described, that means I failed as an assassin."

She responded with a sweet smile. "It's going to happen one day, dear. And when that time comes, you must know how to fight with aggression." She glanced toward the corners of the room. "Hiding in the flames and shadows are good for unsuspecting victims, but for a traditional fight, you must focus more on the skillful side than the creative side. However, even with that said, I'm still impressed. You've managed to hit me and it only took a couple weeks."

Olivia gave her a blank look. "You're not even using your Passion Energy. You're simply evading."

The director laughed. "Look who's talking, young lady. You don't use it either. How can such a tiny girl harbor so much power?" she asked.

"My mother." It was a rapid-fire answer—no hesitation at all.

Venustas's head tilted as she studied Olivia. "Typically, mothers teach their daughters how to be a stereotypical lady, which involves an absence of combat. And even if a mother did teach her daughter how to fight, it's usually an elegant style—much like mine. You, however, use brute force."

"My mother has taught me many things. She said women can be powerful and must show their independence. She also told me to never tap into my Passion Energy. Emotions make you vulnerable and vulnerability makes you weak."

"'Don't let anybody see you while you're weak—especially men,'" Olivia continued, quoting her mother. "'Stand tall, stand strong, stand proud. The moment someone sees you're emotionally weak is the moment they will walk all over you. There is always someone out there evil enough to draw out your emotions ... even when you could have sworn they were locked deep within.' That is what she always tells me."

"That's quite a weight to put on a little girl's shoulders," Director Venustas said quietly. There may have been a scent of pity along with it.

Olivia didn't respond. Meow Meow, however, was displeased. "She can handle it," he said with a stare of ice.

The director's smile returned. "True. Her composure and maturity are unprecedented." She gazed at the kitten hat for a few seconds before she tucked her hair into the back of her robes. "That's it for the day."

11

Lilu's Offer

In the midst of another gloomy day in the Intel Kingdom, a pair of teenagers strolled through the front gate of a beautiful white home. Bryson held the gate open as Lilu graciously accepted his gesture.

While they walked toward the front door, Lilu gazed into the sky and said, "I absolutely adore the suburbs. The clouds aren't as angry as the inner city."

Bryson unlocked the door, and as Lilu stepped by, he replied, "Personally, I don't think they're angry enough."

She took a moment to observe her surroundings once inside the house. "It's quaint, but so beautiful," she said with a smile.

Bryson took the training bag from her shoulder and placed it on the floor next to a group of shoes. "Thank you," he said. He looked at Lilu, who was now curiously staring down the hallway at the light-shielded closet. "Do you want something to drink? Something to eat?"

Her eyes stayed fixated on the light. He leaned in a little closer and added, "Debo is going to work us hard. You're going to need the energy."

A couple more seconds passed until she said, "Yes, water and a banana," in a distracted voice. Bryson understood that the light was odd, but he wasn't expecting her to recognize its peculiarity as quickly as she did.

When he returned from the kitchen with a water and banana in hand, he dropped them with a crash. Lilu was standing directly next to the light. He grabbed her arms and, before he knew it, her entire body was wrapped in his.

"You can't touch that," he said through startled breaths.

"I'm fully aware, Bryson. I was simply getting a closer look to cure my curiosity."

"Is it cured?" he asked.

She gently put her hand on his forearm that was wrapped around her stomach. He felt the velvety skin of her fingertips trace his skin until it reached his hand, entwining her fingers in his. His body temperature skyrocketed, reaching heights in tremendous contrast to the cold he'd felt his entire life.

She looked down at Bryson's fingers, examining each one. Then she saw what she was looking for—a scar on his index finger.

Bryson was numb with shock and bliss. He had his arms around this beautiful royal, and she was accepting his embrace. His chin was resting on her head and he could feel her playing with his fingers.

"You got this scar from this light," she said.

"I did," he affirmed with his eyes closed.

"This is Director Debo's work?" she asked.

"It is. It's an intelight … unparalleled and everlasting. A true testament to his ability."

Lilu stepped away and looked up at him. "That's not an intelight, Bryson, and it's not something that should be just sitting around like this."

Bryson snapped out of his trance and gave her an incredulous look. "It *is* an intelight. It couldn't be anything else."

"I guess that's what makes sense for you to think. If you thought otherwise, you'd know more than a commoner should know."

He was confused, but Lilu gave him no time to respond. She walked into the family room and sat at the piano, tucking her short, yellow dress underneath her. Bryson gave her a weak smile as her fingers drew out an excruciating clashing of tones. His head was aching by the time he was finally rescued by the front door swinging open.

"Who is butchering my poor piano?" asked the tall figure that just entered the house.

Lilu stopped and greeted the new face while blushing. "Hello, Director Debo."

The look on Debo's face was enough for Bryson to cry tears of laughter.

"You're only here for speed training, right?" Debo looked at the piano. "I don't know if I can fix *that*."

Lilu flushed a deeper red. "I'll go get changed," she said as she got up from her seat.

"No, you won't," Debo said flatly.

She stared at him, not sure if he was serious or not, then gestured to herself. She was wearing a sunshine dress, golden high heels, and a yellow daffodil in her hair. "I need to put on proper clothes."

"That's proper enough," Debo said while hanging up his cloak. "Meet me outside."

"He has his reasons," Bryson said. "Don't worry."

Lilu stood nervously on the vast stone patio of the backyard. Her sunny dress was a sharp contrast to the shadows of the overcast sky. The door slid open and out walked Bryson and Debo. Bryson took a seat on one of the wooden lounge chairs and sipped from a tall glass of lemonade. He gave Lilu a teasingly evil smile similar to one of Himitsu's.

"Aren't you training with me?" she asked.

"Nope. I'll be relaxing and observing the comedic display."

The slim girl turned away from Bryson and looked toward the tall Intel Director, who was smiling wide. He had no intentions of wasting time.

"Let's see you walk, Ms. Lilu," Debo commanded.

She made walking in her heels look effortless—as expected from a royal.

"Good," Debo said. "Now jog."

Bryson fought down a giggle as this proved to be more difficult for Lilu. She looked in real danger of rolling an ankle.

"Now run," Debo commanded.

She stopped and looked at him. Through heavy breaths, she asked, "No offense, Director, but are you insane?"

"You wanted *real* training. If you don't agree with my regimen, you can leave and not waste my time."

It was an unusual tone to be taking with someone of royal descent, but Bryson wasn't surprised by it. Debo always had no regard for giving respect if it wasn't given to him—it didn't matter who the other person was. People were so used to seeing his fun-loving, sarcastic side that they forgot how intimidating he could be.

"Making me play around in heels isn't training! I'm not your court jester—I'm a lady! You don't know what it's like trying to walk in these things—let alone *run* in them!"

"Don't piss him off," Bryson said while lazily chewing ice.

Debo gazed at her angry face for a few seconds. "I will disregard your ignorance and entitled attitude. Allow me to prove you wrong. Toss me your heels."

"This will be priceless," Bryson mumbled.

Debo struggled a bit putting them on since Lilu's feet were significantly smaller. Thankfully, they were open-toed, allowing him to force it. Seeing the golden high-heels sitting underneath a pair of lanky, hairy legs was the exact kind of comedy Bryson had been looking forward to. Even Lilu's rage softened somewhat.

"You claim I don't know your struggle because I'm a man." He began to walk very well—disconcertingly well. "You assume I'm asking for the impossible …That's insulting."

"I'm sorr—" Lilu's apology was cut short as she stumbled backward and let out a yelp.

Debo was standing face-to-face with her, the shadow of his towering frame engulfing her. He had gone from where he was pacing, some twenty feet away, to directly in front of her in a split-second.

Bryson smirked, then realized his hand was empty. It was curved as if it was still holding a cup. He looked back at Debo and, sure enough, he now had Bryson's glass of lemonade. Not only had Debo gone from point A to point B within in the blink of an eye, he'd also taken a detour to a third point. And this was all done while wearing heels . . . and neither Lilu nor

Bryson saw it happen.

Debo lifted the glass to his mouth and took a sip, still staring at a flabbergasted Lilu. "False accusations based off misguided assumptions isn't a good look for a royal of the Intel Kingdom, young lady."

Shame crept its way onto Lilu's face. "I'm sorry, Director."

Bryson walked over to Debo and snatched back his lemonade. "Show off," he muttered as he headed back to his chair.

Debo chuckled. "Well, here are your heels. We'll put this behind us."

"I admire your skill," Lilu said, but then added, "However, I'm not completely sure what skill you're showing off."

"Speed alone will not fare you well if you don't have the agility and balance to compliment it," Debo explained as he slipped his feet into his own shoes. "In heels, I was able to move without sacrificing any speed. Not only that, but I was also able to pivot and change direction."

Lilu finally understood. "And this would only improve my speed and agility in normal fighting conditions," she said. "I mean, if I can move in these, I can move in anything."

Debo smiled. "Correct. Training under circumstances that cater to you is not ideal. In order to get better, you must train in conditions that are meant to hinder you."

"That's smart," she said.

"Don't doubt Debo," Bryson said as he lounged in his chair. "Number one rule to live by."

The rest of the afternoon featured a more obedient Lilu and light-hearted Debo. Bryson dozed off for a couple hours, causing Lilu to occasionally give a jealous glance over. After four hours of work, the sun had almost fallen beyond the horizon, and Debo called it a day.

"Whenever you're ready for more, come on over," he said. "I'll be happy to get you to the level you need to be at. Maybe I'll even let you train on the pegs." He nudged behind him, where wooden poles scattered in every direction.

"You don't even let me on those," Bryson said with a pout.

Debo smiled and exited the back yard. The moment he was in the house and out of sight, Lilu collapsed to her knees and snatched off her shoes. She grimaced in pain as she rubbed her toes and the back of her ankle.

"Blisters already," she whined.

"A small price to pay," Bryson remarked from his lounge chair.

She thought about it for a second and said, "I suppose so."

"I went through it too, you know?" he reassured her. "The heels and everything."

"Well, I guess you're proof that it works."

Bryson smirked. "He's fast, isn't he?"

Lilu rose from the ground and sat next to him. "Creepily fast. He must be close to our people's max speed."

"Oh, for sure. And if he isn't at 70% speed, he's at least 65%."

Lilu wiped a bead of sweat from her brow. "He's kind of scary."

"He's kind of awesome," Bryson retorted.

"Awesome …" She mumbled it under her breath, as if she was debating the accuracy of that description. "That light isn't awesome."

Bryson's face soured along with his tone. "Are we back on that now?"

"Of course we're back on *that*. You have no clue how dangerous and out-of-place that light is!"

"Everyone has secrets to protect, Lilu."

"Not to this extent. He's risking hurting somebody he supposedly loves."

"*Supposedly?*"

She didn't back down. "I'm questioning the extent of his love. If his secrecy takes precedence over his love for you, his priorities are backwards."

"I told you … he has his reasons for everything," Bryson said as he looked at the sky in frustration. "I've learned to not doubt him."

She took a moment to consider that, tapping her fingers on the arm of the chair. "What if I told you I could get you in that room?" she finally asked.

"And how would you manage that?"

"My older sister has a method of getting past the light. The difficult part would be convincing her to help you."

His excitement instantly deflated, Bryson sank back into his chair. "There's no way the Princess of the Intel Kingdom would help me with such a petty matter."

"True," Lilu admitted. "However, my father could pull some strings. After all, you're the son of the former Intel General. And I know how much respect my father had for him."

"Is your sister actually that strong?" Bryson asked, ignoring the reference to his dad.

Lilu thought for a second. "She is talented, yes. But her talent has nothing to do with it. It's a perk that comes with being the first-born of a royal bloodline. You know what I'm talking about."

Bryson looked toward the sky again, where he could barely see the crusted underbelly of a floating island. "Her Branian."

"Correct."

"Besides the fact that Branian are Bozani from the Light Empire, what's so special about them?"

She frowned. "I can't answer that, and you know I can't answer that."

"Hmm. Is there anything you're allowed to tell me about them?"

"We're walking a thin line here, but I suppose I can scratch the surface. Branian once belonged to the kingdoms of the Light Realm in an earlier life—just like you and I do now. They are a class of Bozani. They've died before and were reborn on that island you keep looking at above us—the Light Empire. And while they may be the lowest tier of Bozani, they are still far stronger than almost everyone in our kingdoms. They wield abilities we can only dream of—abilities that could help you get in that closet. That's all I can tell you."

"So how are you going to get me in touch with Princess Shelly?"

She grinned from ear to ear. "The annual Generals' Battle is in a few weeks. Biggest spectator event of the year. Lasts a whole weekend. People from each of the Light Realm's kingdoms come. It's quite a treat, and this year our kingdom is hosting it. Parades, epic battles, festivals, plays, and a lot more."

"I've always wanted to go to one," he confessed.

"I will grant your wish. As a royal, I'm permitted three guests. I'll introduce you to the royal family while we're at it," she said with a toothy smile.

Bryson accepted without hesitation. Honestly, he would rather avoid meeting the king, but if that's what it took to unlock the secret behind the closet door, then it was necessary.

Lilu stood up and stretched. "Well, I better get back to campus. Telejunction shuts down in about an hour."

"Do you think my dad is up there?" It was an unexpected question that caught her off-guard.

The beautiful young woman stopped for a moment and looked at him with compassionate eyes. "Mendac was a great and powerful man from what we've all heard growing up. I believe his energy was strong enough for him to be reborn. So yes, I think he is up there right now, happy and care free as a Bozani."

Bryson continued to gaze into the night sky while the crickets sung their songs through the backyard. She studied his face for a moment before wishing him a good night and exiting the yard.

12

A Meeting of Meaning

Bryson was sitting in the lobby of the Lilac Suites at a time of day he was not used to. Rays of light stretched through the windows as the sun slowly peered above the horizon, giving the violet decor a golden hue. Seated with him at the table were two heavy eyed Jestivan, Rhyparia and Himitsu. They sat in silence, for it was too early for conversation. However, someone up above them didn't seem to mind what time it was.

"Wake up! Wake up! Wake up!" came Jilly's screeching voice from the fourth floor. It was accompanied by the sound of fists banging on a wooden door.

Himitsu, who had an already empty mug of coffee sitting in front of him, put his hand to his face and rubbed his forehead. "That girl," he said, exhausted.

"Somehow she seems to be a morning person," Bryson said. "Here I was thinking I had already seen her excitement at its peak."

Himitsu frowned and looked at Bryson. "Be happy you get to go home. I've had to put up with her morning antics every day for the past five weeks. It's always at seven o'clock … never fails."

Rhyparia took a sip of her orange juice and smiled. "It's quite adorable."

Himitsu slowly turned his head with an eerie glare. "She's nineteen."

Rhyparia smiled back. "She's from the Spirit Kingdom."

He slumped in his chair. "Whatever."

"Toshyyyyyyyyyyyyyyyyyyyy!" Jilly was screaming. After some crashing and cursing, a few minutes later she and Toshik walked down to the lobby.

"This doofus," Toshik said with a genuine smile.

Bryson, Himitsu, and Rhyparia got up from their seats.

"Can I at least get a coffee?" Toshik asked.

"No, we're already late because of you," Bryson said. "Let's go."

The lanky swordsman glared at his three group members and turned for the bar. But before he could even take a step, an agonizing pain shot through his ear. Jilly had, once again, given it a solid flick.

"Stop being so rebellious to our captain." She pushed him from behind toward the door, which he reluctantly permitted. "Let's go, mister."

Thankfully, when Jilly was around, Toshik's disobedience wasn't a problem.

*   *   *

Bryson's team darted into the central auditorium where their ceremony had been held a little over a month ago. He could feel the stares of the directors and Olivia's team while racing down the steps.

As they took their seats, Grand Director Poicus said, "Nice of you to join us."

"Sorry, Grand Director."

"Since we're twenty minutes behind already, let's just cut straight to it," Poicus said as he glanced down at some parchment on his podium. "It's nice to see all ten of your faces gathered together again. It's been what, five or six weeks?" He smiled.

"Of course, I've been keeping tabs with the Energy Directors about each person's progress. Overall, it has been nothing but good news. I'm hoping that you have not only bonded well with your respective team, but with your training partner as well." He paused and scanned their faces. "In fact, someone tell me what they've learned about their partner."

To Bryson's surprise, Toshik raised his hand. It startled Director Poicus too, as his eyes widened a bit. "Go ahead, Zana Toshik."

"Sir, I've learned Yama is very talented … at being an uptight witch." He couldn't have said it with a bigger smirk on his face.

A very familiar, strong gust of wind blew through the seats. Bryson knew what to expect—or he thought he did. But when he looked toward Toshik, Yama was not behind him with her sword drawn. Instead a towering figure had appeared among the Jestivan. It was Adrenaline Director Buredo. He had left his podium and was now obstructing her path.

He gazed sternly down at Yama, who for once in her life looked scared. Without averting his glare from Yama, Buredo said, "Toshik, I will see you in my office following the conclusion of this meeting." Toshik's smirk quickly vanished. "Yama, have a seat."

"Yes, Director," she replied.

As Yama walked back to her seat and Director Buredo returned to the stage, Grand Director Poicus cleared his throat. "I should have known better. Moving on. Himitsu, tell me something about your partner, Olivia."

The slender tan boy stood up. He lifted his shirt, exposing a remarkable black and blue bruise that covered the entirety of his left ribcage. Lilu's face cringed a bit at the sight of it.

"Sir, I've learned I'd rather take a punch from a warrior from the Power Kingdom than Olivia."

Passion Director Venustas giggled. "You can't always fight from the shadows," she said playfully. "What better way to teach you this than by going toe-to-toe with one of the most physical fighters in the Jestivan?"

Grand Director Poicus slapped his hands together. "Splendid! We are all becoming highly versatile. Versatility is important." He scanned their faces until he saw Agnos in his familiar white robe. "Agnos, what have you learned about your partner?"

Agnos gazed at him from behind his messy, thick bangs. "I've learned little to none, but I feel as if I've actually learned a lot because of that."

Bryson reran Agnos' sentence through his head, trying to make sense of what seemed to be a major contradiction.

Poicus chuckled. "I find myself unsurprised by the subtlety of your answer. Please elaborate."

"The fact that I know nothing about Rhyparia's capabilities and the fact that Director Senex refuses to allow me near her while she trains lets me know that she is immensely powerful, but lacks any sort of control over that power."

Grand Director Poicus was smiling. "You all think Toshik and Yama are the Jestivan's scariest duo. However, I look at these two here." He gazed at Agnos and Rhyparia. "They are truly dangerous."

Toshik scowled to himself as Poicus continued speaking. "Body and mind. Rhyparia, a humble girl who has potential for the catastrophic destruction of foes, and Agnos, an intelligent boy who can probably manipulate the minds of even the smartest intelligence officers …" Poicus glanced at the Energy Directors and asked, "What do you all think?"

"I would agree," Director Debo replied.

"The way you word it makes me shudder," Director Venustas said.

Bryson looked to his right at Rhyparia. He expected a smile, but that wasn't the case at all. Her face was as grim as ever.

"Alright, let's discuss the two important issues at-hand—the main reasons for this group gathering," Poicus said. He raised one finger in the air. "There has been quite a stir down in the Dark Realm."

The director paused for a brief moment. "There was a shake-up in the Dark Realm last night. The young prince of the Prim Kingdom died. He was murdered in his sleep."

Bryson's eyes widened. *An attack on a royal? Who could be that bold? Or stupid?*

"How could anyone get to the prince in the middle of the night?" asked the snowy-haired Tashami. "He lives in a heavily guarded palace, and it was during witching hours?"

"Good question," Poicus said. "Himitsu, you're the one with assassin's blood. What's your take on it?"

Himitsu thought about it for a second. "Were there any witnesses at all? Any information on what the killer looked like or what his or her ability was?"

"There was one—the general."

"And what information did they get from him?" Himitsu asked.

"None," Poicus responded gravely. "He's dead as well."

"Oh …" Himitsu looked as shocked as most of the Jestivan. The leader of the Prim Kingdom's army was also dead. "Then I don't know, Grand Director."

"Not to worry. I don't expect any of you to know," Poicus responded reassuringly. "There were several odd things about this. Not only is the general dead, there were no signs of a struggle. There were two marks on his body. A hole in his chest and a hole on the top of his head, but no signs of resistance."

"What do you mean by *hole*, Grand Director?" Jilly asked.

"I mean a hole. You could look into each hole and stare directly at the general's heart and brain." Bryson heard Lilu make a subtle noise of disgust. "However, nothing was taken from his body. All organs were left in place."

"As for the prince, it was a simple cut of the throat, so you'd think that was typical. However, his eyes were stark white. Meaning the iris and pupil were completely gone."

Director Poicus took a sip of water as Olivia asked a question of her own. "Does this mean my kingdom is in trouble?"

"You are very intuitive, young lady," he said. "What brought you to this conclusion?"

"The holes sound to be burned in. The method of killing was quick and quiet. Both sound like the actions of a Passion Assassin."

"You're suggesting the killer struck at night because that's the best time to put his black flames to use, and the burns in the victim's chest and temple are the result of his or her fire ability."

Olivia slowly nodded.

"Good to know intelligence isn't an attribute only our Intel and Archaic Jestivan possess," he said. "Now, do we know for a fact that the Prim Kingdom has come to this conclusion? No, but that's what we're speculating. Himitsu."

"Yes, sir," he responded.

Poicus stared him down sternly. "The Passion Kingdom's royal family is currently tracking down all residents with assassin's blood. They are being imprisoned indefinitely without trial. Apparently they are assuming the worst, which is that one of their own did it."

As the Grand Director explained this, Himitsu uncharacteristically lost his calm demeanor. He sat up intently with an unnerved quality in his eyes.

"Don't worry," Poicus said. "Since you're a zana of the Jestivan and all of the Directors can vouch for you, you will be fine."

But this didn't seem to put Himitsu at ease.

"None of this is anything you have to worry about yet. I'm just keeping you up to date. As Jestivan, information is key. Keep your eyes and ears open at all times because you never know when this information will become relevant."

The old director looked toward his notes again. "That looks to be the end of the sorrowful news, so let's move on to something more fun. I'll allow Director Buredo to take over. I know it has been a long wait for a mission, but that wait is over."

Smiles danced their way onto everyone's faces. Well, besides Himitsu's—and Olivia's, of course.

The tall, lean Adren Director stood up. "Good morning."

"Good morning, Director," the Jestivan responded.

Director Buredo's gaze was as stern as always. "Since this will be your first mission, you will not be asked to do much. As most of you know, the biggest event of the year—the Generals' Battle—will take place this upcoming weekend. We will be expecting a record attendance— approximately 300,000 people. Of course, with more people comes more security."

He paused and gently held out his hand toward the Jestivan. "This is where you all will come into play."

Bryson slumped in his chair. Basically, their mission was to serve as security guards. There was nothing dangerous or glamorous about it. If this was a couple weeks ago, he would have been elated to be able to attend the Generals' Battle for the first time, but that was then. Lilu had already invited him to attend as her special guest. Now the only thing he could think about was how this interfered with Lilu's plan to persuade the king.

"You won't have to worry about where you'll room. Taverns have been booked. Money will be given to you for food. As for Friday and Saturday, you have freedom to do as you please. Attend the festivities and enjoy the atmosphere … Honestly, get a bit wild if you want. Not *too* wild. That means you, Mr. Toshik." The brown-haired boy gave a guilty smirk.

"Sunday is the day of the actual battle. For mostly everyone, it is a day of excitement. For all of you, it will be a day of earnest. As the Adren Director and a resident of the Adren Kingdom, I am obligated to fulfill an assignment to the end, so that is exactly what I will expect from each of you on Sunday. The Intel Kingdom's arena is massive—to put it lightly. Each person will be stationed at a different post along the bottom of the stands. Bryson's team will cover the north and east sides. Olivia's team will cover the south and west. Is that clear?"

"Director Buredo," blurted Lilu.

"Yes, Lita Lilu?"

She started to say something, but then stopped as she thought better of it. "Never mind," she said softly as her posture sunk.

Grand Director Poicus's bushy eyebrows slanted sharply, causing his eyes to narrow. "Talk to us after this meeting has been dismissed, Lilu."

The moment he said this, the school's clock tower began ringing. The faint roar of students crowding the halls outside began to leak through the cracks of the auditorium doors.

Poicus gave a toothy smile. "I suppose we'll end the meeting now. The directors will be available for training for the rest of the day. It's optional, but for the next three days leading up to this momentous weekend, you will have a rigorous eight-to-five training schedule with your directors. Prepare yourselves. Friday and Saturday will be your days of relaxation before Sunday."

With that news, the Jestivan began walking up the stairs in a deflated state. Bryson started following Rhyparia and Olivia, but he was suddenly stopped when someone grabbed his wrist. He turned around and saw Lilu's beautiful green eyes staring at him.

"I need you with me when I talk to the directors," she said.

Bryson didn't know what for, but he followed her down the stairs anyways. He wasn't going to say no to her. As they approached the directors, Bryson realized that he had never been this close to all of them at once. They stood still and gazed at the two young Jestivan.

Bryson stayed silent, but Lilu, being the bold girl that she was, spoke up immediately. "Bryson and I had planned on attending the Generals' Battle as spectators. He was to be a guest of mine in the Royal Suites."

"Oh?" Director Venustas said with a giggle, causing Bryson to blush. "A date?"

Lilu's eyes widened. "No, Director! Not at all."

Venustas's red lips curled into a playful smirk. "Say what you want. I find it to be adorable. Young love is the best love."

"Oh stop harassing them, Venustas," commanded a shaky voice. It belonged to the elderly Spirit Director, Director Neaneuma. "You're making them uncomfortable."

"You're simply bitter because you're too old to remember what such youthful love feels like," Venustas responded.

Bryson's eyes widened in disbelief. If he wasn't uncomfortable before, now he was.

The grey-haired director shook her head. "You're lucky I am who I am. Such petty remarks can't break someone like me down. Besides, inner youthfulness trumps outer youthfulness."

Venustas rolled her eyes.

"I have no business knowing," Grand Director Poicus said, "nor do I care, what your purpose is with wanting to be in the suites with Bryson, but that is not something I can allow. You have a responsibility and you're supposed to fulfill it."

Lilu looked upset, but then Poicus continued speaking. "But with that said, your father is the king who is hosting the event, so if he says otherwise, then I'd have to let you do as you please."

For a brief moment, Lilu appeared rejuvenated, but then Director Debo cut in. "No, that's not how this works," he said sharply.

The Grand Director snapped his head around. "Debo, now is *not* the time."

Bryson couldn't wipe the look of shock off his face. He knew Debo to be bold, but he had never witnessed him talk back to the Grand Director.

"The king doesn't have jurisdiction over the Jestivan," Debo said flatly.

"But he has jurisdiction over all of the Intel Kingdom . . . which is where we will be," Poicus retorted.

Debo stared hard at the Grand Director. "I'm putting my foot down."

Poicus closed his eyes and shook his head. "You forget you're below me sometimes. If anyone is putting a foot down, it will be me. Once again, you forget your place."

Bryson was in disbelief. Usually, he supported the man who was practically his father, but Debo was pushing it too far. He connected eyes with the tall Intel Director.

Debo looked at him sternly and said, "Bryson, I trust you to heed my advice. Stick to your responsibility." After saying this, he quickly walked off the stage and up the high-rising stairs.

Next to speak was the normally quiet Archaic Director, Director Senex. "That man has no boundaries. He is a loose cannon."

"Pay him no mind," Poicus said softly. "He loses his place from time to time."

Finally feeling it was appropriate for her to say something, Lilu hesitantly asked, "Should we leave?"

Poicus gave a deep sigh and rubbed his eyes. "Yes, I believe so. The directors need to have a meeting of our own. I will talk to your father when I get the chance, Ms. Lilu."

"Thank you, sir," she gratefully responded.

He gave a weary smile. "Enjoy your day."

13

Shallow Judgment, Shallow Breaths

It was the first cool weekend of November. The air was crisp and the heavy clouds hung low as early evening approached, but this was nothing out of the ordinary for Dunami, the capital of the Intel Kingdom. Girls in playful scarves and boys in feather-light jackets ran through the busy streets as their parents fought to keep them under control, but even they were doing it half-heartedly. After all, it was the first night of the Generals' Battle weekend, so holding back their own excitement proved difficult enough.

Adults of all ages were laughing and conversing throughout the city. Heavy traffic came in and out of taverns, restaurants, and bars. Each time a door swung open, a blast of music would travel out into the cobblestone streets. Scattered among the pleasant commotion, the Jestivan were found all over.

A lanky Toshik occupied one of Dunami's many bars. Surprisingly, he was accompanied by Yama, but he was paying her no attention—not that she cared.

Toshik was drunk, and his normally perfect brown hair was a ruffled mess. He was slashing his sword around in attempt to entertain the wealthy girls surrounding him. It was safe to say none of them had any knowledge as to how a sword should be swung. Otherwise the sloppy, drunken display wouldn't have had them so hypnotized.

The bar's owner, who was a balding man with a beer gut, miserably tried commanding the heedless swordsman to stop, but he was getting nowhere. Guests who had common sense wisely shifted their seating arrangements far away from the flailing six-and-a-half foot man.

Occupying one of the stools at the bar sat a tipsy, yet calmer, Yama. Her sword was wisely sheathed to her hip, and as she took a small sip of ale, an uncommon smirk slipped onto her face.

The blond-haired Jilly sat next to her, and when she noticed her friend's smile, she sweetly said, "I love it when you smile. I wish it wouldn't take alcohol to bring it out."

Yama set her mug on the table, looked at her and said, "I'm not sure if it's the alcohol…. or you."

Jilly's face flushed deep red and she took a hurried sip of her juice in a pathetic attempt to hide her embarrassment. Yama twirled a strand of Jilly's hair and said, "It is a compliment. Not many people can loosen me up like you do."

Yama turned Jilly's head so they were eye-to-eye. She gazed at her deeply and said, "I don't see how Toshik could treat you with such disregard."

At that moment, Jilly could have sworn that Yama was about to move in for a kiss, but she didn't know how to stop it. Thankfully, she was rescued by an unexpected hero.

"Ladies! How dare you waste such affection on each other!" exclaimed an intoxicated Toshik. He had jumped between the two of them and aggressively wrapped an arm around the back of their necks. "That affection should be given to the guys, and when I say guys, I mean me!"

Yama responded with a swift punch to his face. Toshik staggered backward, and the only thing that saved him from toppling over was his gang of fawning women.

Yama's smile had turned into a scowl. "This isn't Phesaw. I will hit you when you cross me, and I will hit you hard."

Toshik waved his finger at the two girls. "Tsk, tsk. What a waste of such beauty."

In the blink of an eye, Yama had hurled her empty mug at Toshik's face, which, despite the amount of alcohol in his system, he was able to dodge as it shattered against the opposite wall. He started laughing hysterically.

This time Yama ignored him and walked out of the bar while holding Jilly's hand behind her. As they entered the bustling street, her purple hair lightly fluttered in the gentle breeze.

"Where was that garden we passed earlier?" she asked.

She didn't receive an answer, so she glanced at Jilly to see that she was pouting. Expecting this, Yama sighed as she pushed to fight her way through the crowd. "I'm sorry, Jilly. I can't stand him."

As Jilly was being dragged, she asked, "Why can't you two just get along?"

"I have zero respect for him as a person. I have zero respect for how he lives his life. I have zero respect for his motives."

"We all have our faults," Jilly said as they walked into the garden.

"And some of us have too many."

They took a seat on a small wooden bench. It was a lot quieter here. "We all have too many," Jilly said. "Some of us just don't hide them well."

The blond girl lay on the bench, staring at the dark night sky above. Her head was on Yama's lap, whose fingers were intertwining with her hair. "He's a spoiled prick who thinks he can get away with anything because of his father's powerhouse of a company. I wish you'd stop defending him," Yama sighed.

"What do you expect? He has protected me since I was a little girl. I owe the world to him."

Yama groaned. "I guess it's no use."

Jilly decided to quickly change the subject. "If only people knew what you're like when you're around me. It's like a mask comes off."

A smile only Jilly could cause once again brightened Yama's face. "I could say the same about you."

"How so?"

114

Yama continued stroking Jilly's hair. "You become calm," she said softly.

Jilly closed her eyes. "Chemistry really is an amazing thing."

The two girls went quiet, both silently enjoying the other's company. They listened to the distant crowd in the street outside the garden. Yama continued to play with Jilly's hair, and Jilly softly gazed at her friend as a cool breeze drifted through the air.

Yama smiled. "Something tells me that wasn't nature's wind."

"I guess you were right. You do calm me. Director Neaneuma would have been proud of that breeze!"

Footsteps interrupted their conversation, causing Jilly to alertly sit up. The intelights at the entrance of the garden casted a dark silhouette. It wasn't until the man stood next to them that Jilly recognized who he was.

"Daddy!" she screamed as she jumped into his arms.

As the man embraced her, he glared at the violet-haired girl, who was just fondling his daughter's hair. When Yama realized how he was staring at her, she returned it with a judgmental glare of her own.

Jilly finally let go of her father, allowing him to stand tall. He had considerable height, but not quite like Director Debo, Himitsu, or Toshik. He had a short, scruffy beard that bordered his entire jawline. He looked like a man of power, but perhaps the most daunting aspect was his gear, which marked him as the second most powerful figure in the Spirit Kingdom's military—second to only the general. It was varying colors of blue with silver trim. However, none of this caused Yama's glare to falter.

Jilly, who was unaware of what was happening, smiled and said, "Daddy, this is Yama. She's from the Adren Kingdom and one of my fellow Jestivan."

The major stared a little while longer before nodding his head in her direction, and as he did so, extending his arm for a handshake.

Yama declined. She stayed seated without averting her eyes from him. She simply said, "We're not going to be fake."

"Yama! Properly greet my father," Jilly upsettingly shouted.

"No, she's right," he said. "I suppose trying to mask my displeasure would only make things worse with her."

"*Displeasure?*" Jilly shrieked.

The man looked at her sternly. "Yes … displeasure. Where is Toshik?" he asked.

"Drunk in a bar," Jilly reluctantly answered.

The man shook his head. "When will he learn?" he muttered to himself.

Yama stood up. "I'm going to head out," she said to Jilly. She looked at the major and added, "Enjoy your father," before walking away.

As Jilly watched her friend exit the garden, her dad asked an unexpected question. "What are you doing?"

"Excuse me?" she asked.

"What are you and that girl?" he asked again. This time he sounded more agitated.

Jilly took a moment, but she finally realized what he was trying to figure out. "We're *friends*," she said.

"That's not friendship."

Disgust crept its way onto Jilly's face. "Who are you to judge?" she asked.

"I am your father!"

She stared at him incredulously. She couldn't believe what her father was accusing her of, and even if he was correct, she wouldn't have expected him to act like this. She thought he was better than that.

When the man saw that he wasn't going to get a response, he decided to make something clear. "My daughter will not portray flirtatious mannerisms with another woman."

Breaking Jilly's spirit was a hard thing to do, but tears began trickling down her face. Her heart was tearing in two. She knew being with Yama felt right, but her father's disappointment made it feel wrong.

It was dark outside, but the defeated girl lowered her sunhat over her eyes as she solemnly followed her father out of the garden, struggling with her newfound dilemma.

*   *   *

A couple blocks over, strolled a once familiar pair of best friends that, recently, had not seen enough of each other. It was a hooded boy and a girl wearing her kitten hat. Bryson had his arm wrapped around Olivia's shoulder.

He playfully leaned his head against hers, which caused Meow Meow to grimace. "I don't like it when your face is this close to my face," the kitten said.

Bryson ignored him and spoke to Olivia. "I've missed you. We rarely get to talk like we used to."

Olivia continued walking with Bryson holding her, paying his embrace no mind. "How have you been?" she asked.

"Been doing well. Spending a lot of time with my team. Actually, been spending a lot of time with a couple of your team members also." Bryson removed his arm.

"Lilu and Yama," Olivia said flatly.

Bryson looked at her and smiled. "Keeping tabs on your team, I see."

"I am the captain. Knowing how my team is progressing is vital. We all update each other with news on our training regiments." Olivia looked at him blankly. "Knowing your teammate's strengths and weaknesses facilitates cohesion in the future."

A slight pout formed on his face. "Why haven't I been doing that?"

"Because you're stupid," Meow Meow scolded.

"Originality is a strong point of yours," Bryson sneered.

"If I tried to be wittier, it won't permeate your thick skull."

Bryson removed his hood. "One day when you're not sitting on Olivia's head, I will shave you bald."

The kitten stuck out his tongue.

"Still dreaming about sitting under a cherry blossom?" Olivia asked.

"Of course," Bryson answered as he scanned the buildings around them in hopes to find a bite to eat. "Why would it change now?"

Olivia looked at him for a brief moment before saying, "Alright."

Finally spotting a beautiful restaurant, Bryson pointed at it and said, "Let's eat."

As they entered and headed toward the host's station, they noticed a group of three waiting to be seated. They were facing away from them, but once Bryson saw the elegant green hair in the middle, he knew who it was. To the right was a girl with brown hair. And on the left was a familiar tall frame.

117

He snuck up behind the girl in the center and put his face close to her ear. "Hi, Lilu," he said.

She jumped with a startled yelp before turning around. When she saw who it was, she playfully pushed him in the chest. "I hate you."

Rhyparia and Himitsu started laughing.

"You're getting better," Himitsu said. "I still saw you were coming though."

Lilu turned and gave the same shove to Himitsu. "Some friend you are," she said.

"So your aspiration in life is to become as big of a stalker as Himitsu," Meow Meow said. "This is what you've been training for these past two months."

That brought everyone's attention to the quiet Olivia. "Hello, Olivia," Rhyparia said with a sweet smile, which Olivia responded to with a silent nod.

Their greetings were cut short as the host finally arrived to guide them to their seats. He was a brunette boy in his upper teens, dressed in a vest, dress pants, and tie. "How many in your group?" he asked in a clipped tone. The place was packed and it was obvious he was feeling the pressure.

"Five," responded Lilu.

The boy looked up at the sound of her voice. When he saw who had answered him, he was aghast. "Lady Lilu! … Or is it Lita Lilu now? I'm sorry about the wait and my poor manners."

Meow Meow cackled. Lilu gave a genuine smile and said, "It's alright, dear. May we have one of the corner booths near the piano?"

"Of course, my lady."

As the group of Jestivan followed the host, Bryson's eyes fixed on Lilu's bouncing green hair in front of him. It was easy for him to forget her status outside of Phesaw because he simply knew her as a fellow student.

The group of five took a seat at a spacious corner booth. Bryson quickly darted to the spot he wanted before anyone had a chance. Lilu laughed at him.

As the young waitress came to the table, she gave a general greeting to everyone—except Lilu, who received a curtsy.

"What can I get for all of you?" she asked with a true smile that the host earlier had lacked.

Olivia was the first to answer. "Eggs and cat food," she said in the most nonchalant way possible.

Laughter exploded around the table as the waitress's expression veered into bafflement. "We don't carry cat food, ma'am."

Olivia didn't seem bothered. "Eggs then," she said.

The waitress, noticing the anger on Meow Meow's face, tried to offer an alternative. "We have fish."

The kitten hat began salivating, but Olivia shut that down quickly. "No. He's not allowed table food."

This time Bryson laughed at Meow Meow's expense. "You know what? I'll take the grilled salmon special."

Himitsu wore a smirk as he leaned back with his menu in front of him. "I see what you did there, Bryson."

Bryson gave him a wink as the waitress walked off with the table's orders. He gazed across the table at a black piano that was obviously very well taken care of. It was likely polished multiple times a day judging by how the candle light flickered off its sleek surface. The urge to run his fingers across the keys arose, but this was not the place.

"Play something!" Lilu demanded while giving Bryson a nudge.

Himitsu gave him a curious look. "You play the piano?"

Bryson didn't reply. His face had turned red. In the Intel Kingdom, it was embarrassing to be known as the artistic type. Thankfully, Meow Meow had decided to drift off into one of his random catnaps, so at least Bryson didn't have to hear it from him.

"He's amazing," Lilu boasted.

"Drop it," Olivia said, and the instant silence indicated how respected she was. Even Lilu instantly dropped the topic.

When their food arrived, Bryson began scarfing down his salmon in front of a defeated Meow Meow.

Rhyparia, who had a bowl of noodles in front of her, took note of the flower pinned to Lilu's hair. "Usually, I know which flower you're using, but I don't recognize that one."

Lilu finished chewing her scallop before addressing Rhyparia. "A chocolate cosmos."

Meow Meow's face twisted. "That explains what I've been smelling."

Giggling, Lilu carefully removed the flower. "You're exactly right, Meow Meow. It gets its name for two reasons, and the smell is one of them. The other reason is the beautiful color transition it has between deep burgundy and dark brown."

Rhyparia delicately examined it between her fingers. "I've never seen one before."

"They're extremely rare in this day and age," Lilu said.

"It's nice ... what money can buy," Himitsu said.

Lilu frowned a bit, but to her credit, she didn't get angry. "It actually had nothing to do with money," she explained. "This was a gift from a legend our realm is very familiar with."

"And who was that?" Himitsu asked.

"The Fifth of Five," she casually said.

Bryson choked on the rice he'd been inhaling. "You knew my father?"

One of Lilu's eyebrows rose. "Obviously. He was the general, my father's top man. However, he was only around when I was very young."

Bryson didn't have much time to ponder this, as a mortified gaze on Rhyparia's face caused him to focus elsewhere. He turned his head to see an older, poorly groomed couple approaching their table.

It was a man and woman who both looked to be in their mid-forties. The man was tall, skinny, and feeble. His face was long and hollow, and a sandy brown mustache sat underneath his narrow nose. And on top of all this, he was dressed in dirty, cheap fabric.

Although her physical attributes were the complete opposite, the woman still didn't fare any better than her partner. She was short and wide. Her features seemed to be scrunched at the center, and the wrinkles and sun-damaged skin gave her face the texture of tree bark. Her hair was dark brown and snug in a tight bun. The one similarity, however, was her attire—more rags.

Rhyparia's eyes glazed with potential tears. She shifted her sweeping bangs further in front of her face in effort to hide her discomfort.

The couple reached the table sporting gleeful smiles. "Hello, dear," the man said.

"Why are you here?" Rhyparia asked coldly.

It clicked. These were Rhyparia's parents. The two people she had made clear, countless times, she hated most in the world. Bryson gave them another glance. Sure, they were filthy, but they didn't seem evil or anything like that.

Her father frowned. "We were invited by the Grand Director."

Rhyparia decided to rephrase her question. "Why'd you come knowing that I don't want anything to do with either of you?"

Bryson wasn't sure what was ruder—the question itself or that she didn't even look at them when she asked it. She just stared at her plate. The tension was palpable, and the Jestivan didn't make a sound. All eating utensils were resting on the table, and it felt like their booth was miles away from any sort of civilization.

The father sighed. "I don't know what I did to you, hon."

Rhyparia didn't respond. The mother still had yet to say anything. She was scanning the faces of the other Jestivan sitting at the table. Then her eyes fixed on Olivia, and she just stared at her.

"I guess I'll introduce myself to your friends since I know you won't," the father said.

As he made his greetings, Bryson couldn't pinpoint why Rhyparia had such a problem with him. He gave off the impression of being a grounded man. His handshakes were firm, and when he made eye contact, he looked at you, not through you. And although his teeth were yellowing and lacking in numbers, his smile was still genuine.

Her mother seemed a little bit like a nut job, but she was also very easy to talk to. Her laugh was a bit obnoxious, but nothing terribly unbearable. Overall, they acted like a lovely couple. They took interest in where each person was from and what their goals were.

However, Bryson knew people weren't always the same in public as they were at home. He was an example of this himself, so he knew to never judge a book by its cover. He kept an eye on Rhyparia throughout the entire meet and greet. Her eyes never unglued themselves from her plate, and there was a wet trail running down her left cheek.

Rhyparia's mother became very intrigued with Meow Meow, which was no surprise. Most people were when first seeing the kitten hat.

"He might be the cutest thing I've ever seen," she said with a playful smile while petting him behind his ear.

"You're the ugliest thing I've ever seen," Meow Meow retorted.

Bryson and Himitsu staved off a laugh. It was rude, but the sort of painfully blunt remark that the kitten was known for.

The mother's eyes widened. "I see it has a sense of humor."

"Please, explain to me why you're talking about me like I'm not right here," Meow Meow said.

She hesitated, but continued smiling. "I'm sorry. This is just new for me."

"You smell like cabbage and you look like it too."

Bryson smiled wide and Himitsu could no longer hold back his laughter. Luckily for them, the father was chuckling as well. The mother was unfazed and ignored the comment altogether. "How did you get this little guy, Olivia?" she asked.

"I don't know."

The woman stared at the kitten for a little while before saying, "I have to get me one."

The moment she said this, the table began to tremble very lightly. Bryson looked at his glass as the water's surface began to ripple. Making sure her eyes weren't deceiving her, Lilu grabbed hold of the table as it shook harder.

Bryson glanced up and noticed Rhyparia's parents were already out the door, but he couldn't think about that. It was getting worse. The table's legs began cracking and the wood's surface was splintering. Then the glass plates and mugs shattered, and Lilu screamed.

Himitsu gawked. "What in the world …?"

The air around them felt thick, and the floorboards underneath them were vibrating violently. The wooden supports that held up the building were also cracking.

"Let's get out of here!" Bryson shouted. But when Bryson tried getting up, it was like he was stuck to his seat. Even Olivia, whose physical strength he had never seen outmatched, was barely able to stand, and was hunched over from the strain at that. Lilu was in fetal position on the booth's seat and crying.

"I can't breathe! My bones hurt!" she gasped.

Bryson tried to pick her up, but it was like lifting a mountain. He could barely stand himself. Olivia stepped over and slung the princess over her shoulder, her expressionless face a subtle red from the effort. Bryson turned to see Rhyparia still seated at the table. As the staff and other customers shrieked in fear and pain, she hadn't moved at all.

"Help me get her out of here!" Bryson screamed at Himitsu. They grabbed her by the arms and started dragging her across the floor.

Bryson followed the stumbling Olivia through the mess of bodies and rubble. Sections of the ceiling were caving in and the wooden supports were buckling. And the pressure bearing down on them was only getting worse. The two boys collapsed to their knees and crawled toward the exit. Even while carrying Lilu, Olivia was somehow the only person still standing.

Bryson climbed over people who were either screaming in pain or not breathing. He wanted to help them all. It was his duty as a Jestivan, but he just wasn't strong enough yet. Something hit him on the head and he almost blacked out. The debris wasn't falling at a normal speed. It was as if it had been shot out of a cannon.

He glanced to his right and saw the host pulling himself across the floor. A ragged chunk of wood ripped itself from the ceiling and hurtled downward, cleanly cutting the boy in two. Bryson tried to look away, but he was too late. He had just witnessed the most horrifying thing he had ever seen in his life.

Olivia and Lilu made it out of the building. But he still had two teammates, and friends, to worry about. Craters were being blasted into the floor. As he tried to crawl around it, the entire front side of the restaurant collapsed, walling them off.

He dully stared at the rubble. It was too much. He was exhausted and his lungs felt flattened. Himitsu had also stopped moving, accepting the same fate. Rhyparia blankly stared into the cloudy night sky through one of the many holes in the roof. Then everything around Bryson began to fade as his eyes slowly shut.

*   *   *

In one of the most crowded intersections in Dunami, a young red-headed boy sat high above everyone else. He gazed across a sea of heads as he enthusiastically shifted on the person's shoulders he was sitting upon.

Observing the buildings surrounding the street, his eyes landed on a rustic one. He squinted in effort to read the tiny sign above the door: BOWS & ARROWS.

His face lit up with joy. "Director!" he yelled above the noise as he looked down at the Intel Director who was carrying him.

"Simon!" Debo playfully yelled back.

"Archery store northbound!" He pointed in its direction. "Move, move, move!"

Chuckling, Debo played along with the charade of Simon acting as a captain. "Yes, sir!"

Debo darted through the tangled web of people, causing Simon's small arms to wrap around Debo's forehead as he held on for dear life.

In an instant, the duo found themselves in front of the shop. Debo crouched down to allow the boy to jump off. Simon looked through the window in awe. Pristine crossbows and traditional bows were gleaming in the glass display.

"One day I'll be the greatest archer in the world!" he exclaimed as he pretended to hold a crossbow on his shoulder, staring down its sights. *"Pew-pew-pew!"*

Debo smiled and put his hand on Simon's shoulder. "Perhaps today is the day to get started."

The boy's posture sunk. "I don't have that kind of money." He thought about it for a second and reiterated. "I don't have *any* money. I'm *eleven*."

"I do," the director said. He rustled Simon's long red hair. "Let's go in. You can pick whichever bow suits you best."

Simon's face brightened. He bolted toward the door, but as he reached for the handle, a loud crashing sound stopped him in his tracks. Clouds of dust were billowing in the distance, but they weren't rising. His smile vanished.

Debo was also concerned. The sounds of destruction weren't coming to an end, and he could hear screams. He scooped Simon onto his shoulders and grasped tightly onto his ankles.

"Hold on like your life depends on it," he commanded.

Debo plunged forward as Simon's head viciously yanked back from the instantaneous acceleration. Holding on was the most difficult thing Simon had ever tried to do in his life. But, somehow, it got worse.

The crowd was impeding Debo's progress, so he took an alternate route that involved no streets—up the side of a tavern. They were now parallel with the ground below as the director ran along the walls, jumping from building to building. Simon had learned in school that this kind of speed existed—speed that defied gravity—but it was so rare, nobody really believed it. His fingers dug into Debo's chest as he closed his eyes to calm his fright, but it was over very quickly.

When Simon reopened his eyes, it took him a second to make sense of the catastrophe. A collapsed restaurant lay before him. Window panes were shattered and missing, piles of wood were strewn on the ground, and bodies were smashed and bleeding in the rubble.

Debo's heart dropped as he saw Olivia was carrying a motionless Lilu away from the havoc. "Was there anyone else with you?" he asked.

The girl looked at him plainly and pointed behind her. "Bryson, Rhyparia, and Himitsu."

Debo knew Olivia very well, but he was still surprised to hear the blandness in her voice. Not even an event like this could drag any emotion out of her.

"Stay right here," Debo ordered Simon. He made a hasty sprint toward the wreckage and he was caught off-guard by the sudden shift in gravity. Instantly, he recognized that this wasn't an accident. But it didn't do much to slow him down. While everyone else twitched feebly, Debo searched through the wreckage. He found them fairly quickly. None of them were moving. Only Rhyparia's eyes were open. But when he touched her face, she continued to blankly stare into the night sky.

Debo was gathering the three of them in his arms when something above him cracked. He looked up to see a gigantic chunk of ceiling crashing down. He dropped the Jestivan and braced himself for impact. The ceiling slammed into him, but he caught it with his upper back and both hands.

His body began to tremble under the added pressure of the gravity and the ceiling, but he refused to give in. Even when his knees buckled, he still held it up. A roar escaped his mouth as he heaved the mass of wood to the side. He swiftly picked up his charges and walked through the weighted atmosphere. Although they were covered in blood, Debo could feel their shallow breathing. There was hope.

When he finally reached the street, he collapsed to one knee. The gravity was back to normal, but he was exhausted. It had been a long time since he was forced to exert that much effort.

"There are still more people barely alive back there," he said through heavy breaths to Spirit Director Neaneuma, who had joined the crowd. "Where is the kingdom's rescue department?"

His question was answered as a couple dozen horses galloped toward them. The mass of onlookers split apart to make way as the riders jumped off with torches in hand.

As the rescue squad took over, Debo noticed another one of the directors. It was the short and balding Archaic Director—Director Senex. His face was grave.

Debo sighed. "It's exactly what you think it is."

14

Hardship

Bryson awoke to a faint beeping sound that gradually grew more piercing. When he opened his eyes, they were assaulted by something just as loud—a room painted in entirely stark white. It took him a moment, but eventually he realized he was lying inside of a hospital room. He also knew which specific hospital he was in. The equipment was all too telling. There was not a single place in the world of Kuki Sphaira that had technology this advanced. In fact, nowhere else could even come close.

The Intel Kingdom originated technological advancement. The people of its kingdom were studious and innovative, and this is what caused it to be a power above the Light Realm's four other kingdoms—although in recent decades, the others had slowly began to catch up. With these advancements came wealth, and with that wealth came more advancement. It was a self-feeding cycle.

There was a hierarchy to the kingdom's spending, as three categories sat high above the rest. Third most important was technology. The machinery surrounding Bryson was evidence of that.

But there were two categories that far outweighed anything else in terms of expenses. And honestly, they could have been grouped as one: science and medicine. More money was put into these two departments than everything else combined, and the Dunami Hospital was a perfect display of that dedication. All of the equipment ran on Intel Energy, which sounded simple enough, but learning the complex methods of weaving Intel Energy had taken centuries of study and trial and error.

Stepping into the Dunami Hospital was like stepping into the future. Most people wouldn't even know what they were looking at. Some of the equipment didn't have proper names. That's how new a lot of it was. Let's be honest, people still struggled with the concept of an intelight.

Noticing none of the medical devices were attached to his body, Bryson concluded that he was simply recovering.

"Hey, buddy," a familiar voice said.

Bryson looked to his right and saw his lanky teammate in a hospital bed of his own. "Hey, Himitsu."

Himitsu appeared to be in decent shape. His knees, hands, and arms were heavily bandaged, but he was sitting up and eating noodles. Bryson looked down to see that he had the same areas wrapped.

Himitsu informed him of their injuries. "We both were fortunate," he said with a trail of noodles dangling from his mouth. "Cuts and scrapes, that's all. Our internal organs, bones, and mental state are all perfectly fine."

Bryson flopped back in relief.

"This place is insane," Himitsu said. "It definitely deserves its reputation. The fanciest medical center I've been in was two stories high and constructed of wood." He looked at the equipment surrounding them. "And there was none of this . . . just a doctor."

"This place is why my kingdom's life expectancy is so much higher than everywhere else," Bryson bragged. He then paused before admitting, "But it also puts people in some massive debt."

He caught a glimpse of another person to his left. It was Olivia and Meow Meow, who were sound asleep in a chair. She had no signs of injuries at all.

Himitsu looked at the girl too. "I only woke up an hour ago, but the doctors said she sat by your side the whole night. She was the only one who got out of that mess uninjured."

Seeing her made Bryson smile. Through thick and thin, he knew that Olivia would always stay by his side. And he would do the same for her.

He observed her resting face. Perhaps it was his imagination, but he had always felt he could see a tiny hint of emotion when she slept.

Then realization dawned on him. "What about Lilu and Rhyparia?" he asked, practically jumping out of his bed.

Himitsu stopped slurping his noodles. "I don't know. They won't tell me. All I know is that they're still in the E.R. ... whatever that is. It sounds bad though."

Emergency room. Bryson put his head in his hands. The sequence of events from the night before rushed through his head, reminding him of how useless he was. Rhyparia was in the E.R. because of his weakness, and Lilu only made it out because of Olivia. Come to think of it, Bryson was at a loss for how he got out. He had no memory of escaping.

His thoughts were put on hold as five people walked into the room. The first four were familiar faces, but the fifth was a stranger. Grand Director Poicus and Directors Buredo, Neaneuma, and Venustas wore somber expressions. The face of the fifth person, a man cloaked in deep burgundy with jet black hair, was inscrutable.

"Good afternoon," Poicus said. "I'm glad to see you've recovered well."

Himitsu gave a half-nod. Bryson simply looked at him.

Passion Director Venustas walked over to the girl and whispered in her ear, "Olivia, sweetie. Wake up."

As Olivia's eyes slowly opened, her peaceful face was instantly replaced by a brick wall. Meow Meow, on the other hand, responded with a hiss, causing Venustas to jump back a bit.

"A lot needs to be explained to you three," Poicus said, "but before we get to that, I will ask you to turn your attention to this gentleman here." He waved his hand in the direction of the stranger. "This is Vistas. He was once a subject of the Dev Kingdom."

Now they had Bryson's full attention. It was the first time he ever encountered someone from the Dark Realm. It made sense that the man was wearing burgundy. It was his former kingdom's color. Bryson had never seen one, but he was aware that there were roughly a hundred slaves from the Dev Kingdom inside of Dunami. They were captured a couple decades ago mostly by the hands of his father, Mendac.

Vistas gave a bow as Poicus explained, "Intel King Vitio is addressing the public in the main plaza today about the scenario that unfolded yesterday. Jilly, Toshik, Yama, Agnos, and Tashami are already attending it, but you three obviously can't attend, so we needed a way for you to view it."

He looked in the direction of the well-dressed slave before continuing, "This is when Vistas comes in handy. As someone from the Dev Kingdom, his Dev Energy and psychic abilities will bring the king's speech into this hospital room."

A large holographic image appeared, and its source was Vistas's eyes. Pictured was the burly Intel King Vitio, as he addressed a crowd that stretched for miles. His speech had already begun.

"—happen unless something catastrophic occurs. Therefore, for me to address the kingdom on such a large scale can only mean the worst. Before I explain what happened last night, which most of you already know about, I would like to say that it was not an act of terror. It was a mere accident caused by a building's aging foundation."

"Are you kidding me?" Bryson exclaimed.

"Shush, Bryson," Grand Director Poicus said.

"There were …" The king paused and sighed before finishing his sentence, "… many deaths. As of right now, the accident area is being cleared by workers. That spot will soon serve as a memorial to the people who lost their lives. There were two high-ranking officials, a few children, and many exuberant parents and couples who were just enjoying a night out.

"Five people made it out alive. They were five of the ten people who were to be our esteemed guests for the Generals' Battle tomorrow. This announcement was supposed to be a surprise, but with this catastrophe, it no longer matters. The second coming of the Jestivan was to stand guard tomorrow, but now only the five who weren't in the wreckage will fulfill that duty. The others are currently recovering in our hospital, which, as all of you know, has the best doctors in all of Kuki Sphaira. Thus we expect them to be perfectly fine.

"With that said, no Jestivan will meet with the public tomorrow. As for the Generals' Battle, it will be held as planned. I spoke with relatives of the deceased this morning, and they wanted the celebration to continue. They explained that this was the one time every year that the Light Realm gathers together in camaraderie. I greatly respect these families and I admire their fortitude.

"Ladies and gentlemen, I don't ask for you to ignore what happened last night. I ask you to do the best you can in enjoying the battle tomorrow, for that's what the fallen would have wanted. Good day, residents of the Light Realm."

With the conclusion of his speech, the hologram disappeared. Bryson was furious.

"That wasn't an accident! It was Rhyparia's parents!"

"Hold on there," Director Poicus said. "We're aware it wasn't an accident, but it works out better this way. As for your accusations, let's not make hasty, irrational conclusions."

Bryson's face reddened. "Rhyparia has told us enough about how awful her parents are, and it was proven last night! The moment even the slightest tremble occurred, they left the building."

Grand Director Poicus sighed. "Bryson, you're angry, and I understand that anger, but I'm telling you to—"

"People *died!*" he interrupted with a shout. "They were *slaughtered!*"

"And you think I don't realize this?!" Poicus shouted back, causing Bryson to quickly shut his mouth. Even the other directors were aghast at the Grand Director's unusual loss of composure.

Poicus took a deep breath. "You three will be spectators during the Generals' Battle tomorrow. Lilu might join you, but that is only because she is demanding to do so. She is in no condition to leave this hospital. Now, as for Rhyparia ... she is incapable of attending."

Bryson started to say something, but Poicus cut him off. "You have noticed Directors Debo and Senex are not here. That is because they are staying by their respective student's bedsides in the emergency room. I'm sure you're wondering how you made it out of the collapse. You have

Director Debo to thank for that."

"Can I go now, sir?" asked Vistas.

"Of course. Thank you for your help."

"My pleasure," he said with a gracious bow before walking out of the room.

The Grand Director turned back to the Jestivan. "Do you want to visit your teammates?" he asked.

The two young men leapt from their beds. That was an answer in itself. Olivia slowly stood up and stretched.

It was quite a walk to the emergency room, which was on the first floor and several stories below them. The journey became longer when they were informed by a nurse that Lilu and Rhyparia had been taken to the Intensive Care Unit, or ICU.

Their new destination made Bryson become uneasy. He was already a cold person, so to feel this type of chill was haunting. It was a vast room—if something so vast could even be called a "room"—of white. Hundreds of hospital beds lined the walls. A nurse's desk sat at the center, where doctors and assistants rushed to and fro with parchment inked with records and diagnoses.

Bryson approached a section of wall that was completely glass, and when he gazed through it, he saw a motionless young woman lying on the bed. Even without her bandana, Bryson knew it was Rhyparia.

They entered the room, and Director Senex, who was sitting next to her bed, slowly gazed toward the group. That was his only acknowledgment of their presence. He didn't even nod. He simply looked defeated.

The three Jestivan stood next to their friend's bed, and Bryson tried saying something. "How are you, Rhyparia?"

No response. "Rhyparia?"

For the second time, silence. Then he noticed something. Her eyes were open, but she still had the same empty stare from the night before. But this time, there was no night sky above her, just a bland ceiling.

Finally, a voice broke the morose quiet. "A coma," Meow Meow said. "I'm guessing from overwhelming shock."

A coma. Bryson glanced back at the Directors behind him to see a canvas of gloom painted on their faces, verifying what Meow Meow had said.

But why did her eyes have to be open? It was deceitful, as if the Bozani were mocking them from the Light Empire above.

Bryson's eyes watered before quickly wiping them. He thought about Rhyparia's determination to excel despite the status and characters of her parents. He thought about her reaction to seeing her parents enter the restaurant. Now he understood her fright.

As these thoughts consumed his mind, he gently swept her sweeping brown bangs in front of her eyes before exiting the room. There was nothing to be gained from staring at her. He didn't want his guilt to build up until it toppled into an unfixable mess.

So he began searching for Lilu, hoping she wasn't anything nearly as injured as Rhyparia. But this was the ICU, so it wasn't promising. Having no luck finding her, he asked one of the nurses at the central service desk, who pointed him in the right direction.

He took a deep breath as he opened the door. Fortunately, while the room looked the same as Rhyparia's, Lilu's health didn't seem to be. Debo was standing with his hands behind his back as he gazed out the window. He didn't turn around when Bryson entered, but it wasn't necessary. He saw the boy in the window's reflection.

"Hey, Bry."

Instead of responding, Bryson darted to Lilu's bedside. He grabbed her hand, noticing how different she looked. Her green hair was a frizzy mess and her eyes had light shadows around them.

Lilu's eyes slowly opened halfway, and she gave him a soft smile. Bryson smiled back. "You're awake," he said with relief.

"I am now," she said weakly, then coughed.

"Keep the words to a minimum," Debo cut in.

Her breathing was irregular and wheezy, and she would occasionally squint in pain. But she was conscious, and that was all that mattered. Bryson looked down at the contraption fastened around her chest.

"Don't worry. A few broken ribs. Rhyparia is who we should worry about." Everything she said sounded like a struggle. "I'll be out of here tomorrow."

Bryson looked at her. "You're not going anywhere."

"Your lungs were punctured," Debo said. "You need time to heal."

"We have commitments," she said.

"Screw the commitments," Bryson replied. He honestly didn't care about the plan any more. Besides, it was Lilu's idea in the first place.

"Director, could you leave for a bit?" she asked.

Debo looked at the two of them for a long moment, as if studying them. "Five minutes," he said before exiting the room.

The silence continued for a few moments as rain pattered against the window. "This is important," Lilu finally managed.

"Not important enough to risk your life," Bryson said. "Besides, why are we still questioning him? He sat by your side all night. He's a good man."

"A good man with dark secrets."

Bryson sighed, careful to not lose his cool. "We will wait for another opportunity."

"This is the *only* opportunity." She started coughing, wincing from the pain.

"And that is why you are not going anywhere," he said. "Besides, do you really want the world to see you like this? I mean … look at your hair."

Lilu accidentally giggled, but quickly stopped, either from the pain or remembering that she was supposed to be serious. "Not funny."

"I won't go through with your plan if I see you at the stadium tomorrow."

Lilu looked at him hopelessly as she realized his mind was not going to be changed. Feebly, she grabbed his hand. "I won't go," she said.

"Good."

"But the plan will still happen," she said. "I'll just have to get in touch with the brothers."

"As long as it involves you not leaving this room."

"Just show up to the Royal Suite tomorrow. I'll take care of everything."

Bryson studied her half-closed eyes. Her persistence was annoying, yet moving at the same time.

"Stop worrying," she reassured him. "I already have one dad. I don't need two."

At that moment, Debo walked back into the room with an apple in hand. "Make that three," she mumbled.

Debo, not hearing her, took a bite out of his apple. "A bit more than five minutes, but I was hungry and couldn't find the cafeteria."

"Thank you," Lilu said.

Deciding to spend the night next to Lilu, Bryson slipped his hood over his head and slumped softly in his chair. It was a rough night. Lilu would wake up in pain every half hour or so. Several times the doctor and nurses forced Bryson to leave, though they practically had to rip him from the chair. And when that happened, he stood outside the room while hopelessly gazing back in … watching her suffer as she screamed loud enough to be heard throughout the entire floor.

15

The Generals' Battle

The next day, Bryson woke up for what probably was the eleventh time, but this time for good. Even with the ever-present overcast skies roiling outside the ICU room's window, it was obvious that it was the heart of morning.

Bryson yawned and stretched more intensely than usual, his body aching from the fitful night. It was reminiscent of his nightmare-riddled nights when he was a child. However, it would be wrong to complain. Lilu was the one who actually experienced the torture. As he gazed at her sleeping face, it was obvious that she still wasn't breathing normally. He wanted to stay, but he knew that would upset her since she was determined to complete their objective.

He walked over to Olivia, who was passed out in a chair opposite Lilu's bed. Before waking her, he took the opportunity to appreciate her peaceful state that could only be seen when fast asleep. It didn't last long though, for her eyes slowly opened. Realizing how strange it was for him to be staring at her so intently, he took a couple steps back. Luckily, Meow Meow was still passed out, so Bryson didn't have to worry about any caustic remarks.

Olivia stared back with her gigantic blue eyes and casually asked, "Shall we leave?"

"Yeah, let's say bye to Lilu."

"No. Let her rest. She is finally getting continuous sleep."

Bryson hesitated for a moment, then agreed. Allowing her to rest was more important than hearing her voice, so he left without a word.

The timing was perfect. As they walked across the busy lobby, Himitsu had just walked out of Rhyparia's room. He seemed to be alright, but his expression was masked.

"Nothing changed?" Bryson asked. He felt he already knew the answer, but it didn't hurt to try being optimistic—something he learned from Jilly.

"No," Himitsu replied.

Bryson peered through the glass. Rhyparia's eyes were still open, motionless, and glued to the ceiling above.

"Let's go," Olivia said.

They were greeted with an empty street upon exiting the hospital. Only something such as the Generals' Battle could clear a city like this. The place was a ghost town. They walked in silence for a good while before Himitsu broke it.

"At least we have an easy day ahead of us."

"Very true," Bryson said. "I didn't really fancy the idea of guard duty anyways—so mundane."

"How jealous will everyone else be, watching us sit in the stands, eat, drink, and just enjoying the show?" Himitsu asked.

"I think they'd be more worried about Rhyparia and Lilu than envying you," Meow Meow said.

Himitsu frowned. "Just trying to be positive."

"You know what would be better than sitting in the stands?" Bryson asked.

"What?"

"Sitting in the Royal Suite box," Bryson said with a crafty grin.

Himitsu shrugged. "I guess we could dream, right?"

"It's no dream. Lilu invited me, but since she won't be there, and I don't want to be there with nobody I know, I'm going to bring you and Olivia with me."

Himitsu threw his arms into the air and bellowed with joy.

Olivia, however, did not have the same reaction. "No, thank you." Her kitten hat frowned.

"You'd rather be crammed into an uncomfortable stone bench?" Himitsu asked incredulously.

"I'd rather fulfill the mission assigned to me. I'm not hurt, so I will ask the directors if they can make an exception for me."

Bryson didn't argue. Knowing Olivia like he did, he wasn't surprised at all.

It was quite a journey from the hospital to the stadium, but they'd left early, so there was no rush. And unlike in other kingdoms, they didn't have to worry about a beaming sun cooking them alive. Bryson was always thankful for the dreary clouds—not that it mattered too much since it was the middle of autumn.

The main entrances to the stadium were flooded with unorganized lines of people. Thankfully, the Jestivan had been instructed to meet at a special guest entrance, so they walked around the perimeter of the towering stone stadium. When they finally arrived, Bryson was happy to not see a giant mass of people fighting over spots in line.

The five Energy Directors and five of the Jestivan were gathered and leisurely talking with each other. Grand Director Poicus had elected to stay at Phesaw over the weekend. A few members of the Intel King Guard were also present. Bryson and Himitsu made a few simple hellos before breaking off from the pack and leaving Olivia behind.

The crowds inside of the stadium walls were even worse. Throngs of people jammed the many food courts and merchandise shops scattered throughout. Children were screaming and playing. A pathetic-looking clown even managed to get a good laugh out of Himitsu.

Finishing their climb to the third floor, they noticed a sharp difference between it and the two lower floors they had just left. First, guards stood by the entrance to grant or deny entry. Luckily, this proved not to be a hindrance as they reacted like they'd known Bryson for years.

"This way," an armored soldier said. The Intel Kingdom's insignia—an array of electrical currents—was molded into his chest plate.

The two Jestivan followed the man through the magnificent lobby. Unlike the dirty cement floors of the coliseum's other levels, the third floor was carpeted in a plush white. The walls were a sunny yellow. A few waiters holding serving trays came in and out of a door that presumably led to a kitchen. Then there were several other doors lining the wall that divided the arena from the outer ring. Bryson suspected those led to the individual suite boxes.

They approached a polished wooden door that was directly in the middle of the rest. The guard knocked three times as Bryson and Himitsu continued to take in the elegant decor surrounding them. A peephole slid open, and a set of green eyes gazed through and scanned over the three of them.

"Lady Lilu's guests are here," the guard said.

"I was only aware of one guest, Jeffery," said a voice through the door. "Who is the tall one?" The eyes in the slit narrowed as she asked.

"I'm Himitsu, ma'am."

"*Ma'am?*" she repeated in disgust.

The peephole slammed shut and the door swung open as an angry young woman stormed into the lobby. Her hair was a familiar green and it was cut very short—boyish short. It worked for her though. She wore an extravagant golden dress with frills at every hem. Her collar was lined with lace. She had a beautiful diamond earring in each earlobe, a shining bracelet on her left wrist, and a diamond necklace. The white belt that hugged her waist and white heels complimented the diamond jewelry perfectly, but it contrasted her golden clothing even better. She was stunning.

She stood directly in front of Himitsu. "I do not know you, so you will address me as Princess or Lady Shelly."

"I'm sorry," Himitsu said in a lightly mocking tone. He saw the woman's face grow sterner, so he quickly added, "... Princess Shelly."

She looked toward Bryson, who was busy observing the physical similarities between the princess and Lilu. "Is he your friend?" Shelly asked.

Bryson gave her a guilty smile. "Yes, Princess. He is one of the Jestivan who were caught in the collapse two nights ago."

She looked up at Himitsu again. "Very well then. Don't expect me to address you as 'Zana' or whatever it is," she said before turning around and heading back into the suite. "Come in."

The guard retreated toward the lobby's main entrance. While Shelly's back was turned, Himitsu cocked his head to the side with his tongue hanging out as he pretended to hang himself, causing Bryson to hold back a laugh. Based off first impressions, Shelly was somehow even more assertive than Lilu. He chalked it up to how they were raised, which wasn't their fault. An entitled attitude was bound to form when growing up as royalty.

The area of the suite box closest to the entrance was heavily illuminated by intelights. To the right sat a small bar area for guests to serve their own drinks. This excited Himitsu, but it meant nothing to Bryson since he wasn't of age. Some furniture rested on the left side of the room, as well as a familiar face that was sprawled leisurely on a sofa.

"Hello, Vistas," Bryson said as he extended his hand.

The man did not shake his hand, but instead lazily looked at Bryson. "I'm not Vistas," he said through a yawn.

Confusion crept its way onto Bryson's face, but Himitsu, who had just walked over with a glass of wine, was the one to respond. "That's funny."

The man looked exactly like Vistas. He had the same facial features, black hair, and colored eyes. Not one thing was different.

"He is Flen—not Vistas," came a new voice.

It was the king. He was dressed in yellow breeches and a waistcoat that represented the Intel Kingdom's colors. He had the sort of build that looked like a thick layer of fat was lying on top of his muscles in his chest and torso.

The king's face flooded with delight as Bryson looked up at him. "What an honor!" the king said as he stretched his arm for a handshake.

Bryson gave it a firm grasp. "Hello, King Vitio."

"Oh, no, no, no!" Vitio playfully yelled. "I will not have the offspring of one of my best friends address me so formally. A simple 'Vitio' will do."

Although he should have expected it, the mention of his father threw Bryson off. He was never going to shake his father's shadow. He internally brushed off the annoyance and attempted a smile. "You and my father achieved monumental things for this kingdom. You were a duo unlike any other."

King Vitio smiled at the blatant flattery. "Is that what they say?" he rhetorically asked with a grin.

"Not where I'm from," the Vistas look-alike sneered.

The king turned to look at the black-haired man sprawled on the sofa. "Well, Flen, we're not concerned about the opinions of the Dark Realm." Flen just smirked.

After remembering what Lilu said the night before, Bryson asked, "Is he Vistas's twin?"

"Let's go with that," the king replied. His eyes looked over Bryson's shoulder. "And who is this well-grown gentleman?"

Bryson had forgotten about Himitsu. He was being oddly quiet, which was probably because he was too busy drinking his second glass of wine. "He is a fellow Jestivan. His name is Himitsu," Bryson explained as he stepped out of the way.

"And which kingdom are you from?" King Vitio asked as Himitsu bowed to him.

"Passion, sir."

"Ah, an emotional one."

Himitsu sat down in a cozy armchair and twirled the thin strand of hair lying on his forehead. "I'm a bit different," he explained. "I must damper any excessive emotions. When your talent in combat is the art of silence, you must silence everything inside first."

A look of understanding graced Vitio's face. "You've been staying safe, right?" he asked gravely.

Himitsu closed his eyes. "Yes, sir."

Vitio decided to change the topic. "Let's go see the view of the arena, Bryson," he said enthusiastically.

Bryson followed the boulder of a king toward the seating area opposite the entrance door. There was no wall on the other end, just an empty space for clear viewing into the arena below. There were seats for a limited amount of guests—ten, maximum. Only three people occupied the seats— the princess and two men. Bryson was introduced to Corporal Peter, an aging man with a grey goatee, and Major Lars, a significantly younger and more handsome man with a rugged jawline.

Meeting these two gentlemen reminded him of something the directors had told the Jestivan a few months back. That their talents were on the level—and, most likely, higher—than the highest-ranking officials of any of the kingdoms' militaries … outside of the generals, that is. Perhaps these two realized this too. Maybe it was common sense to everyone else that a Jestivan was someone who possessed great ability and even greater potential. But to Bryson, it didn't feel that way at all.

The Intel King instructed Bryson to have a seat next to him, which Bryson politely obeyed. He was now sandwiched between King Vitio and Princess Shelly.

"The match should be starting soon," informed Vitio. "Flen!"

After a few moments, Flen lazily walked over to the king. He moved in a surprisingly nonchalant manner for someone who was supposed to be a servant of a royal family.

"Get us connected," Vitio ordered.

Flen rubbed his eyes with a sigh. "Let me see if they're ready." He stared blankly into space for several seconds before a holographic display appeared in front of him. However, his technique was grotesquely odd. Instead of using both eyes to display the picture, he used only one, which was fixed in a certain spot. Meanwhile, the right eye turned a deep burgundy and moved freely on its own.

"Hi, father," said a very familiar voice, instantly jarring Bryson's attention from Flen's creepy eyes.

It was Lilu, who was pictured in the display. She was still in her hospital bed with the metal contraption attached to her upper torso. Bryson finally realized what her plan was, and he took a deep breath of relief.

"How are you feeling, beautiful?" King Vitio asked with a grave tone of concern.

Lilu smiled. "Breathing is still difficult, but I've been perfectly fine. Vistas has been great company."

"Next time we're getting Vistas. Why do I have to get the raw end of the stick?" Princess Shelly whined.

Lilu laughed softly, careful to not hurt herself. "Vistas, say hello to the jealous princess," she teased. A hand waved in the forefront of the screen's vision. Bryson was amused at the thought of Vistas waving his hand in front of his own eyes.

Bryson noticed Flen's free-moving eye rest on him, and that was when Lilu enthusiastically—well, to the best of her ability—said, "Bryson!" He understood: the right eye was recording while the left was presenting.

Bryson couldn't hide his joy. "Hey, Lilu!"

"Don't think just because you're the son of Mendac means you have any chance with my sister," Shelly said with a sneer. Perhaps "assertive" was too kind of a description.

Bryson's face soured immediately. "First of all, stop looking at me as my father's offspring. Second, don't jump to conclusions."

Shelly's face reddened. "How dare you. I don't care if you're a zana. I am a princess! Watch your tongue."

Lilu rolled her eyes as King Vitio jumped in. "Stop this. Mind your manners, Shelly."

Shelly shot up from her seat. "I suppose he's the son you always wanted! Actually, he probably *is* your son! You and Mendac were always so far up each other's hind that he probably planted it while you conceived it!"

Something warm sprayed against the back of Bryson's neck. He turned around and saw that Himitsu had just spit wine all over him and was now laughing hysterically. He made no effort to hold it back.

Flen was also laughing, and Bryson would have reacted the same way if he wasn't so flabbergasted. There wasn't even time for the king to respond since Shelly had stormed out of the suite. He merely sat there red in the face.

"Didn't expect to see you, Himitsu," Lilu said.

Himitsu, who had finally caught his breath, replied, "I'm so happy I was invited. She looks every bit like a princess, but speaks like a sailor."

The rest of the time was spent conversing and bonding with King Vitio. Shelly had come back and taken her original seat, acting as if nothing had happened. The plan started off poorly, but there was still plenty of time to right the ship.

Down below, a tiny man walked toward the center of the arena floor. The crowd went silent.

"Here we go!" King Vitio yelled as he sat up in his seat.

The man was holding a small cone-shaped object, and upon reaching center stage, he put it to his mouth. "Ladies and gentlemen!" His voice was thunderous. It echoed around the stadium's climbing walls of seats.

Vitio leaned toward Bryson. "He's the emcee for the Generals' Battle every year. He's from the Archaic Kingdom, and his ancient piece projects his voice to astounding levels."

"I am so happy to see so many faces!" the emcee continued. "I see fans sporting the colors of their respective kingdoms! The Spirit's blues! The Passion's reds! The Intel's yellows! The Adren's silvers! And of course, the Archaic's browns!"

With each kingdom he named, a different section of the crowd would roar. Bryson gazed toward the bottom of the stands where the other Jestivan were supposed to be positioned. He spotted Tashami in front of his area, but he was the only one. There were too many people and the stadium was far too big for him to recognize the others.

"Shall we welcome the stars of the show?" the commentator asked. The cheers that followed were an obvious yes.

He named off each general, presenting them one by one as they walked into the massive ring. The Intel General was last to be named. "A good man, but nothing like your father," King Vitio remarked.

Bryson's blood boiled, but he bit his lip. "Who could be?" he said smoothly, which Vitio replied to with a hearty chuckle.

The host continued shouting through his ancient: "We all know the drill! A free-for-all! Every man and woman for themselves! The last one standing wins the title of Chief General of all the Light Realm for a year!"

Then he lowered his tone and became more serious. "However, this is *not* a battle to the death. You are eliminated once you are no longer able to *fight*—*not* when you are no longer able to *breathe* … Is that clear, Generals?"

Each general responded with their kingdom's salute, making it clear they understood. There were four men and one woman. She was a brutish-looking lady with shoulders as broad as any man's. It was odd seeing her sporting blue. The Spirit Kingdom was known for its powerful and iconic women, but they were typically dainty and elegant.

"My money is on the Archaic General," Lilu predicted.

"Show faith in your kingdom, dear," her father said disapprovingly. "Our general is fully capable."

"I'm rooting for him, but I'm being realistic."

Bryson gazed at the olive-skinned man in brown, who Lilu just predicted to win. He was holding a long brown staff with a glowing orange ball hovering at the top of it. The bone structure in his face was sharp, and his perfectly clean-shaven head was shining next to the orb's light.

The host walked off the arena's floor, and before Bryson knew it, a raucous shout boomed across the stadium—"*Fight!*"

What Bryson would have expected, which was an epic standoff of five great fighters respecting one another's skillset, did not happen. Instead the action commenced immediately, and the Archaic General wasted no time in putting his ancient piece to work.

Twirling his staff upside-down, he slammed the glowing orb into the ground. The entirety of the arena floor began to shake as if it had been hit with an earthquake. Crevices with smoke spewing out of them extended in every direction.

Clouds of grey obscured the arena floor, but their presence was short-lived, as the beastly Spirit General dispersed them with a heavy blast of wind. Bryson couldn't understand the warrior's intentions behind the Archaic General's opening salvo, which seemed as if it was just for show. An attack had to occur somewhere.

The other generals still had yet to make a move, but then the Adren General shot toward the Archaic General. Bryson could follow his movement surprisingly easily. Perhaps he had underestimated his own talents.

Nevertheless, he was surely too fast for the Archaic General—except that the other man had already planned for it. The moment the Adren General disappeared, a wall of deep red blasted into the air, enclosing the Archaic General in a circle. The Adren General slammed into the barrier and instinctively jumped back while grasping his lava-singed elbow. Now Bryson understood the preemptive move the man had made at the beginning of the fight. He had broken the arena floor to draw up lava from the ground.

"You know better than that, Sinno," the Archaic General drawled. "Look down."

General Sinno had retreated directly on top of a hole. He dove to the side, narrowly dodging another burst of lava. But while he was mid-dive, a surge of electricity collided with his chest. It came from the Intel General, who had entered the fray.

Sinno shuddered as the electric surge burned through his nerves. He looked up and asked, "You two are teaming up on me?"

The Archaic General gave an inquisitive glare to the Intel General. "I must ask the same question. Why are you, out of all people, syncing attacks with me?"

"Because he's a nuisance I can't be bothered with," the Intel General responded sternly. "The sooner he gets taken out, the fewer random variables I must consider. All he knows is speed, and I need structure to fight."

Intrigued, the Archaic General stepped out of his circle and toward the Intel General. He then stood next to him, shoulder to shoulder, and said with a sly smirk, "An odd bonding of two rival kingdoms. Alright then, Lucas, let's give the scribes something to talk about. I suppose getting Minerva and Landon to agree to this will be no problem. They've done nothing but bore the audience anyways."

The two generals who had not been active gave a silent nod, and now General Sinno found himself against terrifying odds. He was crouched and already weakened while surrounded by four highly capable combatants.

"Shall we attack at the same time?" the Archaic General asked.

Another full round of nods were given, resulting in a prompt symphony of attacks. Minerva, the Spirit General, swiped her arm in a clawing motion, creating a harsh, downward-angled strike of wind that cut across the floor and sent Sinno crashing across the arena. Landon, the Passion General, slowly raised his hand in front of him with his palm facing up, summoning flames around Sinno's body.

As the Intel General prepared to finish the hapless man off, something struck him in the back of the head and face-first into the ground—a giant hand of magma. He lay there, unconscious. It was such a marvelous display of energy control by the Archaic General, but the crowd jeered at his treachery.

"And that was Archaic General Inias doing his kingdom proud! He hatched a clever scheme that resulted in two KOs!" the commentator boomed.

Giving a gentle smirk, Inias pointed his staff toward the muscular lady in blue. A wave of lava flowed from the staff and spread thickly across the floor. Bryson felt the heat rising from the arena and could only imagine what the combatants were experiencing.

As Spirit General Minerva struggled to hold back the wall of lava, Passion General Landon took the opportunity to turn on her. He shot a burst of flame from his palms that she swatted away with a gust of wind. Landon ran behind her and sent out flames, completely trapping her in an inferno.

Inias redoubled his efforts, and the wall of lava reached the peak of its ascent, curled inward, and cascaded down toward her. With a single quick twirl of her body, the air around her began to spin, creating a twister of lava. She shot horizontal winds through the thick substance, flinging burning stone fragments at Inias. He dodged several of them, but two made contact. The second projectile was large enough to knock him off his feet.

Inias got up quickly and wiped a trail of blood from his chin. He looked toward Landon and gave a nod. They knew how exhausted Minerva was inside of the inferno, so they simply had to wait.

Finally, the twirling winds subsided, and the lava collapsed around Minerva. The two men were correct. She was keeled over on one knee. The moment she was exposed, the Passion General was already lunging at her with a vicious, flame-coated punch. She fell to the ground as the audience groaned.

Bryson had never experienced such a show of combat. This was not training or play-fighting. It was dangerous, and while they weren't fighting with the intent to kill, those who fell had been pushed to their absolute limits.

"And that leaves the weakest of the generals left for Inias to take out," Lilu said. "I won't say I told you so, Father, but I told you so."

Vitio looked disappointed. "That Archaic General ruins the fun. This will be five straight years. What makes it even more embarrassing is that he uses a different ancient each year."

"He's lucky the princes and princesses can't fight in this battle," Shelly said.

Bryson found her comment strange. She was a princess, not a soldier.

"If you can hang with them, why do you need a general anyways?"

She smirked. "We royal blood first-borns, are actually more talented fighters than any general. We only use them so we don't have to fight. We have to protect ourselves—or more importantly, the future of our bloodline."

Bryson shrugged. In a cruel way, it made sense. He refocused on the final two combatants. With Inias and Landon not having to worry about anyone else, their combat became more technique-based. A kick would be followed up with a punch, which would be followed by a block and a jab. Every few moments, they would launch an elemental attack of lava or fire.

The air rippled in the rising heat, but it seemed to only make the two stronger. The fans in brown wildly cheered on their Archaic General, Inias, while the ones in red did the same for their Passion General, Landon.

However, soon, the Passion Kingdom residents would have nothing to cheer for, as Inias swiped their general's feet with the bottom of his staff. Lava splashed upward as Landon landed in it.

"This could be it!" the commentator yelled. "A final blow might be dealt!"

Inias stood over Landon as he struggled to rise. Inias raised his foot high into the air, readying to stomp. Landon looked up as the bottom of Inias's wooden sandal plummeted toward his face—but then the crowd screamed. Screams of horror.

Blood splashed onto Landon's face. A long metal pole was impaled through Inias's stomach. The Archaic General gaped at his wound with wide eyes. Then a second rod shot through his back and heart. Before he could fall, a third rod went straight into the back of Inias's head.

The Archaic General fell over like a dead tree as the lava swallowed his body. Attached to the final rod, gently blowing in the wind, was a flag. It was burgundy ... the color of the Dev Kingdom.

16

First Blood

The gentle wave of the burgundy flag in the middle of the arena was in stark contrast to the chaos in the stands. Soldiers in burgundy were pouring across the benches, hacking down the spectators as they frantically massed against the exits. Here and there Intel soldiers in gold-trimmed, silver armor fought to stem the red tide, but they were too few in number. And random objects hurtled through the air without anyone seeming to throw them. Rocks, stone, and metal were levitating off the ground before striking down civilians and soldiers alike.

"Damnit!" King Vitio yelled as he jumped out of his seat. "Lars and Peter, go!"

"Dad, go check on the Archaic King right now!" Lilu yelled through the transmission. "He's going to think that we did this!"

King Vitio gaped at his daughter. "But we don't have any Dev soldiers any more. We only kept their intelligence unit."

"Do you think he's going to believe that?! With the history between our two kingdoms? He'll think we used the Dev Kingdom as a scapegoat!"

As Vitio stood motionless, too overwhelmed to make a decision, Shelly sprinted toward the exit. As she reached for the handle, the door shattered into thousands of pieces as a thick pillar of wood blew through it. Shelly was taken off her feet as the base collided violently into her stomach. Her body shot across the suite, and Bryson grabbed her just before she plunged over the railing and down into the stands. For a moment it seemed as if they both would fall as their legs dangled in the air, the top halves of their bodies dangling over the bar. Then Vitio's burly hands grabbed them and pulled them back onto their feet.

Bryson looked down at Shelly. Her face was no longer smug, but momentarily dazed. Her eyes were half closed, but when she gazed up at Bryson, whose golden bangs had fallen in front of his face, they widened.

"Thank you," she said—something he never thought he'd hear from her. Then she looked toward the entrance and her face now flooded with anger.

"*Vitio!* You will *die* today!"

The threat came from a tall skinny man draped in many shades of brown. His head was balding, covered in brown spots, and encompassed by a crown of twigs. He was the king of the Archaic Kingdom, accompanied by the handsome Archaic Prince and two officials.

*   *   *

Utter madness surrounded Agnos, and he was hesitating to join it. Even though he was a Jestivan, fighting was not his purpose, nor did he ever expect something of this scale to happen so soon.

But there was no time to stand around. As he stood in shock at the bottom of the crowd, looking up at the fleeing masses, civilians were collapsing left and right, felled by swords or flying debris. Then the burgundy-clothed attackers began to fall, and Agnos's eyes searched for the assailant. But there was none. Then a presence appeared next to him.

"Zana Agnos, prove useful in some way by assisting in escorting the innocents." It was Adren Director Buredo, who was looking gravely at the scene before them. It explained why Agnos hadn't seen him. Buredo was too fast.

As Agnos ran up the stairs, thankful to receive instructions that did not involve fighting, Buredo bolted from one Dev soldier to the next, effortlessly slashing his sword across the chest of each one. Occasionally, he found himself having to casually dodge a random object hurtling through the air, but his speed and quickness made it easy. As he hacked down the Dev soldiers, none of them skilled enough to even witness his approach, he wondered ... *Where are the big guns?*

*   *   *

Yama, unlike Agnos, was heavily involved in the action, and the Dev soldiers were just as helpless before her as Buredo. She moved fast and killed swiftly. And there was no hesitation as she dealt her fatal blows. This was her job, and the deaths didn't lay guilt upon her shoulders. In fact, even as civilians fell dead by the hundreds, she felt joy. Finally, *real* combat. Actual enemies who gave her the freedom to fight without holding back. For the first time in her life, she was feeling an adrenaline rush like no other as the blood of her victims sprayed across her face like war paint. This caused her Adrenergy to surge to a new level, giving her speed an extra push.

The only problem she encountered was her lack of knowledge and experience of fighting Dev soldiers. She was not accustomed to their Dev Energy and psychic abilities, so the telekinetic attacks frequently caused her to stumble. Twice she almost had her sword completely pulled from her grasp. Yet she continued slashing down endless numbers of foot soldiers as their insides spilled over the seats.

She came to a halt near the middle of her section. Breathing heavily and looking around, she noticed the vast majority of the corpses were enemy soldiers, not civilians. Some bodies that were draped in burgundy moaned as they clung to their lives, but the attack was over.

Then she felt someone's presence behind her. A fist struck her in the back and she stumbled forward from the unexpected blow.

Not even bothering to turn around, she bolted away, but when she came

151

to a stop, a man of average height with brown hair appeared in front of her ... *out of thin air.* This time he shoved his palm into her face, causing her to crash over the bench behind her.

As the man yanked her up and stared into her bloody face, he frowned in disappointment. "Same purple hair, but you're not her."

Yama couldn't comprehend what was happening as they studied each other. *I couldn't see his movements. Is he really that fast? No, he's wearing burgundy. He isn't from my kingdom ... but he's different from the others.*

She sprung away at her fastest speed, and this time, she noticed something. The moment she'd left her spot, the man closed his eyes, and when she stopped, he appeared with his eyes closed for an instant before reopening them. He wasn't moving—he was teleporting, and he was using clairvoyance to track her.

"You're tracking me through an extra sense," Yama said.

He looked impressed. "Intuitive," he remarked. He glanced at her hair for a moment before saying, "However, you are not my target."

Then he dissipated, and Yama fell forward as the toe of his boot connected with her spine. He had teleported behind her. Her sword rattled in front of her as she fell on all fours. When she scrambled to it and whirled around, the man was gone. Her violet hair draped her face as she stared at the ground. Fists clenched, she let out a scream of failure.

*   *   *

On the opposite side of the arena was another swordsman fulfilling his duties. Slashing through the stands, he looked out of place in his white dress shirt and silver tie. Even when on a mission, he wanted to look good for the ladies.

Normally Toshik would have been enjoying the opportunity to display his swordsmanship in the defense of beautiful women, but only one girl was on his mind—Jilly. He simply wanted to clear out his section as quickly as possible, which was not proving to be a difficult task. The soldiers were slow and clumsy, so he was making swift work of them. However, much like Yama, he struggled to fend off the telekinetic objects flying around. He cursed at a rock that slammed into his forehead, but not because of the pain—it was going to leave a noticeable blemish.

After quickly scanning the area to make sure all of his enemies were defeated, he immediately shot toward another section. On his way, he dodged blazing flames as he passed Director Venustas—who was replacing an injured Lilu.

Once Toshik arrived to his destination, he was almost pulled into the sky as winds tugged him in every direction. *Unbelievable. She'll never understand,* he thought to himself.

He found Jilly at the bottom of the stands, and to his unsurprised dismay, she was standing still with her eyes closed and hands holding down her billowing dress as her blond hair whipped violently in the wind.

Jilly not only lacked control of her power, she completely lost awareness when using it. Dev soldiers, Intel soldiers, and civilians alike were being hurled into the air and dashed against the stone bleachers.

A man dressed in burgundy climbed over the arena wall behind Jilly and raised his sword. Toshik shot toward her, stumbling as the gusts knocked into him. As the Dev soldier's sword descended, Toshik slashed off the man's arm at the elbow. Then his howl of agony was cut short as Toshik ran his blade through the man's stomach.

Toshik pulled out his sword as the man collapsed. He gave it a flick to remove the blood before sheathing it again. As he put his hand on Jilly's shoulder, he whispered into her ear, "Jills, that's enough."

Jilly's eyes opened as the wind subdued. She turned to look at her towering friend and beamed at him. "Toshy!"

*   *   *

Olivia was effortlessly taking out opponents with an expressionless face. She threw powerful punches and kicks, breaking the bones of her enemies. Unlike Yama, Toshik, and Director Buredo, she was not about speed, so most of her fights were against multiple opponents, as she did not have the quickness to dash from one enemy to the other.

This, however, wasn't a hindrance. She was fully capable of handling as many Dev soldiers who could fit within her range. With time, she learned that their only ability was manipulating objects through space with their

153

mind. They didn't have the talent with their Dev Energy to perform any of the kingdom's deadlier skills. They were merely cannon fodder.

Olivia had an unusual familiarity with the psychic abilities of the Dev soldiers. In fact, she knew a little too much about them, and if any of the directors had seen her fighting, they would have become curious. With her knowledge of their telekinetic powers, she was fully aware of not only her own fights, but the innocents escaping around her also. She occasionally disregarded her own safety in order to intercept a soaring block of stone from crushing a civilian.

Now she was close to clearing her section. Five soldiers remained, and they were all baring down on her. One of the men aimed a punch to her face from in front, while another kicked at her ankles from behind. She caught the punch with one hand and jumped over the sweeping leg. The power of her jump slightly cracked the ground as it sent her high into the air. She still had a grasp of the man's fist, and at the peak of her jump, she pulled his arm under her before plummeting toward the ground and snapping his arm against a stone bench. As he shrieked, she kicked backward, collapsing the second soldier's ribcage.

"You like that?!" Meow Meow shouted as the man fell.

Olivia turned to her left to see an elbow being swung toward her face. This attack was no different than the others—predictable and simple. She caught it, and as she squeezed the bones in the man's hand to mush, she noticed a female soldier off to the side and a little bit in the distance.

Once again, Olivia's knowledge of Dev Energy proved useful. She swung the man she was holding behind her back—just in time to intercept a metal spike with his forehead.

The fourth man gaped at her and fled. That left one soldier to deal with … the telekinetic. She was shaking violently in fear from what she she had just witnessed. Three of her comrades were wiped out in twenty seconds by a girl who looked to be no older than sixteen.

Then a brunette man of average height had appeared at the top of the stands—the man who had bested Yama. He looked at Olivia from afar and closed his eyes.

Suddenly Olivia was no longer striding toward a frightened Dev soldier, nor was she surrounded by sounds of chaos and screams. She was no longer in the stadium at all.

She was standing somewhere straight out of a dream—nothing but a haze of purple and burgundy in all directions. Olivia stopped breathing and heard the faint echoes of screaming and clashing swords. She realized she wasn't in a different location. To anyone else, Olivia would be looking aimlessly around the stadium. She was caught in the net of an extremely powerful clairvoyant—someone far stronger than the woman she'd been about to strike down. But who? *Who did I miss?*

Realizing there was nothing she could do, Olivia sat down inside of the lucid hallucination. She stared into the endless obscurity with an expression of stone.

"We'll be okay," Meow Meow muttered, his voice trembling.

*   *   *

The suite of the Royal Intel family was now packed with unwelcomed guests. King Vitio stared gravely at the Archaic King, who, like his entourage, glared back with pure spite. Many, many years of history had led up to this …

Lilu was crying tears of many different emotions—anger, hopelessness, and fear were just a few.

Vistas watched her claw at her face in frustration and pull at her hair. "Lady Lilu, may I ask you something?"

"Go ahead," she answered through her hands.

"What is the weight of the situation unfolding over there?"

She slid her hands down her cheeks, smearing her tears. Eyes red, she stared angrily at the ceiling. "Weight unlike anything that we've ever seen … Weight that this kingdom cannot withstand." …

King Vitio spoke carefully. "Itta, this was not our doing."

"*How dare you lie to me!*" King Itta bellowed as he threw a punch from across the room. Again, it transformed into a pillar of wood as it shot through the air.

Vitio quickly sidestepped the attack, but he didn't counter. He wasn't going to give them any reason to blame him for this terrible day.

The onslaught continued as Itta sent endless attacks in Vitio's direction, who continued dodging all of them. Beams of wood were ramming into walls and clattering on top of Bryson, Himitsu, and Princess Shelly, who were hugging the ground.

"Fight me, you wretch!" Itta thundered. "You let others do your dirty work, and now you're too cowardly to fight me hand to hand!"

"I don't want to fight you," Vitio said, "and what happened had nothing to do with me or my kingdom."

"You expect us to believe that?" the Archaic Prince laughed. The young man strode into the room. His laugh only lasted for a brief moment before his face abruptly switched back to an evil leer.

Princess Shelly rose to her feet with a menacing glare of her own. She, unlike her father, would fight if need be.

The prince looked at their group. "Your kingdom, which has been used to getting what it wants, was finally failing in a certain area." He paused. "And what was that area?"

No answer. Expecting this, he answered it himself. "The military. After thousands of years of dominating the rest, your kingdom was finally being brought back down to reality. And every year for the past five years, you've had to witness it during the Generals' Battle as our general proved victorious over and over and over again.

"You became upset that the Archaic Kingdom was finally getting a bit of attention and you couldn't handle the sharing of that spotlight." He gave a death stare to King Vitio. "Therefore, you took care of it." …

"Help me learn," Vistas requested as he took a seat next to Lilu's bed.

She gazed at him—the man who played a vital role in her growing up to be the lady she was. To think a man from the Dark Realm could be so lovely … She had learned to trust Vistas over the years, so she decided to tell him a story of a tainted history.

"There was an era that marks the start of Kuki Sphaira's recorded history, nearly 1,500 years ago. It was a time when two kingdoms held sway over the Light Realm— the Light Knowledge and Light Morality Kingdoms … Known today as the Intel and Archaic Kingdoms. Both were very proud and known for their powerful minds, but for different reasons. While the Intel Kingdom's specialty was technical and intellectual thinking, the Archaic Kingdom's specialty was more geared toward philosophy and mysticism.

"The two kingdoms' symbiotic hatred stemmed from this difference. Refusing to accept

the ideas of the other, each thought its own method of thinking should rule all five kingdoms of the Light Realm.

"While the Intel Kingdom focused on learning about topics that could technologically advance the future, the Archaic Kingdom studied the history of people and tried socially advancing the future based off those studies.

"However, slowly over time, as other kingdoms began adapting based off the ideas and research that the Intel King and his royal family had developed, the Archaic King realized his people were falling behind. Nobody paid attention to the philosophical side of things because inventing things provided all the tangible results.

"But even with all this animosity, not once did anyone try physically attacking the other. It was always a restless battle of differentiating ideas and opinions, and that was it. This passive—yet heated—rivalry has existed for the past 1,500 years, and it is known as the longest war ever ... a war with no spilt blood." ...

The Archaic Prince lunged at Princess Shelly, but she shot him into the ground with a bolt of lightning that slashed through the ceiling from the sky above. Bryson's jaw dropped. It was the most amazing display of Intel Energy he had ever witnessed.

"Manipulating lightning in the clouds ..." the prince remarked as he staggered to his feet. "Considering the amount of overcast this kingdom suffers through, I guess you could call that home field advantage at its finest. However, I'm impressed. Even for a royal, that's not an easy ability to accomplish . . . even if a single bolt is all you're able to muster up. You should have saved it for later."

The Archaic Prince wound his arm behind his head before swinging it forward in a throwing motion. Three balls of a pure white substance exited his hand at an alarming speed. Each made contact with Shelly. One struck her face violently, while the other two simultaneously struck her stomach. King Vitio lunged for her, but was felled by a tree trunk to his torso.

Now the two kings were back at it, but Vitio still refused to attack. Every move he made was an evasive one. Meanwhile, Shelly lay on the ground, clutching her face as she grimaced from pain.

The Archaic Prince flung more balls at her, but a wall of black flames erupted in front of her and absorbed them.

The Archaic Prince looked stunned.

"Fire beats snow," Himitsu said, matter of fact.

The prince, just now noticing the bystander, was outraged. "And who are you?"

"From the looks of things, I'd say your weakness."

The prince's face twisted. He opened his mouth wide and inhaled deeply. Himitsu suspected what the prince was readying, so he decided to do the same. They exhaled at the same time.

A flurry of rock-hard pellets shot out of the prince's mouth as a wave of black fire expelled itself from Himitsu's. The two crashed into each other headlong, and at first the flames pushed back against the melting snow and advanced toward the prince. But Himitsu was soon exhausted while his adversary continued to attack.

Himitsu snapped his hand upward as he tried to protect himself with another barrier of blackened flames. Most of the pellets melted instantly, but several still made it through, pelting the tall Passion Jestivan all over his body.

Then Himitsu's flames extinguished, and the Archaic Prince charged. As his blow was about to land, something tugged hard at his neck, fiercely yanking him backward.

He wasn't prepared for it. He hadn't even seen anyone move. As his back bent, he got a glimpse of the boy who had grabbed his scarf. The boy's hair was a sunny yellow, but he couldn't read his eyes with his bangs swaying in front. All he needed to see, however, was the thin, resentful line that his mouth formed.

It was Bryson, and with a member of his team in danger, he had finally entered the fray. Bryson tried finishing him off by slamming him into the ground, but the prince grabbed his wrist, encasing it in a shell of ice-hard snow. Bryson lost his grip and shrieked at the pain that reached into his bones.

Princess Shelly struck the Archaic Prince with a string of electricity from her palm, causing him to whirl around toward her. Himitsu grabbed Bryson's arm and released a moderate amount of black fire to melt the ice. As they turned to help Shelly, two other men stepped in front of them— one with the insignia of an Archaic Corporal on his collar, the other that of a Major.

"Stay away from the big boys and girls," the corporal teased.

Bryson didn't acknowledge the corporal's taunt. He sidestepped to the right at his fastest speed, extended his left arm, and clotheslined him. The man crashed to the floor, gasping desperately for air through his damaged windpipe.

The action inside the suite was escalating at an even faster pace. A weird sensation took over Bryson's body and he didn't know what was causing it. It felt as if his body was becoming lighter. He searched around for a cause, but nobody seemed to be focused on him. There were two glowing lights beginning to manifest near Princess Shelly and the Archaic Prince; Himitsu was taking care of the major; and King Vitio had fallen to his knees and was coughing up blood. Before Bryson could even think to stop him, the Archaic King hurled another wooden beam …

"So with the murder of Archaic General Inias, it looks to be—at least in the eyes of the Archaic King—the first physical blow dealt between the two kingdoms after a millennium and a half of pent-up hostility.

"Vistas, I can only imagine the tension being felt inside of that suite. A bitter kingdom, which had already been losing for centuries, now believes it has a reason to unleash its repressed and spiteful fury." …

A man stood in front of the Intel King—a man who, just a mere second ago, was not even inside of the room. He was tall, slim, and dark skinned. He wore an elegant suit of silver and had a sword drawn in front of him.

The beam that was supposed to finish off Vitio was extended out of the suite's window overlooking the arena, but it was split cleanly in two. At the beginning of the fork in the beam's path was this man's blade, and he and King Vitio were comfortably situated between the two halves.

Two other presences were holding onto the Archaic Prince and the Intel Princess. One was a young brunette woman dressed in all shades of blue. The other was a very plump balding man adorned in blazing reds.

The Adrenaline King, Spirit Queen, and Passion King had put a halt to the fight and, very likely, saved a few lives.

"Thank you," Vitio weakly pleaded as he struggled for air …

Lilu gazed out the window from her bed, where she could see the top of the stadium in the distance. "So with first blood drawn, this rivalry now properly deserves the title it was given so long ago …

… The Mind War."

17

Missing

The room was no longer distinguishable as a suite. Debris littered the floor and holes peppered the walls. Compared to the loud murmur of the crowds escaping from above and below, the room was quiet. The only audible sound was the heavy breathing of exhausted bodies.

The Adren King stepped over the split tree and glared at King Vitio. "Do not thank me. Your judgment will still come—just not like this."

"I don't care. You saved me and, more importantly, my daughter," Vitio weakly replied.

Itta was not happy. "How dare you, Supido. This is not your war."

King Supido ignored the comment. Bryson watched as the man—who was just as tall as most of the other Adren Kingdom residents—walked to the Archaic Major, who was unconscious on the ground. As Supido observed the motionless body, Bryson wondered if he had seen who attacked that man. Then he received his answer as the Adren King glanced at him out of the corner of his eye.

But he didn't address Bryson. Instead, he looked at Princess Shelly and the Archaic Prince. "Summoning *them*?" he spat. "Both of you are out of your mind. This is enough of a nightmare already. There are thousands of innocent lives in danger here . . . relying on us . . . *thousands*. People are dying by the hundreds." Glancing back at the Archaic King, he added, "I don't care about your petty war."

Itta flushed red, but his lips stayed pursed.

"Is what happened suspicious? Yes," Supido continued. "However, from what is seen on the surface, Dark Realm soldiers are killing Light Realm innocents."

"They're his slaves!" Itta shouted as he gestured angrily toward Vitio.

"Shut up." Supido projected the same aura of anger without expressing it in a childish manner, Bryson thought. Sure, he cursed a few too many times, but his volume was controlled. "All I know is our priority is taking care of the Dev soldiers down there. *They* are the people we should be fighting—not each other. Now is not the time for that."

He gazed out the window to the corpse-strewn stands below. "Queen Apsa and King Damian have elected to keep an eye on you self-indulgent scum. As for me, the Adren King, I will fulfill my natural duty—to protect."

He seemed to contemplate his next words carefully.

"A war between realms is greater than a war between kingdoms." Then he stepped off the edge of the viewing window and plummeted into the ruckus below.

*   *   *

As the day progressed into evening, the battling around the arena began to dissipate. Some of the Dev soldiers managed to escape once they realized they were fighting a losing battle, but most ended up dead or captured.

The sun sat on the horizon, somehow managing to peek through gaps in the clouds. The arena basked in a red hue. It was as if the Bozani decided to contribute their own medium to the already red-smeared canvas.

Bryson and Himitsu took one last look inside the stadium, where rescue teams from all five of the Light Realm's kingdoms were frantically scavenging for civilians and soldiers with a pulse. All Bryson could think about was Olivia. In fact, this was why he had lingered. But after searching her area for nearly an hour, he hadn't been able to find her—or her body.

With Rhyparia and Lilu at the hospital and Himitsu standing next to him, there were six others to be accounted for. Bryson and Himitsu's walk out of the arena was a quiet one. It was a moment to contemplate what had happened and what was to come.

Outside the stadium, a mob of people anxiously waited to begin their journeys home. Guards had set up checkpoints in all directions in effort to weed out any possible Dev Kingdom soldiers trying to sneak past.

"Same spot we met this morning, right?" Bryson asked.

"I think so," Himitsu mumbled.

When they approached the rendezvous point, Bryson's heart skipped a beat. *One, two, three, four, five . . . five . . . FIVE?*

Olivia was nowhere to be seen.

"Yes!" Jilly screamed. "You didn't die!" She jumped to hug the two of them, but Bryson didn't return her embrace.

"Where's Olivia?" he asked.

"We don't know," Director Debo said.

"Then why are we standing around?!"

Debo wasn't rattled. "You're right," he said. "We were just about to start searching for the remaining three, but now that you two have showed up, we only need to find one. For your safety, we will search in pairs."

As the pairs were formed, Bryson became impatient. The moment Jilly was announced as his searching partner, he sprinted toward the stadium, forcing her to try the impossible—keeping up with Bryson's speed.

As he went from body to body, he found himself feeling an odd combination of emotions as he looked at each person's face. On one hand, there was a feeling of relief that Olivia was not one of the lifeless corpses, but on the other, there was despair as each dead person added to the tally.

Jilly searched alongside him—though without the same frenzy. When she turned over bodies, she was more delicate. She would occasionally gaze at the distraught and manic Bryson and murmur soothing sounds. But Bryson did not realize—nor would he have cared—how he was acting. His best friend was missing … the girl who kept his sanity rooted to the ground.

"We'll find her, Bryson. We'll find her alive and well."

Bryson didn't answer. He rolled over a dead Dev soldier and kicked it in the ribs.

The sun sunk behind the horizon, and the other searching pairs left the stadium. Bryson was in disbelief. Of all people, how did she end up missing or dead? He began recalling all the times he witnessed her strength—the many times she had kicked Geno's ass when they were kids, even though he was twice her size; all the painful headlocks she'd given him; Himitsu lifting his shirt to reveal a monstrous bruise on his chest … And her latest, most heroic act, when she marched through the collapsing restaurant with a wailing Lilu over her shoulder. He began to cry as his mind and body approached complete exhaustion.

Jilly stared into the night sky as the second moon sat next to the first. "Olivia is stronger than any of us. She's okay, Bry—"

"*SHUT UP!*" he screamed. "SHUT UP, SHUT UP, *SHUT UP!*"

She shut up. But she stayed by his side.

Bryson let out a howl of anguish and pounded his fists into the cement as tears spilled down his cheeks. "Olivia … Olivia … Olivia …" he panted under his breath.

Then he felt a cool breeze run through his hair. He looked up slowly, and directly in front of him was a pair of feet beneath a blue dress. Each toenail was painted the same shade of blue.

He looked up to see her face, but before he could, she vanished. And as she did so, a voice carried with the wind …

"When the time is right …"

18

The Decision

In a barren field unable to support any natural life lay a camp of burgundy tents—the colors of the Dev Kingdom. And judging by the way the sun blazed down on the bare rock, it was obvious that this area was not part of the overcast Intel Kingdom.

Soldiers in burgundy were stationed throughout the site, but most circled the outer perimeter. The mood was relaxed, with laughter and gossip. There were probably more harlots than female soldiers. Prostitution was more common with Dark Realm kingdoms—not to say the kingdoms of the Light Realm didn't have their fair share.

The largest, most heavily guarded tent rested near the camp's center. A lone young man sat inside of it. Hunched over a wooden table, this clean-shaven, charcoal-haired man was heatedly filling up a third piece of parchment. He depleted the ink on his quill so briskly that he found himself dipping it into the jar every few seconds.

His face was stern, but his penmanship was sporadic as the letters slashed angrily across the paper. As the words came to his mind, he wrote them without hesitation. He was lost in his rage, but he recovered himself when the tent's front curtain parted. A face peeked through.

"King—I mean *Prince*—the general is here to see you."

The young man bit his lip, fighting back the urge to snap at someone for calling him "King."

"Let him in," he replied.

In walked an elderly, yet surprisingly robust, man. It was clear that his hair was once a deep black, but with age, it had started to grey as it receded from his forehead.

"Good afternoon, Prince Storshae," the general said with a bow.

The Dev Prince leaned back in his chair and observed his general. "Ossen, after all these years, why are you the only one who can get my title right?" he asked.

Ossen smirked. "Technically, the title of 'King' is correct."

Storshae didn't return the friendly expression. "I am nothing more than the Dev Prince."

"Your own kingdom may view you that way. However, the rest of Kuki Sphaira isn't fooled. By law, you are the king, so that is how the world views you, sir." General Ossen was choosing his words very carefully as he gazed at a peculiar crown entwined with chocolate cosmos flowers.

The prince noticed this. "Are you upset I took it from his memorial?"

"No, sir. He is your father."

"I take his crown with me wherever I go to remind people that I am not the king. While he may lie in the dirt, he still lives in our hearts."

"That he does," Ossen responded weakly.

"As for the rest of Kuki Sphaira …" The prince closed his eyes and smiled. "Soon, they too will recognize who the true Dev King is, and there is no more Mendac to stop us."

Ossen went silent as the conversation approached a very touchy subject that was best for him to avoid. Thankfully, the prince moved on from the topic.

Storshae placed his quill in the ink bottle and folded his hands on the table. "So what is the reason for this unexpected visit? I suppose it must be important if it drew you from your station—speaking of which, how is she?"

"Telling you how she is would require her showing me," Ossen said.

"Still an expression of stone?" the prince asked with a sly smirk.

The old man gave it some thought before replying. "From what I can see through the bruises and cuts, yes."

Prince Storshae slapped both hands on the table. "Beatings, whippings, and memory torture! She can take it all! I'm thankful for her. She has provided us much needed entertainment while we wallow in this wasteland of a kingdom."

"That she has, sir." He laughed. "It's like a game. Who can crack her stubborn shell first?"

"We should offer a reward!" Prince Storshae exclaimed.

Ossen coughed. "Could that reward be water, sir?" he mumbled.

Storshae sighed "So that's what you came here for."

Ossen nodded gravely. "We have roughly a day's worth left."

"Scout team isn't back with resources?"

"They're back." He averted his eyes as he added, "but without resources."

"It's not their fault. It seems we made a mistake. Our ally set us up for failure. Whether it was purposeful or accidental does not matter. It has been ten days since we had to limp away from that Generals' Battle with our numbers cut by more than half."

Storshae refocused on his parchment while venting his frustration. "Now we've been left to rot in his kingdom in the middle of the Light Realm where we do not belong . . . Ossen, I guarantee that he's at that high council of the five light kingdoms and vowing that he won't back down. That the Intel Kingdom allowed us in, and he, as the Archaic King, will retaliate.

"And he's doing all this while thinking that we still have his back. But he messed up that agreement, and I have an answer for that." The Dev Prince waved his paper with a sneer. "We will no longer stand by his side. The Archaic Kingdom will be exposed and alone."

"That is what I want to hear, sir. The Light and Dark Realms should never coexist."

"We'll just call it a failed experiment." Storshae rose from his seat. "As for the water, take all of mine and distribute it throughout the camp. And send out a second scout team."

Ossen gave a deep bow. "That is awfully generous of you, my Prince."

Storshae waved Ossen out. "I have more writing to do."

Bowing for a third time, Ossen exited the tent. Once outside, he turned to the guards and said, "In the back room of the tent, you'll see several gallons of water. Distribute it to the troops. One quart each for the healthy, half that for the sick and wounded. We don't know how long it will need to last."

As the men scurried away, General Ossen headed back to his station, which was only a few hundred yards east and located directly at the camp's heart. He approached a circular cage surrounded by soldiers and smiled at the prisoner.

Olivia lay awake on her side at the center. Her clothes were filthy and shredded by the Dev soldiers' whips. Her face was swollen, and dried blood stained her body. Yet her expression was as inscrutable as always as she stared into the distance. Unlike Meow Meow, who wore a sharp scowl, she didn't acknowledge the Dev General's return. Olivia simply thought about how her mother was right …

Men are cowardly in the most barbaric of ways.

*   *   *

"We, the five leaders of each of the five light kingdoms, are gathered today because the Light Realm has been declared to be in a state of emergency," the Adren King said as he stood at his place around the vast oval table.

He scanned the faces of his fellow royalty. "As everyone knows, the rule is if the majority of the leaders call for a high council, then it is to be had. Queen Apsa of the Spirit Kingdom; King Damian of the Passion Kingdom; and I, King Supido of the Adren Kingdom, have called for this meeting.

"The rules also state that the meeting must take place in the fairest and most neutral location. Thus, my kingdom was chosen. Although all five kingdoms were affected by the catastrophe at the Generals' Battle, this location was an easy choice. With the Intel and Archaic Kingdoms automatically ruled out, it was a toss-up between the other three.

"When an emergency meeting of this magnitude is called, only the sole leaders of each kingdom attend. Therefore, there are no advisers, generals, chiefs, scribes, or anyone else … Are these rules clear?"

A silent nod was given from everyone except the Archaic King, who was leaning back in his chair with a distracted frown.

King Supido looked toward the burly Intel King. "To start off this council, the floor will be given to the leader of the Intel Kingdom. You will be given five minutes to state your defense—and if desired, an offense."

Itta, the Archaic King, let a small single laugh slip through his lips as Vitio stood. Undeterred, the Intel King cleared his throat.

"First and foremost, I begin with my deepest apologies. As the host kingdom, I take full responsibility for not providing a safe environment. Understandably, the Archaic King is not happy, and he has every right to feel that way. His strongest and highest-ranking soldier was murdered. I also understand his anger toward me. Though I categorically deny allowing the Dev army into the Light Realm, I still cannot ignore how the history of the Mind War could drive him to that conclusion.

"However, as I've stated, this attack was not orchestrated, nor partaken in, by the Intel Kingdom. I have always strived to exist in peaceful harmony with my fellow kingdoms of the Light Realm, and you all know this."

The Spirit Queen gave an approving nod and smile as he continued. "Our kingdoms have been experiencing one of the longest periods of peace in known history, and I would not jeopardize that." He looked at the twig-crowned King Itta. "Inias was one of the strongest generals in recent memory. He was a force to be reckoned with and a shining light during dark times for your kingdom. I had spoken with him several times. He was not only powerful, but smart too.

"Was it that annoying kind of philosophical intelligence that we in the Intel Kingdom instinctively hate? Perhaps, but I knew he wasn't a bad person. I wouldn't stoop to some scheme to murder the man. You must remember that as the hosts, the Intel Kingdom had a constant flow of traffic through its teleplatforms. From Tuesday to Friday—dawn to dusk—hundreds of people were flowing in from all over the Light Realm. It is plausible to say that they could have traveled from another kingdom in the Light Realm."

"Hogwash!" Itta spat as he leapt to his feet. "Dev soldiers have served as slaves of your kingdom for years! They didn't travel to your kingdom. They lived in it!"

Vitio stayed calm. "We returned those soldiers to the Dev Kingdom five years ago. We only kept a handful of their intelligence unit—ones who cannot fight. You know this."

"You lied!" Itta yelled. "You must have hid a few hundred."

"Disobey the decision of you four and risk my kingdom's safety because of it? No thank you. I have pride in my people, but against four other kingdoms, we would perish. People who possess Intel Energy are born with strong minds … for me to try something that stupid would be a disgrace."

"Well, you've certainly made an enemy out of me," Itta hissed. "The only reason we haven't declared war is because I've lost General Inias … but I don't need to state this. That was your plan."

The old Archaic King sat back down. The Intel King followed suit with an exasperated sigh.

Next to stand was Spirit Queen Apsa. She was quite young—in her mid-twenties, perhaps—and had beautiful brunette hair that flowed in natural waves. "I disagree with King Itta—"

"Of course you do, you naïve little wench," Itta interrupted.

"Watch it," Supido cut in.

"That's alright," Apsa said with a charming smile. "'Wench' … 'Queen' … I know who I am. But morals and ethics should be your specialty, no?"

Itta avoided her eyes, which he knew were mocking him in the worst ways. He despised Apsa's vitality.

Next to stand was the Passion King—whose belly rattled the table as he stood. This brought a smile to everyone's face except Itta, who rolled his eyes.

King Damian stared at Vitio for what felt like an eternity, but it wasn't uncomfortable. After half a minute, he smiled broadly, and Vitio nodded in return. Damian then turned to Itta with a frown so pronounced, Itta involuntarily bit his lip. Then Damian sat back down, causing his belly to hit the table again.

Damian was mute, and the people of his kingdom were required to learn sign language in their early curriculum at Phesaw. When communicating with people from outside the Passion Kingdom, he had to use facial expressions. Luckily, he had an expressive face.

"Are you all really that far up his ass?" the Archaic King asked in a calm, controlled rage. "Hundreds of people from each of your lands have died because of that man."

"We have no evidence, Itta," Supido said, equally coldly.

"Then what was the point of this?" Itta asked, bewildered.

Supido shifted his gaze to Vitio. "Because he still will be punished. As he already stated, it happened in his kingdom, so he will take responsibility for not providing a safe environment."

Vitio nodded. "I have a suggestion."

"By all means …" Supido extended his hand, offering the floor to him once again.

Vitio stood. "During an event as big as the Generals' Battle, the teleplatforms are appropriately staffed with escorts and soldiers from all kingdoms. Perhaps we should gather the head escorts from each respective kingdom who were stationed at my kingdom's platforms and question them about what and who they witnessed throughout the day."

"Seeing that these escorts are currently in their home kingdoms, that would take time," Supido said.

"We can schedule another council to be held in one month."

Itta let out a forced laugh. "And give you time to tell your escorts what to say?"

"Not at all," Vitio said. "In fact, none of us will be able to do that. Five years ago—when we last had an emergency meeting—part of the verdict to release all of my Dev soldiers was to give each of your kingdoms five people from the Dev Kingdom's Intelligence Unit, and that was the only condition in allowing me to keep mine. In doing so, I gave one of you a very handy tool."

The attention peaked inside of the room. Vitio looked toward the large Passion King and said, "Damian, when we gather again in a month, bring Marcus. He can extract truths, so anything we might try to tell the escorts would be pointless."

King Damian's eyes widened. "I never told any of you about that ability of Marcus because I couldn't have it be used against anyone else ... which is also why I gave him to Damian," Vitio added.

"And why didn't you keep a weapon like that to yourself?" Supido asked.

Vitio smirked. "So it couldn't be held against me if there ever was a time when I had to reveal that secret."

"So smart!" Apsa exclaimed.

As Vitio sat down for a final time, Supido stood once more. "That settles it. We will meet again in one month's time. Now, in regards to punishment, we think we have reached a reasonable amount. King Vitio of the Intel Kingdom, you will be required to give 200,000 granules each to your neighboring kingdoms of the Light Realm."

Vitio coughed up some of his water. "That's a large sum of money, but feasible and understandable," he said, regaining his composure. He wiped his mouth before continuing, "I suppose each of you will have specific requests for how it will be paid, so we will discuss that through writing or broadcasts."

The Adren King looked at them all and said, "See you in one month," before turning to walk out of the room.

*   *   *

For the Jestivan, it had been two weeks in the routine of classes and training sessions at Phesaw since the disastrous weekend of the Generals' Battle. However, that routine felt different when there were two glaring voids among their numbers.

Both teams were missing members. Bryson's team was missing Rhyparia, who was still in the Dunami Hospital in a coma. The other team was missing its captain, Olivia.

Several of the young Jestivan were beginning to crumble under the stress. Despite Grand Director Poicus's warnings of hardship during the story of Thusia's Sacrifice, they still had not been mentally prepared.

Olivia's team was gathered at a table in the Lilac Suites. The directors, who sensed distraught and disconnect between the Jestivan, had given them the day off to mend bonds. It was done in hopes of morale being lifted, but it was failing miserably.

"What did you even do?" Yama yelled.

Agnos, who was seated calmly across from her, said, "I escorted people out."

"You're worthless," she hissed, her amber brown eyes burning as they locked on his. "What was the body count for your section again?"

He returned her gaze and gave a simple response: "Forty-five."

She slammed her hand on the table. "Forty-five?!" By this point, everyone in the room had turned to their table. "And it would have been worse if Director Buredo didn't come to help!"

Agnos didn't respond immediately. He rested his forearms on the table and gave her a minute to calm down. He knew what she was playing at. He knew why she was actually upset.

"Do I feel guilty for not being able to do my part?" he asked rhetorically before answering it himself. "Yes, I do. I stand for morals. I stand for ethics. I stand for good." Agnos continued to look at her intently. "However, fear struck deep within me, resulting in a loss of what I stand for. And I regret that." After a brief moment of silence—during which neither Lilu nor Tashami made a peep—Agnos leaned back and coolly said, "Do not feign remorse for lost lives."

Yama gaped at him. "What?"

"Of course she's upset, Agnos," Tashami said.

"I'm not denying the fact that she's upset," Agnos replied without taking his eyes from the violet-haired Yama. "But she is upset for the wrong reasons. For reasons of greed and selfishness. She did not look at that catastrophe as a moment to save lives. For her, it was an opportunity to better herself."

"False," Yama said sternly—but then her eyes fluttered and she looked away.

"Oh, the contrary," Agnos said as he pointed a finger up in the air. "Yama is a simple person," he said to Lilu and Tashami. "She once had a Charge. As an Adren Kingdom resident, one must swear to protect their Charge." He looked at Yama. "And we all know how important an Adren resident's duty is to them, don't we?"

Yama's face flushed red. "Shut up."

But he ignored it and continued speaking. "Yama always had one goal, but with a Charge, she found herself in a mental struggle, torn between two things—the need to help fulfill anything her Charge desired and her own desires, as what her Charge wanted was the complete opposite of her own. I would know this because …"

Agnos paused and placidly stared at Yama before finishing his sentence. "… he was my best friend—long before he was her Charge. He was my role model and practically my big brother, and he wanted nothing more than to achieve the highest level of good—of purity. He wanted to discover this world's history and the people before us. He pursued wondrous concepts such as the phenomenon of the human mind, what makes us good, what makes us bad, and how we think. His level of thinking was far beyond anybody's I have ever met in my life.

"And on top of all this, he was physically talented. Not that it mattered, for all he cared about was peace. And that was a completely different mindset than what Yama possessed." His eyes were glazed as he passionately continued his rant: "Yama cares about power—striving to better herself not for the sake of goodness, but to dominate through her fighting abilities. And when she was with her Charge, her drive for power was frustrated because she knew it was her duty to assist and protect him.

"But her charge—my dearest friend—left years ago while she allowed it to happen. And once he was gone, her own selfish desires drowned out everything else. She does not care about saving lives. She looked at that invasion by the Dev soldiers as the perfect opportunity to hone her skills, and it eats at her soul when she sees people, such as myself, not doing the same."

For a brief moment, he became silent as the lounge's piano played in the background. Then Agnos tapped his index finger on the table. "*That* is truly why she is upset with me. She sees me as weak-minded and weak-bodied."

*　　　*　　　*

Three other Jestivan were having a stroll around the perimeter. They formed an odd trio. Jilly and Himitsu frequently spent time together, but

Toshik stuck out like a sore thumb. He never socialized with the other Jestivan, but with the orders from the directors, he had no choice.

He was in the middle, and his displeasure was noticeable as he walked with his hands in his pockets and a harsh expression on his face. An exuberant Jilly wasn't helping. She was doing everything in her power to gain his attention, from pulling on his arm to trying to climb up his lanky back. But Toshik just continued walking without acknowledging her once.

Himitsu was on the left, and his mind was drifting into dark places, but this was nothing new. For the past couple of weeks, darkness had been eating away at his thoughts. If it wasn't the worry about the possibility of his parents being imprisoned, it was the fact that one of his closest friends—and fellow Passion Jestivan—was missing, or that his team member, Rhyparia, was in a coma.

Then there was the issue of their captain, Bryson, who had proven he could not cope with Olivia's disappearance. He had defied the directors' orders to spend time with his team today. Not even Debo could influence him.

"I wish Bryson was here," Jilly said.

"Why?" Toshik asked.

"Because he's our captain."

Toshik rolled his eyes. "Ugh, kill me now."

"Hey! That's not nice."

"He's proving how weak he is. This is why he'll never be captain in my eyes. It's pathetic."

Himitsu's eyes narrowed. He glanced at Toshik from the corner of his eyes, but before he said something inappropriate, Jilly spoke up first.

"So inconsiderate. He lost his best friend."

"I'm supposed to show compassion for a weak-hearted man?"

Himitsu felt his blood begin to boil. "How dare you, a guy who hasn't spent more than ten minutes with us before today, make any judgments about Bryson!" he shouted as he jabbed a finger at his teammate's face.

Toshik just smiled. "You are proving to be just like him ... weak."

The three of them had stopped at the crest of an arched bridge spanning a small stream as the two boys began to tussle. Jilly skipped to the railing and jumped onto it. As she stood there, staring at the quarreling men, she wore a rare grim expression while waiting for her cue.

"Are you saying you don't have a weak spot, emotionally?" Himitsu asked incredulously as he tugged on Toshik's collar.

Toshik eyebrows rose with a mocking surprise. "No. I am a man of the Adren Kingdom—the Light *Courage* Kingdom."

There was her cue. Jilly let out a forced scream and fell backward toward the rock-speckled, shallow stream.

Toshik snapped his head around as his heart dropped into his stomach. He darted toward her and grabbed her trailing forearm. His eyes were instinctively reflecting panic.

Jilly looked up at him with a stern glare as she dangled beneath him. "Every heart—even yours—has a weakness."

*   *   *

If it wasn't for the dripping faucet in the kitchen, Bryson's house would have been completely quiet. The air was still as a chill crept over his body.

He was sitting against the wall on the hallway floor with his elbows resting on his knees. His face was hidden in the shadows of his hoodie. His eyes were red, but more from anger than anything else. His body was rigid, and for the same reason.

Sitting dangerously close to the light-shielded door, he continued debating in his head whether he wanted to commit to something so spiteful and foolish—an idea he had to get back at Debo, who had been refusing to let Bryson and the others search for Olivia.

Even though he had little interest in what was inside the closet, that didn't mean he didn't want to get in for the sake of pissing Debo off. What better way to do that than by breaking his number one rule?

As he thought about it, he caught a glimpse of his scarred pointer finger. He hated it. Every time he saw it, it made him second-guess himself, for he didn't want to relive that pain. He hated it even more than the mystery scar on his chest.

He thought about Lilu's offer once again. But did he really want to find out what was in the closet? In a way, he was afraid of what he might find. Still, he found himself sitting next to the light every day.

Bryson's feelings toward Debo were totally conflicted. He didn't want to see his face, but there were topics he wanted his insight on. Like what the mysterious girl said when he was searching for Olivia … *When the time is right.*

Bryson's train of thought was interrupted when the front door opened. He lazily shifted his head to the left while barely lifting his neck, his hoodie still covering his face. It was Debo, who had come home much earlier than expected, but that didn't alarm Bryson. He couldn't care less.

Debo stood in silence while staring down the hooded boy. Bryson awaited the scolding for not being with his team, but after several more seconds of silence, Debo took off his golden robes and threw them on the rack.

"I would act surprised, but that would require me to actually be surprised," Debo said.

"Any news from Poicus?" Bryson asked as he stared at the floor.

Debo leaned against the hallway's entrance. "We didn't hear from him today."

That wasn't good. The last news they had received was that Poicus had successfully entered the Dev Kingdom three days ago.

Bryson let out a frustrated sigh. "It's been too long. I told you, he needs help. Stop getting in my way—"

"—of death?" Debo cut in, standing up straight. "Poicus told us it would be a few days before he could get in touch, so this is expected. Listen, I understand what Olivia means to you. She means a lot to me too. But you're an idiot if you still think I'd allow you to enter the Dark Realm."

"My father would have more faith in me. I wish he was here."

Debo's expression shifted to something unreadable. "I think you'd regret that wish. And get away from that light," he added as he turned away.

That was it. The decision was made. Bryson was going to get into that closet.

*   *   *

Approaching the kitchen sink, Debo rolled up his sweater's sleeves. He turned on the faucet, cupped his hands underneath it, and splashed the cold water onto his face. Another long day of worry and stress clouded his mind.

From Yama's debriefing to him and Grand Director Poicus after the Generals' Battle, he knew that Olivia had likely been captured by the clairvoyant. She was probably alive, but a rescue mission would be near impossible.

As Debo stared down into the sterling sink, his mind replayed the conversation that doomed any realistic hope of saving Olivia …

"So Yama, is there anything you need to tell us?" Grand Director Poicus asked.

The old man was seated at his desk in his office occupied by two other people. Yama sat across from him while Director Debo was pacing behind her.

As expected from the highest title in the school, the office was big. The Grand Director of Phesaw was the status equivalent of a king or queen of a kingdom. Several busts stood atop stone pillars behind Poicus. These were the sculpted heads of Phesaw's many previous Grand Directors. There were rows of bookshelves that lined the walls, and a couple ladders could be seen leaning against them, for the books seemed to stretch upward to no end.

Yama, who had two large packs of ice strapped to her back and a couple bandages on her face, looked at Poicus with disappointment and responded, "I'm weak."

He gazed over his pressed-together fingertips. "If that was the case, we wouldn't be speaking to you right now," he said.

She didn't respond, so Poicus continued, "Agnos sustained multiple injuries yesterday also, but you don't see him being interrogated in my office."

Once again, she didn't reply, but instead, stared plainly at him while Debo continued to pace.

"And that's because we expect that from Agnos," he further explained. "However, from the likes of you, we're not expecting such injuries from mere foot soldiers."

Yama looked off to the side at nothing in particular.

Grand Director Poicus studied her face for a moment longer before asking, "So tell me, who was it that you had the unfortunate chance of running into? Debo and I know it wasn't just some foot soldier that could do so much damage to the Jestivan's most talented fighter."

She remade eye contact and said, "I don't know who he is."

"What about a description?"

Debo was fidgeting with different modules that were displayed around the office. He became specifically interested in a wired, three dimensional module of the world of Kuki Sphaira that hung from the ceiling. Inspecting it with a stern glare, he listened closely to what Yama was saying.

"Well, he was average height—about as tall as me—and he had brown hair," she said unsurely.

Poicus rested his hands on the desk. "You seem uncertain, Lita Yama."

She slouched. "I am. I couldn't get a good look at him for two reasons. I couldn't believe there was someone that much better than me in that arena, so I was more concerned by that than I was his facial features and physical attributes." She glanced to the side again, avoiding his stare, and added, "Also, he was faster than me, but not because of movement—he could teleport."

Debo immediately looked at her as the sternness wiped away from his face. Poicus' eyes shifted to the tall Intel Director with a look of uneasiness from what she just said.

The Grand Director looked back at Yama and asked slowly, "Are you absolutely sure it was teleportation?"

"Yes, he definitely wasn't moving. I don't think he moved his feet once during our altercation."

Poicus's eyes closed as he sighed deeply. "Did you notice any other of the higher tier Psychic abilities? I know you learned about some of them in classes a few years back."

She thought for a second and said, "He would close his eyes and track my movement through an extra sense."

"Clairvoyance." Debo had finally said something. No longer could he stand in silence . . . Not with all this news.

Poicus stood up and massaged his fingers against his temple. "This would explain Olivia's disappearance. There weren't just Dev soldiers in those stands."

"Olivia is gone because of my shortcoming," she said gravely.

Poicus leaned on his desk and looked at her sincerely. "It wasn't your fault."

"Yes, it is. He is the one who took Olivia."

"It could have been another person."

Yama shook her head. "During our confrontation, he said to me, 'Same purple hair, but you're not her.' He also said, 'You're not my target.'" She glared at Poicus and asked, "Who else do we know with purple hair?"

He didn't give the obvious answer, but instead, quickly turned on his heel and walked toward the window that sat at the front of the room. As he stood there with his hands behind his back, he said, "Thank you, Yama. Rest up and enjoy your day. You are dismissed."

As she walked out the door, Debo quickly said, "This has become more serious than previously thought."

"Indeed so," mumbled Poicus.

"From what she explained, that sounded like a royal … maybe a Gefal."

"Our timetable has shortened," Poicus stated as he gazed at Phesaw's campus grounds. "I will head out tomorrow. If it's a royal, such as the king—or prince—whatever it is he wants to be called, then I shall fair well."

"And if it's a Gefal?" Debo warily asked.

The aging man turned to look at the Intel Director. The tails of his lengthy eyebrows became even whiter as the sunlight hit them. "It's hard to believe a being of the Dark Empire would involve his or herself in such a peculiar matter, but if that is the case …" He trailed off as a soft smile formed. "Well, I've lived a longer life than most already."

Debo nodded. "The Energy Directors will take good care of the school while you're away. You better take care of yourself." He extended his hand.

Poicus extended his own and gave a firm handshake. "This won't be my first trip into the Dark Realm, Director." …

Debo's train of thought was broken by the front door slamming shut. "Bryson?" When he didn't receive an answer, he walked to the front of the house and looked out the window.

Bryson was walking down the sidewalk with his hood over his head and every intention of making it to the palace tonight. With King Vitio and Princess Shelly arriving today, it would mean that Lilu was also there to welcome them.

19

Branian

It took longer than Bryson expected to reach the palace, but that was his own fault. His decision to take a detour by stopping at the hospital to see Rhyparia had slowed him down. Seeing her still in a coma stabbed at him. He had sat by her side and held her hand while reciting a prayer to the Bozani, proving that he was desperate enough to try anything.

As he walked toward the front gates of the palace, a bandana hung out of his back pocket. He had taken it from Rhyparia's side table, wanting to have a piece of her with him. Figuring he already looked suspicious enough approaching by himself in the middle of the night, he decided to remove his hood. He gripped one of the gate's rails and squinted at the grounds beyond, surprised at the absence of guards.

Then a question was shouted from above: "Who goes there?"

Bryson arched his neck, now realizing why it was empty below. A tower sat on each side of the entrance, and the guards were all stationed at the top.

"Bryson, Bryson LeAnce!" he shouted back.

It went silent for a moment, which left him standing awkwardly, wondering if he should just leave. Then a man approached from inside the gate. Bryson recognized the jawline and instantly knew who it was.

"Major Lars, how are you?"

The Intel Major looked disgruntled until he saw Bryson's face, and softened. Looking up, he yelled, "Open it!"

As the entrance slowly creaked open, Lars replied to Bryson's question with a smile. "It has been a wonderful night. Our king is back."

Bryson suited up the fakest of grins as he lied through his teeth: "I can't wait to see him."

As they crossed the castle grounds, Bryson noticed that the previous gate was only the first wall of defense. A second, much higher wall was a couple minutes further in and—according to Lars—this one was lined with archers in its towers.

Once through the second gate, the palace dauntingly towered above them. They walked between two extraordinary marble fountains and up the front steps lined with intelights. The guards opened the main door, giving a courteous nod as the pair walked through.

The beauty of the palace's interior overwhelmed Bryson. It was exactly what he would picture the headquarters of the most powerful kingdom to look like. There was gold everywhere, and the floor was a stunning green and red marble without a scuff or blemish to be seen.

"I'd give you a tour," Lars joked, "but we'd be here for days." Pulling out a pocket watch, he added, "Besides, you're right on time to now be a surprise guest for dinner."

Bryson quickly shook his head. "I don't want to be a bother. I can wait till they're done."

Lars dismissively waved his hand. "Not even I have ever attended a family dinner, but something tells me King Vitio would not hesitate to consider you—Mendac's son—as family."

His stomach churning from another reference to his father, Bryson ignored him.

Lars knocked on a large mahogany door. A deep voice boomed through,

"What is it?"

"It is I, Major Lars. I have brought you a surprise guest, sir."

"Lars, you know the rules about my family dinners."

"I think you'll be happy to make an exception in this instance." Smiling at Bryson, the major opened the left half of the door, allowing the boy to step through.

As Bryson entered the dining hall, King Vitio leapt from his chair. "Bryson!" he blurted out with a gleaming smile. The burly king strode over to the boy. With an energetic shake of the hand, he led him to an empty seat. "Such a visit was unforeseen!"

"Well, I figured I'd welcome my kingdom's royal family home," Bryson lied as he sat down. He locked eyes with the beautiful girl sitting across from him—a girl who had been occupying his dreams for the past few months. Lilu wore a charming smile, and her green hair was done up in an elegant bun with a daisy attached to the front. Bryson's chest ignited as he found himself grinning wider than he had in weeks. For a brief moment, she caused him to forget about all the disasters plaguing his thoughts.

This chemistry didn't go unnoticed. King Vitio's toothy smirk displayed encouragement. Someone else, however, was not so happy.

"Quit gawking at my sister. You've been here for almost a minute now, yet I still haven't heard you greet me." It was Princess Shelly, and she was glaring at Bryson.

"Hello, Princess," he said.

She turned forward and cut into her quail with a disgusted curl to her bottom lip, leaving Bryson to wonder why she pestered him for a greeting if she wasn't going to even acknowledge it.

A voice from the other end of the table made itself heard for the first time. "Dear, aren't you going to introduce me to our guest?"

The woman, whom Bryson presumed to be the queen, had the same intimidating facial expression that he had seen many times from both Lilu and Shelly. *That's where they got it from.*

"I'm sure you know who Bryson is," Vitio said with a chuckle.

Rather than join him, the expression that occupied her face when she slowly turned her head to Bryson was terrifying. She looked exactly like Lilu did when she was angry, but the lines of age on her face made her look even fiercer. "But he does not know who I am," she said in a fake sweet tone.

"The queen," Bryson said a little too plainly.

Vitio guffawed as the queen's face flushed an angry red. "That's quite a set of balls you have," he said as he pointed his fork at the boy.

"I don't know how you commoners do it, but when you meet someone for the first time in a royal setting, you are properly introduced," she said coldly.

Bryson realized that this sort of thing must be a common occurrence when she was around other people as Vitio proved to be a very efficient conciliator, telling a joke at Lars's expense that caused laughs to erupt around the table.

As Bryson enjoyed his dinner of turtle soup, buckwheat cakes with caviar and sour cream, and quail with foie gras and truffle sauce, Shelly struck a few conversations with him about the curriculum at Phesaw. She seemed to be becoming more accepting of his presence. This was good news.

During dessert, Bryson noticed Lilu shift uncomfortably in her chair, and he was reminded of the brace she had to wear.

"When do you get to take it off?" he asked.

"Two months," she groaned. "I keep telling them I don't need it, but they won't listen."

"I heard what you did for my sister," Shelly said.

"What do you mean?" Bryson asked through a mouthful of sponge cake.

"How you saved her."

He turned his head so quickly that he practically snapped his neck. "What?"

"When the restaurant collapsed," she said with the rarest expression he'd ever seen from her—a smile.

"That wasn't—ow!" Someone had kicked him under the table. He looked at Lilu, who was giving him a stare of death.

"Sorry, banged my knee," he said, understanding that Lilu had lied to Shelly. It was Lilu's way of making her sister feel obligated to Bryson—and help them get into Debo's closet.

"It wasn't a big deal," he said to Shelly. "She'd have done the same for me—or anybody."

Shelly shook her head. "She's alive because of you."

It bothered Bryson to hear that. Taking credit—even if it was for a greater purpose—felt like he was dishonoring Olivia. He vowed to tell Shelly the truth as soon as it was practical.

Over coffee, Vitio told several light-hearted stories about the escapes he and Mendac got into when they were young. Bryson was fine with this. He liked hearing stories about his father acting like a regular guy. What he didn't like was hearing about how great his father was, how he received special treatment because of who his father was, or being compared to him. He was eager to learn about his dad's personality. That's what exposed who a person was—not their achievements.

Someone could save lives, but for the wrong reasons. Someone could destroy a kingdom, but for the right ones. A hero could be a bad person, and a villain could be a good person. It was all a matter of perspective: the world was never so black and white.

And now for the first time in his life, he was learning about how his father carried himself. Did he have a sense of humor? Was he raunchy or straight-laced? Compassionate or malevolent? Did he possess self-restraint? He received the answers to only one of these questions through Vitio's stories—that he knew how to laugh—but it was enough to leave him satisfied.

As the clock approached half-past eleven, and Vitio, Lilu, and Bryson were winding down in an intimate little room near the royal chambers. It was mid-December, so a small fire crackled in the fireplace. Bryson found himself sitting on a loveseat with as much distance as he could put between himself and Lilu. It was a bit uncomfortable with her father in the room.

Vitio smiled. "You two are on opposite ends of the couch, but I can tell that's not what you want."

Lilu and Bryson filled the room with an awkward silence. "Young love," the king added with an air of reminiscing.

Lilu blushed. "Director Venustas teases us too. But you're both wrong."

"My family owes you deeply," Vitio said to Bryson, apparently deciding not to embarrass them any further. "Very much so like we did your father."

"Actually, Father," Lilu said, perking up her posture. "About that. You see, there's something very dangerous inside of his house—something that shouldn't be there."

Vitio's eyebrow rose. "And what is that?"

"A light," she said. "A *dangerous* light."

Vitio looked at Bryson with a look of shock. He must have known what Lilu was getting at. "Why? How?"

"*How* doesn't matter," Lilu said. "However, *why* does. It's being used to hide something and has put Bryson in danger. We need a Bozani."

Vitio leaned back in his armchair and took a sip of scotch. "That wasn't exactly the kind of favor I was expecting."

Bryson leaned forward with a look of hunger in his eyes. "I need this."

Vitio studied him for a second. "Your father got that same look when he wanted something."

"Only one person can get us a Bozani though," Lilu said.

The king called for a servant and instructed him to fetch the princess. "The difficult part is getting Shelly to go through with it," Lilu said while they waited.

Vitio took another sip from his glass. "She will do as I say."

"But will *he* do what you say?" The question came from the now open doorway. It was Princess Shelly, dressed in a golden nightgown. Her pixie-cut was flattened out.

"We'll do some convincing," Vitio said as he waved her in.

Shelly didn't sit, just took a couple steps into the room after closing the door behind her. "He doesn't have to do as we say. He is a Bozani. To him, even we royals are commoners."

Vitio flushed. "Yes—it will take some convincing."

Shelly looked at Bryson and said sternly, "Only because you saved my sister."

"Thank you."

"Understand this. What you're about to experience is not of this world—and by law, it isn't something you're supposed to experience at all. Keep this to yourself."

A ball of white light formed next to her, and Bryson instantly recognized it as what she had fought with against the Archaic Prince in the royal suites.

It was what had the Adren King so angry at the two of them.

As the light glowed, Bryson felt himself breathing easier. The air felt as if it was being purified. His mind also felt unclouded, while his heart began to lift inside of his chest. It was euphoric, and he wanted to be trapped forever in this state of freedom.

The light took shape as it slowly shifted into a human's body. It was a young man with greasy hair of a color just like the flames in the fireplace. He wore a long robe that blanketed his entire body. A scimitar was strapped diagonally across his back, which meant that he was once an inhabitant of the Adren Kingdom. *So royal first-borns can have a Branian who isn't native to their kingdom?* Bryson wondered.

The Branian scanned through all the faces around the room until he paused on the unfamiliar one—Bryson. "He is not a royal."

King Vitio stood tall and gave a deep bow out of respect for a higher being. "He is a dear friend of ours and needs the help of a Bozani, Suadade."

Suadade answered quickly and sharply. "No. I am an assigned Branian for the royal first-born of the Intel Family." He gave Bryson a cold stare. "Not some random kid who needs help with straightening out his life."

Bryson stood up and bowed deeply. "I am honored to be in the presence of a Bozani—someone whose energy was pure and strong enough to be reborn into a second life. I know I seem like nothing to you, but I must ask for your help. My name is Bryson LeAnce—"

"LeAnce?" the Branian repeated as he cocked his head at Bryson.

"Yes, LeAnce."

"Then I will help you."

20

Behind the Light

A couple more weeks passed, and with it came the New Year. It was now 1499 K.H., or Known History.

Bryson found himself inside of a lavish horse-drawn carriage and accompanied by two women he had seen a lot of lately—Lilu and Shelly. Today, Lilu's flower was a rose, and her dress was a matching blood red.

As Bryson pulled back a curtain and observed his house's street, heads turned to stare at the royal carriage. For these citizens, this would be the only time they'd ever see royalty. A royal first-born entering the capital's suburbs was frowned upon. The risk of a kidnapping or regicide was too high.

But that fear seemed silly to Bryson. Who could fight better than a royal? Even the ten guards escorting them weren't a match for Shelly, or even Lilu or Bryson for that matter.

Bryson flopped back in his seat. "Worst idea ever," he groaned, "riding in this ridiculous thing."

Princess Shelly glared at him. "I'm sorry that I want comfort."

"This is going to be the talk of my street. I hope Debo doesn't have a change of heart and become sociable with neighbors all of a sudden."

"Well I was hardly going to take your suggestion to wear a hooded jacket and sweatpants. I shouldn't have to sneak around inside of my own kingdom, and I definitely don't need to dress like a bum."

Lilu rolled her eyes.

"You are the Queen of High Maintenance," Bryson sighed.

The princess gave him a sly smile. "That would be my mother."

"Well, we're here," Lilu said. "Let's go."

When the three of them stepped inside Bryson's house, he asked them to remove their shoes. "Debo doesn't like his hardwood floors getting scuffed," he explained to Shelly.

She raised an eyebrow at him. "You're about to break the number one rule in his house, and you're talking about respecting his hardwood floors?"

Bryson stuttered, realizing the flawed logic. There wasn't much time to loiter. If Debo came home early, there would be no calming his anger.

So they got right to it. The three of them stood next to the light. Shelly shuddered. She could feel the power by simply being near its presence. Bryson's heart had dropped into his stomach at the anticipation of discovering something that had been hidden from him for eleven years.

A ball of light appeared as Princess Shelly summoned her Branian, and Bryson felt the same sense of purification as the light took a human shape.

"Hello, Suadade," Shelly said.

"Hey," Suadade said with a distant emptiness as he stared at the light in wonder.

"Thank you for doing this," Bryson said.

The Branian didn't break his gaze away from the light. "No, thank *you*."

Suadade reached toward the light. As his hand was on the brink of penetrating the barrier, Bryson had a familiar flashback to the only time he tried opposing the shield, which caused him to ball his fist around his scarred finger.

Suadade's hand crossed into the light. Bryson flinched, but there was no smoke, no crackling, no screams. Not even the slightest frown or wince crossed the Branian's face. In fact, he smiled. And if Bryson wasn't mistaken, his eyes were bright with potential tears. Where Bryson had experienced agonizing, deadly pain, Suadade looked to be experiencing a joyous dream.

Suadade's hand waved around inside of the light, feeling for something. His smile grew. He stepped all the way in, and his body glowed as it was engulfed by the light. He reached for the handle and turned it slowly.

Bryson's heart felt like it was thumping out of his chest. *What is it? Gold? Some kind of secret or cherished document? Money? The stolen relic? . . . DECAYING BODIES?!*

The door opened, but he couldn't see what was inside. The problem with this infiltration was that only Branian Suadade could enter. Bryson had suggested that Suadade dissemble the light so everyone could pass, but the Bozani had quickly shot that idea down, explaining that he couldn't perfectly replicate the shield. The difference would be too noticeable.

So they had to observe from afar as they watched the scimitar on Suadade's back disappear into the closet.

"What's in there?" Bryson called out, but the Bozani didn't answer. Finally, after the longest minute of Bryson's life, Suadade stepped back through the light while holding something behind his back.

"This is when I depart," he said as he took the object from behind his back and solemnly handed it to Bryson. "Mission accomplished," he added, and then vanished.

Lilu looked on in disbelief as Bryson gaped at what was resting in his hands. Now he knew why Debo never discussed Intel Energy or performed electrical abilities, and why he always trained for speed and nothing else. The reason was resting in his hands … a gleaming katana with an emerald-encrusted hilt.

Debo didn't possess Intel Energy. He was a swordsman of the Adren Kingdom, living his life as a lie.

*   *   *

The sky grew dark as the sun set from behind the clouds. They were in the royal carriage once again as they headed back to the palace in silence.

Lilu hadn't spoken a word since Suadade was summoned. Bryson thought she was trying to refrain from saying "I told you so."

Which she would have had every right to do. She *had* told him so. A million questions flew through Bryson's head as he lay across one of the cushioned benches in the carriage, staring at the roof of golden cloth.

Why had he lied? Did anyone know the truth? At the very least, Grand Director Poicus had to know. He wouldn't just assign Debo the role of Intel Director without his abilities being proven. Why was it necessary to disguise himself? Why has he been raising me? Was he a friend of my dad? Was he assigned to protect me? Was I his Charge?

"How did he become the Intel Director?" Lilu finally asked.

Bryson continued to stare at the ceiling. "Who knows."

"How did he create that light is what I'd like to know," Shelly said.

"Who cares?" Bryson groaned.

"It's important. Sit up and let me teach you something you would have never learned at Phesaw."

"That's not smart," Lilu said to her sister.

Shelly shrugged. "He's already seen way more than he's supposed to." She held out her hand as a perfect sphere of electricity hovered above her palm. "Each kingdom is known for its own energy and ability. For example, our kingdom possesses people with Intel Energy and electrical powers. What we now know to be Debo's kingdom—the Adren Kingdom— possesses people with Adrenergy and the ability of speed."

"I know all this already," Bryson said.

"And there are two islands floating high above us, one of which houses the Light Empire, where the Bozani live."

"I know that too."

"Stop interrupting me!" the princess yelled. "Did you know that there's an energy that everyone is born with, regardless of which kingdom they belong to?"

Bryson looked at her, his interest finally piqued. "What?"

"There's an energy known as *Tahara*. However, it lies dormant for almost everyone. But there are a few rare people in history who were able to tap into their Tahara, gaining them access to the ability of—"

"Light," Bryson interrupted, connecting the dots.

"Very good," Shelly said with a smile. "Typically, it's an ability exclusive to Bozani."

Bryson looked at her as if she was crazy. "Are you implying Debo is a Bozani?"

She laughed. "No, I'm implying one of two options. One, he is secretly the first-born of King Supido and therefore possesses a Branian of his own—one who created the light that guarded his sword."

"Well, that's not believable at all," Bryson said.

"Two, he is one of the rare exceptions I spoke of. Based off the stories from the *Of Five* series, there have been five non-Bozani in history who have been able to tap into their Tahara … even though it's not explained that way in the books. Maybe he is the sixth, and he actually did create that light himself. But that's unlikely."

It didn't sound too unlikely to Bryson. Bryson had seen what Debo could do over the years. He had witnessed his overwhelming confidence—his commanding presence. Shelly hadn't seen any of that. And since there have only been five instances in 1,500 years, he couldn't blame her for doubting him.

It was the idea of a second energy, though, that really got Bryson's mind spinning … *Tahara*. Not once had he ever heard about it at Phesaw. The subject of Bozani was always very vague in school. Not much was known about them.

Bryson was dozing off when Shelly asked to see the katana. He obliged, and she inspected every inch from the tip to the handle. Bryson figured she was simply admiring it, but then her eyes met the hilt and she paused.

As her brows furrowed, he became curious. "What is it?"

Without moving her head, her eyes scanned Bryson. "Nothing," she muttered.

"You have a terrible poker face," he said.

"These emeralds are a very rare type," she said.

"Surprise, surprise. Royals and their obsession with shiny objects."

There wasn't much talking for the rest of the trip, which took about an hour. Shelly slept most of the way, while Lilu and Bryson sat in their thoughts.

It was late, so once inside the palace, Shelly and Lilu split ways with Bryson as they headed toward separate wings. The palace was beginning to become more like home to Bryson. He had been sleeping there about every other night over the past two weeks. So far as Debo was concerned, Bryson had been staying at the Lilac Suites in the attempt to keep the Jestivan together during a difficult month. He had felt bad for lying, but after today, any guilt had disappeared.

He had given Debo's sword to Shelly, who wanted to send it to Brilliance—a city far north, across the Intel River and the northern plains. It was where the Intel Kingdom's top scientists resided, so they'd know what type of value the gems on the hilt possessed. Besides, he wasn't interested in keeping the sword. It was only a symbol of Debo's dishonesty.

The two ladies of royalty walked side-by-side through the moonlit hallway. "What caught your eye on the hilt?" Lilu asked. "I know it wasn't the emeralds."

Shelly paused at her bedroom's door. "Dried blood," she said softly. She then entered her room and closed the door on Lilu, leaving her to ponder in the moonlight.

21

Exposed

"Prince Storshae!" General Ossen yelled as he ripped back the curtain to the prince's tent.

Leaning back with his feet resting on the desk, the prince looked at his subordinate. Next to the prince stood a man of average height and brown hair—a seemingly unassuming man with an inexplicably formidable presence.

The general bowed. "I wasn't expecting to see you here, Bewahr Fonos."

"Hello, Ossen," the Bewahr replied.

Prince Storshae rose from his seat. "I suppose you have barged in here to announce our guest's arrival."

Ossen nodded. "Yes, sir. And quite a lot of his soldiers too."

Storshae shrugged. "As expected. Even under the impression that we're allies, it would have been brainless of him to come without protection. Let him in." He remained standing as he waited for his guest, and when he entered, the prince forced a smile.

"Hello, my friend," Storshae said as he reached across the table to shake the man's hand.

Tall and balding with brown spots speckling his forehead behind a crown of twigs, the Archaic King gripped the prince's hand. "It has been too long, Storshae." The king shot a nervous glance at the Bewahr standing casually off to the side.

"I wonder whose fault that is," the prince replied with a masked coldness, gesturing toward the seat across the desk. All that had been exchanged was a handshake and a few words, but the direction that the conversation was headed was already obvious.

"I'm sorry I couldn't schedule a meeting with you earlier," King Itta apologized as he took his seat.

"It has been nearly a month since you returned to your kingdom," the Dev Prince pointed out. "A month of my soldiers wasting away in this desert." He spoke calmly, but didn't bother to conceal the displeasure.

Itta noticed this, so he matched it. "And I provided you with food and water when I returned."

Storshae laughed. "My soldiers want to return to their families. Instead they're stuck here waiting for you—"

"*YOU KILLED MY GREATEST FIGHTER!*" Itta shouted.

The outburst did not rattle the prince. He gazed mildly at his erstwhile ally.

Itta regained his composure and revised his approach. "I'm sure you can understand that I have been quite beset with difficulties this past month. I no longer have my right-hand man."

Storshae's lips pressed into a thin, resentful line. "I'm sorry that we went a little bit away from the script. Yes, you lost your strongest warrior, but his death took any suspicion away from your kingdom, no?"

"I need to be forewarned about these sorts of things if this is to be a functioning alliance," the Archaic King said.

"Very true," Storshae agreed. "But to be fair, you brought us into a hopeless fight. You informed us of who would be in that arena, and I don't recall you ever mentioning the Jestivan or directors."

"I didn't know they would be there."

Storshae reached into his desk's bottom drawer. "Which is exactly the problem." He pulled out a small stack of papers. "You were so sure of yourself when you told us the plan, but you were wrong. I could have arranged for appropriate staffing to counter the Jestivan and directors— such as the Diatia."

King Itta's eyes were fixed on the stack of parchment.

"The next realm meeting is tomorrow, yes?" Storshae asked. Itta nodded, his eyes still on the papers.

"I'm assuming if you haven't left by now, you don't plan on going at all." The Dev Prince was enjoying the look of fright painted on his guest's face. "You're scared of them extracting the truth from your escorts—or worse, yourself."

The elderly king didn't answer, so Storshae continued his mockery. "I wrote this a month ago." He pressed his finger on the papers in front of him. "But after having weeks to ponder on it, why do I need official documentation for ending this alliance?" A maniacal grin formed. "This scenario sets itself up for a dramatic and believable ending." He tore the documents to pieces. "With the heads of the Light Realm's other four kingdoms gathered in one place, let's expose you properly."

Finally, Itta broke from his paralysis. He jumped from his seat and sprinted toward the exit. As he ran, he turned and threw a punch that extended into a tree back toward Storshae. The prince nonchalantly dodged the attack, but he didn't bother countering.

Bewahr Fonos disappeared and instantly reappeared in front of the tent's exit, blocking Itta's escape as he yelled for help. Itta threw a punch of wood, which Fonos caught bare-handed. As Itta grunted and shook from effort, the Bewahr stood in a relaxed manner before snapping the tree in half, forcing Itta's arm to morph back to normal.

Fonos disappeared again, and Itta wasn't even given a chance to blink before the Bewahr had him in a chokehold from behind. Fonos walked him back to the desk as the sounds of fighting arose from outside the tent.

"It is extremely convenient that you decided to leave your son in the capital," Storshae said, still smiling. "After all, he is the only one who possesses a Branian to counter my Bewahr. It would have been interesting

... seeing one of the Light Empire's Bozani go toe-to-toe with one of the Dark Empire's Gefal. I'm sure you're cursing your age right now. It's unfortunate that one loses their Branian when they grow too old."

Itta's face was a vibrant pink from the lack of oxygen, but he still managed to say through spit, "You will pay."

"Ossen, get in here!" Storshae yelled.

The general rushed into the tent. "Yes, Prince?"

"Grab this worthless scum. Judging from the uproar outside, the clock is ticking. Let's get this done with."

Itta gasped for air as Fonos removed his hold, but he didn't have a chance to regain his bearings. Ossen dragged him behind the desk and sat him down in the prince's chair.

The Archaic King scowled at the two men. "What is killing me going to accomplish?"

"We're not going to kill you," Storshae replied. "Unless you don't say what we tell you to."

*   *   *

Three older gentlemen were seated inside of a dining room that was floored with polished wood and walled with plain drywall. Wooden beams stretched vertically every ten feet or so. An orange hue flickered across the room as several candles flickered atop tall wooden racks in all four corners of the room. There was no moonlight, for the wooden shutters covering the lone window were shut.

In the center of the room sat a low-rising dining table that would look strange if it was in any other kingdom. It sat high enough to lay one's legs underneath parallel to the floor. Silver-colored pillows resting on the floorboards served as cushions for the three kings who sat atop them: a burly man in gold, a gaunt dark-skinned man in silver, and a plump baldheaded man in red. They held a pleasant conversation while enjoying dinner.

"I love visiting your kingdom," Intel King Vitio said as he fumbled with the chopsticks—a utensil only used in the Spirit and Adren kingdoms.

Passion King Damian nodded enthusiastically.

Adren King Supido smiled. "You don't miss the lavishness of your palaces?"

"After a while, lavish becomes normal," Vitio said, taking in the room's modesty. "And plain becomes lavish."

"Strange how that works, isn't it?" Supido asked while deeply hunched over the table. His height practically forced him to fold in two in order to eat his soup.

Vitio placed his chopsticks on the plate. "But it's not just your palace. It's the people and atmosphere. I feel safe here. Your people are polite and respectful, though I must say it's odd to see random duels in the streets."

"Everyone wants to practice whenever the chance presents itself," Supido explained. "As long as they're using the spine of their sword, it's legal."

"I wish my people were like that," Vitio sighed.

Damian gave a remorseful nod, implying he felt the same about the people of his kingdom.

"There's nothing you can do about that," Supido said. "There are even misfits here. We just don't have as many because it's not in our nature to be that way."

"It's also nice not having to deal with children filling the palace with their screaming and fighting," Vitio said as he fumbled with the chopsticks, giving them a second chance despite his better judgment.

Supido stopped slurping his noodles, which hung into his soup. Damian's face clouded with embarrassment.

"I guess that's a matter of perspective," the Adren King said.

"I'm sorry, Supido," Vitio said. "That was thoughtless of me."

Supido wiped his mouth. "No worries. In due time, I will get to experience the joy of what I hear parents complain about so often. And if not simply for the enjoyment of being a parent, then for the necessity of having someone who can carry on the Adren royal blood." The lanky king looked at Vitio and Damian with appealing eyes. "Is that odd—caring more about the joy of raising a strong child than making sure your royal bloodline doesn't die out?"

"No, not at all," Vitio assured him.

Supido held his fellow king's stare for a moment before changing subjects. "Where is Itta?"

Damian shrugged, and Vitio voiced his agreement: "That about sums up what I know too."

"Bastard better be here," Supido threatened. "We're trying to help him. We could have swarmed the Dev Kingdom by now."

The door abruptly slammed open at the hands of a dirty blond–haired man in burgundy. It was Marcus, the truth extractor Vitio had given to Damian five years ago. However, something was wrong. Marcus was distraught and his eyes were bouncing violently. Spirit Queen Apsa peered anxiously over his shoulder.

"Someone is hacking into my broadcast ability!" Marcus shouted.

A holographic display appeared on the opposite wall. The four royal heads stood speechless as they looked on in awe. Pictured in the display was the answer for King Itta's absence.

The man with charcoal black hair, who was seated to the left, gave a delighted grin. "Greetings, royal heads and citizens of the Light Realm. Most of you know me as King Storshae of the Dev Kingdom, but those with proper sense call me its prince. I believe that my esteemed colleague needs no introduction." He looked at Itta and laughed.

Stunned looks were plastered on almost every face in the room. The exception was Adren King Supido. He was fuming.

"It pains me deeply that I can't see your faces right now, but hacking into someone's recording ability is too difficult for even my Bewahr," Storshae continued. "However, this broadcast is going out to every major city in the Light Realm."

"Is that true?" Supido barked at Marcus.

"I wouldn't doubt it. The presence felt strangely powerful. That it's a Gefal behind this makes perfect sense."

"I know a lot of you are possibly confused, but we have answers," Storshae said. He smiled as he turned to look at his ally. "Itta, inform your realm of your traitorous deeds."

The Archaic King looked directly at the recorder. "Six months ago, I contacted Prince Storshae with an offer to unite arms against the Intel Kingdom."

"Unbelievable," Vitio muttered to himself as an uproar from outside the palace could be heard.

Queen Apsa opened the wooden shutters in order to see the streets below. Three holographic displays hovered in the night sky as crowds of angry people swarmed underneath, yelling at the two men in the broadcast.

"So much for a century of peace," she said gravely.

"As most are aware, the Archaic and Dev kingdoms have been cruelly abused by the Intel Kingdom for centuries, so this alliance was clearly to the benefit of our peoples," Itta said. "If anything, it should have been made a long time ago.

"Ultimately, Prince Storshae accepted my offer, and we devised a plan to be set in motion. We had a chance to sever the head of the Intel Kingdom at the Generals' Battle, but this was not successful. And revelation of Vitio's unexpected trump card—an intelligence officer he had stolen from Storshae's kingdom nearly two decades ago—has prompted me to announce our alliance publicly. Here are our conditions, all of them which must be met or we will declare war—"

The broadcast abruptly cut to a different view as Itta's sentence was replaced by gagging sounds. His face filled the image as a pair of hands strangled him. Bewahr Fonos had teleported from the opposite side of the tent and was choking the Archaic King to death.

The image panned to Prince Storshae. His grin was gone, and his eyes were enveloped in the dark shadows of his forehead and eyebrows. "Now, I have an announcement of my own. This King Itta was a pathetic fool. He told me one Jestivan would be at the Generals' Battle, Olivia, a girl he intended on capturing. However, there were a total of six Jestivan in those stands. And not only that, there were four Energy Directors. We entered a battle we had lost before it started."

Itta's gasps for air could still be heard in the background. "So here is my announcement to the Light Realm. This short-lived alliance is over. Do what you like with the Archaic Kingdom. And do what you like with its dim-witted king."

The image panned back to Itta, who was now lying limply on the ground. A boot kicked him in the face, smashing the Archaic King's crown to splinters. "I will keep him alive for you. He'll be here waiting."

Fonos tied up the balding king as Storshae continued: "But I suggest you be quick. He'll die of thirst if you don't get here in time. With that said, it's time to head back home … It's time to return my father—our proper king—to power, and there is no more Mendac to frustrate the resumption of his reign."

With that, the broadcast cut out, leaving the people in every major city of the Light Realm floored.

*　　*　　*

Storshae was preparing for departure of the campgrounds when, somehow, Itta managed to muster up a few words. "You're a fool if you think you're getting away with this," he slurred through broken teeth.

"I am the Prince of the Dev Kingdom. Although a bit dated, what is the other name my kingdom is known by, Mr. Itta?" He paused before answering it himself. "The Dark *Knowledge* Kingdom. Everything I do is highly calculated. Now, I must leave before your darling son hunts me down. I'd rather avoid meeting a Branian tonight." Storshae pulled back the curtain that was behind his desk.

Itta's eyes widened. The Jestivan girl was bound to a chair. Her violet hair was covered in so much dirt that it was on the verge of being brown. Her face was unrecognizable from the bruises, but he still knew who she was. The kitten hat sitting askew on her head told it all.

The Dev Prince instructed Ossen and Fonos to follow him out of the tent. It was time to enter the battle happening outside between the Dev and Archaic soldiers. With Bewahr Fonos entering the fray, massacring the enemy was going to be quick work.

*　　*　　*

Phesaw's campus glowed in gold as the intelights and lanterns illuminated the evening atmosphere. A large crowd of exuberant students gathered at Wealth's Crossroads, all with one goal in mind: meeting the Jestivan.

Eight Jestivan were seated at a long table that had been set up outside of the Lilac Suites. Each of them had a bottle of ink in front of them and a quill in their hand as masses of students approached their favorite members for an autograph. On a normal day, these students would refrain from hassling the Jestivan with star-struck eyes and diarrhea of the mouth. But at this event, that sort of behavior was invited with open arms.

As Bryson signed autograph upon autograph, he still found it odd how he and his fellow teammates were looked at as idols on campus. It may have become routine to walk through a hallway and see kids stare before turning to their friends with awe-inspired smiles, but when he would lie down at the end of the day and think back on it, it truly was bizarre.

A young girl, who looked to be around the age of nine, approached Bryson with a nervous smile. One of her adult front teeth had yet to grow in. Her skin was dark like Adren Director Buredo's, and her hair was straight and deep black.

"Hey there, young lady," Bryson said with a smile.

"Hello, Zana Bryson," she replied quietly.

He took a glance at what was in her hands. "What are the running shoes for?" he asked.

"Sign them! I want to run like you when I'm sixteen."

Bryson stared at the silver leather shoes. He couldn't believe he inspired someone so young in an area he found himself cursing most of the time. As he grabbed his quill and began signing the side of them, he asked, "And what kingdom are you from?"

"Adren," she responded.

A member of the Adren Kingdom envying my speed? Bryson was at a loss for words as, all of a sudden, his appreciation for Debo's training throughout the years grew a little bit.

"You skipped two Jestivan from your kingdom to come to me?" he asked.

She smiled. "I'm going to visit Lita Yama and Zana Toshik too! But I wanted to meet you first."

The little girl stuck out her hand for a handshake, which Bryson humorously accepted. She then looked at a young boy with red hair who was standing behind him, and asked, "Who is he?"

Bryson turned to look at his friend and said, "This is Simon, and one day, the two of you will be the next big things on this campus."

As the other Jestivan calmly signed autographs, Jilly stood at the far end of the table, giving high-fives and enthusiastic bear hugs to her fans. Some challenged her to arm wrestling and thumb war competitions, which she accepted without hesitation. In fact, the students were having so much fun with her that they'd walk away without even realizing they forgot to get an autograph.

A huge cluster of girls waited impatiently to reach the Jestivan's heartthrob, Toshik. Two young women, who both swore they were next, got into a scuffle, tearing at the dresses and elegant hairstyles they'd worn to impress the handsome Jestivan.

"You're not deserving of attention like that," said the snowy-haired boy sitting to his right while continuing to absent-mindedly sign his autographs. "You're a disgusting man."

Toshik laughed. "I enjoy it."

Tashami shook his head in disbelief.

To nobody's surprise, Lilu had drawn the biggest crowd. Not only was she a Jestivan, she was a royal. She had status, money, fame, beauty, and power. She encompassed everything. She was an elegant and benevolent flower, but at the same time, a powerful and assertive avalanche of unyielding rocks that could crush said flower when needed.

As always, her posture was perfectly upright. Her smile was sweet and pearly. Nothing was fabricated. She truly loved this sort of thing. She loved knowing that so many people looked up to her.

Sitting next to Lilu was Yama, who seemed to be just going through the motions. Unlike Lilu, there was no flower present in Yama's soul—just rocks. But this was what people expected from her. So when she'd give a disinterested greeting with a staged smile as she signed whatever was in front of her, nobody was upset. They were just happy to walk away with their heads still attached to their bodies.

Since Agnos was no fighter, he was mostly left alone. The few exceptions were his fellow Archaic students. Most of them were more interested in picking his mind than getting his autograph. A small handful of students huddled in front of him, debating Kuki Sphaira's origins, the existence of consciousness, and many other things.

The Energy Directors mingled behind the Jestivan, doing their best to not talk about work and enjoy themselves for once. But their small talk was cut short when a vast holographic display lit up the night sky—its source somewhere beyond the trees of Phesaw Park. The students stopped and looked up. Some put their hands to their open mouths in shock as murmurs crept through the crowd. They recognized Archaic King Itta. However, the other man was a mystery to most. When he finally introduced himself as Dev Prince Storshae, Wealth's Crossroads was bathed in a frightened silence. Then there were gasps as King Itta announced his alliance, and still more when he was strangled.

When the broadcast finished and disappeared from the sky, Bryson darted toward Debo. "That's who took Olivia!" he shouted. "That teleporter. It has to be. No one else would have been a match for her."

The Intel Director looked at Bryson with sad eyes. "You must stay within yourself," he said.

"Let's go get her!" Bryson shouted above the din behind him—a cacophony of fear and rage. "Who knows what happened to Grand Director Poicus. Your idea didn't work. It's time to send us!"

"You're not going anywhere," Debo replied.

"Why don't you care?!"

"I'M NOT LOSING YOU!"

Bryson had never seen Debo erupt like this, but he didn't miss a beat. *"AND I'M NOT LOSING HER!"*

It wasn't anger that was animating his voice. It was desperation. Bryson had no mother, no father, no siblings. The man who had raised him could no longer be completely trusted. And that trust was dwindling even further as Debo denied his pleas to save his best friend.

Debo's face softened as he stared down into Bryson's blue eyes. "You hate me. That's fine, but you are not going to search for her," he said softly. He shook his head as he walked past Bryson and toward the school.

As Bryson stared blankly into the middle distance, he felt a hand touch his shoulder. He didn't turn to see who it was. He didn't care. Lilu stepped in front of him, but he still gazed through her. She embraced him, and Bryson took a deep breath of her begonia's scent—the same flower she'd worn in her hair when they first met so many months ago.

While standing limp in her arms, a cool wind blew past—a wind he had felt before. Something caught his attention on the roof of the Lilac Suites … a black silhouette of a graceful body and a dress blowing in the wind. Then it disappeared and a message carried through the wind once again …

"Which is almost in sight …"

22

A Familiar Face

The Energy Directors gathered inside of Phesaw's judgment room, the site of students' trials and punishments. With the commotion calmed outside and an early curfew for the night put into effect, it was time to focus on business. A long, curved table that was raised high above the rest of the floor on a platform occupied one side of the room. The rest was vast floor space where a student would typically stand at the center. Tonight, however, it was a Dev servant—their connection to Grand Director Poicus.

Intel Director Debo sat at the center of the table. "Check to see whether it's safe to contact Director Poicus."

The man closed his eyes for a minute before reopening them. "He's ready."

"Start it up," Debo commanded.

A hologram appeared. "For you to contact me so soon after already talking with me this morning, something must have happened," Poicus said, dispensing with any greetings.

"We've learned why you've had no success the past month," Debo said.

His hairy eyebrow rose. "Do tell."

"She's in the Archaic Kingdom, held captive by King Itta. Or was. Storshae may have taken her back to his realm with them."

"What?" Poicus stammered. "But none of the Dev intruders have returned."

"They're on their way now. They've been hiding in the Archaic Kingdom for the past several weeks. Itta had allied with the Dev Kingdom, and he escorted Storshae's army into the Intel Kingdom."

"I guess I'm coming back," Poicus said. "I'm assuming everyone will be sending armies to occupy Itta's land."

"I think you can still prove useful down there," Debo said.

The other Energy Directors eyed him suspiciously. "What more can he do down there?" Archaic Director Senex asked. "Even if Storshae has Olivia, Poicus can't handle a Gefal."

"You haven't heard the last thing that Storshae said," Debo continued, ignoring Senex. "'It's time to return my father—our proper king—to power, and there is no more Mendac to frustrate the resumption of his reign.'"

"So he's still alive," Poicus concluded.

"Correct. Since you're already in the Dev Kingdom, and because of your ability, I ask of you to find Rehn's grave—if there even is one."

"Are you sure this isn't a petty matter?" Passion Director Venustas asked. "Everyone agrees that Mendac obviously killed him."

Poicus thought for a moment, twirling the tail of an eyebrow. "King Rehn was never a petty matter in the past, so we will not treat him like one now … even if he's supposedly dead. I will investigate. And I'll be back before you know it."

*　　　*　　　*

"It's a disgrace that you can't use your Intel Energy," Princess Shelly scolded as she threw an electric ball at a rubber target in the palace's courtyard.

Bryson wasn't offended. "I agree." Shelly looked surprised by his acceptance of her insult.

"Why didn't you go with your father to the realm meeting?" Bryson asked. "You went to the first one."

"I wasn't supposed to go to that one either. If a kingdom's royal head must leave the capital for whatever reason, the successor is obliged to stay."

"Then how did you get away with it?"

She smirked. "One of the soldiers who had a boyish crush on me snuck me into a carriage."

"And you got away with that?" Bryson asked in disbelief.

"Oh, we were found out, of course. The soldier was court-martialed. I believe he shovels manure in the stables now. Luckily for me, my father doesn't know how to properly discipline a daughter, so I received only a half-hearted lecture."

"So why was it so important for you to go?"

"To visit a cemetery. Don't judge me," she added with a laugh.

"You're one of the last people I'd expect to see in a cemetery."

"That whole idea was Suadade's."

Bryson's interest was piqued. "What does your Branian want with a graveyard?"

Shelly's lips pursed. "To visit his grave. To be reminded that he has died already before, that he doesn't need to be scared of anything else."

Bryson decided to not push the topic further, and Shelly reverted to what they were supposed to be discussing.

"I know you have overwhelming speed, but that doesn't mean you should be satisfied. If you have the energy, you can turn that energy into an ability."

"Easier said than done."

"Look at me," the princess commanded.

Bryson obeyed, giving her a defeated look.

"Emitting your energy into a tangible external element requires a lot of control. You should understand this since you can already emit sparks … pretty feeble ones, but they're still something."

Shelly was a good teacher, which was why Bryson continued going straight to the Intel Palace every evening. Debo continued developing his

209

and Lilu's speed after school, and Bryson would accompany her back to the palace afterward. He was overworking himself and losing any bit of a social life he once had. His bonds with his team were weakening as he neglected his duties as captain. But it was all a reasonable sacrifice if it meant becoming strong enough to rescue Olivia.

Continuing her lecture, Shelly paced across the shadows of the palace's towers. "You must be able to manipulate your energy. It's difficult at first, but eventually it becomes instinctive. Each energy has a specific pattern as it runs through your body. They say that Spirit Energy moves in waves. Our energy moves in a jagged path with harsh angles. It's very dynamic."

Bryson glanced at his hand as a few sparks discharged from his fingertips.

Shelly shook her head. "You don't know how to focus on it. Speed and technique are nice, but that focuses on your bodily control—not internal."

Shelly pressed her finger against his forehead hard enough for him to topple backward a few steps. "Internal control requires your mind," she said before turning toward the courtyard's exit. "Think more."

*   *   *

Tashami and Agnos were seated in the grass of Phesaw Park. Agnos was wearing socks with his wooden sandals, as winter wasn't kind to his skin. They were discussing a common topic between the two of them—the Unbreakable.

"I received another letter," Tashami said.

"It's about time," Agnos said through a mouthful of apple. "What does it say?"

"It's pretty vague."

"A vague modifier for the word itself. How ironic."

Tashami's nose wrinkled like he smelled something bad. "Sometimes your intelligence makes you petty, you know."

Agnos ignored the remark. "Could you read it?"

"I'm getting better with your help."

"Good." Agnos retrieved his glasses from his pocket. "Let me see it."

Tashami handed him the parchment, and Agnos scanned through the foreign characters, his glasses instantly translating the text:

Tashami,

A mysterious young man accompanied by an older woman and young girl visited today. Well, everything in this kingdom is mysterious. However, this was different.

Not many foreigners venture into the Cyn Kingdom, but this man and woman chose to—like I did so many years ago. You would think it'd be refreshing to see new faces to sulk in your miseries with, but this couldn't be further from the truth.

They didn't want to sulk. They had an objective—again, much like a younger me did. And even though their mission was a lot more selfish than mine, they still didn't allow this kingdom to deplete their drive. I can admire that.

The man was from the Archaic Kingdom and, from what he told me, had been traveling a lot lately. He's done a lot of bad things—as in murder—but he says it's for a greater good, which I agree with. Although, we may have thought differently about what that greater good was. Whenever you lay someone to eternal rest, you are doing them a favor. Needless to say, I took a liking to the man ... Then I figured out what his goal was.

You see, I don't want to live, but something is keeping me alive. Nobody really wants to live. Think about it. Life is pain. When you die, you are set free from the stress, heartbreak, and uncertainty that plague your thoughts.

Let those lucky people who are rotting inside the crust enjoy their peace. Do not wake the dead, for they do not want to be awakened.

The now broken Unbreakable

Agnos took off his glasses and returned them to his pocket. "This isn't vague at all," he said. He folded the parchment and stuck it in the pocket with his glasses. "I need to borrow this to read it over a few times."

Staring into the scattered trees in front of him, Agnos now knew, without a doubt, that his suspicions of the identity of the Archaic Museum's thief were correct. His once pure-hearted childhood friend, who aspired to the ultimate form of good, was now a thief and murderer. And the woman who stole him away was the catalyst of it all. As for the little girl mentioned, Agnos didn't know who that could be.

But one thing was certain. Agnos had to accept the fact that his friend who had taught him morals, values, and purity no longer followed those teachings himself.

How does someone change that drastically? What did that woman do to him?

*   *   *

Dev Prince Storshae stepped off the teleplatform and took a deep breath. "Home, sweet home," he said to General Ossen with a smile.

To their left, Olivia was shoved from the platform and hit the ground with a thump. She wasn't tied up, for she was no threat to fight back. With how little they had been feeding her, she was in no condition to even stand.

Storshae stared at the limitless sea of yellow prairie gleaming in the first-day sun. The capital sat well over the horizon, at least a week's journey away. Mistrustful of outsiders, his ancestors had built their teleplatforms in the hinterland, in this wide-open landscape with nowhere to hide.

The charcoal-haired prince walked toward a building with about twenty soldiers trailing him. There was a sign above the door: TELESTATION. He instructed the men to stand outside as he entered. It was where the escorts and guards slept between their shifts. It also served as a place for travelers to eat and drink.

Storshae stepped back out with a key in hand a few minutes later. He handed it to one of the soldiers. "Use this to unlock the shed." He then addressed the rest of them. "Prepare the carriage, fetch the horses grazing, and grab some food suitable for two-days' travel."

General Ossen stood still next to the motionless Olivia as the men scurried away. Meow Meow's eyes were almost as unreadable as hers. Beyond the point of exhaustion, he had given up on being angry. And he wasn't stupid. If he said anything that hinted at sarcasm, Olivia would receive the punishment.

"Two days, sir?" Ossen asked when Storshae returned to the teleplatform.

"We're going to stop at Cosmos, then Shreel, then Rence. It has been too long since I've visited the lesser cities of my kingdom … If you can even call Cosmos a 'lesser city'."

Ossen looked at him uneasily. "You sure are taking your sweet time,

Prince."

"First of all, they're probably just arriving in the Archaic Kingdom through the teleplatforms with smaller units. Then good luck to them in trying to find Itta in that desert. And who's to say that they'll attack us? That could spark a world war. They would risk that just to save one girl?

Ossen said nothing.

"They're likely sending ships into the Archaic Kingdom, but that will take months of travel. Yes, they might try infiltrating our kingdom, but that will take an insurmountable amount of time of planning. They can't just throw soldiers through the teleplatforms when it comes to crossing realms. We'd cut them down in an instant. And they can't use ships because the Dark Realm can't be reached through the Light Realm's river system."

"The whirlpools, sir," Ossen pointed out.

"Those haven't been used in centuries." Storshae grinned wide. "We have plenty of time."

The conversation was interrupted as they were approached by a man with sleek, jet black hair and long, burgundy robes.

"Ah, Tristen," Storshae said.

A pair of black boots appeared in front of Olivia. She gazed up in search of the man's face and instantly recognized him, but not as "Tristen". She was sure it was Vistas—the man she met in the hospital the day after the restaurant collapse. But Vistas was supposed to be a servant of King Vitio.

Tristen looked down at the violet-haired girl. "So this was your objective."

"Sorry we had to keep it a secret from you. Only Fonos, Ossen, and I could know."

Tristen looked away from Olivia without showing any signs of knowing her. She would have expected to see some sort of break in his expression—if even for a split-second.

After finally departing and riding for nearly an hour, the sky grew dark as first-night approached. Storshae peeled back a curtain, examining the sky. "I must get used to the day-night cycle again. After months of being in the Light Realm, I've grown fond of their cycle."

"Ah, yes. I remember it from my days of captivity," Tristen said. "A day would only consist of one long period of light followed by one long period of darkness." He thought about it for a second before continuing: "I suppose I did prefer it to our four periods."

"But the Light Realm doesn't get to see Earth," Ossen said.

Looking toward the blue sphere covered in swirling clouds, Storshae agreed with a smile.

Tristen studied the girl crumpled on the floor and the strange kitten hat resting on her head. She continued to stare at him with a blank expression, and he wondered why she was so interested in him.

They traveled a few leagues further before General Ossen complained of an upset stomach. As the carriage came to a halt, Ossen jumped out with his arm wrapped around himself.

Prince Storshae laughed. "I guess I should use this time to empty the bladder."

"What about her?" Tristen asked as he nodded in Olivia's direction.

"Let her piss herself. She's used to it by now anyways."

Storshae left the carriage, and as friendly banter could be heard outside, Olivia mustered up the effort to talk. "Vistas."

His brow furrowed in disbelief. "Who are you?"

"So you're not Vistas," she said. "You would recognize me if you were."

"Vistas is my brother," he whispered, sitting up intently. "So you know King Vitio?"

"I have not met him personally, but I do know Vistas. He is a nice man."

Tristen smiled. "That he is. We both are."

"My name is Olivia Lavender. I am a member of the Jestivan and served as an honorary guard during the Generals' Battle that Intel King Vitio hosted," she explained in her familiar monotone voice.

"I am a spy for King Vitio," he said as he stared at her beaten and bruised face. "Do not worry."

23

An Unsanctioned Mission

King Vitio sat in the Intel Palace's council room with a group of elderly advisers. Vitio, who was seated at the head of the table, fired off questions one after the other. "How far are our ships from the coast?"

"A few weeks away, sir," a wiry haired man responded.

"Any of the other kingdoms' ships arrive yet?"

"Not yet."

"What about the special forces we sent through the portals? How are they?"

"Intel, Passion, Adren, and Spirit soldiers have been scanning the Archaic Desert since they arrived. They found him early this morning."

"And the whereabouts of that Jestivan girl?"

"He is too weak to answer anything. He was on the very cusp of death when he was found. Major Lars is leading our soldiers into the city, Rim, at the foot of the Archaic Mountains. Adren soldiers are headed to the capital. The other kingdoms are headed to different major cities. We are preparing for complete occupation of their land."

"And what about the Archaic Prince?" Vitio asked.

A balding man offered his reassurance. "He has agreed to cooperate. He understands that there is no use resisting."

The door burst open and a beautiful girl with flowing green hair stormed in.

"Lilu," the king stammered. "You should be in school."

"Urgent news, Father," she announced with a look of purpose. She impatiently stared at the old men around the table while purposely tapping her foot on the ground.

"GET OUT!"

The advisers gathered their paperwork and filed toward the door. Several gave her annoyed glares, which she happily returned in an even more exaggerated fashion.

As the final man closed the door, Lilu wasted no time. "Tristen contacted Vistas."

"With what news?" Vitio quickly asked. "It has been so long."

"To connect with him as soon as possible. Apparently we need to see something, and we need to be ready for it at any moment within the next 24 hours. He can't record until it's safe, so there's no telling exactly when that might be."

Vitio sighed as he rubbed his golden beard. "Get Vistas or Flen then. We need one of them to stay close."

"Vistas!" she shouted behind her.

A slender man with black hair and hollow cheekbones entered the room. "I'm here, milady."

King Vitio chuckled to himself. He had three women in his life, and all three were mirror images of each other in varying degrees. He may have been the king, but they almost made him forget that at times.

For the next several hours, Lilu, King Vitio, and Vistas sat in a private chamber, waiting for Tristen to contact them. Finally, Vistas stood.

"He's ready," he announced. "We will not be able to communicate with him, for I will not be recording."

Vistas's eyes instantly dilated as a holographic display appeared. Lilu closed the curtains and waited for her eyes to adjust to the image's darkness. The Dark Realm was currently two hours into their second-night.

After a few seconds, she began to make out shapes and colors. They were viewing the inside of a carriage as it rattled along. However, the angle was awkward. Everything was turned on its side and their point of view was lower than normal. Also, the image was blurry.

The king squinted at the display. "I guess this is the best he can do?"

"He's trying not to get caught," Lilu said. "He's lying on his side, probably pretending to rest. The blurry narrow picture means he's squinting to hide the burgundy color of his eyes. In fact, he's being stupidly reckless. I thought he'd have something safer in mind."

They only caught a glimpse of Prince Storshae relaxing on the other side of the carriage before Tristen closed his eyes completely, causing the display to become a wall of black. But they could still hear, which was all that mattered.

"Have you spoken with Toono since our arrival yesterday, Prince?"

"I should speak with him when we arrive in Cosmos. However, I believe he's still attending to matters in the Cyn Kingdom."

"He has been there for a while now … like four months."

There was soft laughter. "Killing a royal isn't easy. It involves planning and, most importantly, actually executing the plan."

"He made quick work of the Prim Kingdom's prince. A simple cut of the throat."

"Yes, well, he has a connection that made that an easy job … The rest won't be so easy."

"Aren't you afraid he'll come after you?"

More laughter. "He can't kill me. Unlike everyone else in Kuki Sphaira, I actually know his plan, so he knows I'm prepared for anything. And you forget that this is a two-way street."

"I'm aware."

The voices fell silent, and all they could hear was the carriage bouncing along the ground.

"This is why we can't kill her. Nobody gets what they want if she is dead. The Dev Kingdom, nor Toono, will come out of this satisfied."

"If I recall, Toono didn't want her hurt either."

"Meh, as long as she's alive to serve the purpose, who cares?"

Then Tristen opened his eyes a crack, and to Lilu and Vitio's horror, they saw a battered Olivia curled up on the floor.

"My goodness," Lilu cried. "That's Olivia, father. That's Olivia!"

"Ossen," said a voice in the hologram, "it seems Tristen's stay in this world has come to an end. He is recording us."

Lilu jumped out of her chair. Vitio, although still seated, looked just as horrified.

"Shame, shame," the voice teased.

By this point, Tristen's eyes were wide open and he was now upright. Ossen was furious and no longer seated. A plank of wood ripped away from the carriage's floorboard and hovered in the air. The jagged end pointed directly at Tristen as he, along with Lilu and Vitio, stared his death in the eye.

"Despicable. Helping the Intel family, I imagine. To betray your home kingdom—your home realm—for the kingdom that abducted and enslaved you ... where is the logic?"

Prince Storshae flicked his wrist, and the splintered plank of wood hurtled toward Tristen. The hologram instantly disappeared, and Lilu sobbed. Vitio's face was drained of color. He wanted to do something, but he couldn't wage a war on a Dark Realm kingdom because of a girl. None of the other royal heads would even entertain such a proposal.

He looked at Vistas—a normally impassive man. But the king could have sworn that he saw a subtle hint of anguish cross his face.

"May I be excused?" Vistas asked a little too quietly. "I must inform Flen."

"Of course."

As Vistas exited the room, Lilu exploded. "We need to get Olivia!"

Her father looked down at the floor. "We can't."

"Of course we can!" she shouted. "We're a world power!"

"Your anger is taking control of your intelligent mind, sweetie. You know that's a simplistic view for a complex reality. The other families wouldn't back us on this. She's just one girl."

"We'll do it ourselves," she pleaded.

Vitio embraced his daughter, pressing her head against his brawny chest. "I wish we could."

Lilu sniffled a few times. "What about for the sake of stopping their plan? She is the key."

"A plan we know nothing about."

"Olivia is the reason why I'm alive. She carried me out of that restaurant. She is my captain, and I owe her a huge debt."

"And Bryson ...?"

She shook her head. "That was a lie—my lie, mind you—and I apologize. He and Himitsu helped their own teammate, Rhyparia."

Vitio studied his daughter's face as a plan crossed his mind. "That Himitsu boy I met in the suite, bring him to the palace tomorrow."

*   *   *

Four o'clock approached as a hooded Bryson strolled between the fountains of the palace's front courtyard. His pace slowed when he noticed it wasn't Shelly waiting for him at the front door. "Hello, Vitio."

It wasn't the welcoming that Bryson was used to. "Bryson ... how was school?"

"Besides the fact that Lilu was truant, it went well. Trained as a unit today—all the Jestivan together. It was a valuable session that we never get, so it's a shame she missed it." Bryson looked around the courtyard. "Where's Shelly?"

"I told her to take the day off," Vitio said. He looked up the palace's walls. "But I assume she's snooping up there, spying out one of the windows. As for Lilu, she had unexpected matters to attend to here."

"I crossed paths with her just an hour ago at Telejunction. She looked so distraught and didn't say one word to me."

Vitio stared at him for a moment before turning toward the garden. Bryson followed.

"Remember when you asked me if Flen and Vistas were twins?"

Bryson nodded. "And you said 'let's go with that.'"

Vitio sighed. "They're actually triplets. They have—or had—a third brother."

"And what happened to him?"

"He died today at the hands of Dev Prince Storshae. Five years ago, when it was decided that I had to send most of my Dev slaves back to their kingdom, some of them didn't want to leave. We allowed them to stay. Although they were not made citizens, we agreed to pay them a wage. In this group was a set of triplets: Vistas, Flen, and Tristen. Originally, all three were to stay here in the palace. However, a very impressive mind changed that plan, realizing the opportunity we had. We could send one back as a spy."

"And whose plan was that?" Bryson asked.

"Lilu."

"*Lilu?* She couldn't have been more than twelve years old."

Vitio gazed down at the boy. "That should not surprise you. Lilu is one of the sharpest minds in our kingdom."

Realizing he had insulted the king's daughter, Bryson quickly apologized. Vitio brought the focus back to the intended topic. "Typically the people of the Dev Kingdom cannot link their Dev Energy in order to broadcast between realms, but blood relations are an exception. The closer the relation, the more effective the communication can be."

"So by sending one of the triplets, you had a flawless means of communication between the Dark and Light Realms."

"Exactly," Vitio replied. "We sent Tristen back home while Vistas and Flen stayed here. His job was to be a spy, which nobody would ever expect … A man choosing to betray his home kingdom for the people who enslaved him? Absurd."

"Nobody knew he was a triplet?" Bryson asked.

"Not anyone in the capital. He'd go unrecognized as long as he stayed away from his hometown of Tames."

"So how was he discovered?"

They took a left and stepped between two towering hedges that stretched for a long while. Vitio lowered his voice considerably. "He was recording information for us. He was caught in the act by Prince Storshae. Lilu, Vistas, and I witnessed his death."

Bryson stopped in his tracks, now understanding Lilu's deflated demeanor.

"That's not it," Vitio said even more sternly. He leaned in close as they stared each other in the eyes. "What is Olivia to you?"

Bryson's heart raced. "She's my best friend and the only person I can fully trust. She has been in my life since we were six. Do you have news?"

"Yes, it's the information he died trying to give to us."

"What is it?" Bryson pressed.

"She's not in good condition. I assume she has gone through months of abuse. She's currently in a carriage with the Dev Prince."

The young Intel Jestivan stared at his king with an empty rage. The thoughts that came to his mind were too fast and jumbled for him to even try making a coherent sentence.

"Are you willing to risk your life for her?"

"Yes," Bryson answered, more certain than he had ever been in his life.

*   *   *

The next morning, Bryson was slumped on the top floor of the Lilac Suites. As his head tipped to the side for the hundredth time, the door jarred open, causing him to snap his head back into the wall with a thud.

"I'm so sorry, Bryson!"

"It's okay, Jilly," he groaned, rubbing the back of his skull.

"What are you doing here?" She bounced on her toes. "Do you want to get some coffee? Coffee gets me going!"

By some miracle, Bryson cracked a smile. "No, thank you. I'm good," he said. "But we can go down to the lobby and talk while you have some."

Jilly beamed. "One-on-one time with my captain? Let's go!"

Bryson weakly smirked at the thought of her needing coffee. She ran down the stairs with a hand sliding down each rail. The squeaking from the friction pierced the quiet early-morning lobby. Besides the barkeep, the lobby was empty, but that would change soon.

After grabbing a seat, Bryson stared at the piano while he waited for Jilly. As scrambled as his life had become, he hadn't played in what seemed like forever.

Jilly took a seat at the table and sipped from her mug. "How are you?" she asked.

"Nervous."

Her face softened. "They will be okay. We'll get everyone back."

Bryson decided to cut straight to it. "I will be entering the Dark Realm today."

A spitting sound echoed inside her mug as her eyes widened. "*What?*"

"Olivia is there, and King Vitio is allowing me to go. He told me to ask whichever Jestivan I wanted to help, so I've decided to ask my team."

Jilly curiously gazed at her captain, but didn't say anything.

"It's your choice," Bryson said. "You don't need to be told that you'd be risking your life."

"Olivia is a fellow Jestivan," she said. "When do we head out?"

"Four o'clock. This gives you the rest of the morning and early afternoon to do something else for me." He gave her an uneasy look.

"What's that?"

"Convince Toshik," Bryson begged.

Her face brightened with an evil smile. "If I'm going somewhere that puts me in danger, he's going to go too. That's just how it works with him. Don't worry."

"One more thing," Bryson added. "When you say goodbye to Yama — and I know you will—lie to her. Tell her we're going on a fun trip somewhere in order to rebuild our team's morale."

Jilly gave her kingdom's salute and yelled a hearty, "Yes, sir!"

*   *   *

Students in the bustling cafeteria forked down plates of food in preparation for the second half of the school day. Windows stretching from the floor to the ceiling lined the two side walls, and sunlight blanketed the stone surfaces. Four red drapes hung on both the back and front walls, each adorning the Passion Kingdom's emblem of fire.

It was loud, as students anticipated the weekend that was only a few hours away. But there was one anomaly in the crowded room. An eighteen-year-old Jestivan sat at the far end of one of the corner tables. The closest person to him was five chairs down. His cheek rested in his palm as he lazily bit into a slice of bread. A few thin strands of black hair had fallen in front of his eyes.

The same topics ran amuck in Himitsu's mind: his parents' whereabouts, Olivia's imprisonment by Archaic King Itta, Rhyparia's coma, and the lives of his fellow Passion Assassins, who were being held prisoner by Passion King Damian.

While staring aimlessly ahead, Himitsu noticed the conversations around him die down into mumbling and whispering. He followed the eyes of his fellow students to the cafeteria's main entrance. A beautiful girl with a flower attached to her green hair stood at the entrance.

Lilu briskly walked over to him, ignoring the trailing stares of the students. She cupped her hand around his ear. "If you want to save Olivia, come with me," she whispered.

Himitsu's chair toppled backward as he sprung from his seat. He grabbed his blazing red coat and chased after her, itching for the opportunity to finally lay one of his worries to rest.

*　　　*　　　*

The clock had just struck noon as Bryson arrived at the door of the Grand Director's office. He was to meet with Debo, who had been occupying Poicus's office while he was away. This was the final and most crucial part of the plan before departing from Phesaw. Lying was something Bryson could normally do on a whim, but with Debo, it was a lot more difficult. He took a deep breath before entering the room.

Debo was seated at the desk with an open book in front of him. He looked up. Although his expression remained undisturbed, his tone hinted at surprise. "Bryson … hey."

Bryson shut the door and took a seat in front of the desk. "What are you reading?"

"A biography."

"Yikes." Bryson smirked. "You must be bored. Who about?"

Debo laughed. "It's actually interesting. I find myself shaking my head at the absurdity of some of the stuff in here." He held up the book so Bryson could see the cover: *Ataway Kawi: The Third of Five*.

Bryson arched an eyebrow. "*That* fairy tale? I'll admit it was one of my favorite childhood stories."

"You always asked me to read it to you … almost every night." Debo smiled at the memory. "You'd run into my room, eyes wide with excitement, jump on the bed, and shove the book in my hands. 'Debo, Debo! Read me *The Turd of Five*!'" He laughed. "You couldn't pronounce 'third.' It was always 'turd.'"

Bryson doubled over with laughter. But another part of him was cringing. Debo wasn't making this easy.

"But we never got to the end," Debo said once Bryson had regained his composure. "You always fell asleep on my chest before learning why Ataway was a hero."

"I assume it's the same as every other fairy tale. The hero wins along with a happy ending."

Debo continued studying the boy who was practically his son. "That does seem to be the common theme of fairy tales." He placed the book on the desk. "I won't pretend like I expected a visit from you. Why did you—"

"I'm sorry." Bryson cut him off. Just a few minutes ago, that would have been a lie. But now Bryson wasn't sure. Another long silence followed as they stared at each other.

"I'm sorry too. I know how much Olivia means to you, but it's not only me who can't afford to lose you. There are eight other Jestivan who need you."

"I understand that," Bryson said. "That's why I'm going to spend the weekend with my team instead of going home. Kind of like the beginning of the school year when I stayed in the Lilac Suites during our first break."

"Great!" Debo beamed, ripping a hole in Bryson's stomach. "What are you going to do?"

Bryson looked off to the side. "Jilly talked about camping in Phesaw Park for one of the nights." He quickly thought of another lie. "Toshik said he'd teach me how to pick up girls."

"Sounds like fun!"

A loud knock came from the door, causing Bryson to flinch. The excitement was wiped from Debo's face as he looked at the door. "You have fun this weekend. I have a guest who doesn't like waiting."

Bryson stared at Debo before getting up. He made sure to take in every feature, every memory. He smiled weakly at the man who raised him before turning to walk out. As he reached for the handle, he was stopped in his tracks.

"I love you, Bry."

Bryson paused, staring at his distorted reflection on the brass handle. There was fear in his eyes. Another knock shook the door. Bryson turned to look at Debo, careful to rid the fright from his face. He smiled before turning the handle and exiting the room.

The moment he was in the hallway, his eyes glazed over. As he wiped his cheeks, he looked up at the person who had been knocking. He or she was fully concealed in a brown traveler's cloak. Not one inch of skin was visible. The hood, which was tattered at the hem, hung low over the person's face.

The person pushed past him, causing their shoulders to collide. Instantly, Bryson heard a woman's gut-wrenching scream inside his head as a frostbitten cold shot through his entire body. It lasted for close to three seconds.

When the moment finally passed, Bryson gasped for breath as if he had just surfaced from an ice-capped lake. A white cloud of cold air escaped as he exhaled.

He turned around to see the person had paused at the door with their back facing him. The figure didn't turn around, but Bryson knew that he or she had felt something too. Then the cloaked person walked into the office and slammed the door shut. Bryson continued to stare in bewilderment as he debated what had just happened. But he was running low on time. He sprinted away, ignoring the shouts of anger from within the office.

*　　*　　*

Bryson, Jilly, and Toshik walked up the front steps of Dunami Hospital. It was time to pay a visit to their friend and teammate, Rhyparia. Toshik had tried to talk them out of this, but he had no choice. Where Jilly went, he would follow.

"We'll be quick," Bryson assured him. "We still have almost two hours before we're supposed to depart."

"We have to look at the bright side of things," Jilly said. "Perhaps while we're away, Rhyparia will wake up! And when we come back, she'll be waiting for us!"

"Maybe," Bryson said with a smile as they entered the ICU. Toshik's face soured as he looked around the room full of nurses and doctors scrambling in every direction.

"Not a fan of hospitals?" Bryson asked.

Toshik cringed at the sight of a nurse holding a huge needle. "This is stupid. She won't even know that we're here."

"You don't know that. And it's good to support our teammate."

"And what do you know about that?" Toshik snarled. "Some captain you are. You spend all your time crying. Or trying to screw Lilu."

Bryson's face stiffened. "You can stay for all I care." He stormed away and headed straight for Rhyparia's room. He paused to regain his composure before opening the door. Once calm, he pushed it open and looked at the bed … it was empty.

Bryson hurriedly walked to the center desk where Jilly was scolding Toshik. "Which room is Rhyparia located in?" he asked a nurse.

"She awoke three days ago … and was discharged two days ago," the man explained.

"By who?!"

The nurse's brow creased with irritation. "There is this thing called confidentiality, young man."

Bryson stormed out of the hospital, forcing his teammates to chase after him. "What's wrong?" Jilly asked.

"Rhyparia's been discharged."

"Where is she?"

"I don't know, but there's nothing we can do about it. We need to get to the palace."

"Is she okay?"

"I don't know," Bryson quietly said. The hospital wouldn't release her to a stranger. But what if they'd handed her over to her parents?

Once they arrived at the palace, Bryson sped through the outer courtyard and up a staircase. Jilly and Toshik straggled behind, taking in the beautifully manicured gardens and lawn.

"Hurry up," Bryson called down to them. "You'll get lost."

Bryson took a route he had never taken before, down a corridor to a door that opened to a spiraling stone staircase. Prior to today, the door had always been bolted shut with a huge lock. He walked down into the blackness. It was a bit creepy.

He reached the bottom and called out, "Hello?" A candle ignited, exposing the faces of Lilu and King Vitio.

"Punctual. Very good," Lilu said.

There wasn't anything royal about the room. No gold, silver, or marble composed any of the structure. Crude, uneven stone sat beneath their feet and surfaced the walls. The depths of the room couldn't be seen, for the flickering light of the candle waned before reaching that far.

"Where is Himitsu?." Bryson asked.

"In the Dev Kingdom. He left three hours ago with Vistas."

Bryson gaped. "He went alone?"

"He had to go first. He has the appropriate skillset needed," Vitio explained. "Don't fret. He did his job. Vistas contacted us just an hour ago. They are both alive and waiting for you three."

Lilu snapped her head around. "*Three?*"

"Yes, three. You aren't going anywhere," Vitio said firmly.

"Yes I am!"

"Actually, no you're not." This time, it was Bryson who said so.

"And what gives you that authority?" Lilu demanded with a threatening look in her eyes.

"Your father told me to choose which Jestivan to take with me. And I chose my team. I'm not putting you or any other members of Olivia's team at risk. That is not my right to do. Add on the fact that your ribs still aren't fully healed and it's an easy call."

She held her ground. "I don't care."

"I do," said a voice from the dark staircase. "As your big sister, I will literally restrain you from getting on that teleplatform."

Lilu's eyes darted between Bryson and Shelly. Too angry to respond, she stormed up the stairs and out of sight. "That went about just as expected," Shelly said as she reached the bottom of the stairs.

King Vitio shook his head. "She'll regret not saying goodbye."

The princess smirked at Toshik, who returned the gesture.

"Nice to meet you, milady," Toshik said with a gracious bow.

She playfully ignored him and looked at Bryson. "Don't die," she said.

Bryson smiled. It felt good to know that Shelly cared ... even if it was in a morbid kind of way.

"Enough pleasantries," Vitio said. "It's four o'clock—just two hours left of the Dark Realm's second-night." He stepped to the side as a ring of intelights sparked to life behind him. They revealed a teleplatform—a rather makeshift one constructed of wood.

"This is a secret teleplatform that Mendac built. You can port out, but not back in." The three Jestivan stepped on. "Perks of once having the Fifth of Five as your general."

"We're ready," Bryson said, gripping onto one of the support beams. He gave it an uneasy look as it wobbled in his hand.

"If you need to contact me, go through Vistas," Vitio said. "We have Flen. Please, be smart and stay safe."

"We'll be great, Mr. King!" Jilly said.

Vitio smiled as the platform picked up rotational speed. Princess Shelly gave an ironic little wave. Everything became a blur, and Bryson caught a glimpse of a somber Lilu standing at the foot of the staircase.

Slowly, Bryson regained his bearings. It was night, and the only light came from the stars and moons. The three Jestivan hesitantly stepped off the teleplatform, and not a second passed before Jilly screamed.

"What is it?" Toshik asked.

She looked down and gasped. "A body."

As Bryson's eyes adjusted to the darkness, he realized that that was hardly the only one. Corpses—roughly twenty of them—were scattered in the grass. Who had done this?

"About time." They all jumped at the sound. They turned and saw a lanky young man with silky black hair casually sitting in the tall grass, staring up at the night sky.

Jilly jumped on him and gave him the friendliest of hugs. "*Himitsu!*"

24

Pursuit

It was a little past four P.M., less than two hours until the Dark Realm's second-day. Jilly and Vistas were outside preparing for their journey. There wasn't much time, as the teleplatform would reopen at six.

Bryson, Himitsu, and Toshik were inside Telestation, sitting at the bar. On the other side was a teenager in an apron, his face white with terror.

"Why didn't you kill him?" Toshik asked. "He could rat us out."

"He's just a civilian," Himitsu said. "An unable. He can't tap into his energy. From what he told me, they are treated quite poorly here."

Toshik snorted. "Soft," he said.

"Five of the men I killed out there were on their knees as they begged to surrender," Himitsu said, his voice carefully even. "I will do whatever it takes to complete this mission. If he's not working when the teleplatform reopens, they'll quickly figure out that we've attacked. Besides, he has information he can tell you." Himitsu got up from the bar and walked outside. "I'll be cleaning up out there."

The young bartender pointed at the map. "This is the land of the Dev Kingdom. As you can see, there are two routes from the teleplatform to the capital. King Storshae has taken the long way—due west, toward Cosmos. He's announced a tour of that city, as well as Shreel and Rence."

"What's the Region of Demons?" Toshik asked.

"Precisely what it implies."

Toshik smirked. "So you mean to tell me it's a region … of demons?"

"Yes," the boy said, with a hint of annoyance in his voice. "It will serve you well if the prince is alerted to your presence here."

"So if he tries to cross through, he'll be attacked … by *demons*?" Toshik mockingly asked.

"No. You can't get in and they can't get out," the boy explained. "You'll see what I mean."

"So we'll cut Storshae off at Rence," Bryson said. "Easy enough."

"Maybe not," the boy said.

Bryson's eyes narrowed. "Elaborate."

"King Storshae could risk crossing through Necrosis Valley."

Toshik laughed. "'Necrosis'? These names, man."

The server's face became grave. "It's not a laughing matter."

"How many men does he have with him?" Bryson asked.

"General Ossen, a major, a lieutenant, two corporals, and roughly fifteen lower ranks."

And his Bewahr, Bryson thought as he rose from his seat. He looked at the boy and extended his hand. "Thank you."

Bryson walked outside and gazed around the field that showed no signs of a battle. "What did you do with the bodies?" he asked Himitsu, who was throwing a sack of supplies over a white horse's back.

"Threw 'em off the Edge."

Bryson looked beyond the teleplatform, where he could see the ground suddenly stop. Cliffs that fell into the infinity of empty space ran around the perimeter of the floating island. In the Light Realm's kingdoms, one couldn't get too close because the Edge was gated off and heavily secured, but it seemed as if the kingdoms of the Dark Realm didn't bother with such precautions—or at least the Dev Kingdom didn't.

Himitsu walked up to the horse and patted the saddle. "Get on," he said to Jilly.

She smiled and hopped onto the horse's back. "Pony!"

Toshik and Himitsu were still practically eye-level with Jilly, but Bryson had to crane his neck upward.

"It's a Hackney—not a pony," Toshik said.

She brushed some falling hairs behind her left ear and stuck out her tongue. "Anything that has four legs, hooves, a long hairy tail, and a long nose is a pony."

Bryson laughed. "You can't beat that logic."

Himitsu grabbed a few bags and handed them around.

"I don't think so." Toshik rudely pushed the bag into Himitsu's chest.

Himitsu shoved it back harder with a cold look. "Either you do or we will leave your ass to rot, and if you choose to follow us, we'll beat you senseless until you're unable to follow."

Toshik returned his gaze for a few seconds—as if he was sizing him up—before reluctantly throwing the bag over his shoulder.

They departed from the station and headed southwest toward Rence. The road was a rather narrow trail between the tall prairie grass. Bryson and Himitsu led the way with Jilly and her horse a few yards behind. Vistas walked beside her and Toshik took the rear, instinctively keeping his eyes peeled for any sort of danger to his Charge. The sun had partially risen, and golden rays shone against the tails of Jilly's blond hair. Most of her head was shaded by her large sunhat.

"Stop!" she shouted.

They looked at her as she dangled her feet before jumping to the ground. She reached into the brown sack hanging against the horse's ribs and pulled out a green apple. She gave it to the horse and caressed its mane before struggling to climb back on the saddle.

Himitsu scowled. "We're not stopping every ten minutes for you to feed it an apple."

Bryson scanned the ground ahead of them, still seeing nothing but rolling hills of thick grass swaying in the breeze. "I suppose we can jog for a bit. It would cut the trip into only a day or two's worth of travel time."

"Yes, run!" Jilly said. "I don't want to sleep in a tent."

"You're starting to sound like Lilu," Himitsu sighed. Bryson smiled at the accurate comparison.

So they jogged while Jilly shouted "Giddy up!" and "Hee-yaw!" as her horse trotted beneath her.

Before long, a strikingly tall structure rose into the sky ahead of them. When they got closer, they saw that it was a sturdy black gate with bars too narrow to squeeze through. They slowed their pace to a walk as they looked up, searching for its pinnacle with no success. The clouds swallowed it. Across the gate, the prairie grass had been replaced with scattered shrubbery and trees, but mostly the hard crust of the land.

Toshik's voice carried from the back of the pack: "The Region ... of *Demons!* Dun, dun, dunnnn."

The moment Toshik's sarcastic remark concluded, a hair-raising roar scattered birds from the treetops and shook the ground beneath their feet. Jilly fell off her horse from shock.

"What would you call that? A rabbit?" Himitsu cracked.

Bryson would have laughed, but he just wanted to get away. Beyond that fence was where Thusia must have died to save his father's life some 25 years ago. His stomach was doing flips.

Vistas hadn't said much—not that anybody tried to force him to. They understood how difficult this must be for him. One of his identical brothers died and now he was in the kingdom he once called home.

They made it through the rest of second-day fairly easily—a couple of bathroom breaks, a few friendly hellos to people they passed, and the all-too-frequent hiccups to feed the horse an apple. Jilly had named it Bobuel—a mixture of Bob and Samuel. She thought the fusion was clever, but no matter how many times she said it, it never sounded less silly. Bryson and Himitsu would break into a fit of laughter every time they heard it.

As midnight passed, second-day ended and first-night began. They camped in a forest a few hundred yards from the trail. While Jilly, Toshik, and Vistas slept inside the tent, Bryson and Himitsu sat next to the dying fire, whose light reflected in the canopy above.

"It's truly amazing how she can manage to make us smile at a time like this," Himitsu said.

"The directors were right. The first lesson they tried to teach us was that each of us was important in our own special way." Bryson glanced at the tent. "She's the one who never needed that lesson in the first place." He paused for a second before adding, "Much like Thusia was for the original Jestivan."

Himitsu grimaced. "But why Toshik? What is his purpose?"

Bryson's smile faded. "He's skillful. However, his main purpose is probably to protect Jilly. The directors realize he'd die for her, and she's too important to die. She keeps us going."

"You're right. Sounds like Thusia."

"That's exactly what she is." Bryson poked at the fire with a stick. "When Thusia died, so did the Jestivan. Mendac's love wasn't enough to protect her. So the directors took a different track this time, hoping Toshik's sense of duty is enough to protect Jilly."

Himitsu sprawled out on his back and stared at the cloud-covered Earth in the black sky. "What is stronger in holding together the glue of the group—A.K.A. Jilly? They found out it wasn't love, so now they test out duty."

Realizing Toshik's role, the inky-haired Jestivan rolled on his side to look at his captain. "That's strange," Himitsu teased. "You sounded just like Agnos for a second there."

Bryson's appreciative smile flickered in the firelight. "Thank you."

Himitsu pushed himself off the matted grass and let out a massive yawn. "I'm gonna try to get some sleep. Wake me when it's my turn to keep watch."

Bryson gave a nod. "Good night."

*   *   *

A dorm room door in the Lilac Suites slammed shut as an aggravated young woman prepared to wind down for the night. Her makeup was flawless and her lips a light pink, which was odd for a girl who always rejected the image of a delicate lady. But it was worth it for what was supposed to be a night of fun with one of her favorite people in the world. Her plans, however, had fallen through. Jilly hadn't shown.

She yanked the flowers from her elegant bun, and her violet hair crashed down her back. She undid her bra, pulled it through her sleeve, and angrily tossed it across the room. She followed its path as it landed on her pillow, where a piece of parchment caught her eye. Picking it up and unfolding it, her eyes widened when she saw Jilly's handwriting.

Dear beautiful, scary, too serious, alcoholic, voluptuous (Agnos taught me that word), back-talking, feisty (as Toshik always says), and absolutely perfect Yama,

I'm hoping you won't read this until you arrive back at the suites late at night after realizing I was going to be a no-show to our little dinner date … And by that time, I should be far away. But I will be back!

Bryson decided to take our team on a getaway trip. With everything that has happened, we want to rekindle (Agnos is so smart!) our relationships. It should only be a few days over the weekend, which is why we left on a Friday. This way, the directors won't find our absence disturbing. Oh! Which reminds me …

Don't tell the directors. K? K. I miss you already as I write this, so by the time you're reading this, just know I'm dying of not being able to spend time with you. If you're wondering why I didn't just tell you this in person, it's because I would have cried like a baby, and then you would have called me a clingy, pathetic little girl because you wouldn't have been drunk enough to say what you're really feeling.

And that's another reason why I hope you're reading this at the end of the night. I suppose you had a few drinks alone while you waited for me, so I know you're reading this and thinking, "Oh, I miss you too, silly Jilly!"

Or you're completely sober and reading with a scowl … Either way, I'll see you soon!

LoooOOOoooOOOoooOOOoooove,

Jilly!

P.S. I put this on your pillow because, no matter how many times, I know exactly where your bra lands when you toss it away at the end of the night. And I say this with the biggest, most exaggerated wink.

Yama smiled. She *was* a bit tipsy.

* * *

After a couple days of speedy travel, Vistas, Toshik, Jilly, and an exhausted Bryson and Himitsu—who had been alternating shifts of guard duty while the group slept—saw a gap in the trees ahead. They stepped into the sunlight of second-day as they passed the final trees. It was nine P.M. on Sunday, and they had made excellent time.

The small town of Rence lay in front of them. Buildings reached no higher than two stories and the roads were dirt. Bryson couldn't help but imagine how many towns of this size could fit into Dunami—*probably 40*.

"Hopefully the women aren't as ugly as the town," Toshik said as they walked through a street flanked by rickety houses.

Bryson and Himitsu didn't react, having learned to ignore his shallow remarks. Jilly, however, pegged him in the back with an apple she was eating. They were looking for the tavern that the young bartender at Telestation had told them about. As they reached an intersection of another dirt road, they turned the corner to see a building with three carriages, several horses, and scattered packs of people outside of it. Rowdy noises carried down the street. It was strange to see such nightlife while the sun was still shining, but it was approaching ten o'clock, so it made a certain sort of sense.

Toshik smiled for the first time in days. "See ya!" he yelled, bolting toward the tavern at his highest speed percentage.

"He's an idiot," Bryson said flatly. "Does he even realize that those carriages and horses are draped in burgundy? There are Dev soldiers in there … or worse, Storshae."

"Storshae can't be there," Himitsu said. "One, he couldn't have made it here yet, and two, I doubt he would be in the mood."

Bryson gave it some thought. "I don't think he knows who we are anyways." After thinking about it a little while longer, he finally made up his mind. "Alright then, let's go in and take a look."

As Himitsu helped Jilly dismount and tied her horse to a wooden pole, he saw that Bryson was correct. There were soldiers everywhere. Most of them mingled with each other, while others rudely advanced on uninterested women.

Bryson was expecting to receive judgmental glares as he walked inside, but nobody even took a second glance. Back home, if a sixteen-year-old walked into a bar, it would be frowned upon. But here, no one seemed to care.

Vulgarity was tossed around like the cheapest whore in a brothel. Men drunkenly laughed in groups as they dug into different meats. Hard liquor sat at every table and lewdly dressed women were scattered throughout. This type of scene would definitely not be approved in Dunami's taverns.

Unlike in the Intel Kingdom, there was no steel here. All the architecture was wood. The windows were tiny squares, and the glass inside was almost as filthy as the stone floor they were standing on. A drunken band of men in the corner played various string instruments that looked like they had been dragged over rocks for centuries. A few men and women danced in front of them, and one woman's dress was caught in her knee-high hosiery's buckle.

But Toshik stood out most of all. The lanky, 6'6" swordsman circulated among the tables with a mug of beer in his hand, laughing and conversing with people like he had lived in this town his whole life. He was doing a great job of providing a cover—though he surely wasn't thinking of it that way.

A server walked past with a tray of beers raised above his head. Himitsu swiped one and took a sip. "One won't hurt," he said through a smirk. "Now, let's do some snooping."

Bryson scanned the packed expanse. He needed leads on Storshae. He saw four heads in the far corner behind a low wall. Unlike the rest of the crowd, they appeared to be in control of their actions. An empty booth sat in front of the wall, so Bryson motioned for Himitsu, Jilly, and Vistas to follow him over.

Before Bryson took a seat, he looked across the divider to see sober faces. One of the men quickly met his eyes. He was young and strong with a perfectly edged goatee of deep black. The man's eyes widened as he stared at the young Jestivan, but he didn't say anything. He simply dropped his gaze back to the soldiers he was seated with.

Bryson slid into the booth, wondering why the soldier reacted that way. Did they know who the Jestivan were and what they looked like? If that were the case, wouldn't they be fighting for their lives right now.

"What's wrong?" Himitsu asked.

"I think one of them recognized me," he whispered.

"Impossible!" Jilly shouted.

Himitsu snapped his hand over Jilly's mouth with a look of disbelief. "Careful!"

A calm voice made itself heard for the first time all night. "I think I'll go find us a room," Vistas said.

Bryson nodded.

It was hard to hear what the men across the divider were discussing. They seemed to be talking about their families and home. Bryson listened for several minutes before he heard something of value:

"It'll be nice to have the king back," one of the men said from the other side of the wall.

"Tell me about it. His advisers have made a botch of things."

"He never should have left in the first place. What if he had been killed? He has no children."

"Have faith. He'll return to the capital soon."

"How much longer?"

"Not long. He's in Shreel, or so I've heard."

The group fell silent for a few seconds. "Then something's got him spooked. He's not the type of man to rush when he doesn't have to."

"Well, if he's still in Shreel, we have plenty of time to make it back to the capital before he does. He won't even know that we were here."

"Not as much time as you'd think. I heard he's going to cut through Necrosis Valley."

"What?!"

"Like I said—he's spooked."

"Then we must leave tonight."

"No need to panic. He won't be leaving Shreel for at least a day. He has to allow his group time to mentally prepare for such a journey."

"Room 207."

Bryson and Himitsu jumped, startled from their eavesdropping. It was Vistas.

Bryson slid out of the booth, satisfied. His group had at least two days of rest before heading west to cut Storshae off in Necrosis Valley.

Jilly also decided to call it a day, but Himitsu stayed in the bar to have a couple more beers—and keep an eye on Toshik.

Vistas unlocked the door to a rather dingy room. There were two twin-sized beds, and to their surprise, a bathroom. It even had faucets. It was a mystery how such a poor and tiny town could have indoor plumbing.

"A shower!" Jilly shouted before darting in and slamming the bathroom door closed.

"I'm going to go to sleep," Vistas said in a dull, empty voice. He curled up on a mass of blankets that he had laid out on the ground. Bryson plopped onto the stiff bed with a wince. He allowed his mind to wander with the pattering of the shower water as a backdrop. He thought about his all-too-frequent dream—sitting underneath a cherry blossom, staring at Phesaw's campus below. He thought about the two mysterious messages he had received in the past three months from—what he could only explain as—the illusion of an unknown woman …

When the time is right …

Which is almost in sight …

It was so cryptic, but there had to be a reason for that. Stressing about it helped nothing. If he hadn't come up with an answer by now, he never would. So he allowed sleep to creep upon him.

A few hours passed, and the tavern finally was quiet. It was two A.M.— two hours into first-night—and the room of the Jestivan was bathed in moonlight.

Jilly slept in a bed to herself, Bryson and Himitsu occupied the other, and an inebriated Toshik was passed out on the floor in a puddle of his own drool, his limbs awkwardly splayed in all directions.

The door unlocked.

Being the light sleeper that he was, Bryson lazily opened his eyes at the sound of the door unlatching. He closed his eyes again, attributing the noise to his imagination.

Then the door creaked as it opened.

Bryson sprung out of bed. Standing in the doorway was the soldier who had stared at him in the bar. He instantly bolted toward the man with a punch readied. This foot soldier had made a grave mistake by trying to confront the Jestivan—

Or not. Not only was the man prepared for Bryson's speed, he had the strength and reflexes to catch his punch. Bryson followed with a kick, but that was blocked by the soldier's forearm. Black flames erupted where the man had been standing, but he dodged it with a simple side-step. By this point, everyone in the room was awake except for Toshik.

"Stop it," the man snapped. "I know your methods of fighting."

What kind of infantryman is this? Bryson wondered. "And how would you know that?"

The man didn't answer. Instead his face and body morphed into someone else, causing jaws to drop around the room.

Lines began crowding his face, and his skin tone lightened from tan to pale. His hairline crept backward, revealing more of his forehead and scalp. His black goatee transformed into a long pure white beard. Then there was the most notable feature—eyebrows sprouted until they hung in tails down the sides of his face.

It was Grand Director Poicus.

25

Debonicus

Jilly hopped up and down. "That was so awesome, Grand Di—"

She was cut short by a chorus of hushes. There was no end to her cluelessness. Some people in the tavern might not have known the Jestivan by name, but they definitely knew who Grand Director Poicus was.

"After not seeing the lot of you for so long, I would typically display my excitement with a fit of warming pleasantries," Poicus said quietly. "But I must say these weren't the circumstances I had envisioned. What are you doing down here?"

"Rescuing Olivia," Bryson said, not bothering to lie.

Poicus sighed. "I should have known. I suppose your plan is to take on Prince Storshae, his general, and his Bewahr—a Gefal?"

Bryson didn't respond. The Grand Director gazed at all of their faces, then landed on a man lying awake on the floor on the far side of the room. A look of understanding graced his face. "Vistas," he mumbled. "The directors would not have sent you on this journey. King Vitio sent you."

No one spoke.

"It's too late to get in touch with the directors," Poicus continued, "but at the break of first-day's dawn, we will have a sit-down with ..." His voice trailed off as footsteps sounded outside the door.

The Grand Director morphed back into the young soldier as the door swung open. A Dev soldier stared at his comrade with a skeptical look.

"It was getting late," the man said. "I heard noises, so I came to take a look." He studied the faces in the room and then looked at the disguised Poicus. "Why are you in a roomful of children in the middle of the night?"

Poicus staggered and slumped against the wall. "Wrong room? I was wondering what they were doing here."

The man rolled his eyes and grabbed Poicus's arm. "Let's go, dimwit."

The door slammed shut. "Repack and get ready," Bryson said. "We're heading west within the hour. If we stay, Director Poicus will be dragging us back to the Light Realm by morning." He looked at the passed out Toshik. "Wake your buddy up," he said to Jilly.

*   *   *

At eight A.M., a distressed Poicus was standing in an abandoned building in the outskirts of Rence. He was accompanied by a pale brunette woman.

"Get in touch with your son, so we can broadcast," the director commanded as horses neighed and men shouted in the distance. "And make sure Debo is with him. He'll be wondering why half the Jestivan aren't showing up for school."

After a couple minutes, her right eye turned burgundy while her left eye dilated and projected a hologram. Debo was sitting in an office that looked rather familiar.

"Is that my office?" Poicus asked.

Debo smiled. "Makes me feel important." Then he registered the look on Poicus's face. "What's wrong?"

"Do you know where Bryson's team has been the past few days?"

"Trying to mend bonds. I think they went camping." Debo's face clouded. "Oh."

"That's right. They're here, at a tavern in Rence. Vistas is with them."

"Vistas?!" Debo repeated. "So Vitio's behind this. Get them out of there. I'm not losing four Jestivan to try to save one." The volume of his voice was controlled, but the aggression was unmistakable.

"About that," Poicus said carefully. "They're gone. By the time I was able to get away this morning, their room was deserted."

Poicus winced as Debo slammed his fist into the desk. "What was that fool thinking?" the Intel Director muttered. "He'll get his, I swear it."

"I don't know what to do," Poicus said. "I think they may be headed west, but I can't leave my unit."

It took a minute for Debo to respond. "You continue the task I asked of you. Follow your fleet to the Dev capital. Make sure that he's really dead."

"And the Jestivan?"

"I'll take care of it," Debo said in a tone that sent chills down Poicus's spine.

The broadcast cut off, and Debo instantly formulated the steps he needed to take before crossing realms. There was no time to waste, but he knew how important it was to pace his energy.

First stop was Passion Director Venustas.

Debo headed toward the Emotion Wing while effortlessly weaving through Phesaw's halls. Students stood dumbfounded as their books were blown from their grasp by sudden gusts of wind. To their eyes, there was no cause.

Debo barged into Venustas's office without knocking. She didn't jump at the intrusion, but her eyes widened as she stared at her guest while brushing her hair. "Director De—"

"Talk to the Dev servant," Debo said, cutting her off. "He'll explain. I'm leaving for a while."

"Why?" she asked. "What is this about?"

"I apologize, but time is of the essence. Just do what I ask of you. Hopefully, I'll be back." He paused and stared at her before saying, "Good bye."

Without waiting for a response, he disappeared. He exited Phesaw and ran to Telejunction, where he ordered an escort to commandeer him a teleplatform at once. The young man wisely obliged.

When Debo arrived in the Intel Kingdom, he hopped off the platform before it even stopped spinning. He headed west to his home and, once there, stopped in front of the light-shielded door for a brief moment. Then he took a deep breath before crossing the threshold.

He turned the handle and pushed it open, and as he looked at the opposite wall, his stomach dropped in horror. The mantle was empty. He disappeared as his fist ended up in the wall. Who had gotten through the light?

But there was no time to dwell on his anger. He darted to his next location—Dunami Prison. He sprinted at a speed that approached recklessness. He blew over a traveling carriage, its occupants tumbling from the doors onto the street. Once in the capital, he headed toward the west end of the city, slicing through the midmorning crowds in the markets.

He didn't want to fight, so he picked up speed when he saw the prison building. He scaled the forty-foot-wall with ease before falling into the grounds. He flew by the guards and even snagged a loop of keys from one man's waist.

That's not to say that the staff didn't know what was happening. They had been trained for this sort of thing—a man capable of high speed percentages. But this was far beyond anything they were capable of dealing with. There was, quite literally, nothing they could do. You can't catch what you can't see.

Debo skated down multiple flights of stairs to the most secure floor of the dungeons. He stopped on the landing to compose himself. He wanted to hunch over and breathe, but he forced himself to stand tall with his back arched and hands on his hips—a much better position for replenishing his lungs with oxygen.

Two very big men approached him down the torch-lit stone hallway. They were built like boulders and even taller than Debo. An electrical wave lit up the space.

Debo didn't bother to dodge the attack. His body flickered as it absorbed their energy. Then he popped up behind the guards before their brains registered that he had moved. He pinched the base of their necks with each arm and gently guided their bodies to the floor.

Continuing down the shadowy hall, he walked between prison cells of some of the vilest and most notorious criminals in the Intel Kingdom. Crazed men and women reached through the bars in a desperate effort to grasp onto him. There were cries for help, shouted death threats ... one even vowed to have him for supper. Eventually, he reached the final cell at the dead-end of the hallway.

"Go away," muttered the curled-up ball in the cell's back corner.

Debo fumbled with the keys before unlocking the gate and walking inside. "I need you."

"I'm the opposite of what anyone needs. I hurt people." Her voice was shaking.

"Your team is in trouble. Your *friends* are in trouble," Debo corrected himself.

The girl finally looked up, exposing one bloodshot eye, her brown bangs sweeping across the other. Her face was oily and her shirt was somehow dirtier than usual.

Debo held out his hand. "Please, Rhyparia." A few seconds lingered past before she grabbed his hand and was pulled to her feet.

"Let's go," he said as he picked her up, holding her in his arms. "We need to travel faster than you can run."

Debo ran north to the Intel Palace, but he was slowing down. Fatigue from already sprinting countless leagues and the added weight of a fifteen-year-old girl were getting to him.

Nevertheless, it was still well before noon when he reached the palace's first wall of defense. He set Rhyparia down and yelled, "I advise you let me in!"

"I think not!" A soldier yelled back.

"I'm being polite! I could easily let myself through!"

A chorus of laughter rained down from the tower. "Go for it!" one shouted.

Shrugging, Debo prepared to run up the wall, but a command from the other side stopped him. "Open the gate!"

The man had authority, for the gate opened immediately. Debo's face softened as he saw a young man with greasy red hair. "Suadade," he said quietly.

Princess Shelly's Branian walked slowly toward Debo and Rhyparia with a reminiscing smile. "It has been entirely too long," he said before coming to a halt a few yards away, careful to keep a certain distance. "I assume you're off to save Bryson."

"How could you let that man send him on such a mission?" Debo asked.

Suadade pursed his lips. "My job is to protect Shelly. You know that. However, trust me when I say I warned Vitio of what an awful ideal it was." He briefly went quiet. "I imagine you're here to confront him. However, I'm not allowing you beyond this point."

Debo sighed. "You're lucky I can't waste any time or energy confronting you, someone who is not the enemy." He picked up Rhyparia, readying to sprint out of the city. "Be well, Suadade."

"I helped Bryson get into your closet."

Debo turned around with a look of utter shock. "I did it out of spite," Suadade said. "I wanted to get back at you, but believe me when I say I would never allow my spite to get so bad that it would put that boy in danger. Infiltrating the Dev Kingdom is stupid, and I know how much he means to you ... You made that obvious when you abandoned us for him."

"I had to."

"Spare me the rubbish," the Branian snapped.

"I'm sorry for what I did. I really am," Debo said. "Well, so long."

"Will you come back, Debonicus?"

Debo froze. This question was dangerous. He couldn't go back to that place. He had made that final decision a long, long time ago. He hadn't been Debonicus for eleven years. Unwilling to answer, he simply bolted out of sight.

Branian Suadade wandered aimlessly through the palace grounds, thinking back to his visit to the graveyard with Princess Shelly ...

The sun was setting across a cemetery outside of a small town in the Adren Kingdom. This town sat at the far end of the kingdom, as close to the Edge as one could possibly get. It was hundreds of leagues away from any other civilization, with forests and plains stretching between.

Two large oak trees extended their orange and yellow-draped branches above the center of the cemetery, where two memorials rested, one at the base of each tree.

Princess Shelly and Branian Suadade stood in front of the gravestone on the right. "This is what we came out here for?" she pouted.

HERE LIES A PUPIL.

HERE LIES A HERO.

REST IN PEACE,

LEON SUADADE

930-960 K.H.

Shelly couldn't fathom why anybody would want to visit their own grave and be reminded of their death.

"You can't forget who you are," Suadade said softly as if he was distracted by other thoughts. "You can't forget your roots. And by remembering that I've died before, I realize that I shouldn't be scared of anything."

"And what has you, a Bozani, scared?"

Suadade smiled. "I forget that down here we're thought of as some kind of gods. Just because there is a lack of a physical threat, doesn't mean there isn't a mental one. Often times, what scares us the most is internal. And that is humanity at its finest. We aren't Gods."

Suadade's smile was replaced by a solemn gaze. "I'm scared because I've lost him. Whether it was before or after I was reborn, he was always guiding me. A best friend and an inspiration. We died together. We were reborn together."

"Who?" Shelly asked.

The Branian turned and walked toward the headstone beneath the other tree. There were more flowers, a much bigger polished slab of marble, and a more delicately carved message. It didn't have to be said. The man buried here was the friend Suadade was yearning for.

"I thank you for coming out here," he said as he knelt by the grave.

Shelly kept her distance, allowing him this moment. But she had another question: "You said he was reborn with you, so where is he?"

"He left."

She stepped forward to read the gravestone. Engraved on it was the name of a legend. A man who was a hero to all the active imaginations of children in the Light Realm, the hero of The Third of Five. He was one of five people in Known History to attain a Bozani's power level without actually dying.

She stood in awe as she realized the man she grew up hearing stories about, whom she and everyone else had chalked up to being nothing more than a fictitious character in a fairy tale, was actually real. She wondered whether the story was exaggerated, and if so, by how much. But one thing was for certain … he had existed.

HERE LIES A TEACHER.

HERE LIES A LEGEND.

REST IN PEACE,

ATAWAY DEBONICUS KAWI

925-960 K.H.

26

Bryson vs. Ossen

Over the course of two days, Bryson and his team had been traveling toward Necrosis Valley from the east. His original plan to wait a couple days before intercepting Prince Storshae's route had been changed by the unfortunate encounter with Grand Director Poicus.

This time, there was no road to follow. And why would there be? Even in the Dark Realm, who would voluntarily enter a place named 'Necrosis Valley'?

A day ago, they arrived at a vast crater that had been blasted into the earth. They situated their tent close to its edge, which had a sharp slope ... although it didn't plunge straight down.

They could see for dozens of miles across the crater—though its opposite edge was far out of sight—as well as miles to the left and right. Since the land around the crater was flat and barren, seeing Storshae's approach wouldn't be difficult. And even if Bryson's party attacked by night, Himitsu could conjure his black flames to mask their presence.

It was half-past five on Wednesday morning, marking the approach of first-day. The Jestivan and Vistas were wide awake, which they had been for a couple hours. Storshae and his men should have been arriving soon, and they had to be prepared. However, their alertness was mostly because of nerves.

They lay on their stomachs in silence next to the ledge, staring through gaps in Himitsu's flaming black wall. They were spread out widely—each positioned to serve a specific purpose.

Bryson was in a spot that allowed him to look across the canyon in search of the main unit. Jilly and Toshik were on the flanks, where they could scan the level ground to their left and right.

Even in the middle of his own kingdom, Bryson didn't think Storshae would be stupid enough to funnel all of his soldiers into the crater and surrender the high ground. He predicted that Suadade would send a few of his common foot soldiers to encircle the perimeter of the crater.

It proved to be a correct theory. As a hint of daylight stretched over the horizon, Jilly spotted shadowy figures in the distance. They were several lackadaisical soldiers who were probably too tired from their journey.

"Soldiers from the north, *captain*," Jilly announced—quietly, thankfully.

By this point, Bryson was used to Jilly calling him captain. He just wished she wouldn't say it like that. It made her sound like she wasn't taking this seriously, but playing war instead.

Bryson scanned the floor of the crater, and as the day brightened, he saw a thin trail of dust in the distance. Soon, it revealed a carriage draped in deep burgundy trundling across the crust. Two ebony horses led it with a man holding the reins.

Bryson looked to his right and gave a nod to Himitsu. The only way they were going to do this effectively was by ambush. They were already concealed, so now, it came down to timing. This kind of tactical maneuvering was Himitsu's specialty, so it wasn't a surprise that this was his plan.

"How many soldiers are on our level?" Bryson asked.

"I think I see twelve," she replied.

"Toshik?"

"Nothing to our left."

If Bryson was to go by the information the young unable back at the teleplatforms had told him, that meant Storshae had dispatched most or all of his soldiers up here, and only Storshae, General Ossen, and Olivia were in that carriage ... and Storshae's Bewahr, of course.

Jilly waited a few more minutes, allowing the enemies to come closer. Once she was satisfied, she signaled to Bryson. "You're up," he said to Himitsu.

The slender Passion Jestivan rose to his feet. "Remember to be quick. My energy is running thin."

"Quick?" Bryson repeated. "You forget who you're talking to."

Himitsu smirked as he leaned his weight aggressively onto his back leg, bending his knee nearly to the ground. Taking in one of the deepest inhales Bryson had ever seen, Himitsu's upper body sprung forward as he blew out a blast of Passion Energy into the wall of flames he had conjured to conceal them. A trail of fire shot out the other side, down the cliff's sloping wall and across the bottom of the barren valley.

"Go," Himitsu instructed.

A space in Himitsu's original wall opened, and Bryson shot through it. He plunged down the cliff like a hawk from the sky before sprinting across the crater floor to the other side. He jumped behind a boulder the Jestivan had identified the day before. Himitsu's covering fire had dissipated, but Bryson judged that he had concealed himself in time. He had sprinted a good three miles in no more than ten seconds. Debo would have been proud. Although, he would have laughed at how winded Bryson was.

The group atop the cliff was now exposed, as according to plan. All Bryson could do was wait for his signal. He couldn't allow his eyes to leave the approaching carriage ... no matter how much he wanted to make sure his friends executed their roles correctly.

Himitsu, Jilly, and Toshik stood next to each other at the edge of the crater. Jilly stood in the middle, while the two taller Jestivan flanked her, each a few yards apart.

Toshik leaned casually on the handle of his sword, the point of its blade stuck into the dirt. Jilly's sunhat was on, but in the dim light, it was probably more for an intimidating look—or what she thought was intimidating.

Himitsu stood tall, but casually—though not as insouciant as Toshik. Vistas had fled out of sight as instructed, for he was useless in combat.

There was a row of four soldiers in front, followed by another row of four behind them. This group of eight stepped apart, allowing the third row of four to step through to the front. These were the bigger guns—two corporals, a lieutenant, and a major.

"I suggest you move," the major said, smiling wryly at the young faces.

They didn't.

The major waved his hand in a shooing motion. "Run along now."

The Jestivan continued to stand in silence.

"You're going to regret it if you don't get out of our way," the major threatened.

Once he finally realized they weren't going to budge, he ordered his men to attack.

The first row of foot soldiers charged, their burgundy coats flapping behind them as they ran with swords drawn. The Jestivan had been expecting something a little more refined, such as telekinesis, but they couldn't complain.

The man who targeted Himitsu caught a fist of flames to his stomach, which then engulfed his entire body. Another approached Jilly, who effortlessly slipped past his slashing sword and knocked him to the ground with a twirling kick to the back of his head.

The two men who charged Toshik fell even quicker than the rest. Before they could register what was happening, their heads were blinking in the dirt, decapitated by a single swipe from Toshik's sword. Then he distorted into a blur of color. When he returned to his original spot, he smiled sardonically at the four other foot soldiers, who looked down to see intestines spilling from the clean slashes across their stomachs.

Himitsu, Jilly, and Toshik didn't break their cool demeanor as the four higher ranks gaped at the carnage. "We have an issue up here," said the major, his eye briefly shifting to burgundy. "Eight men are down."

*　　　*　　　*

Bryson was still watching the carriage, unsure of what was happening above. Then the horses stopped trotting along—the signal he was waiting for. The back curtains opened up as three men stepped down. One of them was easily recognizable as Dev Prince Storshae.

Ossen was identifiable by the general's insignia on his burgundy cape. He also matched King Vitio's description of him: old, yet fit and robust. That left Storshae's Bewahr as the third man. But his ordinary height and rather scrawny build made that kind of hard to believe.

"The situation is critical," Bryson heard a voice explain to Storshae.

"How critical?" asked the prince.

"Well, um, we've been taken prisoner."

"By whom?"

There was grunting, and then a squeal of panic. "He says he's a Jestivan from the Adren Kingdom. And he has demands."

"Very well then," Storshae said. "And what is the request?"

"They want … Olivia. The girl in the carriage."

Storshae cracked a smile. "Indeed. By all means, invite them to come down here."

"He says he's going to kill us."

"That would serve you right—a dozen grown men cut down by … children."

As soon as the negotiations began, Bryson had snuck into the back of the carriage. Now he stared at his dearest friend's unmoving body with a look of despair. He knelt next to Olivia with tears of rage forming in his eyes as he took in every scar and bruise on her skin, every hole and cut in her clothing, and the outline of her ribs poking through her malnourished frame. It was as if she was lying on her deathbed.

Part of him wanted to march straight outside and inflict as much agonizing pain as he possibly could to those three men—even if it would surely lead to his death. But as he continued to stare at Olivia, her face, impassive even in unconsciousness, reminded him to keep his composure. He gently scooped her up, noticing the drastic difference in her weight. Even still, he wouldn't be able to reach high speed percentages while carrying her. He didn't have the balance or strength training for that yet. He had to count on his fellow Jestivan to give him enough time to get away.

The sun was now a quarter of the way over the horizon. "Are you coming down here or not?" Storshae was roaring. Fonos stood next to him with his eyes closed. Then the Bewahr disappeared. Storshae whirled around toward the sound of an abrupt collision behind him. Bryson was on his back in the dirt. Bewahr Fonos stood in front of him, one open palm extended.

*　　　*　　　*

"Something's gone wrong," Himitsu murmured.

"Wh——?" Toshik started to ask, and then was arm-barred by the major and flipped to the ground. Then he whirled and struck Himitsu with an energy blast that knocked him over the edge of the cliff.

Jilly ran at the brute of a man, but Toshik leapt to his feet and cut her off. He looked down at his Charge with forbidding eyes and instructed. "Run."

It was a rare look of menace in Toshik's eyes—so rare, it seemed bizarre. And it only took Jilly's life being in immediate danger for it to be unmasked.

Jilly removed her sun hat, allowing it to hang down her back. She looked up, matching his sternness. "No."

While they argued, the major freed the other three officers. Ignoring Jilly, the four of them advanced on Toshik in a semicircle, forcing him to retreat from his Charge. "*GO!*" Toshik shouted at the top of his lungs.

Meanwhile, Himitsu scrambled to the top of the cliff. Exhausted, he leaned forward with his hands on his knees and contemplated what to do. He was almost out of his Passion Energy, and although the training he had received from Passion Director Venustas and Olivia did help, he still had a lot of improvement to make in regards to head-to-head combat.

Then a huge blast of wind kicked up dirt, blinding him. Wiping the burning grit from his eyes, he saw Jilly standing next to Toshik, whose face was black with rage. Himitsu wearily stumbled toward the fray.

*　　　*　　　*

On the floor of the crater, Bryson stood swaying with Olivia in his arms.

Bewahr Fonos gazed at the boy, intrigued.

As for Prince Storshae, he was on the verge of a fit of laughter. "*This* was your plan?" he asked.

Bryson didn't answer. He looked down at Olivia's battered body and Meow Meow's sleeping, exhausted face. The rage was boiling over.

"Your plan was to ambush the most dangerous warriors in the Dev Kingdom? A bunch of teenagers? You think you're Mendac? And that's Thusia you're holding?"

Ironic. Little did Storshae know, it was the son of Mendac he was talking to. Bryson's fury intensified at the sound of his father's name. But when he spoke, his voice was cold and controlled. "You're right. I'm not Mendac, but I can end you the same way he ended your father."

Fonos teleported and connected with a vicious punch to Bryson's chest, knocking Olivia from his arms and sending him skidding a good ten yards across the blasted earth. The boy clutched at his chest as he staggered to his feet.

Bryson knew he was being stupid, but he itched with a compulsion to attack. If he only landed a few blows on Storshae, it would be worth it …

He tried to clear his head. If he stalled long enough, maybe Toshik, Jilly, and Himitsu could win their battles and then come to help. But even then? The Gefal could take out their whole group himself.

"Let me kill him, Prince Storshae," General Ossen begged.

Storshae's eyes shifted sideways to his right-hand man.

"I watched a Jestivan wreak havoc on our kingdom many years ago," Ossen continued. "That man, Mendac, is the most hated person to our people. You were too young and cannot remember it. So please, this will be the closest I'll ever get to being able to avenge our kingdom."

The prince thought about it for a second more before saying, "Go ahead."

The general's eyes widened at the opportunity. As he advanced on Bryson, Fonos teleported back to Storshae's side.

"Are you sure this is wise?" he asked.

"He's just a boy," Storshae replied.

Bryson carefully watched the approaching general. His burgundy cape was adorned with silver and gold medals. He swallowed with difficulty, trying to compose himself. He had sparred with Debo many times, but this was a fight to the death. If he allowed his mind to wander toward anything that didn't involve his immediate enemy, he would die.

"I enjoyed beating the snot out of your friend there," Ossen said with a sneer. "I don't know why you would want her back. The smell is putrid."

In any other circumstance, Bryson would have attacked at full speed by now, but here, he couldn't, not with Storshae and Fonos looking on. He was going to have to fight a technique-based battle with Ossen. He couldn't show his cards.

"It will feel so good to kill a Jestivan," Ossen said with a scary thirst.

Ossen threw a punch, but that wasn't what Bryson was worried about. He was more focused on the two rocks levitating in the periphery of his vision. He hadn't forgotten how Archaic General Inias was murdered at the Generals' Battle. He parried the punch with his forearm as the rocks plunged at him from the left and right. He extended both arms to the side, and as the projectiles landed in his grasp, he swung them forward, sandwiching them against Ossen's head.

Ossen stumbled backward, clutching at his ears as blood gushed out. Before the man had a chance to recover, Bryson thrust his right knee into the general's face, spun, and swung his extended leg down into Ossen's back like an executioner's axe. Both connected, but he was attacking too rapidly, and Ossen swept the young Jestivan's ankle from underneath him.

As Bryson fell parallel to the ground, Ossen grabbed his face and thrust the back of his head into the crust. The boy let out a muffled, agonized shout, but he countered by grabbing Ossen's wrist and emitting a surge of electricity. He had Princess Shelly to thank for this newly gained tool.

Ossen's grasp weakened, allowing Bryson to kick up his legs, grab Ossen's neck between his calves, and toss him to the side. Ossen slid a couple yards on his left hand and both feet—a flawless recovery.

"The irony," Prince Storshae remarked to his Bewahr. "Seems the boy's from the Intel Kingdom, just like Mendac was."

Standing upright, Ossen smiled. "Oh, that makes this kill even sweeter." A trio of daggers shot out from beneath his jacket.

Glancing left and right for projectiles, Bryson saw the daggers too late. He dodged two, but the last one plunged into his left shoulder. He cringed as he clutched at the dagger's handle and ripped it out. Then he unknowingly made another terrible error—he threw his hoodie to the side.

The moment Ossen saw this, he flicked his hand, and the jacket clotheslined Bryson, dragging him across the floor before slamming him into a boulder.

"Do you see that on his chest?" Storshae asked Fonos.

The Bewahr narrowed his eyes.

Bryson was now pinned by his own hoodie. He pried hopelessly at the jacket, his vision dimming as he futilely gasped for air.

Ossen stood a good fifteen feet away, wearing a wide smirk. He had three more daggers in his hand. "Let's make this even more fun," he teased. "Target practice? I won't even use my telekinesis, for throwing will prove a little more . . . *unpredictable*." He sent a blade flying with a flick of his wrist, and all Bryson could do was squirm and watch helplessly as it soared toward him.

*   *   *

On the rim of the crater, one of the corporals lay dead in the dirt. The other was pressing Himitsu hard as his arms became heavy. The Jestivan's movements were getting slower, and the corporal could see this. He recklessly pressed forward as Himitsu began to lose his footing.

Himitsu jumped over a sweeping kick and grabbed the man's shoulder as he landed. Yanking the Dev officer into a hunched position, Himitsu heaved his knee into his stomach. The corporal let out a hoarse groan as he slumped to the ground. As Himitsu swung a boot toward the fallen man's prone head, the corporal sent a dagger flying. Himitsu bent sideways, but the blade slashed his cheek. He put his hand to his face to observe the damage. While gazing at his blood-soaked fingers, he made the decision.

Wanting to have some Passion Energy to help Toshik and Jilly with the two higher ranks, he had been storing a tiny amount. Now he realized that he didn't have that luxury. So when the corporal extended his hand to fire another dagger, Himitsu grabbed his wrist and pulled him forward. He squeezed the man's face with his other hand as black flames engulfed the corporal's head. The bloodcurdling screams lasted for a few seconds before the Dev officer collapsed to the ground. Himitsu dropped to his knees and gazed weakly over at his two teammates.

Neither the lieutenant nor major had flanked the two Jestivan. They attacked in the same pattern again and again. The lieutenant would fling a dagger at Jilly. Then when Toshik parried the blade, not trusting his Charge to defend herself, the major would let loose a blast of Dev energy at the young swordsman. Toshik's face and minimal armor were scorched and stained with his blood.

The major—second only to General Ossen in terms of military power—seemed almost offended. "Let the girl fight," he said. "It's your only chance, vanishing though it may be."

The tall Jestivan dashed forward, but his speed percentage had been drained by his wounds. The major contemptuously punched him in the gut as the lieutenant went for Jilly.

He swept his leg at her knee, but she blocked it with her thigh and hopped back a few steps. The two began sparring while Toshik struggled to get up. The major's boot pressed him back down to the dirt.

"Your efforts to fight in that girl's stead are foolish. You have too much pride."

"Pride shouldn't be mistaken for commitment," Toshik said coldly.

The major casually ground his boot into Toshik's chin. "We are committed to only one thing, my boy: Our journey from life to death. Your commitment, I'm afraid, will be paid today." He ran his thumb across the edge of his dagger, bent down, and grabbed Toshik by the scalp.

As Toshik glared into the Dev officer's beady eyes, some strange force tugged him away. Jilly, who had been handling the lieutenant with relative ease, felt the same sensation—as did Himitsu.

The three Jestivan looked around. They were still at the edge of the crater's rim, but some distance from the Dev officers.

"What was that?" Toshik asked.

"Maybe they teleported us," Jilly said.

Himitsu shook his head. "No, something or someone grabbed us. I felt it."

"My sword!" Toshik exclaimed as he twisted and turned. "Where is my sword?!"

Paying him no mind, Himitsu's eyes narrowed. Next to the lieutenant and corporal stood a third person—a girl.

His eyes widened. "Guys … it's Rhyparia."

*   *   *

Bryson winced as shards of rock stung his eyes. Ossen had missed! Bryson reached across his face with his left hand, yanked the dagger from the rock, and slashed downward, slicing his hoodie in two. And before Ossen could comprehend what happened, Bryson had disappeared, for he had finally decided to crank his speed percentage up.

Ossen wasn't prepared, as he couldn't fathom the existence of someone outside of the Adren Kingdom having such speed. The general didn't even have time to brace himself before a forearm knocked him backward and into the hard ground.

Prince Storshae gaped in disbelief at what he was witnessing … even to his trained eyes, Bryson's arms were a blur. He sat on top of Ossen, pulverizing his top officer's skull and brains to a paste.

Bryson had lost any awareness of Storshae or Fonos. Ossen was dead already, yet he continued to pound away. *Like kneading bread*, he thought absently, alternating fists with a maniacal satisfaction. Then a hand grabbed his shoulder and threw him backward. An unhappy Prince Storshae had entered the fight.

"Arrogant brat," the prince spat.

Bryson gazed up at Storshae from where he lay in the dirt, too tired to move. Storshae opened the front of his cloak, where ten steel blades were hooked to his waist. They hovered gently.

It was an uncanny display of skill. A world-class fighter like Ossen could telekinetically control three objects at once; Storshae was handling *ten*. Even discounting Bryson's exhausted state, there was no way he could escape the wide area that ten daggers thrown simultaneously could encompass.

Bryson's thoughts raced to his friends and how he had led them to their deaths. He thought of Debo, the only father he'd ever had, whose love Bryson's foolishness had thrown away …

Storshae ducked his shoulder, pivoted, and a wide wall of steel swept toward Bryson. Once again, the boy closed his eyes, surrendering to his inevitable death.

And then he heard a clash of metal, like a royal carriage crashing to the ground from a great height. He squinted, then cautiously opened his eyes to see a familiar lean back and ear-piercings shimmering in the sun. Shards of broken steel littered the ground around him.

It was Debo, and Bryson had never been happier to see him. Storshae looked angry, but Fonos reacted differently. His eyebrows scrunched together as his mouth dropped in, what looked to be, disbelief.

"Debonicus …" Fonos muttered.

"Get back, Bryson," Debo commanded without turning his head from Storshae and Fonos. Bryson happily obeyed and scrambled back to Olivia's body.

"Kill this fool while I finish the boy," Storshae barked.

"Easier said than done," Fonos said, his voice distant as if lost in thought.

"What?" the prince snapped. "You're a Gefal!"

Fonos was careful to not look away from Debo. "If we are to fight *him*, I will need your help."

27

Discovery

Four Jestivan entered Phesaw's main auditorium. This meeting had been orchestrated by the Energy Directors, who had promised a visit from an esteemed individual.

Lilu, Yama, Agnos, and Tashami walked down the steps with uncertainty in most of their eyes. They were hoping this gathering would give them the answers as to why their fellow Jestivan and Director Debo had been mysteriously absent for the past couple days.

As they reached the bottom, they saw a boulder of a man with blond hair and matching silk robes—Intel King Vitio. The directors were standing in front of the first row as they waited for the Jestivan to take a seat.

"To be forthright, Bryson, Himitsu, Jilly, and Toshik have all been inside of the Dev Kingdom the past several days," Archaic Director Senex began, "hunting down Dev Prince Storshae and his soldiers in efforts to rescue Olivia."

Shock blanketed the faces of the Jestivan.

"Obviously, we would never have sent four Jestivan into the Dark Realm by themselves, so the question becomes, who allowed them to do so?" Senex turned and extended his arm to the man on the stage. "I introduce to you King Vitio of the Intel Kingdom."

While the directors took a seat in the first row, Vitio remained standing at the stage's edge. He took a deep breath. "I'm sorry. I sent four teenagers into the Dark Realm to pursue someone much stronger than any of them. I did it with thoughts of the original Jestivan in my mind and, more importantly, a specific zana we are all familiar with—Mendac. He was unparalleled in talent, and I thought, perhaps, that his offspring possessed the same ability. But I was blinded by my memories of an older Mendac ... Bryson is only sixteen. Even Mendac, at that age, could not have handled such a mission—I think.

"Of course, the decision was Bryson's. I did not force it upon him. I don't know Olivia personally, but I did know how desperate he was to save her. I warned him and his friends of the dangers—the almost near-certain death—and they still wanted to go, so I let them."

The Jestivan wore varying expressions. Yama was angry at Jilly's lie. Tashami simply looked flabbergasted. Agnos wore a look of disgust, probably casting moral judgment on the king. And Lilu ... since she already knew about all of this, she was more focused on her fellow Jestivan's reactions, scared of what they thought of her father.

"So they will die," Agnos pronounced, "and you will have the lost lives of four youths on your shoulders."

Vitio turned pale, though undoubtedly he had considered this many times before.

"That's no sure thing, Agnos," Passion Director Venustas said. "Director Debo departed immediately when he learned the news."

"That means nothing," Agnos said. "First of all, he has to find them. Second, he has to make it there in time. And third, as much as I respect each of you Directors, the truth is that you're not a Bozani or Gefal."

Venustas's rosy red lips pursed, but she didn't try to deny what he had said.

"T-There is something else," Vitio stammered. "Now, I wouldn't burden you with this under normal circumstances, but with our invasion of the Archaic Kingdom, I simply cannot put all my attention toward what I'm about to tell you. Therefore, I ask for your help.

"There is someone in Kuki Sphaira who is a threat to every royal family in both realms. He is responsible for the assassination of the Prim Kingdom's prince a few months back and now he is in the Cyn Kingdom stalking a royal there as well. And recently, I received a major tip … His name is Toono."

The name sent chills up the spines of Yama and Agnos. Agnos glanced at the violet-haired swordswoman, who was looking back at him with furrowed brows. All of her denials of Toono's involvement were wrong.

As Vitio recounted the conversation between Storshae and Ossen, Agnos thought back to the most recent letter from the Unbreakable. And the more he heard, the more he wanted to find Toono—but not to forgive. He didn't believe in forgiveness for sins that were too severe. That was his understanding, and he had learned that way of thinking from none other than Toono.

Agnos stood up. "May I speak?" he asked.

Director Senex granted him permission. As Agnos took the stage, he reached into the front pocket of his white robes. He held up a folded piece of parchment. "If the Energy Directors recall, during the captaincy test back in September of last year, I read a section of a book written by the Unbreakable. Over the past several months, Tashami has been receiving letters from him, which I have been deciphering.

"Now, most of these letters were mindless babbling about pessimistic and morbid matters. There was no doubt that the uniquely macabre atmosphere of the Cyn Kingdom sucked enough life out of this man that he simply was not right in the head."

Agnos shook the parchment in his hand. "That was until this particular letter. This contained valuable information. Information about a man I once knew when he was a boy."

Opening the letter and equipping his circular framed glasses, he recited it word for word. He looked back up after finishing.

"Toono was my friend," Agnos continued. "We were orphans at a foster home. But don't apply that label to our minds, as we were far beyond any normal child's mental capacity—especially Toono. He eventually became Yama's Charge. But several years ago, he met a woman … and he changed.

"I still tried to keep tabs on him, and I knew that he was working at the Archaic Museum as a guard. There's no way he could have escaped that museum without help from the outside, so I'll go ahead and assume that he's still with this woman."

Agnos began to pace. "Then there was the assassination of the Prim Prince in late October, early November. When we learned of it, I didn't think much of it besides that it was an outrageously impure act. … That was until this letter.

"The Unbreakable spoke of a man who was accompanied by a woman. He said the man was from the Archaic Kingdom. He said the man had done bad things—the royal assassination, it seems likely to me. He said he had a mission. Now, he didn't say what that mission was specifically, but consider the context clues. He repeatedly mentions how the dead should stay dead. How he didn't agree with the man's mission.

"Clearly, Toono wants someone alive again. The question was, *who?* Why, Dev King Rehn, of course. Storshae said that his father would be returning after he strangled Itta, and after what King Vitio has told us, we know that Toono and Storshae are working together. Toono is helping him resurrect King Rehn … and, somehow, Olivia is the key to it all."

The room sat in silence. Agnos returned to his seat, and Spirit Director Neaneuma took the stage, her sky-blue robes cascading down to the floor. "Bringing someone back to life seems farfetched and, quite frankly, a bit impossible. With that said, if there's a threat of it, we still must act. Dev King Rehn cannot return."

"But why not?" Tashami asked. "There is always going to be a Dev Kingdom, and it's always going to have a king … if Storshae wants his father back, why would that be such a disaster?"

Neaneuma blushed slightly. "Truthfully, it's a mystery. Grand Director Poicus always said, 'that man knows too much.' He knew things nobody should know, and it put the entirety of our realm in danger. Therefore, depending on the safe arrival of the rest of the Jestivan, the four of you will be sent on a group mission into the Cyn Kingdom to contact the Unbreakable."

As the Jestivan sat up intently, the other directors started to murmur. "Perhaps we should discuss this amongst ourselves first," Director Venustas said.

King Vitio also voiced his disapproval. "My daughter is not going to the Dark Realm."

"Yet you have no problem sending her friends there," Director Neaneuma retorted, causing Vitio to flush with embarrassment.

"Besides, they won't go alone," Neaneuma said. "Two Energy Directors will go with them, and I will be one of them. And we won't be taking on any royal heads, or looking for a fight at all."

The baritone voice of Director Buredo made itself heard for the first time. "Let's discuss this privately first, Lorna."

"We will."

Buredo stood and turned to look at the Jestivan. "Run along. Don't stray from the campus the next few days."

Lilu, Tashami, Yama, and Agnos exited the auditorium with clouded minds. Each of them had different issues. Tashami thought about finally meeting the Unbreakable. Yama and Agnos were focused on the possibility of seeing Toono again. And Lilu …

She continued thinking about her friends and how likely it was that they were dead.

*   *   *

Just before dawn, Lilu—against the wishes of the Energy Directors—lay asleep in her bed in the Intel Palace. She had chosen to stay there instead of the Lilac Suites so she could receive updates from Vistas from Flen. It had been several days since they last heard from him, and Lilu was becoming more stressed as each day passed. She was never happy and made no effort in faking it.

Princess Shelly stood outside Lilu's door, preparing to wake her little sister. She had been standing there for a good fifteen minutes, for she didn't want to tell Lilu the news she just received from the city of Brilliance. It seemed as if everything continued to pile up.

Shelly—still draped in her nightgown—knocked three times. "Sister," she called out.

Lilu's eyes opened for what seemed like the millionth time that night. "Come in."

Shelly opened the door but didn't enter. Lilu didn't try to sit up. She just lay in the same position she had spent the entire night: her cheek in her tear-stained pillow and her body twisted in the blankets.

"We have to talk," the princess said softly. "It's about the blood on Debo's sword ... it's Mendac's."

28

Pogu

Bryson picked up Olivia and staggered away from the fight that was about to begin between Debo, Dev Prince Storshae, and Bewahr Fonos. He felt like he was abandoning Debo to a certain death, as no commoner, not even a director, stood a chance against a Gefal. They were the Dark Empire's equivalent to the Light Empire's Bozani. Still, Fonos had asked for help—and called the Energy Director "Debonicus." Why did that name sound familiar?

"Do something," Storshae ordered his Bewahr.

Debo stood tall, towering over the prince. "You are naïve, young man."

The prince looked him up and down. "You look to be only a few years older than—*aargh!*"

Debo was directly in front of him with his sword impaled through the prince's shoulder. Storshae hadn't seen him move. In fact, he hadn't even seen him disappear. He gazed at the man in horror.

"I'm centuries older than you," Debo said. "You are a child, and you're lucky I can't kill you." He ripped the sword away, leaving a hole in the prince's shoulder much like the one Ossen put in Bryson's.

Storshae clutched his wound and staggered back. "*DO YOUR JOB!*" he shouted at Fonos.

"Yes, do your job," Debo mocked with a stern glare.

Fonos finally stepped forward, but he approached with a question. "What are you doing down here?"

Debo disappeared again, and just as quickly, Fonos vanished too. In a blink, the Bewahr was standing casually some thirty feet away.

It was a battle of instant teleportation and blazing speed. Neither Bryson nor Storshae's eyes could follow the madness. The only glimpses they could catch were the moments of impact—when Debo and Fonos locked blades or grips. Then they'd disappear again and pop up an instant later at a completely different location.

Bryson shook his head to clear his thoughts. He had to get Olivia out of here—but where should he take her? The battle between Debo and Fonos seemed to take up the entire floor of the crater. As he turned in a circle, trying to decide, Storshae swept his arms forward, causing the daggers lying on the ground to kick up dust as they sprung directly at the boy. Before Bryson could react, they were deflected once again by the slashing sword of Debo.

The Energy Director crumpled to the dirt, and Fonos stood over him. Debo's sword vanished, but so did the Bewahr. Then Storshae grabbed Debo's other wrist, and for a moment, the Energy Director seemed paralyzed. The Dev Prince swept four daggers into Debo's chest. Bryson screamed.

"What are you doing?" Fonos asked, incredulous.

Storshae sneered at his Bewahr. "Something you can't do, apparently: Killing him."

Suddenly, Debo was gone again, and then his sword was jammed deep into the prince's other shoulder.

Debo pulled it out, allowing more blood to spill. "Your mistake is not knowing your enemy. You should have kept me in that trance. In fact, I'm impressed you have that kind of talent to perform such a feat on someone like me … making me relive my worst memories."

"What are you?" Storshae gasped.

Debo thought about it for a second before replying, "An Energy Director."

This obviously wasn't the case, so Storshae redirected his question to his Bewahr. "What is he, Fonos?"

"He is a Pogu," he replied, still staring at Debo. "And I'm confused as to why he hasn't done away with us by now."

"Pogu?" the prince repeated.

"Branian is the lowest tier of the Bozani hierarchy. Pogu is a tier higher."

A Pogu? Bryson always knew that the man who acted as his father had secrets, but of this magnitude? He hadn't even heard of a Pogu before.

"My goodness, why are you struggling to defeat me?" Fonos asked.

"Because of how long I've spent away from the Light Empire."

"And she allowed you to come down here?"

"Yes, eleven years ago."

"Eleven years," Fonos repeated with a smirk. "And you still can fight me toe-to-toe. That is very frightening."

The conversation was interrupted by the roar of falling rocks. High above them, the crater rim was collapsing as broken rock and dirt cascaded into the valley. The ground at their feet reverberated with each explosion. It went on for less than a minute before it stopped and dust clouds began to rise in front of the sun.

Fonos's mouth flattened. "That, too, is very frightening."

*   *   *

The lieutenant and major looked at each other, not sure of what had just happened. One moment, there were three Jestivan in front of them. The next moment, a lone girl, who looked even younger than the others, was the only one in sight.

She had an umbrella in her hand, but the bandana that she typically had wrapped around her head was missing, for Bryson had it in his pants pocket. One eye was visible—one cold, sad, green eye. The other was hidden behind her sweeping bangs.

Rhyparia broke the silence. "Hello."

"Another Jestivan?" the major asked.

"Their friend," she corrected.

"Well, you're going to end up just like your friends."

Her eyebrow climbed up her forehead. "Oh, you mean perfectly fine?" she asked, nodding her head at the Jestivan in the distance.

The major turned around, and sure enough, there were the three Jestivan he was previously fighting. His teeth grated against each other.

Rhyparia scanned her surroundings with a professorial air. "It seems my friends were not at their best here. From their tracks, it seems Toshik was fighting to stop Jilly from fighting more than he was paying attention to you. And based on the wounds in your dead corporals, I'll assume Himitsu's energy had nearly been depleted before this contest began."

"Or perhaps the lot of you aren't as strong as you would like to think," the lieutenant spat. "And you ... you are irrelevant. Your presence is almost nonexistent. I feel nothing."

"Because when my switch is turned off, I am quite possibly one of the least threatening people around," Rhyparia said. "However, it only takes a trigger, and then all control is lost. I don't want to sound like I'm bragging. It's definitely a flaw."

"*A switch?*"

His answer was an umbrella thrust through his torso. The lieutenant stared with wide eyes as his blood gushed from the wound. Rhyparia pulled her ancient free, and his body collapsed with a thud.

Then the weight of the atmosphere intensified, and the major grabbed his throat as he gasped for air. He panicked as he realized what her ability was.

The feeling drifted into his bones. At first they ached, then they cracked under the pressure. His ankles snapped first, bringing him to his knees as the joints all over his body were dislocating. His hands and feet were crushed, turning them into nothing but dust-filled bags of skin. His excruciating screams of pain blended with the crunching of his collapsing skeleton. Then they were drowned out by the roar of Kuki Sphaira's crust cracking and collapsing. Rhyparia was sculpting a new landscape.

It didn't take long for Rhyparia's body to overexert itself. She fell to the ground as the gravity instantly shifted back to its normal balance. But for the major, it was too late. His mangled body was contorted in the rubble. Rhyparia's eyes were barely open as she incoherently stared at nothing.

A man with sleek, jet-black hair crouched beside her. Finally, the girl's eyes moved. She weakly looked up at the stranger's face.

"Young lady, that was overwhelming and unprecedented power," the man said. "My name is Vistas, and I am a friend."

*   *   *

Bewahr Fonos was tiring. He had already sustained several slashes to his forearms. As his mind hazed, he began to teleport more or less at random, desperately hoping to somehow be delivered from Debo's relentless assault.

"You may have the ability to travel from one spot to another instantly," Debo said, "but your mind can't react instantly. I may not be as fast as I once was, but I'm still too fast for you!" He swung his sword, and when Fonos reappeared several feet away, he was missing something—an arm. It had fallen to the ground where he had previously stood.

"Fonos!" Storshae cried.

The Bewahr grimaced as he looked down where his left arm should have been. Blood was spurting from the wound. Then Debo pushed off again, reaching his maximum speed percentage instantaneously.

Fonos remained deathly still with no effort to teleport away. Debo swung his sword as violently as he could, and he felt its blade rip across the enemy's stomach.

Debo's sword fell from his grasp and clattered against the hard ground. For the first time in eleven years, tears were forming in his eyes as he watched the intestines spill from the rent he had torn … into Bryson.

The boy fell to the ground on his knees as he clutched his organs in his hands.

"No … No … No, no, no, no, Bryson," Debo pleaded.

Bryson gazed up at him with a look of disbelief before falling flat on his face. As Debo stood in shock, Fonos grabbed the Pogu's neck with his remaining arm.

Now Fonos and Debo were no longer in the crater, for Fonos had teleported them to the rim, not far from where Himitsu, Jilly, and Toshik stood.

"Director!" Jilly screamed.

Debo's lanky frame dangled over the cliff's edge, suspended by Fonos's grip. The Pogu wasn't struggling. He hung limp.

Fonos gave Debo a curious look. "We'll see just how much damage eleven years away from the Light Empire did to your Tahara." He let go, and the Jestivan watched hopelessly as their director's body tumbled through the air.

A scream came from the canyon floor: "*DEBO!*"

Debo gazed blankly in the direction of the shouting. It was Bryson. He was standing on the crater floor, pinned in a headlock by Prince Storshae. But he had no wounds. His stomach was intact.

Debo realized what had happened. Fonos inflicted a hallucination upon him. A mixture of feelings swept over him: frustration for being so careless and unaware, relief to see Bryson alive, and helplessness. Fonos was correct. If only he were the man he had been eleven years ago …

Bryson, on the other hand, was in a state of shock at the sight of Debo's flailing body. He didn't understand how the tides had been reversed so abruptly. All he had seen was Debo randomly breaking down in the middle of a finishing blow.

Fonos teleported back to the crater floor, between where Bryson stood and where Debo was falling. Bryson's dirt-and-sweat-lathered face reflected sheer horror as he watched it happen … Debo's body smashing to the ground with a blast like a clap of thunder.

Bryson wailed as he hopelessly tried to tear himself from Storshae's grasp.

"Your last resort is dead," the prince sneered. "What are you going to do now, cry? That's the fight you're going to put up?"

Bryson let out another agonizing sob and stopped struggling, allowing himself to hang listlessly in Storshae's arms.

Fonos was on his knees, holding his bleeding shoulder. He looked up at Bryson with a white face. "You must have been something extremely special to him. Whether the Light or Dark Empire, for a rank above a

Branian or Bewahr to leave is extremely rare. And for eleven years? That is unheard of. What was he doing here?"

Bryson just stared at the dirt, too disconsolate to answer.

Fonos slumped onto his backside. "Just like the Dark Empire's Gefal, each tier of the Light Empire's Bozani hierarchy has a purpose, its own way of protecting the balance. The Pogu ... they are executioners. Once in a great while, they are ordered to kill potential threats to said balance." He coughed. "But that's it. They are to go straight back to the Light Empire. And here on, Kuki Sphaira, they are not to be seen. They are assassins. So I ask again, what about you made him break that rule?"

Storshae cuffed Bryson on the cheek. "Answer him, boy. He'd like to know before he bleeds to death."

Realization dawned upon Fonos as his brows furrowed. "Debonicus said that he arrived eleven years ago. That would put us right at the time of Mendac LeAnce's death."

"You're implying he executed him?" Storshae scoffed.

"Who else could have? Mendac was the Fifth of Five. And Ataway Debonicus Kawi was the Third of Five."

Ataway Debonicus Kawi. Bryson rolled the name through his battered brain. *Debo.*

"But why would the Light Empire have one of their own realm executed?" Fonos asked himself, his voice weakening. "It couldn't have been simply because of his talent. Debonicus had unmatched talent when he was human too, but nobody was sent down to kill him. He sacrificed himself."

"A pathetic way of trying to glorify a suicide," Storshae spat. He swept Bryson to the ground, pressed his knee into the back of the boy's head, and drew his sword. "Is there a point to your rambling?"

Fonos looked at the prince with his dying eyes. "The messy blond hair ... blue eyes ... electrical abilities. That boy. He's Mendac's son. I'm sure of it."

"Is that so?" Storshae flipped Bryson over and laughed. "This will be even more enjoyable than I had imagined."

He grabbed Bryson's chin and stared into his face. "How would you like to relive your deepest, darkest memories? Let's see if they're as twisted as your little lady friend's.'"

Storshae sunk his fingertips into Bryson's scalp. Bryson's eyes rolled to the back of his head, exposing the whites. His temple began to pulse and his breathing became heavy. An array of subconscious memories began to seep into the forefront of his mind:

He was inside the hallway of his house, standing next to the light-shielded closet door. An eleven-year-old boy whose curiosities had finally gotten the best of him. He stared at the light as if it was the strongest opponent he would ever fight in his life.

He thrust his finger into the light. He screamed as his skin shriveled and burned. The popping sounds scared him even more. He collapsed to the floor, writhing in pain—

He was grasping at a wooden floorboard, trying to pull himself forward. The air felt like a boulder crushing the life from him.

He looked to his right and saw a young boy pinned to the floor. A chunk of ceiling fell and split the boy in two—

A stadium, bathed in blood, echoed clashing metal and dying screams. Innocents who had only wanted to enjoy a holiday weekend were being hacked down left and right—

He fumbled across rows of seats as he scrambled to find his best friend. The sun had sunk below the horizon, making it harder to decipher facial features as he turned over countless corpses—

The next vision was the worst. It was a nightmare he hadn't experienced since he was maybe ten years old.

He was looking at the back of his eyelids, but he couldn't open them. Not because he physically couldn't, but for fear of what he might see.

He braced himself for the pain, but screamed when the blade carved deep into his chest. Slowly, cruelly, the blade cut horizontally, then vertically. He could feel the warm blood seep out of the wounds and drip down his cold body—he was always cold. All the while, Bryson continued to scream. He was young—very young. His screams were childlike.

The carving switched to his left pectoral, and this was even worse, as there was a curve to its path. The boy kicked feebly. His tiny hands clutched at the wooden table he lied upon, splintering beneath his fingernails ...

Storshae was forced to strengthen his grip as Bryson's body violently convulsed. It looked as if he was going into a seizure as bubbles of saliva foamed between his lips. The scars on his chest began to bleed, running up and over his abdominals.

Eventually the foaming stopped, and Bryson lay still. Sweat matted his hair to his face. His body was about to shut down, but his next memory took him to a different place—a peaceful one:

He was sitting in a spot he had sat so many times before in countless dreams. He looked up, knowing exactly what to expect. Sure enough, there was the canopy of cherry blossoms that cast him in a cooling shade. Phesaw's bustling campus expanded at the foot of his green hill. He inhaled fresh air from a calming breeze.

He knew what came next, readying himself for disappointment. This was when the dream always stopped.

His head turned. His view panned to the left ... and kept going. He pressed his hand into the lush grass and pivoted to look behind him.

A man stood with his hands clasped behind his back as if he was lost deep in thought. His hair was blond and messy.

Then Bryson spoke, but the voice that escaped his mouth was a woman's: "How many times are you going to bring me up here to watch the grass grow? You're the most boring date I could ever ask for."

"I'm not watching grass grow, love. I'm planning," the man said.

"Oh yes, and what was that completely fantastic and awesome name you plan to name it?"

"Don't patronize me," he said through a chuckle.

She guffawed. "Let me have my fun. 'Telejunction' is okay ... I guess." She paused. "You know I love you, Mendac."

The man turned his head—as if in slow motion, so anxious was Bryson to see his father's face.

Mendac's face was chiseled. His bangs flirted with his eyelashes just like Bryson's, and there was scruff bordering his jaw. His eyes were more aggressive than his son's, and his nose was narrower.

A couple tears dripped from Bryson's white eyes—tears of happiness. The experience was euphoric, and he didn't want it to stop.

Mendac beamed. "I love you too, Thusia."

Then his dad's face vanished as Bryson's vision was erased by a blinding white. An unnatural breeze ran across his neck—a breeze he had felt twice before. And a woman's voice carried through. It was so calming, yet rejuvenating.

"I shall descend from the Light."

Bryson's hair whipped against his face as the gentle breeze intensified.

His eyes were still rolled in the back of his head.

Dev Prince Storshae could no longer keep his grip on the boy's scalp. He let go, his heels sliding in the dirt as he struggled to brace himself in the tornado-like winds. Bewahr Fonos fell on his side and slid bonelessly across the ground.

"What is happening?!" Storshae screamed over the noise.

The windstorm formed a clear, upside-down tornado. The widest part sat at ground level. As it reached higher in the air, the funnel became smaller and more concentrated. A blinding light shined at the top, which was parallel to the crater's rim. Himitsu, Toshik, and Jilly held their arms in front of them to shield their eyes from the light.

"Don't look directly at it!" Himitsu yelled.

Rhyparia could see it from where she lay in the dirt. Her eyes were barely open, but even if they were closed, its intensity would have turned her eyelids a bloody red. Vistas, who was crouched next to her, stared at it in astonishment.

Each of them experienced a sensation they had never felt in their life. It was a sensation that Bryson had felt when he first met Princess Shelly's Branian. Their hearts lifted. They felt no worry, no pain, no fear. They breathed deep and easy, inhaling the purest, cleanest air that could ever exist. They felt feathery—as if they could sprout wings.

Storshae had a different reaction. "What is this?!" he yelled with a mixture of disbelief and rage. "How is this happening?! He's a plebeian!"

As the torrential winds continued, the light began floating down to the crater floor, softening as it descended. Bryson's eyes finally rolled to the front of his head.

As the glowing orb reached ground, it began to take shape. A pair of feet formed first. Each toenail was painted sky blue. Two slender calves stretched upward until her legs disappeared behind a blue dress that rippled in the winds. A single white bracelet hugged a tiny wrist, and she wore a white collar around her neck with a diamond set in the front. Her blond hair whipped violently in the storm.

Then the winds abruptly stopped, casting the crater in stunned silence. Her hair fell down to her mid-back. It was perfectly straight—much like Jilly's.

She fixed her sight on various things. She looked at Bryson. Then Debo's body lying near the cliff's wall. Finally she looked at Fonos, who was somehow still alive.

She casually waved her hand in his direction, and an intense blast of wind sent him flying into the crater wall head-first.

The woman turned to look at the prince, not bothering to hide her disgust.

His voice trembled. "I don't understand."

"You don't need to understand," she replied coldly. "I'm here to protect Bryson LeAnce. My name is Thusia, a Bozani of the Light Empire, and I am bound to him as his Branian."

*　　　*　　　*

Jilly was leaning so far over the edge that she was in danger of falling off. Little did she know that the woman was her childhood idol and hero—much like many other girls'—Thusia.

"Who is it?" she asked.

"Our ticket out of here," Toshik said.

"What's happening?" Rhyparia whispered to Vistas.

"I'm not sure how, but it appears as if Bryson just summoned a Branian," he replied.

"A Branian …"

For the first time since his brother's death, Vistas smiled. "Victory. Your captain rose to the challenge."

Perhaps Vistas had been blinded by the hope he felt in his chest, but when he looked at Rhyparia's debilitated face, he could have sworn, that for a brief moment, the right side of her mouth curled upward a tiny bit.

"And we were supposed to be the weakest ones," she said.

*　　　*　　　*

Thusia and Storshae continued to study each other. The prince eyed Debo's sword lying in the dirt and wondered whether he should bother trying to telekinetically fling it in her direction. Better to go down fighting, he thought.

"Run," Thusia commanded.

"You're just going to let me go?" Storshae asked with a suspicious glare, narrowing his eyes.

"I have no choice," she said, venom in her voice. "Hopefully you'll die of exhaustion or thirst before you reach safety."

Storshae's eyes danced with a delighted scorn. "Scared to commit an Untenable, eh?"

"I know the penalty for such an act."

Storshae stared at her for a moment longer. "Seeing a Bozani express fear sickens me … Makes me wonder why people pray to the likes of you." He then turned and purposefully began his journey south.

Bryson had crawled over to Debo's body during Thusia and Storshae's confrontation. Somehow, he knew that what Fonos had said was true, that Debo had killed his father, but he still felt a huge hole in his heart for this man—the man who raised him for eleven years of his life. Who had taught him everything he knew. Who provided for and protected him—and above all, loved him.

Debo was still clinging to his final breaths. It was a shock to see the man who had always been the strongest, most assertive person Bryson had ever met appear so frail.

Debo gazed up at the boy and smiled. "I love you, Bry."

"Why'd you do it? I'm confused, Debo. Execution?"

"I was told to. I carried out an order."

"Was my dad a bad man?"

He didn't get an answer. Instead, Debo looked above Bryson as a shadow engulfed the pair. "It's about time," Debo said. The life in his eyes faded. He was gone.

A teardrop landed on Debo's cheek. It wasn't Bryson's, so he turned to look up at who was standing over them.

It was Thusia. Her face was perfectly impassive, but a couple of tears were dropping from her bright blue eyes.

Looking back at Debo, Bryson broke down and laid his head on the man's chest like he did when he was a little kid. When he would listen to Debo read *The Third of Five* every night—the legend of the same man whose chest he used as a pillow—the only place to properly fall asleep after a night full of nightmares …

Only this time, instead of feeling the man's chest rise and fall and the warm air hitting the back of his neck with each breath of slumber, he felt nothing …

Nothing but memories of what once was and never would be again.

29

The Void

The sun was setting as second-night approached. A lavish carriage, draped in burgundy, traveled across a barren road.

It was led by the same man who headed the carriage when Dev Prince Storshae was riding in it. He wasn't a soldier and had no intention of confronting the Jestivan, so he offered to help them get back home by acting if the prince were still inside.

Trotting next to the carriage was a white horse—the horse Jilly had named Bobuel a few days back. Vistas rode atop it, as he allowed the Jestivan and Thusia time alone inside of the carriage.

However, they spent this time together in silence. The mood was glum, and the looks on most of their faces reflected that. The only exceptions were Rhyparia, Toshik, and Olivia.

Rhyparia was still recovering. Olivia was sleeping—still. Meow Meow had woken up for a brief moment to express his gratitude and inform them that Olivia was alright. She was just very tired.

Toshik was leaning forward in his seat with his sword in his hands. Bryson had retrieved it from Debo's body when he recognized whose it was. Toshik's eyes were on his blade, but they were unfocused. "I was a fool," he murmured. "The greatest warrior in the world ... and I neglected his training."

Then there was Jilly. She couldn't keep her eyes off of the slender woman who had graced them with her presence. Thusia's golden eyelashes curved long and thick above her cerulean eyes. Her blond hair fell perfectly down the sides of her lightly freckled cheeks, and she wore a white neckband—almost like a collar—with a giant blue diamond at the front. Her entire appearance was bright.

"You've been staring at me for quite some time now," Thusia said, turning to look at Jilly. Several of the battle-weary Jestivan flinched at her voice cutting through the stillness.

Jilly opened her mouth, but the only sound to escape was an awkward half-stutter. She was speechless—a first for Jilly.

"I'm sorry I'm not myself," Thusia said. "Typically, I'm a lot more fun to be around, but under these circumstances ..."

"Are you Thusia?" Himitsu asked for Jilly since she couldn't seem to ask it herself.

She forced a small, friendly smile. "Yes, I am."

A dull thud reverberated in the carriage. Jilly had fallen off her seat and onto the floorboard.

Thusia looked at her with a smile, this time a genuine one. "Priceless."

*   *   *

A lone barn house sat in a moonlit field of tall prairie grass. The house was rickety and weathered, and looked to be abandoned—then again, every building in this kingdom looked abandoned. The tall blades of grass stood deathly still in the moon's deep bluish hue. Wind didn't exist in this kingdom. The air was cold and eerily thin, and gave no resistance to those moving through it.

Three figures lay still in the field, hiding in the grass. Even the slightest twitch would disturb their surroundings and signal their presence. Normally, speaking would be prohibited as well, but the thick grass allowed them to at least whisper. In this kingdom, if someone were to even breathe while occupying an open space, the sound would carry for several hundred feet, reaching the ears of anyone nearby—and even the dead.

A young man with a bandage circling the top of his head stared intently at the house. All it took was one glance at his face to realize the wear and tear this kingdom had done to him over the past few months. His eyes were sunken into his face with heavy shadows of black surrounding them. His lips were dry and split in several spots. And though he looked to be in his twenties at most, his dirty blond hair was greying at the roots.

"Kadlest, I can't take this much longer," he whispered.

"We're almost done, Toono," said the middle-aged woman lying next to him. "We just have to wait a little while longer. Then we'll be gone by first-night."

Toono's eyes darted away from the house, toward random spots in the field where he could make out human shapes. "Three months in and I'm vividly seeing the dead roam around us."

"It certainly takes a toll on you," Kadlest said. "They call it the Void for a reason." She glanced to her right where a little girl with long black hair hid in the grass. "But Illipsia is experiencing it the worst because of her age."

"If I keep my eyes closed, it's not as scary," the girl whispered. "But I can feel them touching me."

The barn doors opened with a piercing scream. Every sound was magnified in the Cyn Kingdom's atmosphere. Candle light filtered through the open doors and spilled onto a dirt path in front of it as horses could be heard neighing from within.

A couple minutes passed before two horses trotted out of the giant barn doors. An open carriage followed behind them. Two people occupied its seats—a woman and a man. The parents of their target.

As the carriage passed by Toono, Kadlest, and Illipsia, Kadlest clamped her hand over Illipsia's mouth, for the young girl's breathing hitched at the sight of the horses.

The right side of one of the horse's face was skinned down to the bones. The ivory color of the bones practically glowed in the lucent light of the moon. Its right hind leg had been stripped of hide, muscle, and veins as well.

The other horse was even more horrifying. Its body was fine—equipped with silky brown hair and all. But its entire head from the neck up was composed of blood-lathered muscle. And its eyes were missing.

Toono looked away. He wanted out of this kingdom as fast as possible. He listened for the clacking of the hooves to grow distant. Once satisfied, he stood, finally disrupting the stillness surrounding them. He listened closely, and sure enough, he could hear the faint breaths of slumber from within the barn house. Their target was asleep.

He withdrew his ancient from his robes—a bubble wand. He blew into the middle hole of the three at the top. A bubble with a diameter of about half his height was produced. It hovered in one spot, and Toono climbed onto it. Its surface sank in a bit from his weight, but it was as strong as steel, so it didn't pop.

Toono leaned forward, causing the bubble to accelerate in that direction. If he walked, his footsteps would wake the person inside. He leaned back, causing the bubble to rise to a window on the barn's second floor. He shot forward and through the open window. He didn't jump off once he was inside the room, but the boy in the bed instantly awoke to the sound of Toono's breathing.

"Who are you?" the boy asked. He was probably in his late teens.

Toono sighed. "It would have been better if you hadn't woken."

"Sleep is not easily obtained here," the boy replied.

Hopping off the bubble, Toono walked toward his target and pulled a knife from within his cloak. "To make what I'm about to do feel less painful for me and you, I would tell you that I'm granting you an everlasting slumber. But I have learned that in your kingdom, your Cynergy keeps a part of you alive … if you can call it that. I must admit, that makes it even harder for me to do this. I hate killing enough as it is."

"Are you aware of who I am?"

"You are Chelekah, a member of the Dark Realm's Diatia—a group designed to counter the Light Realm's Jestivan."

"So you know I will not simply allow you to kill me as easily as you make it seem," Chelekah said.

"Titles mean nothing to me. In fact, I despise them," Toono replied with an unfazed stare. "It's comparable to the stamp found burned into a cow's hind parts, designating it for an unfulfilling life before it's led to slaughtered meat."

Chelekah stood up. "This kingdom really has gotten to you."

"You think?" With that, Toono reached back, grabbed his bubble, and flung it at the snowy-haired boy. The collision sent him flying through the wall and into another room as wooden planks shattered in every direction.

Toono strode forward, stepping through the hole in the wall. Chelekah was sprawled face-down on the floorboards. Toono knelt down, straddling the boy's ribs with his knees. He wanted to get this over with. There was no joy in prolonging a death. He yanked up Chelekah's head, placed his blade against his neck, and swiftly sliced across.

Blood spurted from the wound as Chelekah made a hopeless gargling noise. His blood saturated into and then pooled on top of the porous wood. Toono let go of the boy's head and stood as Chelekah's blood stained his ivory hair.

Toono sheathed his knife back in his pocket and sat down in an armchair. He took out a gem and held it up. Twirling the gem between his fingers, he frowned as it remained lifeless. He started to get up, but the gem's sudden glow made him return to his seat. His mission in this kingdom was finally over.

Toono sat tucked away in the shadows as he stared intently at the corpse lying in the moonlight. "Poor kid," he mumbled.

"It was necessary." said Kadlest, who had just entered through the doorway.

She was tall for a woman, and her subtle muscle definition made her look like she was once a fighter.

"Which kingdom is our next?" she asked.

Toono rubbed his eyes. "An easier one than this, I hope."

"What did you expect? I had connections in the Prim Kingdom. That won't be the case anywhere else."

Toono held his face in his hands. "I underestimated the stories about this place ... brushing them off as nonsense. Let's go back to the Light Realm for a bit. I haven't been there since September."

"Has it really been that long?"

"A month in the Prim Kingdom. Two months scouting the Power Kingdom. And the past three months in this disaster."

Kadlest gave it some thought. "Alright then, how about—"

She was interrupted by a pebble smacking the window. She stared at it for a moment before walking over, opening it, and acknowledging the girl who stood outside.

It was Illipsia. She was tiny—just ten years old. So tiny, in fact, her onyx hair was longer than her body.

"Ms. Kadlest!" the girl half-whispered, half-shouted.

"What is it?"

"Dev Prince Storshae has contacted us."

Kadlest looked back at Toono, who was still gazing at the corpse. "It's Storshae."

He rose from the chair. "About time."

"Connect us," Toono commanded as they walked out of the house.

One of Illipsia's eyes turned a deep burgundy while the other dilated and gazed upward a tiny bit. A holographic display of a charcoal-haired man appeared.

"Hello, Storshae," Toono greeted flatly.

The prince gave a nod. "Toono. How are things over there?"

"Just killed one of the Diatia."

Storshae's right eyebrow arched. "Interesting. Well, I figured I should update you before I visit my father. Need to drop something off."

Toono forced the conversation forward. "Where is Olivia?"

With an all-too obvious stare of defeat, he replied, "I lost her."

"How do you *lose* her?" the young man reacted with calm frustration. Off to the side, Kadlest was shaking her head in disappointment. For a pair of people who had committed some heinous acts, they possessed shockingly composed personalities.

"The Jestivan," Storshae said.

"You were overtaken by teenagers? What about Fonos?"

"Dead. It wasn't just the Jestivan," Storshae rushed to explain. "We had them in hand—although, I will admit one of them was talented enough to take out Ossen. I was on the verge of killing the little pest … until a Pogu showed up, which was my first time of even hearing about such a being."

Kadlest snickered. "What was his name?" Toono asked.

"You know what a Pogu is?" Storshae asked.

"I'm not an idiot. *What was his name?*"

"Ataway Debonicus Kawi," Storshae recited. "From your realm's little fairy tale."

"If it were a fairy tale, why would Mendac be a part of it? You, of all people, should know he was real."

"Yeah, yeah …We killed Debonicus though … well, Fonos killed him."

"He killed a Pogu?"

Storshae retold the story.

"The boy who summoned a Branian—what did he look like?" Toono asked.

"Messy blond hair. Long bangs. Blue eyes. Strange scar on his chest that read 'T2.'"

Toono's eyes widened. "What was his name?"

Storshae let out a single forced laugh. "I didn't catch it. But Fonos said he was Mendac's son."

His mind spinning, Toono went silent for a moment.

"At least we surely left a scar—or several hundred scars—on that girl," Storshae mumbled.

This snapped the young man out of his trance. "I told you not to hurt her."

Storshae laughed. "As long as she's alive, she's still useful. We can still get King Rehn back."

Toono's body swelled, then subsided. "We'll never get him back with her lost or injured beyond repair." He gave the signal to Illipsia to cut the transmission.

"Mendac's son … this changes a lot of things. I didn't know Olivia had a bond with such a person." He turned to look at Kadlest. "We go to the Passion Kingdom."

Her interest piqued as a smile formed. "Does that mean what I think it means?"

He nodded. "It's time we find Miss Apoleia Lavender."

30

Memory Transfer

Somewhere between Rence and the Dev Kingdom's teleplatforms, Bryson and company gathered near a small pond at the foot of a hill. Jilly was splashing frantically in the water. Although the weather was becoming somewhat warmer, it was still ill-advised to do such a thing. But this was Jilly, and nobody expected anything less.

In fact, Thusia jumped in and dunked Jilly underneath the surface. Her spirits had already lifted. Bryson was quickly learning that having Thusia around was the same as having a second Jilly—just a smidge more mature version.

Toshik was sitting in the reeds lining the stream that fed the pond with his elbows on his knees. He too was observing the blond-haired duo. His eyes had the same empty stare as Olivia's always did.

Bryson walked up the grassy hill with a satchel of flasks that he had filled to the brim. The stream was a bit murky, but with Olivia and Rhyparia

286

both desperate for water, and with Storshae on the loose and possibly sounding the alarm, he wasn't going to hazard entering any town.

Himitsu had disappeared into the scattered trees behind the pond. He had said something about needing to clear his mind.

Then there was Vistas, who squatted among the rocks of the stream, as far from the others as he could get. He cupped both hands into the cold water and splashed his face. He did this a few more times before straightening his back and taking a deep breath.

He was doing everything he could to calm his nerves—something he was unused to as he was, by nature, a very calm man. But that was before the foreign memory that now resided in his mind. A memory that didn't belong to him. A memory that he had to hold onto until the time was right—according to the instructions Debo gave to him the day before ...

Vistas crouched behind a rocky outcrop as he watched the battle. Himitsu had successfully taken out two of the Dev officers, but he had collapsed from exhaustion. Toshik was bleeding from multiple wounds and his opponents were harrying him toward the crater rim as he tried to keep Jilly from the fray. Then a Dev officer knocked Toshik to the ground and drew a knife. Vistas ground his teeth, but he couldn't do anything. He was no soldier.

Then a sudden blast of wind knocked him clear off his feet. He scrambled onto his back, prepared to die. But the figure standing over him wasn't an enemy.

Intimidatingly tall with a face drenched with sheer fury, Debo loomed over Vistas with a young girl by his side. Vistas remembered her from the hospital.

Debo knelt down and lifted the man by his armpits. "Can you do something for me?" he asked.

"Yes, sir."

"Are you capable of memory transfer?" Debo asked.

"It's been a while, but yes."

"I have a memory for you to take. I ask for you to hold onto it until Bryson figures out the truth about his parents. That could happen in two months or ten years ... It may never happen. Can I trust you with this?"

Vistas hesitated.

"Can I?!"

"Of course. Bring the memory to the forefront of your mind. Do not think of anything else until I remove my finger from your temple."

Debo closed his eyes and did as he was told.

Once the memory transfer concluded, Vistas opened his eyes and glared at Debo with furrowed brows. The emotion on his face was out of place for the phlegmatic man.

Debo's ear piercings jangled as he grabbed Vistas's shoulders, slightly squatting to make eye contact. "I just trusted you with information that will get you killed by beings like me if they were to find out you have it. Keep it to yourself until the time comes for you to tell Bryson, and only Bryson."

With that, Debo scooped up Rhyparia and bolted toward Necrosis Valley. Vistas, meanwhile, backed against a tree and slid down to the patchy grass, mind running at a hundred miles an hour …

*   *   *

Within a spacious room of golden floors, walls, and ceiling, a lone coffin of matching gold rested at the center.

An elderly man walked down the stairs. His white eyebrows hung down the sides of his face. Streaks of red stained his cheeks. Blood soaked his burgundy robes, and his breathing was ragged.

The Dev soldiers had discovered who he was. They were growing suspicious through the last leg of their journey from Rence to the capital, and they finally figured it out several days after their arrival when he asked too many questions about their king's grave.

Poicus had slain more than a hundred guards off as he forced his way down into this tomb, leaving a breadcrumb trail of lifeless bodies behind him.

He placed his hands on the coffin and pushed its heavy gold lid to the side. His eyebrows arched as he gazed inside. The body was wrapped heavily in layers of fine linen bandages.

How was he supposed to know if this was actually Dev King Rehn?

He was given his answer as a voice from behind made him jump. "I had planned on visiting my father's grave and returning his crown today. I've had it for entirely too long. Being greeted by Phesaw's Grand Director was not something that I had foreseen."

Poicus turned to see a young Dev Prince Storshae standing at the doorway. Storshae was playfully twirling his father's chocolate cosmos–entwined crown around his finger.

"Have you come to pay your respects to my father?" the prince asked.

Poicus didn't reply.

Storshae's eyes narrowed. "Something tells me that would be a silly assumption."

31

Her Darkest Secret

At the head of a polished mahogany table, a brawny man sat hunched over with his finger and thumb pressed into his eyes. King Vitio's hand dragged down his face and began impatiently tugging at his blond beard. His frustration was growing by the second. Not requesting Vistas's presence was starting to seem like more of a mistake.

But he didn't want to ask anything of Vistas. His Dev servant had been through enough and deserved his rest. So Vitio simply bit his tongue and continued waiting, trying to ignore the fact that he was several minutes late for his broadcast meeting.

Finally, the doors slowly opened as a pale, skinny man with long black hair waltzed in with a lackadaisical stride.

Vitio gave his guest a hardnosed stare. "No need to rush on my account."

Flen smirked as he took a seat at the opposite end of the table. "No refreshments?" he asked. "I'm starving."

"And no longer breathing if you don't connect me right now."

Flen rolled his eyes, then one colored burgundy while the other dilated. A holographic projection sat in the air.

"It's about time," said the deep voice of the Adren King.

"I'm sorry, Supido," Vitio said.

The display cut from Supido's face to that of a beautiful young lady. "We decided to go on without you since there isn't much time. A four-way broadcast quickly depletes the Dev Energy of our servants."

Vitio nodded. "I understand, Apsa. Damian is connected with us, correct?"

He was answered by the broadcast cutting to a plump, bald man smiling quietly at the screen. "Alright, what are we discussing?" Vitio asked.

"Rhyparia," Supido immediately replied.

"I'm not locking her up again," Vitio fired back.

"She is responsible for the murder of 24 people. Children died when she flattened that restaurant."

"I get that. But it was an accident. A loss of control. She has a power that is difficult to tame."

Supido shook his head. "That makes it even worse."

"It's hard for me to agree with you here, Vitio," Spirit Queen Apsa said. "The act of taking even one life is enough to send someone to the gallows."

Damian gravely nodded his head in agreement.

"She's a Jestivan … and one of the more talented ones," Vitio pleaded. "We need her."

Supido tapped his finger on the table. "If I recall correctly, one of the Diatia was assassinated last week. So we could afford to lose her. Numbers would stay even."

"Half the Jestivan would be dead if it wasn't for Rhyparia!" Vitio shouted.

A short pause followed before Apsa spoke up. "Archaic Director Senex needs to do his job. He's the one who's supposed to be developing her … teaching her control. Perhaps we give her another chance—a final chance. After all, she's only fifteen. But if it happens again, both of them will receive the strictest of punishments."

Hope flashed onto Vitio's face. "That's all I ask."

Supido's face remained rigid as he debated it in his mind. "What do you think, Damian?" he asked.

The Passion King stared at the ceiling. One side of his mouth crinkled at the edge as he stroked his chin. Then he returned his gaze to the broadcast and gave a thumbs-up. A sigh of relief escaped Vitio as he realized that was the majority.

"I will send a letter to Senex about our discussion today," Supido said. "Inform him that Rhyparia has one more chance, and we will come down hard if she screws it up."

"This is a wise decision," Vitio reassured him. "After the Grand Director's warnings of a higher war, we need all the talent we can get."

*   *   *

Children and adults of all ages were flowing out of Phesaw's many exits. It was a sea of black, as everyone was dressed to mourn the great man who had died ten days prior. To them, he was Phesaw's Intel Director—a man named Debo. In reality, he was a Pogu of the Light Empire's Bozani—Ataway Debonicus Kawi. And to Bryson, he was the closest thing to a father he would ever have in his life.

The ten Jestivan, who found themselves together for the first time since October, headed toward Phesaw Park. Thusia also accompanied them, relieved that she could finally remove her black hat and veil. Bryson had introduced her to the Jestivan, but no one else—not even the directors knew.

Separate groups formed and walked at their own pace. Yama and Jilly walked as a pair. It turned out that Yama exerted an even greater pull on the irrepressible girl than Thusia did.

Jilly was humming the tune that she had sung at Debo's funeral. She said it was a song her nanny always sung to her when she had nightmares as a little girl:

Evil bleeds,
Including its leader,

We fight for Good,
So we will not fail,
And even though,
Our hearts are aching,
For you, we will prevail.

Olivia was still recovering, but she had insisted on coming to the funeral. She had regained some of the meat on her bones and her wounds had begun to heal over—although the scars were a livid purple. She walked next to Tashami, Agnos, and Lilu. Needless to say, her team was excited to have her back and refused to let her leave their side.

Himitsu and Rhyparia walked side by side. Toshik, meanwhile, kept off to the side. His expression was glum, and he would occasionally throw a glance at Jilly from afar.

Then there were the two stragglers from the pack—Bryson and Thusia. Bryson looked at his Branian, who was smiling reminiscently and stuffing her face with a very generous portion of apple pie. If there was one thing he had learned about Thusia over the past week and a half, it was that she had an appetite unrivaled by anyone's he knew. And each time he watched her shovel down a five-course meal, he'd stare at her flat stomach in search of where it all went.

"Do you want to talk about anything?" Bryson asked.

"Nope," Thusia said happily through a mouthful of pie.

Bryson's frustration was apparent. "How long are you going to avoid this?"

"What do you want me to say? Mendac was a great man and was wrongfully murdered? Frankly, even if that was the case, I don't think you'd want to hear that because, well … that would mean Debonicus was a bad man." She spun her pie plate into the woods. "But let's say Mendac *was* a very bad man, which—let's face it—is not improbable, then that would imply you've been lied to about him your whole entire life; your dad, who is revered around the realm, was a psychopath. Would you rather hear that? That Debonicus was right to kill your father? Maybe you would; I don't know."

She paused for air before looking at Bryson with a serious stare. "Either way, you'll still end up disgusted by one—if not both—of the men you think you could call your father."

She was right, Bryson thought. He would end up hating either Debo or Mendac—maybe both.

Thusia's face crumpled. "I'm sorry, Bryson. This has been a lot for me to take in too. I'll say this—I fell in love with a part of Mendac. Unfortunately, there were many parts to him. He was a complex man, and that complexity only worsened after I died."

That was an answer, and Bryson knew that would be the best one he'd get from her, at least for now.

The Jestivan stopped at a grassy clearing in the park. Students milled in the distance, some curious for a first look at the young elites, others curious to see how they were handling Debo's death.

It was still cool outside, and the trees were bare. Bryson found himself sandwiched between two girls while sitting at the base of one of the trees. He was leaning on Olivia's shoulder to his right while Lilu rested her head on his left shoulder.

They were happy—or it seemed so. One could never tell with Olivia. Even after all that she had experienced, her face was as rigid as stone.

Playfully blowing strands of Olivia's purple hair from in front of his face, Bryson watched the blond-headed duo of Jilly and Thusia spar with fallen tree branches against Yama and her actual sword. Despite herself, Yama couldn't hold back. She would disappear and reappear, and each time she did so, Thusia and Jilly's sticks would be an inch shorter as a sliced section fell to the grass.

Lilu, who had a black petunia pinned to her hair, adjusted her head on Bryson's shoulder. A beautiful scent curled into his nose. There wasn't a word to describe what he was feeling. He had his best friend back, and the girl of his dreams was snuggled against him. Although he wasn't sure how or why, he had a Branian now, and he would be lying if he tried to tell himself that the thought of her becoming some kind of mother-figure hadn't crossed his mind. But of course, his happy thoughts were interrupted.

"*Ahchoo!*" went Meow Meow, and it may have been the most fabricated sneeze of all time.

"Ah, damn, Bryson. I'm sorry," the kitten lied. "Maybe you should—I don't know—get away."

Lilu snorted. Bryson frowned as he felt the mucus sprinkle in his hair, but he kept quiet. He wasn't going to allow the kitten to ruin his peace. "How long until you leave to the Cyn Kingdom?" he asked Lilu.

"Two months," she replied. "They're going to train us hard. Make sure we're ready."

"Directors Neaneuma and Buredo?"

"Yes, but no Olivia. It was decided today … Not after what she's been through."

"Dumb," Olivia cut in plainly.

Bryson smirked as he tilted his head toward his friend. "That's my friend. Always ready."

Olivia returned his gaze for a moment, then abruptly stood up. "I need to head home."

"I wonder what it's like living in your household," Bryson said. "It seems to have such strict rules."

"It does," she said. Meow Meow frowned.

Bryson decided it was time to ask the question that he'd been curious about throughout the entirety of their friendship. "When will I ever get to visit?"

Olivia gave him her all-too-familiar empty blue-eyed stare.

"You can't," she said. "You are my darkest secret."

Printed in Great Britain
by Amazon

69681991R00177